EVERGREEN
TIDINGS
from the
Baumgartners

EVERGREEN TIDINGS

TIDINGS

from the

Baumgartners

GRETCHEN ANTHONY

PARK
ROW
BOOKS

PARK
ROW
BOOKS

Recycling programs
for this product may
not exist in your area.

ISBN-13: 978-0-7783-0786-0
ISBN-13: 978-0-7783-0841-6 (Library Exclusive Edition)

Evergreen Tidings from the Baumgartners

Copyright © 2018 by Gretchen Anthony

This is a work of fiction. Names, characters, places and incidents are either the product of the author's imagination or are used fictitiously, and any resemblance to actual persons, living or dead, business establishments, events or locales is entirely coincidental.

For questions and comments about the quality of this book, please contact us at CustomerService@Harlequin.com.

ParkRowBooks.com
BookClubbish.com

Printed in U.S.A.

3 2901 00647 4507

To Dad. Thanks for laughing.

EVERGREEN TIDINGS

TIDINGS

from the

Baumgartners

Be it labor great or small, do it well or not at all.

—CHILDREN'S RHYME

June

ONE WOULD THINK being treated like a daft old Betty by a police officer with mustard on his lapel would top Violet's all-time list of humiliations. But after the fall of Gomorrah she'd just witnessed, it barely registered.

"Mrs. Baumgartner," he said, as if repeating her name would help. "Why won't you tell me who threw the first punch?"

"Like I told you, Officer, I couldn't see. I went momentarily blind."

"But you can see now?"

For heaven's sake, she said she'd gone blind, not soft in the head. "Of course I can see now—" She raised her finger to his name badge. "Officer Clive Bailey."

She paused to let him absorb her demonstration of faculties. "Officer Bailey, I couldn't see who threw the first punch, but believe me, I know very well it wasn't my husband. Nor could I see what happened next because of the stars. And the buzzing. Like a swarm of bees in my head and before my eyes."

"Bees." Officer Bailey made a note.

"No, not bees." Now that she was on record she thought she ought to be exact. "Like pins—hundreds of tiny, sharp pricks piercing the blackness. And then a million streams of blinding light. Really, I thought my brain was about ready to rip in two."

She noticed the officer's right eye had begun to twitch ever so imperceptibly where lid met lash, but he did manage to record the words *blinding light*. That would have to suffice.

"Okay. So if you were blind, how did you manage to leave the scene?"

"My husband, of course. Edward Baumgartner. He's a distinguished scientist so I can assure you that he has no tolerance for violence. A man like Edward only uses his hands for the good of others." She paused, and then added, "Even when he would have had every right to punch the man groping his meaty fingers across his wife's backside."

The twitch in Officer Bailey's eye escalated to full-blown mutiny, and he began to worry at it with the back of his wrist. "I'm confused. A man groped your backside? Or he groped his own wife's backside?"

"How on earth could he have groped his own wife's backside? She was off pawing at Pastor Norblad like a Parisian streetwalker."

Officer Bailey's hand was so busy controlling the twitch in his eye that none of this was making it into his notes.

"Aren't you going to write that down?"

The officer sighed and shook his head. "I've got enough." He closed his notebook with a defeated *slap* and went to slip it into his breast pocket, then stopped. "One last thing, actually. A few people reported something I can't seem to make sense of. They reported hearing a woman scream—" He flipped back and forth through his pages of notes. "Here it is. They say she screamed, 'Was it intercourse?'" He raised a single eyebrow and looked directly at Violet. "Any idea who that might have been?"

Yes, Violet knew. Of course she knew.

The last six months, however, had painted in stark contrast the difference between *knowing* and *understanding*. Six months ago, she knew she was married to a world-class scientist. She knew their daughter was on track to exceed her father's success. Violet knew that she, herself, had meticulously navigated motherhood, raising a successful child during an era when it was both necessary to direct her every move, while acting as if Pinocchio had no strings.

But what did she *understand* about this family of hers? Not her shockingly secretive daughter, who used her mastery of science for far more than professional advancement. And certainly not her bending willow of a husband. Would it break him to stand up for once?

Imagine. A woman of Violet's stature faced with such fundamental questions. It was disorienting. Distasteful. Her cheeks burned as if she'd been slapped. Her family's health, its very survival, would forever fall squarely on her shoulders alone.

Yes, Violet knew who'd shouted the question Officer Bailey was asking about. She knew, too, about the pills, and the vodka, and the backside grabbing, and the sobbing, and all of the jokes for which her family would forever be the butt.

She also knew there would be no explaining it away in this year's Baumgartner Christmas letter.

Part
One

Seven Months
Earlier

1

Violet

Christmas 2017

Dearest loved ones, far and near—

Evergreen Tidings from the Baumgartners!

By the time you open this letter I'm sure it will be old news that 2017 has been a monumental year for our family—one that we're certain to treasure until the end of our days. So tonight, as I sit tucked into my warm house with a steaming cup of Christmas tea, I feel nothing but blessed. And while I know that my modest little Christmas correspondences can't hold a candle to the day-to-day joys and sorrows of your lives, I do hope you'll indulge this meek attempt to share a glimpse of our year with you.

The biggest Baumgartner news, of course, is dear Ed's retirement from BiolTech after 30 extraordinary years. How proud we are of you, Ed! Though you know I'm loath to brag, I can hardly constrain myself. How can the Good Lord expect me to go humbly about while congratulatory cards and letters flood our home? I can't help but repeat here what's been said to us in those notes—that millions of people around the world are living healthier, happier lives because of this dear man's research into FBD. And to think that I am the lucky girl who gets to wake up next to him every day!

But as each of us knows, all good things must come to an end, including my brilliant husband's career. This could mean only one thing: Time for a party! And was it ever! We welcomed hundreds of guests, including many of you reading this letter now, and we thank you from the bottom of our overflowing hearts for joining us in celebrating my dear husband's life and achievements.

The night included all the trappings, of course. A select few from the St. Paul Chamber Orchestra charmed us with Mendelssohn and Brahms while we nibbled on shrimp cakes and (wickedly expensive but wildly popular!) Brie-en-croute. Later, a jazz quartet, fresh in from their latest tour of New York, Los Angeles and Toronto, rang in the midnight hour while we popped corks for the Champagne toasts.

Now, if you'll permit me just one modest name-drop (those of you disinterested in the gossipy comings and goings of local celebrities may skip ahead to the next paragraph)...the evening included a most unexpected and wonderful guest! Imagine our surprise when the ballroom doors opened and who should walk in

RING!

Violet nearly leaped from her chair at the sound of the phone.

Good Lord Almighty, she thought. *Are You trying to take me home with a heart attack?*

An hour or so earlier, before sitting down at the computer to write, she'd paused to consider disabling any possible distractions—doorbell and phone included—but decided no. She wouldn't put the day's To-Do list in jeopardy. Silence was a poor trade for accomplishment.

She took a deep breath and ran the tips of her fingers across the nape of her neck to gather herself.

"Hello. Baumgartner residence. Violet Baumgartner speaking." It struck her that she'd been answering the phone in this manner for more than thirty years.

There was an audible pause on the other end before a man finally cleared his throat and spoke up. "Yes, Mrs. Baumgartner? Harvey Arpell from the *Minneapolis/St. Paul Standard.* Returning your call."

Outstanding.

Arpell was top priority on the day's list. *Draft Christmas let-*

ter was second, followed by *Confirm menu*, and those tasks were both well underway. Her mind buzzed with efficiency.

"Now, Mr. Arpell. I need to know if you will be bringing a photographer along with you on the sixteenth. If not, we will need to hire one to meet you there."

Arpell cleared his throat again. She hoped this wasn't a chronic condition; phlegmy encounters were so off-putting. She couldn't expose her guests to that.

"The sixteenth?"

"Yes."

"November 16? As in, next week?"

"For heaven's sake, no." Next he'd be asking if she were catering her party with Costco party trays. "December 16. The retirement party for my husband, Ed Baumgartner. You'll recall that we discussed it at length during the Overbergs' fund-raiser for the Minnesota Orchestra last month. You expressed quite an interest in attending."

"I'm afraid I—"

"I've assembled a press kit with Ed's biographical information, as well as a list of career highlights. I had planned to drop them in the mail to your office today. Unless you'd prefer I have the package couriered."

Of course he'd remember; he'd commented on Ed's Medical Legion of Honor lapel pin, which Ed hadn't wanted to wear but which she'd strongly encouraged. Their *wear it or don't* discussion had made them almost late, and yet, here she was, taking calls from one of Minnesota's premier reporters.

"Mrs. Baumgartner, you'll forgive me. Remind me who your husband is again?"

Violet grabbed the locket at her throat and wrapped it tightly in her palm. This wasn't at all the conversation she'd been expecting and she began to doubt her choice of reporters. He showed no grasp of the facts nor the opportunity before him.

Nevertheless.

"My husband, Edward Baumgartner, is retiring after thirty

years with BiolTech. He is a premier researcher in his field and holds several patents for FBD treatment devices. You likely have heard of the F8 Tri-scope Method, which he developed, and which proved foundational for all subsequent FBD treatment methods."

Violet had invested no small bit of her life mastering the subtle language required to describe a condition as sensitive as the one to which dear Ed had dedicated his work. His career was her work, too, after all.

"And, by FBD, you mean—what, exactly?"

Good Lord. Violet shook her head. She was most definitely rethinking her choice of reporters.

"Functional Bowel Disorders."

"Ah, of course."

"FBD is actually a category of disorder, inclusive of several subcategories of gastrointestinal disorders, including irritable bowel syndrome—which, thanks to all the advertising with which we're assaulted these days, is more commonly known as IBS—and FD, or functional dyspepsia." She paused to let him absorb the details and to come to terms with the fact that, yes, she did in fact know what she was talking about. "IBS, alone, is estimated to affect nearly twenty percent of the American population."

Arpell *hmm*'d. "That's an awful lot of—well, you know..." He paused, and experience told her he was weighing his choice of words. There wasn't a punch line she hadn't heard—bowels were such an easy target—and she hoped he'd rise above.

"Stomach pain," he said, finally.

She smiled. Perhaps he wasn't as thick as he'd begun to sound. "Indeed it is, Mr. Arpell. And my husband, Ed, has been doing his best to soothe that pain for millions of affected people most of his life."

Arpell was quiet on the line, though Violet believed she could hear the ticking of his keyboard. She had him intrigued.

"Is he one of the company founders?" Arpell's keys ticked

away. "I'm looking at their website right now, and I don't see his name listed along with the other executives."

Did this man ignore everything she'd just said? Ed hadn't sacrificed his laboratory for the politicking claustrophobia of the boardroom. He applied his life to science, to improving lives. He'd made the world a better place. Certainly not even a man made dumb with phlegm would argue otherwise.

Violet felt a sudden pang of sorrow for the reporter's wife—imagine living a life of not being heard.

"Mr. Arpell, let's not get hung up on titles. Certainly we can agree that a scientist of my husband's stature deserves a bit of public recognition at the close of his career. And I believe you're just the man to tell his story."

The keys stopped clattering and Violet could tell immediately from the tone of Arpell's voice that she would not be striking this task from her list today.

"Look, Mrs. Baumgartner. I'm sure everything you've told me about your husband is worthy of a wonderful retirement farewell. I just don't think it's something that falls into the category of news."

Violet took her pencil and wrote *f/u* for *follow up* next to Arpell's name on her notepad. Then she placed the pencil quietly on her desk and rested her fingertips gently on the warm locket at her throat. She would let a week pass, then call again. If experience taught her anything, it was the necessity of easing into a subject like FBD. The reporter needed time to let the subject marinate. Right now, she knew his mind couldn't help rubbernecking at the horrors of intestinal distress.

"Very well, Mr. Arpell. But I do ask you to rethink your decision the next time your dinner disagrees with you." She paused, exercising her belief that to be the first to hang up from a phone call was to admit defeat. "By the way, would it affect your decision if I happened to mention that national broadcaster Rhonda Nelson was scheduled to make a surprise visit?"

Let him chew on that for a moment.

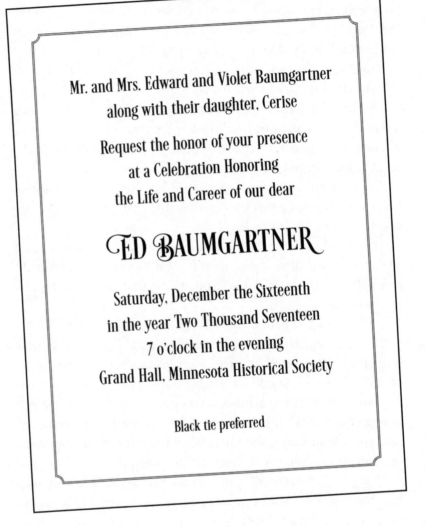

Mr. and Mrs. Edward and Violet Baumgartner
along with their daughter, Cerise

Request the honor of your presence
at a Celebration Honoring
the Life and Career of our dear

ED BAUMGARTNER

Saturday, December the Sixteenth
in the year Two Thousand Seventeen
7 o'clock in the evening
Grand Hall, Minnesota Historical Society

Black tie preferred

2

Cerise

CERISE BAUMGARTNER THUMBED the edge of the invitation. Hundred-pound card stock. Bronze ink engraving. Red and blue border—the BiolTech colors.

Not bad, Mom.

She tossed the card onto the pile of mail flooding her kitchen counter and noticed, as it fell, the utility bill, unopened and at risk of drowning amid the flotsam and jetsam. She plucked it out and shoved it into her back pocket.

Was that a— Yep. A dollar bill in the pocket of her jeans, folded in on itself and toughened by its washer-dryer tormentors. She unearthed it and pushed the utility bill down in its place. Hopefully she could be trusted to pull that out before laundry day.

As if there were a day for any sort of normal human behavior anymore. She glanced around the kitchen. They obviously didn't observe *Load the Dishwasher Day*. When had they eaten spaghetti? Two days ago? Three? She walked over to the stove and ran a fingernail along the crusted edge of their best sauce pot. Must have been closer to a week. She sucked the sauce flakes from her nail and her stomach growled its approval.

God, she was hungry.

She stepped around a pile of orphaned shoes and opened the fridge. A beer would taste heavenly, but she was relieved to find that there wasn't any. Several people—qualified and not—

had assured her that a sip or two wouldn't hurt anything, but she couldn't justify even the smallest risk. She was just three months along.

Baby felt at once unreal and impossibly tenuous.

She leaned in over the half-empty shelves, inviting the chilled air to rush her face and down the front of her shirt. Cerise had never quite *blossomed*—as her mother had called the rounding hips and growing breasts on Cerise's classmates—until now, thanks to baby. Never mind that she was almost thirty and had spent her life looking like a rectangle with legs. Now hormones swarmed her bloodstream like evangelizing zealots, bustling, stockpiling, preparing and bringing with them the start of real, hand-to-God boobs and curves.

I love you, baby. I love you. What do you want to eat?

Baby wanted a green olive sandwich and yogurt.

Several sandwiches, actually—enough to wipe the fridge clean of olives—and Cerise finally had to drag herself from her sodium- and carb-induced coma to stand and add *olives* to the curling grocery list stuck to the front of their fridge.

The back door opened and she heard Barb drop her backpack to the mudroom floor.

"Hi!" called Cerise.

"Hi back." Barb appeared in the doorway, her light meter still dangling from its industrial cord around her neck. If Cerise remembered correctly, she'd spent the day shooting a commercial for a local restaurant chain—she thought maybe a seafood place. Who ever knew?

Her partner had been one of those creative types whose parents often predicted would be on their payroll until she was in her thirties. But she'd actually become a go-to videographer in the Minneapolis advertising scene. Whereas Cerise had a lab coat and drove five days a week to her nine-to-five job—more like seven to six, if she was being honest—Barb worked more like a client jockey, guiding companies of every size—Fortune 100s to mom-and-pop shops, alike—across the high-def finish line. From the smell of her, today's client made its income the deep-fried way.

Of the two of them, they had both known Barb was better suited to be the day-in, day-out manager of all things social and emotional for baby. As a human being she was warmer, calmer, a better nurturer, a better teacher than Cerise, the sort of person who could talk to any random child at the park or the grocery store as if they were the most interesting person holding the most wonderful piece of sticky candy in the world. But it had been Mother Nature, Herself, who'd raised a willowy finger, pointed it at Cerise and thundered, "You first."

Cerise and Barb obeyed.

These days, Cerise thrilled at the prospect of motherhood more than she ever imagined. She felt a pull, a purpose she never knew existed, something that must have lain dormant in her cells, waiting for the right hormone to come along and light it up. And had it ever.

Yesterday she stopped by the deli at lunch and welled up with tears at the tenderness with which a young mother offered her son a bite of her sandwich. She pictured herself as the tender young mother in flip-flops and a slightly rumpled shirt. It looked like a few days had passed since she'd had a shower, but the grime didn't look at all the same on that new mom as it would have on a hipster or an old man. Motherhood carried with it a sweetness, an air, and she couldn't believe it was actually coming true.

Nevertheless, she still prayed the housekeeping gene would kick in for at least one of them before baby came.

Barb pulled the light meter from her neck and dropped it to the pile of mess on the counter, then made her way across the kitchen, kicking aside a pair of abandoned slippers as she went.

"How's Shrimpy?" She leaned over, lifted the hem of Cerise's shirt and kissed her belly.

Cerise could smell layers of butter and deep fat fryer and garlic on Barb's neck. She breathed them in. Yes, today's shoot must have been the fish place.

"Baby is full of olive love."

By SEVEN THIRTY, Cerise had called it a night and crawled under the covers in bed. All this boob, baby and hip growing sapped her energy most days before dinnertime, and it took all she had to fill her stomach before sleep.

She rearranged the pillows beneath her head and, thanks to the twisting and thumping, burped up the taste of green olives and toothpaste.

You're a strange one, baby.

Barb walked in holding a mug of something steamy. She lay down on top of her share of the comforter, holding the mug carefully at her chest, not spilling a drop. Her body was twice the size of Cerise's, long and broad, like Cerise's mother, Violet, but without the oversize clown feet—both women more imposing than your typical *gal.*

Cerise had not missed the fact that she'd chosen a partner with the same physical stature of her own mother—hair excepted, as Barb had the luscious red hair reminiscent of a Femme Noir while her mother, Violet, nursed an unwavering commitment to short, *wash 'n' wear* cuts. Wasn't there some saying about daughters choosing to marry their fathers? Well—go figure. Cerise already was her father. She couldn't marry herself.

"Tired again?" Barb fumbled about the covers in search of Cerise's hand.

"Pregnancy equals exhausting." She yawned a voracious tornado of breath, effectively shredding the sweet whiffs of cinnamon rising from the steaming mug. Barb grimaced and recoiled.

"God, what did Shrimpy have you eating tonight? Smells like cat food."

"Good thing we don't have a cat or it might have been." She unearthed a hand from the depths of her cocoon and reached for Barb's mug. "Safe for me to have a sip?"

"Plain ol' cinnamon apple tea." Barb handed it over, and Cerise watched as she sat up and bent at the waist to pull the socks from her feet.

"How long do you think it will be before I can't do that anymore?"

Barb tossed the socks to the floor and looked at her. "Do what?"

"Bend at the waist. See my toes."

Barb smiled. "A while, I'd assume. Though, who knows? Virgin terrain for both of us."

Cerise snorted. She took a sip of the tea and felt it glide down her throat. Her stomach settled, though until that moment she hadn't known it was upset. Baby had taken over everything.

"We got the invitation to my dad's retirement party today." She handed the mug back to Barb and hunkered down, rustling the sheets as she burrowed.

"Yeah, I saw it downstairs. Beautiful stationery."

"Nothing but the best," agreed Cerise. She smiled and crooked her elbow, holding her head up above the rise of the bedding.

"How long do you think it'll take till your mom and dad drive each other crazy?"

"I think everyone is concerned." Cerise rolled her eyes. "I imagine they'll break up the time as best they can—Mom's already planning a trip to Scandinavia." True fact: she'd received no fewer than a dozen emails from her mother proposing various dates that she hoped might allow Cerise to join them. "She wants me to go along."

"Oh, I'm sure she does," said Barb, nodding. "Little does she know Shrimpy gets the final say."

"Little does she know…"

Barb smiled gently and held her gaze. "I get that you haven't told your mom, but how come you haven't told your dad?"

"You told your dad yet?"

Barb snorted. "Last time I talked to my dad he claimed to be in Pamplona for the Running of the Bulls. But I know he was just dodging my call. I could hear a *very American* barista in the background calling out coffee orders."

"Why Pamplona?" Then Cerise waved off the question, as if admitting she wouldn't understand the answer even if there was one. Barb's semiestranged relationship with her trust-fund-turned-hippie parents provided for a steady flow of cash and cocktail party anecdotes, but little else. There wouldn't be a warm, congratulatory call coming from them anytime soon.

"Anyway…" Cerise returned to the subject at hand. "I thought I ought to let my parents get through the retirement party first. Plus, that's not news I want to drop into our typical conversation—price of gas, interest rates, hey-Dad-I'm-pregnant. Baby deserves its *own* moment."

"All right." Barb sighed. This wasn't the first time they'd had this conversation. "Your mother at least knows I'm coming to the party, right?"

Cerise laughed. "Knows, yes. Acknowledges, no. Same old story."

"Same old story, then." Barb drained the mug and sat up. She eased her legs over the side of the bed and sat for a moment, her back to Cerise. "We kissed at Christmas dinner last year, right in front of her. On the lips." She turned and smiled. "Ostriches can't hold a feather to your mother."

"Aw, c'mon. Admit it." Cerise teased Barb's backside with her foot. "You ain't nothin' but a phase."

Barb rolled her eyes. "Okay, Daisy Buchanan."

"Wait—" Cerise held up a hand, stopping any clues. Barb was steeped in the classics, but the only literary references Cerise knew came from the mandatory hours spent next to her mother watching *Masterpiece Theatre* on PBS. All that time invested and the only things she had to show for it were a decent British accent and a canny ability to let her thoughts wander behind open eyes.

"Henry James?" she guessed.

"Close, but no. That's Daisy Miller. Daisy Buchanan is Fitzgerald. *Gatsby.* The *come what may, life is a party* girl."

"God." Cerise pulled her legs back, tucking them up under her hips like a nest. "That's an unfair comparison."

"I'm just saying, maybe your mother isn't the only ostrich in your family."

Cerise paused, still smiling, though barely. She knew the right response would be to engage, be a big girl and work through her partner's worries. Instead, she took her cue from Mrs. Buchanan.

"Actually, I think if the Baumgartners were to be any sort of bird, we'd be wrens. A little bit plain, but loyal as they come."

Barb sighed and stood. Cerise knew she'd let her down but didn't have the energy to correct course.

"If the Hesse family were birds, we'd be California condors."

"Nice. Majestic and powerful."

"No, members of the vulture family and nearly extinct."

Christmas 2010

Dearest friends, far and near—

Evergreen Tidings from the Baumgartners!

I do hope that everyone reading this letter has had the wealth of blessings that 2010 brought our family. I am truly humbled and I hope, as I write this, that you'll sit with me for just a moment so that I can share a few of the highlights with you.

My dear Ed and I continue to "plug away," as they say, on the day-to-day work to which the Good Lord calls us. Ed is working as much as ever in his BiolTech laboratory, advancing the world's understanding and treatment for those who suffer from the pain and humiliation associated with gastrointestinal distress. And I, in turn, do the Lord's small work—taking care of house and home and volunteering my time with the Dorcas Circle and the Heritage Council at church. Pastor Norblad, our longtime minister, scared us this fall with a minor heart attack, but I am pleased and relieved to report that he has returned to the pulpit the picture of health. And not a minute too soon, as I worried I was going to have to add Pastor Search Committee *to my list of duties. We welcome you back, Pastor Norblad!*

But let's get to the real news! And that is, of course, that our daughter, Cerise, graduated with honors from the Engineering School at Rensselaer Polytechnic Institute in New York with a Master of Science degree in Materials Science. I cannot believe that it was just five short years ago she left home with nothing but a fresh high school diploma, a laptop and a new Laura Ashley comforter (no one should leave for college without good bedding). And now here she is, a young woman and a scientist, soon to be an inspiration to young girls everywhere! Ed reports that her graduate work into the timed molecular breakdown of composite biological adhesives was nothing short of inspired (my words, as I'm sure you already predicted, since everyone knows how my dear Ed is long on smarts but short on conversation (the delightful old poop!)).

I, of course, had quietly hoped Cerise would focus her studies on biomechanical engineering, so as to follow in dear Ed's footsteps (Rensselaer's program is ranked among the best in the world by U.S. News & World Report), but she is happy with her choice of degree, nevertheless. Please join us in congratulating our determined daughter. As you can well imagine, her father and I are both so proud!

As if that weren't wonderful news enough, Ed, with the help of his outstanding network of fellow scientists, has secured Cerise a position as Junior Materials Engineer at none other than Minnesota's own 3M Company. Just what products she'll be working on there I cannot say—even 3M moms aren't privileged with that sort of competitive information! But I can only imagine that by working in the world-renown 3M laboratories, she'll be at the forefront of the scientific innovations we'll have in our homes soon. Even the inventor of the Post-it Note (yes, a 3M product!) started as a Junior Engineer, too, I'm sure!

Now, if you can stand even more excitement, I'm thrilled to report that Cerise's job will be bringing her home to Minnesota! (Take a minute if you need to absorb the news...) I'm sure you can relate when I say that I was practically breathless when she called to tell us. I had to sit down and hand the phone to Ed so that he could get the details (imagine leaving "the details" up to a man—that's how flabbergasted I was (and, thank goodness, too, that our Stickley dining set had just returned from the reupholsterers' (you know how critical it is to maintain their veneer), or I would have fallen straight to the floor)).

Cerise begins her new job on January 15th, so not only will she be with us for Christmas this year, but all year-round, as well. I have contracted the services of everyone's favorite Minneapolis Realtor, Irving Schumacher, who—as you likely know—specializes in properties near Lakes Harriet and Calhoun. Obviously, young twentysomethings flock to the areas around

Minneapolis lakes. Who am I to stand in my daughter's way of doing the same? I am not the least bit blind to the handsome young men jogging and biking the parkways during warm summer afternoons! And yet, Ed and I also feel it vital that she put her Junior Engineer salary to work immediately by way of a real estate investment, and we plan to do whatever we can to help. A scientist, an engineer and a homeowner she will be! (Plus, how could I resist an excuse to decorate a house? What fun! Watch for details in next year's Evergreen Tidings...)

Cerise also reports that when she returns home, she'll be bringing with her a dear friend named Barb, a fellow Rensselaer classmate and Fine Arts major whom Cerise took under her wing during their time together on campus. Both Cerise and Barb traveled to their New York school from Midwest upbringings (Barb hails from Cincinnati, where I believe her great-great-grandfather started a shipping company that's still in the family today), and both young women seem to have found kindred Midwest spirits in each other. Let's hope the young men of Minneapolis and St. Paul are prepared, as I suspect these two beauties are about to give them a run for their money and attention! We think of you like a daughter, Barb, and we welcome you to our modest Minnesota family.

And now, my good friends, the telephone is ringing and the pile of letters I've yet to answer grows, so I must sign off. But I do so with the deepest joy and most sincere wishes of Evergreen Tidings to you and yours, tonight and throughout the coming year.

Ed and Violet Baumgartner

3

Violet

THE PHONE CALL to the caterers would have to wait; Violet was late for her Dorcas Circle meeting at church. Not that they'd start without her—the Faithful Redeemer Lutheran Church Christmas Fair for the Homeless, of which she was this year's chairperson, comprised nearly the entirety of today's agenda.

Purse. Tote. Overcoat. Shoes. She took one last inventory of herself to ensure she had everything she needed, then slid into the driver's seat, pulling the car door shut behind her. She loved the silence of a still car. The near-echoing quiet allowed her to gather her thoughts.

She'd start with a serious review of the volunteer roster. Last year's fair had relied too heavily on members of Faithful Redeemer's high school youth group, a demonstratively unreliable bunch who showed up late and inappropriately attired—only teenage hubris could be blamed for flaunting about among those in need while wearing two-hundred-dollar jeans. And some of their crew hadn't shown up at all, which, after chasing home several girls who looked like they'd melted into their jeans like chocolate into a mold, Violet thought perhaps was more blessing than curse.

She turned her key in the car's ignition and backed carefully to the end of the driveway, where she stopped, put the car into Park and pulled her pen and a copy of the day's agenda from her tote bag. She made a note in the margin: *Volunteer Dress Code.*

Now, then. Onward.

Down the block, Mrs. Donaldson, her neighbor of nearly thirty years, stopped plucking the dead blossoms from the autumn mums on her front porch to wave hello.

The fair committee would need time to review the flashy language in the special insert for Sunday's bulletin. Unfortunately, the church secretary had submitted an early draft that encouraged church members to "Come one, come all." *For gracious' sake.* Didn't she know the difference between a Christmas Fair and a hootenanny?

Violet pulled over to the side of the road. She again pulled out her agenda and pen and made a second note: *Too flashy.*

Violet engaged her blinker and turned right at the end of the block.

This was the ninth Christmas Fair she had overseen, each year more successful than the last. And she suspected it might be her final hurrah. Who could predict what adventures would sweep her and dear Ed away after retirement? They needed to seize every moment before disease and old age took their toll. Not that she or Ed were old yet—heavens no. And she'd already made a doctor's appointment for Ed to receive a physical the first week he was home. Health and adventure would be top priorities for them in their golden years—carpe diem, indeed.

She drove one block farther, slowed to a complete stop at the stop sign and turned left.

Truth be told, if anyone had predicted that her professor father would drop dead of a heart attack three months after delivering his final lecture, Violet would have made an appointment with his doctor, too. Her mother had always blamed his death on a lack of direction following the end of his career. "What was left for him to achieve?" she used to say with a melancholy Violet found ripe with self-pity. Violet, herself, was much more reasonable. She blamed her father's death on the fact that her mother fried two eggs for breakfast every morning, and then drove the man to campus so she could have the car for shopping and errands. No wonder his heart stopped. He hadn't exercised a single gram of cholesterol out of his arteries for forty years.

No, Violet wouldn't tolerate any unwelcome surprises when she and her husband had both worked so hard to achieve the life they had now. Ed knew that. But did the Lord? She certainly hoped He did.

It was true, yes, that she'd nearly turned down the opportunity to head this year's Christmas Fair committee, since she knew planning dear Ed's retirement party would require most of her energies. Even so, she'd agreed to one last year. In fact, she'd already kicked off the donations drive by personally buying three American Girl dolls—a Kit, a Rebecca and a Samantha—along with each doll's accompanying storybook set. It was the perfect Christmas gift—to the tune of $450 dollars, no less—and any girl would love to have it. Cerise never favored dolls as a child, of course, but then, she was always so busy reading the set of medical school texts Violet found at the used-book store for a dollar.

At the end of the third block, Violet turned right into the nearly empty church parking lot.

The hard truth was, Violet couldn't step down from the committee yet. She needed one more year to prime her friend and committee cochair, Eldris Endres, to properly take over. Violet's concerns over Eldris's readiness weren't so much a question of loyalty—she could trust her age-old friend to maintain the fair's traditions. After all, the Baumgartners and the Endreses were of the same school of thought, the same old-home wisdom that placed the church at the heart of all things. They served side by side on the Dorcas Circle and had brought their children up through Sunday school and high school ministry together. Richard Endres was even dear Ed's VP during his two-year term as president of the church council.

No, Violet's sole concern was with Eldris's judgment. Several years ago, for example, she'd actually suggested that they send each family home with a poinsettia plant in addition to their gifts.

"And have Faithful Redeemer get blamed," Violet protested, "when hundreds of children end up in the hospital from eating the poisonous plant?" That was the end of the poinsettia debate.

It was just before two o'clock when Violet walked through the church doors.

From the street, Faithful Redeemer was postcard perfect: clapboard and brick with a steeple that could be seen for blocks. It was the sort of building that conjured up images of devout, hardworking folk dressed in muted colors and driving American cars. It even had a cornerstone that read, "Erected in 1870." A hearty vintage for Lutherans.

The early Minneapolis families who began the Faithful Redeemer history—mainly first-generation Swedish-immigrant storekeepers and livestock traders with family names such as Aasgaard and Ruud and Torsen—were an earnest and practical bunch. They built the original sanctuary themselves—Violet had always pictured it in an Amish barn raising sort of way—and for nearly a hundred years, the congregation wanted for nothing.

But no congregation should have to function without space to gather both in worship and in fellowship. Finally, in 1964, Faithful Redeemer families funded the addition of Sunday school classrooms, a church office and the Fellowship Hall.

That's where the trouble began.

In Violet's estimation, nothing could have been as contrary to the style and intent of the original building—not to mention its founding families—than the modernist rubbish of the new addition. All rounded edges and dome ceilinged, it adhered to the side of the classic sanctuary like a tumor, hungrily metastasizing into the hillside on which it sat. And that was only the outside.

The 1964 designs inflicted the families of Faithful Redeemer with a Fellowship Hall in which the walls were carpeted in burnt-orange shag—or, as her dear Ed had once called it, "the color of my retinas burning." And the attached kitchen couldn't have been designed by anyone other than a man, since every food-related event had the women of the church bumping elbows and crawling on hands and knees to unearth serving dishes from dark and ancient depths. Arthritis flared with every potluck, tempers with every coffee hour.

Until Violet stepped in.

Just about ten years ago now, the women of Dorcas Circle took it upon themselves—under Violet's leadership—to raise the funds to transform Fellowship Hall. Once a room of temperance and fire, today it was appealing, practical and beige. The walls were cleanly textured and painted, and the carpet, restricted only to the floor, was no longer shag but Berber. They'd even raised enough money to expand the kitchen and equip it properly with three ovens and two industrial refrigerators.

Violet felt a sense of relief and pride every time she opened its doors.

"Good afternoon, ladies!"

The Christmas Fair committee members had already arrived and they'd helped themselves to coffee from the commercial-grade stainless steel pot in the kitchen. Violet shook her coat from her shoulders and sat down at the head of the table. Eldris handed her a steaming mug of black coffee.

"Is that a new skirt, Violet? I haven't seen you in pleats before."

It wasn't a new skirt, but a very old one that she'd been holding at the back of her closet until the next charity clothing drive at church. She'd been so busy with her various projects lately, though, that she'd neglected to put the dry cleaning out for the delivery driver and now neither she nor dear Ed had anything pressed and ready to wear.

"Pleats are coming back, apparently," Violet said, flouncing the skirt about her knees. "What fun!"

Eldris smiled and turned her attention to organizing the notebook and pen in front of her. Violet watched her quietly, trying to gauge the moment. Why the sudden interest in her shopping habits? New skirt or not, her friend seemed to be making a point. Eldris was always full of questions, yes, but there was something about her tone. Not judgment, exactly. Was it envy?

Violet silently scolded herself for leaping to such a petty assumption.

Then again.

Richard Endres, Eldris's husband, had been laid off nearly six months ago from a very senior position at a large Minneapolis advertising agency, and one could only assume money was quickly becoming an issue. A man like Richard was too old to start over and too young to retire. Not to mention, too proud to ever admit they were in trouble.

Violet resented awkward moments like this. Ed had been very responsible with their investments. Retirement would be comfortable for them. And Violet, too, had played her part—never paying full price and always remembering the value of a dollar. There was nothing she could do to fix the Endreses' financial woes.

And to think that they soon had their son's wedding to pay for. Violet shifted in her seat just thinking of the bills. Perhaps luck would favor them and it would be one of those affairs where the bride's family paid for everything.

Violet made a mental note: *No new dress for the Endres wedding.* Moving on.

She smoothed the stack of agendas in front of her and straightened her pencil, then passed her fingertips across the locket at her neck and let the smooth cool of the gold calm her.

"We're here, of course, to bring a touch of Christmas joy to any neighbors in our Cedar-Isles community who've fallen on hard times this year." She passed the agendas to Eldris, who stood and distributed them around the table.

"The event will remain largely unchanged from years past.

We'll spend the month of December collecting donations and the fair will be held on the last Saturday before Christmas. Everyone will be issued two tickets. The first allows them to choose a gift for themselves, and the second, a gift for someone else."

The women at the table murmured their consent.

"Now, last year we discovered that several families had more children than tickets. So this year we'll set aside a stock of tickets to hand out as circumstances require."

Eldris nodded fervently and scribbled in her notebook. No one, Violet noted thankfully, mentioned aloud the commotion they'd encountered last year when a single mother marched through the door with seven children in tow. Each child wished to use their second ticket on a gift for their mother. That was fine. The real issue was the volume with which their mother began to question volunteer staff about just which one of her children she was supposed to use her extra ticket on. "The Lord blessed me with each and every one of them," she'd hollered, "but now you ladies, here, seem to be asking me to choose." Violet had shoved a fistful of gift cards into the woman's pockets and ushered her out the door as quickly as she could.

They wouldn't risk that scene again.

Violet continued, "And there is, of course, the issue of video games. I have long been vocal about my desire to make it a policy that we neither solicit nor accept electronic donations of any kind. It is unfathomable that we—especially the members of the Faithful Redeemer community—would spend good money only to encourage the decay of young minds." She paused, letting her point sink in. "Can I get a second on the motion?"

Silence.

Just like last year. And the year before. She shouldn't be surprised at the moral cowardice in the room today, and yet she was. Where was their indignity? Like she'd said all along, goodhearted kindness such as their Christmas Fair was nothing more than displaced pity if it encouraged the decline of a whole generation of children.

After a moment, Eldris cleared her throat and raised a sorry hand. Violet nodded in acknowledgment.

"It's not that we disagree with you *per se*, Violet..."

Per se. Did Eldris really think flowery language made her sound more convincing? Violet folded her hands and placed them in her lap. She would just have to ride this out.

"But it comes down to a matter of judgment. If a child has his heart set on a video game, who are we to decide that it's not good for him? That's the parents' job, I think."

Another committee member, Meg—who sat holding her toddler daughter—spoke up. Violet noticed she hadn't waited to be called on. "There are loads of educational video games available these days." She nodded at the blond-headed girl in her lap. "Sylvia here is learning her ABCs from Elmo on my iPad."

Hearing the name, the child raised expectant eyes to her mother and clapped. "Elmo?" She was squealing now.

"Oops! Shouldn't have said his name aloud." Meg reached over and pulled a bright pink rectangle from her diaper bag. It was an iPad, as far as Violet could tell, but it was encased in several inches of foam and had a pair of bunny ears sticking out the top.

The child squealed with renewed vigor and the committeewomen watched as Meg quickly turned on the screen and located Elmo. Sylvia grabbed one of the bunny ears, slid off her mother's lap and toddled off into the corner, eyes glued to the screen in her hands.

"See what I mean?" said Meg. "Video games aren't all bad."

The women murmured their agreement. Not Violet. She was thinking that the child had been a perfect angel until her mother gave her an excuse to misbehave.

She and Ed had allowed their daughter, Cerise, only thirty minutes of television every day, and only after homework was completed and reviewed, and only if the program was educational. Their diligence paid off. Cerise had been the only child in her fourth grade class to do a current events report on the disturbing rise of antibiotic-resistant bacterium strains, as documented in the PBS program, *Nova*.

"Be that as it may," said Violet, "I think we can all agree that the gentle monsters of Sesame Street are unusual in the world of video game characters. Just last week I was forced to watch a child in the dentist's office shoot zombies with grenades. The gore was appalling."

Meg piped up, again without waiting for Violet to yield the floor. "I really can't believe the members of our congregation wouldn't exercise good judgment when selecting a gift. Have we had trouble with violent donations in the past?"

Eldris shook her head. "Only the once—someone donated a G.I. Joe doll."

Meg laughed. "G.I. Joe isn't violent. He's basically a Barbie doll with muscles."

Violet was stunned at the young mother's ignorance. "A doll that promotes war and comes with his own machine gun." She made a mental note to keep an eye on young Sylvia as she grew up.

In the end, the women of the Dorcas Circle found a comfortable middle ground on the question of electronics, deciding that all promotional materials would include a list of *Recommended Donations* and *Not Recommended Donations*. Violet gave the decision a B+.

After the meeting, Eldris took her aside. "I know we didn't reach an ideal solution, Violet. But let me assure you—our son, Kyle, played every sort of video game throughout his teenage years and he turned out just fine."

"Thank you, Eldris. Your words mean a great deal to me." She smiled. Eldris was a waif of a thing—she pushed her food around on the plate rather than eat it—but she was as stalwart a defender of family as Violet. Judgment was one thing. Values were quite another.

Which meant, of course, she would never admit to poor Eldris that, contrary to his mother's esteem, Violet would give Kyle Endres a C+. Just *fine*, was right. He was pleasant enough, and he'd managed to graduate from university and begin a career as an optometrist—the variety of eye doctor, Violet was keen to remember, that did not require an MD. But he was boastful and overly pleased with himself, always bragging about the trips to Africa he'd taken with EyeShine, the fledgling nonprofit he'd founded to collect used eyewear for third world countries—and that stayed afloat only because his mother haunted her friends for donations and because the good people of Faithful Redeemer changed their eye fashion so frequently.

He wasn't a bad person. He just needn't be so forthright about his virtues.

Cerise disagreed, of course, always squelching Violet's opinions on the matter as quickly as they arose. Cerise and Kyle had been friends for ages and in her daughter's eyes, the budding Mr. Endres could do no wrong.

"I'm nothing but thankful for Kyle," Cerise liked to tell her. "My life would have been entirely different without him."

Which was poppycock, of course. But Violet knew that on certain matters, there was no telling Cerise anything. She also knew—rest assured, she and Ed had both kept a very close eye— that the friendship never breached the bounds of romance. Not once in all the years of rainy afternoons spent together in the Baumgartners' TV room or over a board game at their kitchen table did Violet or her husband ever walk in to find the two of them canoodling. There was Cerise and there was Kyle and there was their friendship.

And the fact that Kyle had managed to live twenty-plus years without falling madly in love with her daughter was just one more strike against the boy.

What Kyle *did* have to his advantage was his engagement to Rhonda Nelson, a local girl turned Channel 4 meteorologist, who'd recently gone national with a new job and a prime-time spot on The Weather Channel. Violet had always like Rhonda's style. She was the sort of handsome, educated woman who could be trusted to deliver the weather honestly, without the commercial hype so common in today's meteorology—every storm ending with "-mageddon" or "-tastrophy." Not to mention that she hadn't fallen victim to the low-cut, tight dresses worn by every other newscaster in the business.

No, Rhonda Nelson was the real deal. After all, both Violet's husband and her daughter were scientists. She could spot a phony a mile away.

"By the way, Eldris," she said, touching her friend's wrist gently for emphasis, "I've asked Rhonda to say a few words at Ed's retirement party and she's agreed. Can you think of a more fitting tribute? One nationally known scientist bidding another farewell?"

"She's a weather broadcaster, Violet. I don't think a weather person qualifies as a scientist unless you're a meteorologist."

"Semantics," said Violet. "No one's the wiser if we don't mention it. And anyway, in my opinion she has a PhD in style."

2017 FAITHFUL REDEEMER LUTHERAN CHURCH CHRISTMAS FAIR FOR THE HOMELESS
Saturday, December 23

———— ✧ ————

Your generous donations are once again being sought for the annual church Christmas Fair supporting our less fortunate Cedar-Isles neighbors. Last year's fair provided gifts to nearly 50 families. This year is expected to bring an even greater demand.

Donation bins are located in the narthex.

RECOMMENDED DONATIONS

Dolls	Small stuffed animals
Children's books	Warm socks
Winter gloves, hats, scarves	Small appliances
Shaving kits	Tool kits

NOT RECOMMENDED

Video games
Toys or books that glorify images of violence or war
Knife sets
Fireworks

EyeShine Thanks You for Your Generous Support

———— ✧ ————

FRLC member Kyle Endres, founder of EyeShine, a non-profit that provides prescription eyewear to the poor in Africa, would like to thank the members of Faithful Redeemer for donating over 200 pairs of used eyeglasses this year. Says Kyle, "Think of all of the people who will now see God's creation, thanks to you!"

4

Richard

RICHARD ENDRES ENTERED his fourteen-digit password and clicked Submit. He dreaded this part of his week more than anything, but he forced himself to do it—every Monday, without fail. If he didn't look... Well, he'd done that before and it led nowhere good.

$1,867.37. They had enough to pay the mortgage. If they didn't go out to eat, they'd be fine until next week when the utilities came due. Plus, there was the weekly $547 unemployment deposit coming next Monday morning. He checked the transactions list to ensure that this week's deposit had already cleared. It had.

At least the government was finally paying him for once, instead of the other way around.

It wasn't that he and Eldris were poor. God, no. He'd been a Senior Vice President at Peter+son Communications managing an eighteen-million-dollar client portfolio, for chrissake. This was no more than a hiccup. They'd navigated choppier financial straits. Setbacks were nothing more than opportunities gaining steam.

God, he was starting to sound like a motivational poster.

Eldris, though—she had to get on board with this new, temporary reality. Just this morning, she couldn't stop going on about what in the world she was going to wear to Ed Baumgartner's retirement party.

"The invitation says, *Black tie preferred*, Richard! We can't show up in just any old thing."

Fine, he'd said. He'd wear his tux. He'd been a Senior Vice President. He owned a tuxedo.

"No, I'm not talking about you, for once. I'm talking about *me*. Just what am I supposed to wear when everyone else is waltzing about in black tie?"

God, he hated when she got hysterical. As if there wasn't a single piece of clothing in one of her two—yes, two, goddamn it—closets that she couldn't put on for the twenty minutes he planned to spend at that ludicrous party.

Not that Ed Baumgartner wasn't a good guy. He was a hell of a guy—accomplished all sorts of medical breakthroughs for people with god-awful shitter problems. Not that you'd hear any of that stuff from Ed. His accomplishments were the sorts of things you read in the newspaper or heard about secondhand on the eighth hole of the Faithful Redeemer Charity Golf Tournament. Ed was just another stand-up guy: he wore a good suit, ushered at church most Sundays, kept his mouth shut.

No, it was Baumgartner's wife who bugged Richard: Violet. Queen of the Baumgartner Realm, Overseer of the Kingdom of Her Own Creation.

Violet was one of those people who started conversations in the middle of a sentence, who never gave a backstory, always just assumed you cared about what she had to say mostly because she was the one saying it.

So, fine. Eldris and Violet had been friends for who knew how long. What did he care what his wife did with her own time as long as it didn't cost him money or his sanity? But that was just the problem. Violet Baumgartner cost him more than his fair share of both. Today it was Eldris going on about his failures in black-tie wardrobing. Last week it was *couldn't they possibly redo the kitchen cupboards* because Violet had made some crack about the outdated handles. What the hell should she care about how a man opened the cupboards in his own goddamn house?

If it were only Eldris, maybe all this Baumgartner talk wouldn't feel like a shadow over his life. But it wasn't just her. Kyle, too. Their son had been Cerise Baumgartner's best friend since... Well, he didn't exactly know when, but definitely long before the poor kid was old enough to see the dead end waiting for him on Best Friend Street. Ah, God, he'd watched Kyle spend entire years trying not to wet himself over that girl.

Of course, now he knew. He'd pieced that puzzle together. No one had to tell him outright why Kyle never set her hormones burning. But back then—

One night he came home to find the two of them side by side on the couch, watching a movie so intently you'd think the alien attack unfolding on-screen was the only excitement their teenage brains could manage. Richard couldn't believe it. He walked into a dark house to find his teenage son alone on the couch with a girl and taking advantage of exactly none of it. No empty beer cans stuffed in the trash. No pretending they'd *fallen asleep* that way, all tangled up into each other. Not even a pizza box on the floor.

Since when had his house become a high holy monastery?

"Kyle," he'd said later, closing the kid's bedroom door behind him. "This thing with Cerise."

"What thing?"

What thing? He didn't corner his son very often, and he could tell he was practically scaring the fool half to death.

"You know." He guessed he should have done this long ago. "The thing. The hanging out. The being best friends."

"Yeah?"

Oh, for Pete's sake, this kid.

"What's it... What're you... What's gonna come of it?"

"What do you mean?"

And so the conversation went. An eternity of hemming

around a subject the way Richard Endres never hemmed, of not coming right out to talk about the bases when you weren't talking about baseball. Goddamn it, fatherhood was painful.

"Best friend never turns into boyfriend!" He realized he was yelling and immediately regretted it. "Look. If you and Cerise haven't started doing the stuff your mom and I don't want to hear about, you're never gonna get to do that stuff with her."

Kyle lowered his head and Richard felt the surrender like a kick in the gut. He wanted his kid to know there was no shame in rejection, but some people just weren't wired to see it that way. Kyle had his mother's softer side. That wasn't all bad, but still. Life happens. You buck up. Tomorrow comes.

"Nobody wants to do that stuff with me, Dad. It's not just Cerise."

"You'll find someone, kiddo. I promise." Because everybody eventually found somebody. He'd found Eldris. Maybe she was an odd bird sometimes, but she was loyal. And if there was one thing Richard Endres knew, it was the value of loyalty.

Or, he had.

Loyalty these days was nothing but a word, nothing but goddamn spin reserved for CEO crooks and financial planners. He used to think it was a valued commodity. Just like he used to be an SVP at Peter+son. Now he was just a guy with a late-middle-age paunch standing in his kitchen on a Monday morning while his wife waved the mail in his face.

"This has to be 150-pound stock, at least. And linen!" Eldris had gone on and on about the paper Violet had Ed's invites printed on. As if Richard gave a shit about card stock.

What he did give a shit about was that a single damn square of 100-pound—Eldris and her exaggerations—linen card stock had given him a migraine.

And they were out of Scotch.

This new world baffled him. *Fluid* was the word now. Data fluidity. Techno fluidity. Gender fluidity. What the hell was he supposed to make of that? Back when he was coming up, the only talk about flow was when you were told to *go with it*, and that was only fun because you were probably high. These days, strong was bad and bend was good, fusion was on the rise and steel was sinking fast. This wasn't a world he knew anymore. In it, he wasn't strong. He wasn't intimidating. He wasn't anything.

Everyone blamed the economy, of course. "I'd love to bring you on board, Richard, but it's the economy. The ad billings have practically dried up." Same shit, different lunch.

It's what they'd said to him at Peter+son that day, too, only he'd watched that shit storm crossing the horizon for months. And there hadn't been anything he could do about it. First his financial services accounts shuttered—in less than a week, three major US banks pulled ad revenues totaling more than six million dollars annually. Then it was the Consumer & Retail segment, then Travel. By the time Richard walked into the CEO suite that fateful day back in May, his client portfolio totaled less than five million dollars.

"I hope you know how much we'll miss you, Richard." He watched as his soon-to-be-former boss, a toad of a guy who kept his dermatologist busy with retinol treatments and mole removal, straightened the pin tethering his Dolce & Gabbana tie to his Burberry shirt. Richard wasn't one for men's fashion— aw, hell, yes he was. So he knew that this toad, the man who was about to dismiss himself so that some HR neophyte in a tight skirt and heels could talk Richard through his separation agreement, would walk out of the room wearing no less than a few thousand dollars' worth of thread.

"We're all hurting. I want to assure you of that." He gave Richard the same bullshit *If only there was something I could do* smile that he'd seen him give hundreds of suckers over the years—vendors who were expected to take the shit end of a raw deal, clients who weren't worth the paper their bills were printed on and saps like Richard about to land face-first on the unemployment tarmac.

I hope you croak, Richard wanted to say. *I hear that's what toads do.*

Instead, he stood up and shook hands with him like a damn fool, then watched him hop out of the room in his Italian leather loafers.

Just before the HR girl came in, Richard walked over to the desk, found the toad's gold pen and pocketed it.

5

Cerise

CERISE PROMISED HER mother that she and Barb would arrive at the retirement party no later than seven o'clock. So far, she might be able to keep her word. If only she could get her dress zipped.

"It's your boobs." Barb stood behind her, pulling at gaps in the fabric, trying to gain as much leverage as she could while she tugged at the zipper. "When did you grow boobs?"

"Don't tell me you haven't noticed." Normally, Cerise would have welcomed the banter, but she wasn't feeling playful. There wasn't another dress to choose from, and time was ticking.

"Of course I noticed, but these are like—" Barb grunted and pulled "—real boobs."

The zipper suddenly crossed its last threshold and glided to a quick stop at the base of Cerise's neck. Success. She released the air from her lungs—her tummy hadn't been the problem but she'd sucked it in, anyway.

Breathe.

Barb came around from behind and took her in. "You look great, all shimmery in red. Busty, even." She cocked an eyebrow. "You're walking into bombshell territory."

They'd gone shopping for the dress together and chose this one because of the plush ruche at its waist—plenty of baby disguise, just in case. But neither one of them had been pregnant before; how were they to predict that Cerise's top half would grow before her belly?

"The boobs aren't too much?"

"Not nearly."

Cerise didn't laugh. "I'm serious. Every dress I've ever put on my whole life made me look like a gift-wrapped shoebox. Flat and fancy. Now suddenly I'm in 3-D. My mom's got to notice."

Barb swatted away the concern. "I'll tell her you finally broke down and bought those silicon chicken cutlets from the Nordstrom women's department. She's been after you about them for years."

Cerise groaned. But knowing her mother, she might just believe it.

Shoes, coats, purses, and they were heading for the car. Cerise handed Barb the keys.

"I'm too anxious to drive."

"First time out in the world with boobs," said Barb. "Talk about pressure."

IT WAS 7:05 P.M. when they walked through the doors of the Historical Society's Grand Hall. The room was stunning, and her mother had obviously pulled out every last stop. The ceiling glittered with twinkle lights so faint they looked like stars. Crystal Champagne flutes adorned every table. The sound of the string quartet filled the room and floated down the stairs to the street. And the windows—floor-to-ceiling glass with a clear view of the state capitol and the state mall surrounding it.

It was a fitting tribute to the man she and her mother both loved so dearly.

"You're late." Her mother pounced from behind the head table as soon as they arrived. Cerise saw that she'd been redirecting a waiter holding a tray loaded with appetizers and she couldn't help but smile at the look of relief that passed over his face when Violet turned her attention elsewhere. It felt good to help a fella out.

Not to mention, Cerise was the tiniest bit flabbergasted by how beautiful her mother looked. She wasn't a particularly pretty woman—she had a deep chin cleft and a shallow jawline that, coupled, left the impression of her mouth sinking into her neck. But there was no disputing her innate elegance, and she carried herself with a fluid grace that Cerise had always envied. Tonight, she was radiant in cream satin and pearls.

"You look wonderful, Mom. Really lovely."

Her mom smiled and tilted her cheek for a kiss. Cerise complied.

Violet turned to Barb. "Well, Miss Hesse. You look as lovely as always."

Barb shot her a sparkling grin.

"Let me see you spin," ordered Violet.

She acquiesced. Hers was a floor-length emerald gown with a modest neckline and an open back that plunged all the way to her hips. Cerise suspected her mother had already spotted the naked zone and was performing a covert propriety check.

"Risqué, no?" Barb winked. "I figure I have to wear this sort of thing while I'm still young."

Violet nodded primly. She couldn't have liked it, but she apparently didn't consider it worth a fuss.

"Mom, what can we do to help? Everything looks just beautiful."

"I'd like you to stand near the door and welcome guests as they arrive. Direct anyone you know—or *anyone you suspect is important*—over to your father." She waved a hand toward the middle of the ballroom where Cerise saw her dad, awkwardly engaged in conversation with their minister, Pastor Norblad.

"Direct anyone you don't know to the hors d'oeuvres." She gestured dismissively toward several tables lavished with towers of food against the far wall.

"And where will you be, Mrs. Baumgartner?" asked Barb. "In case we have any questions."

Cerise shot her a look. *Suck up.* Barb smiled back.

"Everywhere." Violet fluttered her hands about the room, indicating that her territory as hostess extended to every corner and everyone. "I go wherever I'm needed." And with that, she was off, heading for the waiter with the appetizers, who saw her coming and turned on his heel to flee.

Over the next hour, guests trickled in by pairs. It was most fun to see old family friends, people she'd known as a child and who'd watched her grow up. She greeted Mr. and Mrs. Abelson from church, who owned a State Farm agency and who'd sold her the insurance for her first car. And she saw her parents' neighbors, Mr. and Mrs. Carlson, who'd always given her banana-flavored Popsicles on hot afternoons and who spent their summer evenings chatting in matching lawn chairs on their back stoop.

Finally, just before eight o'clock, Mr. and Mrs. Endres walked through the doors.

"Mrs. Endres!" Cerise gave her a warm hug. "Thank you for coming. It's wonderful to see you."

Eldris nodded and sputtered something about being thankful she had something to wear. Cerise had forgotten this quirk of hers. It was as if her head was a Boggle cube that she had to shake and wait for the letters to settle before making words.

"I just hope we're dressed appropriately." She fluffed the folds of her elaborate, black velvet skirt, then turned and straightened Mr. Endres's cuffs. "Your mother has such good taste, you know."

Cerise reached for her elbow, reassuringly. "You look wonderful."

Eldris continued to bobble and fuss. Cerise turned her attention to Richard, who snatched his cuffs away from his wife's worrying grasp. "Hello, Mr. Endres. Great to see you."

He reached out to shake her hand. "C'mon, kiddo. Call me Richard. We're all adults now."

"Fine then... *Richard.*" She smiled and took his hand, noting that he'd just called her *kiddo* and an *adult* in the same breath. "I'm sure you've met my partner, Barb." She put her hand on the base of Barb's back and ushered her gently forward.

"Of course. Good to see you again, Barb." He shook her hand. Almost too formally, with a little nod and a bow, as if making a point that their relationship didn't bother him.

It happened all the time. Barb seemed to spot it, as well, because she nodded and bowed back as if to put him at ease.

"Kyle and Rhonda should be here anytime now." He peered over Cerise's head at the faces in the room. "I got a text that said they were on their way."

"I'm glad," she said. "I made sure Mom put them on the list. I need some of my friends here, too!" She laughed playfully, hoping to keep the moment light. She couldn't help but notice the strain between Mr. and Mrs. Endres. Eldris was now fussing with the shoulders of Richard's jacket and he looked about ready to bodycheck her. The Endreses had never been a particularly placid couple, Richard forever barking orders and Eldris never seeming to know how seriously to take them. Maybe the tension was all in Cerise's imagination. Then again, she knew Richard was out of a job—Kyle had told her months ago.

"Please," said Cerise, gesturing toward the center of the room, "go say hello to my parents. They'll be thrilled to see you."

The Endreses made their way through the crowd and Cerise found herself breathing a sigh of relief.

"That was chilly," said Barb, watching them.

"Arctic cold," agreed Cerise.

"Ironic that they're both wearing black and white tonight." They turned to each other and said in unison, *"Penguins!"*

"Come on," said Barb, taking her hand. "Let's go see if any of those Champagne flutes are filled with plain old sparkling cider."

"And get some food," added Cerise. "Shrimpy wants a few of those shrimp cakes."

Violet Baumgartner knew food. The spread on the evening's banquet tables was proof, though Cerise had already known it to be true. Her mother served Brie and Buffalo mozzarella and handmade, hand-fired salsa back in the '90s before they were *things*. Tonight's delights were no exception.

Cerise piled a plate with shrimp cakes, Brie-en-croute and sun-dried tomato chutney, then layered smoked trout onto wafer-thin baguettes and slathered them with chilled cucumber-dill sauce.

"Oh, my god," moaned Barb. "Taste the Havarti. It's as rich as ice cream." She held up a piece and gave Cerise a bite.

It was. She loaded a few slices onto her plate, too.

While they stood, sampling and eating and reloading their plates, Cerise saw her mother excuse herself from conversation and make her way toward them from across the room.

"Incoming," she said to Barb under her breath. "She's spotted the boobs. I'm sure of it."

Barb laughed. "Let's see how this goes."

"Enjoying the food?" Violet appeared quickly. She always did have the power to part a crowd.

"Wow, Mom. This Brie-en-croute is amazing. Everything is amazing."

Her mother smiled graciously and smoothed the pearls at her neck, but said nothing more.

"You have wonderful skills as a hostess, Violet," said Barb. "The food, the setting—the entire evening has been lovely."

"Well, our dear Ed deserves every bit of it. He's been nothing but generous to Cerise and me." She turned and eyed Cerise. "You look different. I'd ask if you'd done something with your hair, but I know it isn't that."

Cerise stiffened and slowly turned so that she was fully facing her mother, eliminating her profile. "Well, it's not often you see me dressed up like this." She held out one of her shoes to show off her high heels. "Plus, I gained an inch or two."

She saw Barb out of the corner of her eye, watching the exchange carefully. "Violet," Barb said, interrupting the moment, "will you please tell me who your caterer is? I have some friends planning a wedding and their taste is nearly as fine as yours."

Nearly as fine. How did Barb ever manage to get so good at sucking up? Maybe it came as an accessory to the prep school uniforms she wore in all her childhood pictures. Or maybe it was the result of what her mother would have called *good breeding.*

"Remind me next week and I'll give you their card." Violet snapped from her study of Cerise's *je ne sais quoi.* "But for now, I have to get things started on the Champagne toasts." And again she was off.

"Thank you for saving me," whispered Cerise, taking Barb's hand.

"Anything for Shrimpy," she whispered back.

The sound of a finger tapping a microphone quieted the room and a gentle spotlight brought the guests' attention to Violet, standing beside the head table, urging the microphone into her husband's hands.

"Just welcome everyone and thank them for coming..." She was whispering, but the microphone was strong enough to pick up her voice, nevertheless.

A few guests tittered. Another hollered, "Speech, Ed! Let's hear from the man of the hour!"

Guests made clinking sounds, knocking their wedding bands against their glasses, and calls of *"Hear! Hear!"* rose throughout the room.

Cerise felt a warm glow at the sight of it all, pride and joy and love—everything at once. Her mother was right: Ed Baumgartner was a brilliant but simple man who asked for little and gave much. She had been lucky enough to be on the receiving end of his great generosity her entire life.

She knew without looking that her chest and face flushed red with emotion.

"I—well. Huh." Her father had taken the microphone and begun to speak. Cerise wasn't surprised he didn't appear to have prepared anything in advance. "This is all...wonderful. A wonderful night. Wonderful friends. Violet and Cerise, thank you." He paused and turned to Violet, his hand on his heart. She returned the gesture, beaming at him.

Cerise wasn't far from where they stood but she knew he wouldn't be able to quickly spot her in the crowd, so she raised her hand and blew him a kiss.

"Ah, there's Cerise," he said, pointing at her.

"Congratulations, Dad!" she called.

He smiled and waited a beat for the room to settle again before continuing. "I know I'm not a man known for many words, so when I do speak, I like to make them count. Which is why I just can't resist telling this joke one last time."

The crowd groaned. They knew what was coming. Cerise's father had told the same joke for as long as she could remember, the only arrow in his comedy quiver.

"What happens when a clown passes gas?" Then he held the microphone out to the audience, an invitation to join in on the punch line. Only to have Violet snatch it from his hands. The amplifier squealed in protest and everyone in the room went for their ears.

Violet thumped the microphone back into submission with her fingers. *BOOM. BOOM.*

"Now, Ed. We know how you feel about that joke. But before you go on, I need to announce that we have a very special *surprise* guest tonight who just walked in. And I know she would love to say a few words."

The confused audience gave a spattering of disappointed shouts, but Violet ignored them and swept her arms open to welcome Rhonda Nelson, rising Weather Channel star and fiancée to Cerise's best friend, Kyle Endres.

Cerise waved to Kyle as he stood off to the side of the room talking with his parents. He shot her a happy, relaxed grin. She hadn't seen him since his engagement party several weeks ago and it already felt like ages.

Cerise had known very little of life without Kyle in it, all the way back to their days in the Faithful Redeemer kinder-choir when he wouldn't stop kissing her cheek as they sat all lined up in the front pew, wearing their angelic white robes and waiting to sing,

Jesus loves the little children,
All the children of the world.

Her mother had later ensured that Kyle never be allowed to sit next to Cerise again, but the spark had been lit.

They were friends throughout elementary and into middle school, weathering together that period of adolescence when even the most well-adjusted kids spent entire years hating their faces and their clothes and every single thing in their whole lives. They were friends in high school, when Cerise started to think about dating girls and Kyle actually did it. And they remained friends when, in college, Cerise told him why she'd never acquiesced to the handful of hints he'd given her about them kissing each other.

Now Kyle was engaged and Cerise was having a baby. And they were still friends. Somehow, with each other's help, they'd managed to open the doors to adulthood and walk on through.

Cerise's mother, however, had never warmed to Kyle, even despite his long-standing loyalty to her daughter. The highest compliment Violet ever paid was to call him "not unpleasant," which Cerise knew was also how she would have described white sheet cake—necessary for a potluck, but never a dinner party standout. Tonight, however, Violet was keeping her mouth shut about Kyle, as his engagement to Rhonda Nelson had provided her a direct path to the evening's celebrity emcee.

Rhonda took the microphone like she was born to it. "What a marvelous affair! Am I right?"

Her charm was contagious, and Cerise and Barb exchanged impressed glances as the room again came to life with cheers and applause.

"So first things first. What does happen when a clown passes gas?"

Now it was Rhonda holding the microphone out to the crowd, and they merrily followed her lead.

"IT SMELLS FUNNY!" they all called. And again the room erupted.

Cerise saw her father double over, laughing at his own signature joke. She then caught sight of the smile pasted to her mother's face. Was she happy? Or was that the look of disgust? She couldn't tell. But Cerise did know that if her parents had ever decided to divorce, that joke would have been her mother's chief complaint.

Rhonda continued, "Now, Mr. Baumgartner. This is your night. And while I haven't had the pleasure of knowing you well over the years, I believe we can all join in celebrating and thanking you for your extraordinary medical achievements." She paused for further applause.

"As happens in every book, one chapter has come to a close and a new one begins." She held up her glass of Champagne for a toast. "So, without further ado, here's to as wonderful a tomorrow as your yesterdays."

The room raised their glasses and toasted in kind.

Rhonda then turned her attention to Violet and continued, "Now, if I may add one tiny more thing…"

Violet opened her palms by way of saying, *Go on!*

"A little birdie tells me that the two of you aren't likely to be bored during retirement."

Violet and Ed looked artificially horror-struck at the passively sexual innuendo, and Ed waved his hands at Rhonda as if to say,

Say no more! Say no more! It was the closest Cerise had ever seen her parents come to hamming it up.

More laughter. A few bawdy hoots from boisterous men.

She noticed then something on Rhonda's hem—a torn strand of sequins, like she'd snagged them with the heel of her shoe or a hurried fingernail. Then again, maybe it was just the light bouncing off the dress and playing tricks on her eyes...

Cerise heard the room go silent and realized, *crap*, she'd quit listening. What just happened? Rhonda had been talking, her parents laughing and Cerise had been taking it all in. But now Cerise was still struggling to register the moment when she heard her mother cry, "Holy GOD!"

Then the crash of crystal and the electric *crack!* of her mother's head hitting the floor.

6

Violet

ED AND THAT foul clown joke of his. *Of all nights.* To think he was still telling it, decades after he and Cerise found it in an issue of *Highlights Magazine.* Had Violet even an inkling of what that joke would do to her family, she would have immediately written the publisher and demanded her money back.

But then, as if on cue, there was Rhonda Nelson, fresh faced and stage ready, emanating from the crowd like an angel. Violet's salvation.

"So first things first," Rhonda cooed. "What does happen when a clown passes gas?"

Oh, for heaven's sake. The woman was supposed to elevate the evening, not continue its desultory spiral. Violet steeled her spine against what she knew came next.

"IT SMELLS FUNNY!"

The room exploded in laughter. Of course it did. This was precisely why she'd opposed a cocktail hour. Alcohol and good sense never mixed. But the caterer overruled her. "These are sophisticates," he'd said. "They'll expect a drink."

Why hadn't she followed her instincts? An evening that started as a ballroom filled with Minnesota's best and brightest had suddenly degenerated into a bloated gaggle of grown men and women surrendering themselves to the spells of a broadcasting bubblehead.

Well, Violet would not succumb. Rhonda may have a certain appeal, but Violet possessed something far more powerful. She had manners.

"Always a pleasant face, Violet," her mother had taught.

"Never forget that family is the face we bear to the world," her father had said.

So, Violet brought her chin up, her chest out and her tummy in, and there she stood, smiling until her face hurt, chuckling for the whole room to see as Rhonda carried on with her nonsense.

Always a pleasant face, Violet. Do it for Edward. For Cerise.

She smiled at Dr. Samuel Alcott, the state's leading orthopedic surgeon and the man who singularly reconstructed dear Edward's elbow after his disastrous fall on the ice three years ago, and who now stood hooting and thumping his wife on the back with such meaty force that her martini rained from its glass, thump by awful thump.

She gazed pleasantly at Elaine Overberg, Chairperson for the Minnesota Symphony Orchestra Fund and personally responsible for clawing the foundation's coffers from red to black with a series of fund-raisers so wildly successful she was now rumored to be forbidden from resigning. And to think Violet had just heard her *snort*, piglike, at a joke about a gassy clown.

Finally she spotted Cerise, rose cheeked and smiling, her pinkie finger entwined in Barb's. Cerise was happy, clearly, and Violet felt the briefest moment of relief wash over her. But something else struck her about Cerise tonight, an angle in her face that hadn't been visible before. Was it in the chin, the way it rose into her jawline? Or maybe the way her cheekbones filled the once-hollow curve just below her eyes. Whatever she saw, it was new, and at the same time, familiar. The face, she realized with a start, reminded Violet of her own father.

For heaven's sake.

Here she was, a grown woman—a *married* woman—watching her husband cross into retirement and thinking of her father. *Of all things.* This was Ed's moment—*their* moment. A Baumgartner celebration. It was not the time for reliving ancient sorrows.

But still. Her father had died a month after his own retirement party. How could she not think of him? How could she, even at this moment of great achievement, avoid asking the questions that draped themselves over his every memory? Would life have unfolded differently if her father had lived? Would he have defended himself where others did not?

Scandal was near enough impossible to fight during one's lifetime, but to see him attacked so viciously after death was nothing short of cruel. Mere weeks after he'd passed, the whispers turned to words, the words to howls. Why couldn't the university have let the questions go unanswered? What did it matter if the research wasn't his alone? He was gone, dead and buried.

Her mother should have fought harder. Violet would never quit holding her to account for what unfolded. There was so much more she could have done to save his work and legacy. And yet, she'd let it die, gave up, failed him as quickly as his heart. "There's no sense in getting ugly," she'd said. "I won't let this shadow the life I have left."

Always a pleasant face.

Somehow, thankfully, Violet had made it this far with her own family intact. Dear Edward retiring at the pinnacle of his career, Cerise grown and happy. Her family was stable. Responsible. Reliable. Barb was unexpected, yes, though Violet had to admit she invited little fanfare. Most people didn't ask, and their closest friends didn't need to—people in the Baumgartner orbit were smart enough to piece together the Cerise and Barb picture for themselves. And anyway, whatever news Violet chose to share about her daughter, it certainly would never have included a discussion of her bedroom life. That sort of business was no one's business.

Of course she would have loved grandchildren, but that was an emotional hurdle for another day. At least Cerise would never experience the pain she'd experienced on the road to parenthood. That journey had nearly gotten the best of her.

She shuddered and pushed back against the dark. *No sense in getting ugly.*

"A little birdie tells me that the two of you aren't likely to be bored during retirement."

Violet snapped from her thoughts. *Oh, for—* Weather girl could not have possibly moved from jokes about clown flatulence to the subject of one's postretirement sex life. Enough of Rhonda's indiscretion. There would be no more talk of clowns or sexual shenanigans or what in the world she and Edward were planning to do in the privacy of their own bedroom.

She opened her mouth to say as much but quickly thought the better of it. Let Rhonda Nelson be her own most embarrassing moment.

"*Because* before my fiancé, Kyle, and I even have the chance to tie the knot...you two are going to be busy *grandparents!*" She would, most certainly, however, speak to Cerise first thing tomorrow morning. Her daughter's best friend was about to marry a woman with absolutely no boundaries. No, Violet had raised her daughter better. Cerise would never have stood in front of Minnesota's greatest minds and made jokes about...

Grandbabies.

Oh, for gracious' sake.

Cerise is pregnant?

Cerise is pregnant!

Cerise is pregnant.

Part
Two

Christmas 1990

Dearest loved ones, far and near—

Evergreen Tidings from the Baumgartners!

1990. What a year of blessings this has been! I hope you feel the same. This morning I rose early, managing not to wake dear Ed or our little Cerise in the process, simply to find a quiet moment in which to share some of the highlights of our year with you. Sit with me, and I promise to do my best to honor the timeless traditions of the family Christmas letter.

Our dear Ed is working as diligently as ever on his medical research into the cause and treatment of gastrointestinal disorders. His team has been on the verge of a breakthrough for months, a new fiber-optic scope and laser combination (please excuse my unsophisticated explanation, as I am hardly a scientific or medical professional!). When finally put to use, the new tool will allow patients to avoid painful and costly surgery. I am so wonderfully proud of my husband.

Needless to say, there have been many, many days when little Cerise and I don't see him at all—coming home after we've gone to sleep and rising before we wake. I worry about his long hours. When we do see him, he's so very tired. I even considered buying him a pillow and blanket to keep in his laboratory, but I feared that would only keep him away from us longer. A man should sleep in his own bed.

But I am vigilant against the temptation to nag, whine or fuss about his job. I will not become that sort of wife. After all, it is Ed who is sacrificing his time and energies. The least I can do is to make a home for him where he feels warm, and happy, and rested.

All those years ago, when dear Ed asked me to marry him, I said "Yes!" without hesitation, secure in the knowledge that he was a man of integrity, a man who would never turn his back on God or family or responsibility. So, even though little Cerise and I miss him dearly, I know that the hours he spends away from us are hours he's giving to a greater good, to improving lives. He is putting to use the remarkable skills the Good Lord gave him. I could not be more blessed.

Even the weighty responsibilities of dear Ed's work, however, cannot erase the joy little Cerise brings to our lives. She is three years old now, as bright and as quick a young girl as I've ever seen. I predict that she will be an early reader, as she's already picking out letters of the alphabet and repeating their sounds. Just recently, she piped up from the back seat of the car and said, "Look, Mommy! That red sign has an S on it. S says sssssssss, like a sssssssnake." It's a good thing we were stopped at that stop sign, or I would have driven off the road in my shock! I went straight home to call dear Ed and tell him all about it.

Sadly, there were frightening moments in our year, as well. On February 27th at 2 o'clock in the afternoon, I was putting little Cerise's nap time to good use cleaning the kitchen (a mother gets so little free time!) when I heard the most alarming crash from above. Needless to say, I rushed upstairs to find little Cerise hysterical, a wounded bundle on her bedroom floor, blood veritably rushing from a gash in her head.

There was no time to ask questions. I grabbed a baby blanket to staunch the bleeding, and rushed our little girl to the hospital.

I regret to say that the doctors on duty (and may I be so brazen as to call out the hospital by name: Swedish General) were less than appropriately alarmed by the injury or its cause, electing to shortcut the care owed to our daughter. They attempted to proceed with nothing more than stitches. I stopped them before a single needle could be threaded.

After all, had they even considered the cause of the accident? Our little Cerise had never fallen from her bed once in her life. In fact, she'd hardly fallen, ever (she was sturdy even as an early walker). I demanded a CT scan. They resisted, attempting to assure me that any child of any age can roll out of bed in the midst of a dream. I, in turn, advised them that our daughter, Cerise, was hardly any child.

I proceeded to list my concerns: skull fracture, hematoma, brain bleed or (heaven forbid) a tumor. Had they considered any of these possibilities? Yes, they said, of course they had. But little Cerise was cheerful and happy and, ultimately, only in need of stitches.

At 6:45 p.m. that evening, our daughter, Cerise, walked out of the imaging lab, happy as a lark, bearing CT scans as clear as the sky on the day she was born. (To be safe, you can imagine that I requested a follow-up MRI, which, despite my obvious objection, they patently refused.)

I called dear Ed immediately at the lab to share the good news with him.

My husband and I have said many prayers of thanks for the guardian angels the dear Lord sent little Cerise that day. We are truly blessed. And I hope, in turn, that our trauma serves as a reminder to each of you, however young or old, to listen to your fears, to never take no for an answer and to always look out for the ones you hold so dear.

Christmas blessings to each and every one of you,
Ed and Violet Baumgartner

7

Richard

NOW THAT WAS one hell of a party.

Sure, Richard felt sorry that Violet had to be rushed to the hospital. From the sound of it, she took a pretty decent crack to the head. Everyone, including him, grabbed their own skulls as soon she hit the floor, a sort of mass commiseration. It was a scene, all right.

She took a fair bit of crystal and china with her on the way down, too—must have grabbed for the head table, only to end up pulling the tablecloth and everything on it to the floor. From where he'd stood, all anybody could see was Violet, lying in a jumble of broken glass, spilled Champagne and blood.

What a mess. What a bloody, expensive mess.

He really felt sorry for Ed. It was his retirement party, after all. The guy worked his ass off for thirty-some years and just when he's ready to celebrate, he gets stuck with a bill for damages and an ambulance. The insurance deductibles alone were going to be less fun than a prostate exam.

According to Eldris, Violet was still in the hospital. She'd been over to visit three or four times at least, even though the party had only been two days ago. She brought flowers the first time, but apparently the smell aggravated Violet's headache, so she brought them home again along with half a dozen other bouquets from Baumgartner sympathizers. Now the whole damn house smelled like a funeral home.

Then Eldris made a huge batch of Richard's favorite chicken tortilla soup but wouldn't let him have any of it, saying it was for Violet and Ed. Apparently Violet was refusing the hospital food and Ed hadn't eaten since popping shrimp cakes at the party. How this became Richard's problem, he'd never understand. But according to Eldris, he was supposed to keep his *greedy, grubby self* away from the pot.

So he'd have an egg salad sandwich. Tomatoes gave him heartburn lately, anyway.

In the meantime, Kyle was pacing their house like a bored lion at the zoo. Going on and on to his mother about how she had to convince Violet that Rhonda didn't know Cerise hadn't told her parents about the baby—on and on about *how could they not know?* And really, Richard had to agree with the kid. It wasn't normal for a woman her age to suddenly grow boobs. He'd noticed—sure. She'd looked like a skinned cat in that tight red dress.

And, yes, he knew there was surgery for that kind of thing. God, of course he knew that. But those boobs weren't surgery kinds of boobs. They were normal lady-with-boobs sort of boobs. Plus, lesbians—were they even *into* that artificial sort of thing? He sure as hell didn't know.

Which, of course, brought up the question of how Cerise got pregnant in the first place. And who the hell got her that way? (Someone at the party asked him who he thought had *knocked her up*, but Cerise struck Richard as too nice a girl to deserve that kind of visual and he ignored the damn fool.)

He could pretty much guarantee that Eldris hadn't dared ask Violet about the father. And he damn well wasn't about to ask Ed. Their conversational bandwidth ended at quarterbacks and the PGA. When their kids were graduating high school, maybe they talked about paying for college, but those checks were cashed long ago—*thank god*. No, to ask Ed that question, that was like taking a dump in another man's toilet.

Definitely not.

This was the Baumgartners' own damn mystery, anyway. He had bigger issues—money and a job and figuring out how the hell to keep thirty years of his life and career from pissing away down the toilet.

He'd had lunch yesterday with his former Peter+son colleague, Bill Benson, who told him, while eating a salad, no less—a god-awful fig and crap-something salad—that the agency had dismantled most of his accounts and handed them out to junior execs like bubble gum at a birthday party.

"Chad Handlers took BiolTech."

"Handlers! He's a goddamn twelve-year old." In fact, Richard had hired the kid no more than—what was it? "I hired the damn kid in 2007."

Benson shrugged. "That was years ago. Plus, he came over from across town at Olson. Even then he was hardly a baby."

Justice. Richard suddenly very much liked the sound of that word.

"What else? Who got the new Vikings stadium?" If Richard had ever had a baby, this was it. The Minnesota Vikings, the NFL and the City of Minneapolis—along with a scattering of citizen advocacy groups—had been in negotiations for years to replace the Metrodome with a new, state-of-the-art football stadium. These weren't million-dollar conversations, but billion-dollar ones. With a *B.*

Needless to say, he wasn't the only guy who wanted in. You could pick them out wherever you went—tight clusters of men in suits in the darkest corner of every restaurant in town, spending their Account Development dollars on guys who offered potential, but no promise. It was anyone's guess back then which way the wind would blow, and Richard wanted a farmer in every field.

He wormed his way into the negotiating scrum all the way back in 2007, gaining an invite to a closed-door session on the recently completed land-use feasibility study, thanks to his buddy in the state legislature, Dan Higgs. From there on out it was nothing but lunches and golf and drinks with the shifting list of names that meant anything and everything to the deal.

And he'd done it, goddamn it. He'd won the advertising contracts on the whole damn stadium. The money would start flowing in the very day the quarterback threw his first pass.

That was March. Just three months before they gave him his walking papers.

"Who got it? Who got the new stadium account?"

Benson dropped his napkin to his bowl and fell back in his chair. "No one. The stadium canceled the whole damn contract. Took it across town to Olson."

Richard felt a bitter aftertaste rise in his mouth. Not just today's lunch, but the taste of so many lunches, so many martinis, so many asses kissed. That was it, was it? Everything he'd ever accomplished in his entire career amounted to no more than slips of paper, traded about, one exec, one peon, one agency to another. All the energy he'd invested. All the sleep he'd lost. And the *hair*—he'd gone both bald and gray landing the goddamn stadium deal. All of it, now nothing more than figures on a page in some other guy's book.

God, maybe it wasn't the tomatoes giving him heartburn.

Where was the justice in it all? He was growing increasingly fond of that word—*justice*. There sure as hell wasn't any justice in his little corner of the world. No, those blowhards up in Washington could talk all they wanted about bringing America back. It was all just noise, just a distraction to keep us deaf to what was really going on. But he knew—he knew they took money from whatever dirty, grubby hand would feed them. Who cared about little guys like him? Mr. and Mrs. American, be damned. Republicans touting entitlements reform nonsense to banquet rooms full of millionaire cronies—as if Richard had ever taken a handout in his life. Not that the Democrat fools were much better. They were so busy pretending to understand the poor guy's troubles they kept forgetting not to have their picture taken on their favorite yacht.

The latest election was finally over, but did he expect anything to change? Of course not. When had it ever? They were still fighting the same wars that the last guy started, still drinking tax dollars through a straw and burping injured soldiers up in return. Poor bastards.

No, the world had no sense of justice anymore. If you didn't believe him, just ask Ed Baumgartner.

8

Violet

TREACLE TART. THE words emerged, sticky but resonate, from a gauzy haze. They drifted. She drifted. How fun. How lovely.

She wanted to know them. The words, *treacle tart*. There they were, there, just in front of her.

They wanted her to know them.

She had, at one time, known them. *Treacle tart*. Such lovely sounding words, all soft and generously curvy. No sharp corners in the words *treacle tart*. No, they would be just fine. She'd like the feel of them on her lips. She'd like the taste of them falling from her mouth.

Treacle. Tart.

She thought she ought to at least try.

She opened her mouth.

"Oh, you're awake, are you?" Ed's voice tore into her head like a seam ripper. Ripped the quiet right in two. Like pants, the pants she'd been mending. Had she been mending pants?

No. At least, she didn't think so. She'd been—
What?

"Another bouquet, love."

Ed was here. They were both here. Yes, she and Ed were both here.

"From the Heritage Council at church. Nice of them."

"Don't—" Violet held up a hand. It felt only remotely connected to her body. "My head." Her voice was hoarse. She felt it on the way up. Heard it on the way out.

"Right. I'll bring them down to the nurses' station. See if anyone else on the floor needs the cheering up."

Ed. Wonderful Ed.

WHY WAS HE WHISPERING?

"Been in and out all day. Doctors say that's a good sign—means she's healing. Not nearly as agitated as she was when they first saw her. All that shouting. Terribly agitated."

Agitated. That was sort of a lovely word, wasn't it? Soft but strong. Like the sound of a sneeze... *Aaaaa-jeh!*

On second thought.

"WE'VE BEEN REDUCING the sedatives for twenty-four hours now."

Oh, dear. This was not a voice she liked. No, this voice needed to blow its nose or take a warm shower. Flush everything out. Seek medical help if all else failed.

"Now that she's resting on her own, we'll watch her. I imagine she'll start to perk up within the next several hours."

Why was this voice in charge? This voice needed to see a doctor. Where was Ed? She ought to tell Ed to advise the voice about a good saltwater gargle.

"The scans are clear, so once she passes her balance test, you'll be free to take her home."

Home. This voice ought not to be coming home with them.

"Salt, Ed. Tell him about the salt."

Then Ed's hand was on hers.

"It's the sedatives wearing off," said the voice. "That should clear as she perks up. Like I said, next few hours."

⁂

"Mom?"

Little Cerise. Lovely, little Cerise.

"How are you feeling?"

That was sweet of her to ask, wasn't it? Little Cerise playing make-believe, a child caring for her parent.

Warm. She was comfortably warm. But her neck ached. This pillow was awful. And her head…

"My head is splitting."

The taste of disinfectant on the air brought her crashing back. To the hospital. To her sinus-infected doctor. To the presence of memories she could not yet see or reach. She scowled, and then winced anew from the radiant waves of pain racing across her face and skull.

Cerise took her hand and caressed a thumb along its surface. Violet could feel it bump as it passed over each vein and knuckle.

"The nurse is on the way with your pain meds. That should help."

This was not a game, it was not make-believe, and she swallowed back the panic threatening to rise in her throat. She forced her eyes open. The room wasn't too bright. The flourescent daylight wasn't painful anymore.

Well, at least that was something.

Her overnight bag was on the windowsill. Packed. She was going home today. To her own bed. To the quiet of her own house. No more assaults by nurses obsessed with her blood pressure.

Ed had promised a freezer stocked full of Häagen-Dazs mango sorbet.

Finally she could see the pieces lining up obediently in her mind.

"I stopped by the house." Cerise again. Why was everyone whispering at her?

"I made sure your favorite robe was washed and ready. And I bought you these." Cerise pulled a soft pink bundle from the bag beside her chair. "The woman who sold them to me said they're the world's softest pajamas. But I like them because they don't look like pajamas at all." She smiled reassuringly. "I know how much you hate lounging around."

Violet reached out a finger and touched the fabric. Soft, yes.

She pushed them back into the bag with as much force as she could muster. She didn't want pajamas. Soft was not a virtue. These words mocked her.

"This isn't a game of make-believe, Cerise." The thoughts, mere seconds ago arranging themselves into an orderly space in her head, threatened to mutiny. She could feel them, shuffling and jeering.

"Of course not, Mom—"

"Cerise," she said, looking at her lovely, pink-faced daughter. Cerise met her eyes. "Such a sweet girl. My wonderful girl." She touched her cheek. It helped. Yes, the quiet was good. One more piece of her thoughts took its place in line. "You're about to make me a grandmother."

Cerise let out a long breath. "Yes."

"Which means you are about to become a mother."

"Also true, yes."

The truths fell from her mouth without warning. She hadn't known them until, suddenly, there they were.

"Promise me this pregnancy wasn't a—" She grasped for the words flitting across her addled brain, but they were too quick. "I mean, you want this baby? It's a baby you want?"

She thought that's what she wanted to say. The words, though. They weren't cooperating.

Cerise was close now, her cheek nearly touching Violet's.

"Yes, yes, of course. This baby is very much wanted. Very much loved."

"Because it was a surprise, you know. We were surprised. We weren't ready."

"I know, Mom. I'm so, so sorry. If I'd known..."

"That's just it." There, she felt something click. Neurons connecting. "I didn't know. I didn't know about the baby."

She paused, the clarity lifting her, pushing her forward like the opening of a curtain onto the morning sun. Then, memory. Rhonda Nelson blinding in sequins. Samuel Alcott thumping his wife's back. Martini rain. Cerise's cheeks. Her father's face. Pinkie fingers.

And there. The final connection. The truth standing in silent vigil awaiting her arrival.

Her daughter had gone and gotten herself pregnant and Violet hadn't even known.

9

Cerise

"Mrs. Baumgartner! If you don't lie down we'll be forced to restrain you."

It took two brawny orderlies and her mother's no-nonsense nurse nearly ten minutes to restore peace.

"What set her off?" the nurse barked, her voice cresting the din of the orderlies' tussles. "What upset her so suddenly?"

"I'm not sure," Cerise said. "She was calm, asking me questions, and then *bang*! Something flipped. I think her memory is coming back."

Her mother stopped thrashing, then turned and glared at Cerise with a look she hadn't seen for years. As teenagers, Kyle had dubbed it "the Watchtower," and it held a place of preeminence among her mother's tricks.

"You better find some kind of way outta here," Kyle would sing, channeling Hendrix as they made their escape to his hand-me-down Buick. "Said your mother with her glare."

They knew her mother deployed the Watchtower only rarely, and always strategically. It was a look that said, *You can't hide from me*, and when it came, they ran.

Today, Cerise withered.

She reached out and smoothed the bandage wrapped around her mother's forearm—eight stitches from a broken Champagne glass. And after she'd been so adamant with the caterer—"absolutely no plastic."

"Mom. Please relax. I don't want you to get hurt again."

Her mother closed her eyes.

"Well, she seems to have calmed so I'm going to see where the doctor is," the nurse said. "We can't release her until a final consult and he's going to want to know about this. Call the nurses' station immediately if she shows any more sign of agitation."

Cerise nodded and fell into the chair beside her mother's bed. She kicked the bag of pajamas away with her foot. She'd spent all last night arguing with Barb, the trauma from the party continuing to take new forms like an emotional shape-shifter, relentless in its hunger.

"Didn't I warn you?" Barb said, not yelling but close enough.

"Warn me? No. You hinted. Called me Daisy May and talked about my screwed-up family instead of your own."

"Buchanan!"

"What?"

"Daisy Buchanan, not Daisy May!"

Because fictional accuracy was what mattered. Cerise threw up her hands and went to bed to not sleep.

Now she welcomed the quiet of the hospital room. Her mother hadn't stirred for several minutes and Cerise watched her rest. The bruises on her cheek were deepening—Cerise figured she must have hit a table as she fainted. The goose egg at the back of her head would take some time, too. She tossed in her sleep trying to find a comfortable position. Maybe Cerise should buy one of those foam neck pillows they advertise on late-night TV.

That would probably go over as well as the pajamas.

Beads of perspiration ran from her mother's forehead and streaked her face like tears. Maybe there were tears, too. Hard to tell. Her mother rarely cried, but Cerise knew the pain must be awful.

And because she caused it, she knew she'd also have to fix it.

They were taking her home today, but what came next, she didn't know. Her dad would need some sort of help.

Her poor dad. By the time the ambulance had arrived, he'd gone white, his skin nearly translucent, holding her mother's hand, oblivious to the quiet chaos swirling around them. Cerise didn't know what had upset her more, the sight of her mother lying on the gurney, or her father, forlorn as a child.

He was finally sleeping at home again. She'd convinced him to leave after two nearly sleepless nights in the hospital recliner that left his back so torqued he couldn't stand up straight.

"She's going to need you when she comes home, Dad. You've got to get some good rest."

That's where he was now, paying a few bills and answering phone calls so that he would be distraction-free as soon as Violet left the hospital.

Cerise's cell phone buzzed.

"Do you know where your mother keeps the queen-size sheets? This darn sheet I pulled out is far too small—keeps pulling up at the corners."

"Don't worry about it, Dad," she whispered. "I already changed them. Just put the old ones back on. Or leave it. I'll make the bed up when I get there."

"No, I'd like everything ready when she gets home. I'll put the old ones on, like you said." She could hear the sheets rustling against the phone as he spoke. His voice was confused with irritation but quick with the urgency of an incomplete to-do list.

Had her father gotten old while she wasn't paying attention? He was only sixty-eight. Just weeks ago he was running a world-class laboratory; now he couldn't change the sheets on the bed.

She tucked the phone into her pocket and looked over at her mother, who appeared to be still asleep. Her skin was growing thinner with age, too. Not yet translucent, but nearly paper fine.

"I can feel you looking at me, Cerise. I'm not dead." She opened her eyes and looked at her. "I was resting my eyes."

"I didn't think—anyway. Dad's at home taking care of a few last things. Hopefully the doctor will be in to see you soon. Then we'll sign your discharge paperwork and bring you home."

Her mother hmm'd approvingly. "He didn't have the wrong sheet," she said. "It was sideways. He was trying to stretch the horizontal edge across the length of the bed. He's always done it. That's why I make the beds."

Apparently she and Kyle hadn't been the only targets of the Watchtower.

"He'll pay the bills, sort the mail and fill the car with gas on the way to the hospital," said her mother. She smiled, and then began, gingerly but determinedly, the process of sitting up. "He'll be here within the hour."

Cerise put a gentle hand on her shoulder, stopping her. "Mom, no. You're under strict orders to take it easy."

She scowled and looked Cerise in the eye. "Are you interested in changing my bedpan, then? Because if not, you need to walk me the restroom."

Right. Of course.

Together, they eased her legs over the edge of the bed, and then paused to give her head time to adjust to being upright. Gradually, Violet transitioned her weight to her feet.

"Please make sure the back of my robe is closed, Cerise," she said, swatting at the fabric closures along her back. "You can spare me at least that one small indignity, can't you?"

And so it had begun, the subtle jabs Cerise knew to expect until their collective power exhausted itself. She could ignore this one, but it wouldn't be the last and she was prepared to swallow the bitter pill of her guilty fate.

She couldn't help but wonder if her mother actually had lost her memory, it would have made the situation just a tiny bit easier. She was going to tell her parents about the baby *when the time was right*—after the retirement party, after her father had had his time in the spotlight.

She felt her spine arch as her thoughts began to spin anew.

After all, Rhonda Nelson owned a big fat slice of responsibility for this mess, too. And Kyle—Rhonda had to get her information somewhere. Kyle had been calling Cerise nonstop for three days, begging her not to blame Rhonda, that she didn't know the baby wasn't common knowledge, that she felt so unbelievably bad and did she think her mother would appreciate a visit from Rhonda in the hospital?

"Ow!" She felt her mother flinch. "My arm is not a lemon, Cerise. You needn't squeeze so hard."

Cerise loosened her grip and let out a long breath. "Take all the time you need, Mom. I'm right here."

CEDAR-ISLES NORTH STAR SAILOR

April 18, 1996

Cerise Baumgartner, age 8, took home the blue ribbon in the Cedar-Isles Elementary School Spelling Bee. She defeated 24 fellow schoolmates to advance to the Minneapolis Public Schools Elementary Spelling Bee Finals in May. Baumgartner is in third grade. Her winning word was *fortuitous.*

CEDAR-ISLES NORTH STAR SAILOR

May 9, 1996

Cerise Baumgartner, age 8, of Cedar-Isles Elementary, won a blue ribbon in the Minneapolis Public Schools Elementary Spelling Bee, defeating 28 fellow students representing elementary schools throughout the district. Her winning word was *indefatigable.*

There are no further levels of elementary competition within the district, so Baumgartner's parents have petitioned the school district to allow their daughter to participate in the Secondary Schools Spelling Bee Finals scheduled for May 18. According to her mother, Violet Baumgartner, "It's irresponsible for a school board to stifle a child's abilities and desires. No wonder the Chinese are beating us in education. Any mother in China would do the same."

CEDAR-ISLES NORTH STAR SAILOR

May 23, 1996

Cerise Baumgartner, age 8, of Cedar-Isles Elementary, is scheduled to appear at the Minneapolis Public School Board meeting on Thursday, May 25 at 7 p.m. The Board held a special, out-of-session vote late Sunday evening to allow Baumgartner, who recently won the Minneapolis Public Schools Elementary Spelling

Bee, the opportunity to display her exemplary spelling skills by spelling nine challenge words, one selected by each member of the Board. The event is open to the public.

CEDAR-ISLES NORTH STAR SAILOR

May 30, 1996

Cerise Baumgartner, age 8, was awarded a $5 gift certificate to Swenson's Ace Hardware, as well as a Certificate of Accomplishment by the members of the Minneapolis School Board at their May 25 meeting. Baumgartner, recent spelling bee champion, correctly spelled eight of the nine challenge words selected for her by the members of the Board, faltering only on the word *deferential*. Her mother reports that she will donate the gift certificate to charity.

10

Violet

VIOLET HAD A choice to make. She could obey doctor's orders to sit quietly at home and thereby surrender the Faithful Redeemer Christmas Fair to Eldris and her assorted crew, or she could layer on a good concealer and surprise the do-gooder church gossips who would otherwise spend the day spitting the Baumgartner reputation out the blunt end of the social meat grinder.

There didn't seem to be any choice about it.

"I most certainly will *not* drive you to church tomorrow." It was already 9 a.m., but Ed was still in his pajamas at the breakfast nook. He had his laptop open next to him and Violet could tell he'd been checking for BiolTech news. An artist's rendering of intestines emanated bold and pink from his screen.

"My head hasn't hurt for days, Ed."

"Wonderful. But you're still on strict orders to take it easy." He closed his laptop, as if to punctuate the refusal.

Violet flinched.

They'd had this discussion at least a half-dozen times since she'd returned home, yet here she was, still confined within the same four walls because some doctor with a nasal condition decided he knew better than she did about her own health.

Not to mention that Ed, just a week into retirement, was also stuck at home, forced into the roles of caretaker and traffic cop. *All this fuss.*

"You heard the doctor, Violet. You are to do nothing but rest until your exam next week. A Grade 3 concussion is nothing to mess around with."

"Nor is providing Christmas to more than a hundred people. All I'm asking is—do *not* roll your eyes at me, Edward Baumgartner."

He may have thought she wouldn't see, but she had. Or at least she thought she had. She was still forced to squeeze her eyes closed from time to time when her vision blurred. This morning she blamed his plaid pajamas—they were too busy and awful. Her mind couldn't make sense of it.

"Never in my life have I rolled my eyes at you, Violet. I wouldn't dream of starting now." He stood and emptied his coffee mug into the sink, then took her hand and eased her into one of their kitchen chairs. He sat down beside her. "We're about to become grandparents. We need our health so we can enjoy every minute of it."

He smiled and placed a gentle hand on her knee. She covered it with her own. His hands had always been a bit rough—all those chemicals in the lab, she'd figured. Now they were already softening.

"Healing takes time, Violet. Give it time. That's all I ask."

"But people are talking, Ed. The fiasco at the party. The baby. Cerise. Doesn't that bother you?"

He shook his head no. "Let them. It's just talk."

She couldn't believe her ears. How could he say such a thing after what they'd experienced? Here was a man who hadn't voluntarily picked up the telephone since the day they married, but now carried it with him wherever he went—even, she shuddered to admit, into the bathroom. He had to. It rang all day and night. And every time it did, she was forced to listen to him recount the details of that awful evening.

She could see the phone sitting beside him right now, atop the legal pad on which he'd scrawled the speaking points she insisted he use.

Violet suffered a serious concussion, though is feeling much better now.

Her doctor expects her to make a full recovery. She's already bouncing back beautifully.

The fall was caused by her sheer excitement about becoming a grandmother. We could not be happier about the news.

Cerise and the baby are both healthy. She is due in May.

We are blessed to have so much support from friends and family. The phone rings day and night.

The best thing you can do to help us is to support the upcoming Faithful Redeemer Christmas Fair for the Homeless on December 23. We have all that we need, but so many people in our community are hurting.

The notes were meant to help Ed manage his answer consistency. Every caller asked the same series of questions and it was crucial they each receive the same information, given that each person's next call would be to a friend with whom they could compare notes. He'd balked, of course, but she'd worn him down after insisting he call Lois Jacobsen back to correct a number of his statements.

And now to hear him say, *let them talk.*

"Honestly, Edward. I suppose you'd let the inmates run the asylum, too?" She stood, but too quickly, and the world buckled under her feet. She grabbed the back of her chair to steady herself.

"Are you all right?" He was suddenly next to her, a hand under her elbow.

The change in position provided her a perfect opening to snatch the telephone up when it rang no more than a second later.

"Baumgartner residence. Violet Baumgartner speaking." This time she saw it. Ed had most certainly rolled his eyes.

"Violet! Wonderful! Oh, it's just super to hear your voice."

Who on earth was squawking at her? "May I please ask who's calling?"

"It's Meg. From church. From Dorcas Circle."

Of course. The toddler mother who sounded like a toddler herself. "Meg, how lovely of you to call. I took a bad fall, as you know, but the doctor expects me to make a full recovery. In fact, I'm already bouncing back—"

"Holy cow, Violet, I could hardly believe my ears when I heard the news. I can't even imagine."

Violet *hmm*'d pleasantly to buy herself a moment in which to locate her thoughts. Where had she left off with her speaking points? She wished she'd been following Ed's page. Oh, yes. "It's just wonderful news. Ed and I could not be more excited."

"It all must be terribly confusing, though! How did it happen?"

"Well, I simply fell—wait, how did what, dear?"

"Oh, it's just so awful. Not what you expected at all. You must be heartbroken."

"I, of course, well, no..." Violet couldn't make heads or tails of what this woman was saying. Her stomach rose at the insinuation that she and Ed would be anything but overjoyed about their impending grandparenthood. And yet—oh, for heaven's sake, there was no making sense of this woman. "Pardon me, Meg. I'm not following."

"Well, of course not, Violet. That's what I'm telling you. You just rest. We've got this. You don't worry about a thing. You take care of you."

The words spun from Meg's sentences like debris tossed from a tornado. Violet felt dizzy. Exhausted. "Of course, dear. By all means." She squeezed her eyes closed and took a moment to calm the storm in her head.

They had been talking about her fall.

Then the baby.

Then. Wait. She was confused again.

It was time to close this conversation down.

"The best thing you can do to help us is to remember to support the Faithful Redeemer Christmas Fair for the Homeless on—well, I forget the date but it's coming soon."

"Absolutely! You have my word. We'll miss you this year, Violet, but you just focus on getting better. Don't give the Christmas Fair a second thought. We'll just see you when you're back on your feet."

"Excuse me?" There was no mistaking what Meg was telling her now.

"Oh, I know. I've kept you far too long. Be well!"

She heard the line click as Meg hung up. Violet stayed still, lingering with the dead phone to her ear until it began to wail its off-the-hook siren.

Ed took it gently from her hand and pushed the off button. "Violet?" he said gently. "Who was that?"

"The start of the mutiny."

"MOM, I'M SURE Mrs. Endres and the committee have it perfectly under control. I don't know what Barb and I could possibly do."

That evening, Cerise and Barb sat side by side on the couch in her family room. They'd arrived soon after dinner, though Violet assumed the two of them had not yet eaten, as Barb was still in the baggy, industrial pants she'd only seen her wear when returning home from a shoot. From all appearances, they'd come straight here, as she'd requested.

"There's leftover chicken tortilla soup in the refrigerator. I'll have Daddy bring you each a bowl."

"Mother—" Cerise began to protest, but Violet saw Barb put a halting hand on her knee.

Cerise shifted, twitching her shoulders about like she did as a child when trying to make up her mind. Finally she settled, placing a hand on her gentle slope of a baby bump. "All right. Thank you. Soup would be lovely."

Ed had been hanging up the girls' coats, but he took his cue and headed to the kitchen. Violet leaned back into the blankets and pillow Cerise had left for her before she came home from the hospital, which still sat neatly folded where she'd placed them. Ed insisted Violet leave them there—his way of encouraging her to rest. But really, if she were going to lounge about like someone with nothing better to do, she'd do so in the privacy of her own bed. The family room was a public space.

"I'm sure Eldris will do a fine job, Violet," said Barb. "Though no one could fill your shoes."

Violet eyed her. Even all these years later she still hadn't decided if she was a kiss-up, or if her propensity toward flattery was the result of fine breeding and all her years of private preparatory schools.

"You and I both know, dear, that *fine* is not a label to strive for." She waited a moment, letting the point sink in.

Barb demurred. "Of course not. My apologies."

"The result of all this mess is that the two of you must uphold the lion's share of responsibility until I'm back on my feet."

"For the Christmas Fair?" Cerise's voice was edging toward a whine. She clearly needed to eat. "You have a whole team of capable people—Mrs. Endres especially—eager and ready to help."

Violet held up a hand, her patience wearing thin. "I don't like asking this any more than you like hearing it." She dabbed gently at the corners of her eyes, now watering from pain and frustration both.

"Mom, please don't make this about the Christmas Fair if it's really about the baby."

She stared at her daughter. "Of course this is about the baby, Cerise. From now on, everything in your life—every choice you make, every dollar you earn, every book, every vacation, every meal, every word you utter will be *about the baby*." She reached for the locket at her throat, closing it in her palm. "You will never again do anything *without* thinking about the baby."

And she wasn't exaggerating. Cerise had no idea how much her life was about to change. Her mother had told her the same when she'd tried so desperately to become pregnant, but Violet had ignored her then just as Cerise gave every indication of ignoring her now.

Still, that wasn't the reason she'd called the girls here tonight. Instead, Violet had a strategy. She may have been stripped of the Christmas Fair but she would make it absolutely clear to the Faithful Redeemer community that the Baumgartner family refused be pushed quietly aside. They would not be shamed into isolation. This baby was a miracle and her daughter a brave champion. She would earn them the respect they deserved.

Barb took a long sip from the glass of water in front of her, then smiled. "That's the best part about becoming a parent, isn't it? The permanence. The absolute dedication."

"The responsibility," Violet added.

"Yes," agreed Barb, nodding. "That, too."

"Then you get what I'm asking. You get why it's important to get ahead of this sooner than later. It's for the sake of the baby, for the sake of the family."

Barb's head stopped nodding.

"Mom, you're being cryptic."

Violet sighed. She had tried. She had tried so very hard.

"I want you to announce the pregnancy in the church bulletin."

Barb choked on her water. Cerise snorted with laughter.

"You're not serious, Mom."

"I most certainly am. Do you know how many phone calls I've gotten since the accident?"

"Well, I'd hope lots. You were hospitalized for three days."

"Hundreds. Hundreds of calls, Cerise."

Her father, obviously still following the conversation from the kitchen, called, "Now, Violet. Don't exaggerate."

"Calls every day, and every single one of them wanting to

know how you got pregnant. Wondering if this was your *plan* all along. This is your chance to stand proud."

Barb now. "They ask that? They say, 'How's your head? And by the way, Violet, how did your daughter and her lesbian partner manage to swing that making-a-baby part?'"

"Of course not."

Vulgar. She'd never know Barb to be so…direct.

"They're not asking, Mom. You're asking. You can't stand not knowing everything there is to know about this baby." She brought her hand back to her belly protectively. "Except we're not telling."

"Why on earth not?"

"Because that's not the point. You wouldn't ask Amy Meyers to publish an announcement about how Jason managed to knock her up. *It was the big snow back in December that had every road closed between here and Rochester. There was a bottle of wine and a fire—*"

"Cerise Applewhite Baumgartner!"

Now Barb snorted with laughter. Violet couldn't be more appalled. The indecency of the room was practically causing her to break out in a sweat.

"Now you're getting insolent." You could never reason with Cerise once she became sarcastic.

Barb leaned forward, placing her elbows on the two giant canvas patches covering her knees. Violet was almost certain she was smirking.

"Please understand, Violet. We don't believe it's anyone's business how, or with whose help, this baby came into our lives. Cerise and I alone are the baby's parents. Just like you said. From now on—every thought, every decision, every move we make—the two of us. All about the baby. Isn't that what matters?"

Violet met Barb's eyes, second for second refusing to break her gaze. The grandfather clock in the front hall ticked.

"If you don't tell, people will assume. And believe me, girls, it's never good when people are left to their assumptions. Consider it the first gift you give your child—to be born with an enviable story and a bright future."

She saw a scowl flash on Barb's face, but she said nothing.

Cerise sighed, the look on her face full of regret. "I'm sorry I didn't tell you about the baby, Mom. I should have. I know that now. I didn't want to overshadow the party, is all—and now look. I'm really sorry."

Her voice caught, tight with emotion, and Violet felt her heart lurch at the sound of it.

Ed emerged from the kitchen with a tray loaded with two steaming bowls. "Who's ready for soup?"

Cerise and Barb raised their hands.

"Cerise," Violet said, watching her daughter blow cooling ripples across the surface of her bowl. "Do you remember the elementary spelling bee?"

"Don't you mean the school board meeting where I was asked to compete against myself?"

Violet did not rise to her bait. "You made your displeasure clear, yes. But do you remember what I told you that night?"

"No, but I remember the winning word. *Fortuitous. F-o-r-t-u-i-t-o-u-s. Fortuitous.*" She winked at Barb and smiled, then tucked into her soup.

"Yes. And I told you that we insisted you compete at the school board meeting for one very important reason. You honestly don't remember?"

Cerise shook her head. Violet looked to her husband, but he'd made what she assumed to be a convenient retreat to the kitchen. She was on her own.

"Your father and I insisted you be given that experience so you'd learn one thing." She paused, waiting until her daughter met her gaze and gave her complete attention. "We said, 'Always remember, Cerise. You can't win the battle if you don't show up.'"

11

Cerise

"She's kidding about the talking points, right? Tell me she's not serious." Barb held the car door for Cerise as she edged into the passenger seat. "And you can pretty much guarantee that I'm not reporting back to her about who asked what."

Cerise waved her off. She'd promised Mrs. Endres they'd be at the church by 10 a.m. and they were already late. There wasn't time for debate. "You know my mom. Always suggesting something. Don't take her too seriously right now—I'm just trying to focus on what we can do to help. I mean—" she snapped her seat belt into its lock "—we're sort of the reason she can't be at the Christmas Fair herself today."

Barb was quiet as she backed the car out of the driveway into the street. "You don't really believe that, do you? Are you seriously blaming yourself for what happened?"

Cerise looked at her. "Blaming *myself*? I'm not the only one expecting a baby here."

Barb flashed her a fiery look and started to say something, but snapped her mouth shut and turned her eyes back to the road. It had snowed last night, just in time for Christmas, and the streets were slick.

"It's complicated, Barb." God, Cerise hated it when they fought. Getting along was so much easier. "I tell myself that it's not our fault, but I keep replaying the scene over and over in my mind. The sound of her head cracking against the floor. It was so awful."

"I was there, Cerise. You don't have to explain it to me as if I didn't see any of it." She was pissed now. Cerise could see it in the set of her jaw, the way she never moved her face when she was trying hard to keep from exploding. Each turn of the steering wheel became just a little sharper than the last.

"I didn't mean to imply—anyway. I'm sorry." It was all Cerise had been saying to anyone lately.

"I prodded you to tell your parents about the baby but you wanted to wait. And I respected that. I let you take the lead. I was patient. But now I'm stuck between your guilt and your mother's fury and it's getting more than a little frustrating not to be able to do a damn thing about any of it."

Fury. That was an interesting choice of word.

"I don't know that I'd exactly call her furious. She's upset, not to mention she's recovering—"

"Oh, she's absolutely furious. About it all—that her perfect party was spoiled, that she can't pretend anymore that you're not gay. Although, I wouldn't put it past her to find a way."

"Hey, that's not fair."

"Oh, c'mon, Cerise. I know you and your mom have some sort of metaneutrality about each other, but you're lying to yourself if you don't think for one moment she wouldn't prefer you knocked up and straight over happy and gay."

That wasn't true, but truth didn't seem the point to this discussion.

"Well, we could offer to throw a big white wedding. That would keep her busy for a while." Cerise poked Barb playfully in the ribs, but she didn't smile. "Look—you're right. She's never going to love the fact that I didn't grow up to be the girl she envisioned me to be. But this is a lot for anyone to come to terms with, and she was forced to do it in front of two hundred people. All I'm saying is, I can cut her some slack while she processes."

"Fine. But at least respect that I see it differently. And I say she's so mad, she's about to bubble over."

"Like a little teapot, short and stout?" There she went again, trying to lighten the mood.

"Like Glenn Close boiling the pet rabbit." Barb finally turned to look at her. "Like, don't be surprised if she shows up at our house and wants you to try on a new pair of Mary Janes she just bought for you at the Buster Brown store."

"Well, make up your mind. Is she furious or is she crazy? I haven't shopped at Buster Brown since I was six."

"Exactly. When you were still perfect and adorable and presumably straight."

The thought struck her like she'd hit a funny bone, made her focus wobble. "Did you know?" She sucked in a breath, as if shocking her brain with oxygen would help her sort it out.

Barb turned to her again. "Did I know what?"

"The picture in her locket. The one she's always kept there. It's my kindergarten picture. From school. From when I was six."

Neither of them said another word until they pulled into the church parking lot.

THE FELLOWSHIP HALL was full to overflowing by the time they arrived. Cerise craned her neck looking for Mrs. Endres, but the room was thick with people. "Well, what do you think? Find someone and ask what we can do to help?"

Barb shrugged. Cerise realized she was going to have to accept the fact that this was her clown car and Barb was just along for the ride.

"All right, well let me…" The feel of her cell phone vibrating in her pocket interrupted her thoughts. The caller ID flashed her mother's number.

"Hi, Mom."

"How many people are there?"

"Well, the room is certainly full."

"That's not what I asked, Cerise. Isn't anyone keeping a tally at the door?"

"Um, not on the way in, at least." Cerise turned to look back at where they'd just come from. "I think they must be keeping a count some other way."

Her mother huffed so hard Cerise imagined she could feel the rush of breath on her ear through the line. "I must have told Eldris a hundred times—you have to track the numbers on the way in and on the way out. It's basic."

"I think I see Mrs. Endres, Mom. I have to go." She hung up before giving her the chance to respond.

"Hi, Mrs. Endres. Looks like it's a great turnout. How can we help?"

"Oh, I'm in a state, Cerise. Your mother always has everything so under control." She bobbled her head and closed her eyes, formulating her next thought.

Cerise and Barb waited and watched.

Finally, after several seconds without an answer, Cerise chimed in. "How about we stand at the door and keep a count of the people coming in? We can welcome them. Tell them how the room is laid out."

Mrs. Endres's face brightened with delight, then fell just as quickly. "Oh, dear. Your mother must have reminded me a million times." She continued bobbling and sputtering about to-do lists and traditions and G.I. Joe, none of which seemed pertinent to their role as greeters, since everything they needed to know about that job could be learned in a single visit to Walmart. Cerise turned and pointed Barb in the direction of the entrance.

It really was a great tradition, the Christmas Fair. Tables were lined with wonderful donations—board games and stuffed animals and blankets. Cerise watched as a young girl, probably no more than eight, ran a gentle finger along a pink box containing a brand-new Barbie Bride doll. Then she picked up the box and hugged it.

"Look at her." Cerise nodded in the girl's direction. "It's sweet."

A few tables over, an older woman caught her eye, smiled her recognition and headed in their direction. Cerise noted the choice of sneakers with the knee-length skirt. Very Fellowship Hall practical.

"Cerise," said the woman, the wobble in her voice commensurate to her age. "Do you remember me? I had you in Sunday school."

Cerise's mind was blank but she hoped enough fake enthusiasm would fool her brain into spitting up a name. "Of course! Yes. Mrs.—" *Darn.*

"Walters. Evelyn Walters. My husband was Maynard Walters. But you may not remember him. He passed."

"Oh." Cerise gently touched her wrist. "I'm sorry. When was that?"

"It was 1989."

Cerise nodded and *hmm*'d consolingly, doing her best to avoid looking at Barb, who was busy making wild eyes, obviously less concerned about maintaining her decorum.

"Anyway, such sad news about your mother," said Mrs. Walters. "And all that upset."

Barb raised a curious eyebrow. Cerise ignored her.

"Yes, well, she's doing better every day. Doctors expect her to be fully recovered soon."

"Well, our Patrick never married, either. Says he's too busy traveling here and there for work. I guess that's just the way of the world these days."

Her voice trailed off into a melancholy hum. Cerise couldn't quite pick out the tune.

"Anyway…" Mrs. Walters turned to address Barb for the first time since making her appearance. "Hello."

"Hello," said Barb.

Mrs. Walters nodded. "Yes, well…" Then she turned and headed back to where she'd come from.

"Interesting," said Barb under her breath.

"I haven't the foggiest," answered Cerise.

Her phone began to vibrate again.

"Hi, Mom."

Barb shot her a look and rolled her eyes. Cerise ignored it.

"Do they have the boys' toys separated from the girls'? If they're even close to each other they get muddled into a horrible mess and we have girls thinking they have no choice but to go home with some sort of remote control monstrosity."

Cerise scanned the chaos on the tables. "It looks as if everything is going wonderfully, Mom. No need to worry. Love you." Her mother was still talking as she hung up.

The calls continued. Had she checked on the number of additional tickets being handed out? Were the high school volunteers behaving themselves? Had anyone remembered to make the coffee?

Just as the clock was edging up on the end of the day, her phone, unsurprisingly, rang again.

"I need you to make sure someone donated a Bible. We can't host a church Christmas Fair without at least pretending it's not all about the gifts."

"Well, Mom, the tables are nearly picked clean by now. I don't have any way of knowing what everyone donated."

Barb shuffled in her boots and straightened her ponytail. Cerise could tell she didn't want to let on about how much she was enjoying watching her squirm with every phone call. Not that Cerise could blame her.

She turned and imitated a flapping beak with her hand as her mother expended every last ounce of worry over the donations. Barb raised an eyebrow, but didn't laugh.

"All right. I'll do what I can, Mom."

The shoppers were nearly all gone and the room hummed

with the activity of volunteers cleaning up and breaking every-thing down. Cerise was torn between telling her mother that the event was over and withholding that information, for fear the news would result in another round of reminder calls.

A few of the volunteers laid a picnic blanket against the wall by the entrance and spread it with an array of snacks. Small children began appearing from every direction, hungry and drawn to the food.

"Look," mouthed Cerise, waving at Barb and pointing at the children amassing on the blanket. Her mother was still talk-ing but she'd quit listening. "They're like minnows in a pond."

Finally Barb cracked a smile and laughed. It felt delicious.

"Mom, I—" Cerise tried to interrupt but Violet carried on. "Mom? Mom."

One of the mothers tending the minnow pond overheard her and looked up.

"Is that your mom on the phone, Cerise?"

Cerise nodded, though she didn't have the slightest clue as to who this woman was.

The woman took two gingerly hops across the blanket and landed at Cerise's side. "Hello, Violet!" She lined her face up with Cerise's and spoke into the phone. Cerise could smell the Goldfish crackers on the woman's breath. "It's Meg here. We miss you something awful, but it's so wonderful to see your daughter! I've been telling everyone the congregation is going to have a two-mommy family!"

For the first time all day, Cerise could tell that she hadn't been the first one to hang up.

12

Richard

THERE WASN'T A damn thing to eat in the whole house.

"Eldris!"

Not that she was even home. No, she was still over at the church cleaning up the mess Violet left with the Christmas charity fest, or whatever they called it. Violet was always handing work to Eldris and she was forever taking it, claimed she *enjoyed* helping others. To which he wanted to say, *Well, if that's the case, Eldris, how come there isn't a goddamn thing to eat in the whole house?*

Not that he did say that, of course. That would've had her in tears and him feeling like the worst. Still. Since when did he stop being someone his wife liked to help?

Richard grabbed a box of stale saltines from the back of the pantry and got to work looking for peanut butter. It'd better be creamy. That chunky crap just broke the crackers in half and made a mess of everything.

Well, all right. Something was actually going his way for once. He pulled an unopened jar of creamy peanut butter from behind a can of kidney beans. *Kidney.* Didn't Eldris know he only ate black beans?

Their regular dinner plates wouldn't be big enough to hold all the peanut butter crackers he was going to make. Maybe he ought to pull out a serving tray. That should be adequate. Where did Eldris keep that sort of holiday-only crap, anyway? Hell if he knew. He only paid for the goddamn stuff.

Ah, hell. This was his house. His money, his food, his house. Who said he needed a plate?

He picked up the jar of peanut butter and the box of crackers and headed for the silverware drawer. Did he need a knife? His house. He made the rules.

Not to say that he was a slob, though, either. He wasn't some Neanderthal who ate with his fingers. No, he'd been a goddamn SVP with an expense account and a corporate Amex card. He ate lunch at five-star restaurants and ordered whatever he liked. He knew the difference between a salad fork and a dinner fork. No one would have stared at him across a white tablecloth and wondered whether this was his first time at bat.

Damn it. Since when had he started mixing metaphors?

No, he wouldn't give anyone the satisfaction of seeing him get lazy. He grabbed a knife out of the drawer and headed for the couch.

The box of crackers didn't last nearly long enough. He was still hungry.

"Eldris!"

Not that she was even home yet. He knew that. He just liked having the freedom to let off a little steam when he wanted to. Yelling seemed like as good a way as any.

"Eldris!" Christ, that felt good. "Eldris! Eldris! Elllllldrissssss!"

"For heaven's sake, Richard, you sound like an old man in the senility ward."

Goddamn it!

He jumped from the couch, jar of peanut butter in his hand, aimed and ready. "You nearly gave me a heart attack."

"Well, of course you wouldn't have heard me with all that bellowing. What on earth is wrong with you? I could hear you practically halfway down the block." She dumped a worn grocery tote on the kitchen counter and did a double take in his direction. "Is that my sweatshirt you're wearing?"

Richard glanced down. Right. The university logo was stitched in pink and gold. So what?

"There wasn't any clean laundry."

"As if you're too busy to do a load for yourself. Kyle could manage that by the time he was twelve." She put her hands on her hips. This was Eldris on a roll.

"And you're eating on the couch again! Seriously, Richard?" She marched over and grabbed the jar of peanut butter with one hand and brushed the cracker crumbs from the couch cushion with the other. "What has gotten into you?"

She marched back to the kitchen and opened her grocery sack. She pulled a loaf of bread out of the bag and made him a sloppy sandwich, then dropped it on a plate at the kitchen table.

Man, it looked good, even without the jelly. But he wouldn't take it yet. He wasn't that simple. In fact, just this morning he'd gotten a very interesting email. An offer of sorts. Not the kind of offer one gets after a networking lunch or seeing an ad in the paper, but it paid. Cash.

"Richard, do you know who I just spent the day with? People with *real* problems. People who lost their homes, their jobs, some of them even their kids. The least I can do is show them a tiny bit of Christmas cheer. And now I come home to find that you won't even get off the couch long enough to do laundry!"

It wouldn't be easy, this deal he'd been offered. So he'd sat on it. Mulled it. Took his time. Thought it over. Had a bite to eat. He knew better than to rush a decision.

Eldris dug into her bag again and began dumping the contents onto the counter. Cornmeal. Tomato sauce. Kidney beans. *Kidney.*

"You know I hate kidney beans, Eldris!"

She slammed the last can down on the counter. "You need them for vegetarian chili and vegetarian chili is cheap!"

And there it was. Eldris's talent for reminding him of just how much of a loser he was. Couldn't get a job, couldn't even afford the expensive beans—aw, hell, not even the goddamn meat—for his chili.

He'd had it.

He walked into the office and slammed the door behind him.

The same email lit up his screen as soon as he touched the mouse. "All right. I'm in," he typed. "See you tomorrow night."

Feds Receive Most Unusual Welcome Gift

by Harvey Arpell,
staff reporter, *Minneapolis/St. Paul Standard*

December 28, 2017

Minneapolis, MN—Members of the Federal Reserve Bank, who gathered in Minneapolis Tuesday for a three-day summit on the nation's monetary policy, were greeted with a most unusual welcome gift—an eight-foot statue on the lawn facing the Federal Reserve Building. The statue, depicting a begging child, was constructed of chicken wire and eyeglasses. According to Minneapolis Police, a group calling themselves "The Watchers," claimed responsibility for the installation via multiple social media sites, writing, "We see the vulnerable among us, but who will speak for them?"

Other than this incident, the group does not have a history with law enforcement.

No arrests have been made and the installation has been removed.

13

Cerise

CERISE FLEXED HER fingers to relieve the cramping in her joints. Who knew week-old mashed potatoes were crazy difficult to scrape from the pan? Maybe if she'd realized she was eating glue...

The point was she was tired of living in chaos. Neither she nor Barb was particularly hung up on housecleaning. This was great in theory—they never fought about trivialities like who left their socks laying in the middle of the bathroom floor—but it also meant that their house was a rolling disaster zone. It wasn't just the dirty dishes or the forsaken shoes or the piles of life's miscellany. It wasn't even the fact that Barb regularly bought new underwear in lieu of doing laundry.

It was time to get their crap together.

"Come New Year's Day," she'd declared last week over dinner, "we pick up after ourselves. Every day."

Barb frowned. "I've never been one for New Year's resolutions. If we're intent on change, why not just start now?"

Cerise looked around the kitchen. "Okay. You first."

How had they gotten here? Any stranger would assume they were tidy, meticulous people. After all, they were both in detail-oriented professions—Cerise even working at the molecular level. You couldn't get more finely detailed.

As for Barb, she could spot discrepancies between cuts in TV shows and movies even when they flashed on-screen for no more than a second or two—a coffee mug facing the wrong direction, a glass of wine that grew from nearly empty to nearly full, a necktie that went from straight to askew to straight again. She was wired for consistency.

Only, neither one of them seemed to crave the same in their home environment. Cerise didn't know why.

Barb blamed her privileged childhood and the fact that she'd never known a time without a housekeeper.

"But wouldn't that have just created an expectation in you? Like, wouldn't you just expect someone to always take care of your mess for you?" Cerise was endlessly curious about Barb's family life. Her parents seemed the stuff of novels.

"Maybe. My mother certainly hasn't been able to survive without a maid and a generously flexible income." Her mother was forever landing herself at the spa to escape the stresses of life, despite never demonstrating responsibility for a single thing other than managing her husband's "idiosyncrasies."

"But I was always a little annoyed that someone kept moving my stuff. Lay a book down on your bed to go get a glass of water and it wouldn't be there when you returned five minutes later."

Cerise's mother had been the same way. Only, she wasn't just picking the book up, she was also frowning and *tsk*ing at Cerise. "Clean space, clean brain," she used to say. What did that even mean?

Of course, Cerise had never truly understood just how much time and energy her mother had invested in maintaining their home. When the dishes were always done and the laundry always clean and folded, the results looked effortless. She was fourteen before she realized how unusual it was for socks to customarily bear a crease.

"I'll bet you're nesting," Barb had said. "Feeling the need to get the house ready for Shrimpy." Then she stood, stretched and left the room. Cerise couldn't believe it. Never mind her half-eaten plate of turkey meat loaf or the nibbled crusts of bread littering the table.

"Fairies?" Cerise called after her. "Is that who you think is going to come in and clean all this?"

The fairies never showed. Unless it was them ringing the doorbell just now.

She crumpled her dish towel and tossed it onto the mounting laundry heap at the top of basement stairs. One of them was going to have to tackle the laundry, and quick. After her shower, Cerise had toweled off with a T-shirt.

She went to the door and peeked out the side window to see who was ringing the bell. A small part of her was actually hoping for fairies. Instead, there stood Kyle and his fiancée, Rhonda Nelson, bundled in matching cotton fisherman sweaters and hunched against the December cold.

Oh, god.

It had been a few weeks since the accident—enough time that she'd gone from simply needing a new bra to having to unbutton her pants between meetings—and she still couldn't bring herself to return Kyle's phone calls. The best she'd done was answer one of his pleading texts with a "Thanks. I'll call you."

Now she'd waited too long to make good on her promise and the living L.L.Bean advertisement on her front stoop was her penance.

"Barb!" she called. "Company!" She opened the door and hurried their guests in ahead of the wind.

"Wow," she said. "I thought you two were spending the holidays in New York." She'd squeezed that nugget of information for weeks, trusting it to save her from this very moment.

"We did." Rhonda answered, though Cerise had been looking at Kyle for explanation. "It was just lovely. An intimate Christmas Eve dinner with dear friends and a candlelight vigil at St. Patrick's. Santa even stuffed my stocking on Christmas morning!"

"Hmm, not sure where to begin on that one," said Barb. "Except to congratulate Santa, I guess?" She winked at Kyle, who was too busy shaking his head *no* to blush.

Cerise was having a hard time getting past the "intimate dinner with dear friends." Rhonda hadn't moved more than six months ago. How intimate could her New York friends be?

"Well, come in. Come in," she said, gathering her senses. "The fire's on in the living room."

It took nearly an hour to exhaust Rhonda of small talk—the recent Weather Channel trips to South Carolina and South Africa, her chances of nabbing the coveted 8 p.m. time slot, the frustrations of finding a New York wedding planner willing to coordinate with the Minneapolis wedding team.

"Brutal," said Barb.

"You can't even begin to imagine," said Rhonda without losing her smile. "And anyway, Kyle had an urgent issue come up at the foundation. So between the need to micromanage the Minneapolis wedding team and his needing to deal with work, here we are!"

"What happened with EyeShine?" said Cerise, taking care to lock eyes with Kyle before speaking.

He shuffled his loafers against the grain of the carpet. "Oh, it's not urgent so much as our treasurer suspects we may have double-counted a portion of our donations. Just want to get on top of it before year-end."

Cerise nodded. This time she saw that Kyle was blushing.

"Well," said Rhonda, reclaiming the floor. "Call me a pushy New Yorker–type, but I think it best we all speak to the ghost in the room."

"Are you a New Yorker yet?" said Barb. "What's the time statute on that?"

Rhonda charged ahead, ignoring her. "Needless to say, I never would have mentioned the baby had I known."

Needless to say? Cerise felt her face flush. Nothing about her pending apology felt needless. It felt, in fact, very, very much needed.

"Bad reporting on my part. I didn't do my homework." Rhonda shot an impish glance at Kyle. He reached out and stroked her hand.

"Are you for real?" Barb thumped her coffee mug down on the side table and leaned in. "Violet spent three days in the hospital with a serious concussion. You chalk that up to *bad reporting*?"

Kyle edged up in his seat, obviously primed for defense, but Rhonda blocked him with an elbow.

"I'm certain I couldn't have predicted the depth of Violet's reaction." She flicked a dismissive hand.

Cerise and Barb exchanged amazed glances.

"I'm sure what we're trying to say here—" Kyle managed to outswerve Rhonda's elbow this time, but not her firm hand on his forearm. He retreated.

Rhonda's manicure, Cerise noticed then, was the exact color of her skin. It had an eerie effect, making her pale, porcelain fingers look seamless, like they could wrap with infinite length around anything they touched.

"Look, Rhonda," she started, and then she paused. She hadn't woken up this morning looking for a fight. Just the opposite— she'd started her day looking to reboot. And she'd made progress on her intentions, judging from the stack of dishes drying on the kitchen counters. Plus, this crazy intervention of sorts was probably her fault, anyway. If she'd just returned even one of his phone calls.

She looked directly at Kyle and changed tack. "It was terrible for a while—my mom was pretty out of it in the hospital. And my dad—well, he's had his hands full trying to keep her from running the world from their living room. I'm sure your mother told you how much she's tried to help out."

"Yeah," he said. "You know my mom. All the news that's fit to print."

Cerise laughed. "Yeah. And you know mine. Never let a good drama go to waste." The two friends locked eyes and smiled and it felt like a gear finally settling into place.

She didn't want to not like Rhonda. Moreover, she didn't want Rhonda to know just how hard she was having to work to get there. Rhonda and Kyle were now a package deal and Cerise liked any package Kyle came in. He seemed happy. Barb thought he was simply starstruck, but Cerise found it hard to believe that one could be struck by someone who wasn't actually a star. The Weather Channel wasn't exactly Oprah territory.

Plus, he and Rhonda met in his optometrist's chair—Rhonda the patient and Kyle the doctor—which Cerise still called him even though he, as her mother liked to point out, wasn't. Shouldn't that dynamic put Rhonda in awe of him?

"Rhonda's in it for Rhonda," Barb liked to argue. "Just you watch. Flash forward thirty years and those two are going to be just like his parents, one in total servitude to the other's ambitions. Only this time, Kyle's going to be the one doing the serving."

Cerise always hoped she was wrong.

"Well..." Kyle put his coffee mug down on the table and patted Rhonda swiftly—*one, two*—on the knee. "This one here has a plane to catch. Shall we?" He stood and offered his hand to his fiancée. She didn't immediately take it. She paused a beat, then two, three, letting her silence fill the room like steam.

Finally she stood and she looked to Cerise as if she'd never felt anything but charmed.

"Be on the lookout for your 'Save the Date' card," she said, slinging her tote across her shoulder. It looked big enough for a week's worth of wardrobe changes. "The planning team is due to mail them on the nineteenth."

And as quickly as they'd appeared, they were gone, the scent of Rhonda's lingering perfume and two empty mugs the only signs that they'd been there.

"Did you get a load of that purse?" said Barb. "I bet if you looked in it you wouldn't find anything but binged Snickers wrappers and a tube of two-hundred-dollar lip gloss."

Cerise gathered the dishes from the coffee table and wandered with them into the kitchen. "You think?"

"Absolutely," said Barb. "That was the wrath of a hungry woman."

Cerise shrugged. Rhonda was hungry for something, all right.

Christmas 1978

Dearest loved ones, far and near—

Evergreen Tidings from the Baumgartners!

It brings me such joy to sit down at the typewriter tonight. As if the thrill of becoming Mrs. Edward Baumgartner weren't enough, I'm now able to join in the most revered of traditions: the family Christmas letter! I look forward to sharing our Baumgartner news with you as the years pass, and I pray that the dear Lord will allow me to do so for a long time to come.

Now, onto news of the wedding! Our deepest thanks to each and every one of you who joined the celebration. I really can't believe it's over. It felt so long in coming and then, suddenly, it was gone, over in the bat of an eye. For the briefest moment in time we were happier than we'd ever imagined.

As most of you know, it was a simple affair at dear Ed's home church, Lake Hennepin Lutheran. Pastor Paul Berendtsen presided over the ceremony and, as the final chords of "Love Divine, All Loves Excelling" rang from the organ, the Ladies Aid Society opened the doors of the Fellowship Hall for cake and punch. Guests greeted us with cheers, tears and best wishes, until finally you all bid us farewell and we ran through showers of rice and confetti to our getaway car. To say it was a girl's "dream come true" may sound cliché, but how can I not say it when it's the truth?!

Now, have no fear—we didn't go far! As Minnesotans, tried and true, we elected to stay close to home, knowing that our northern lake country in June rivals the beauty and tranquility of nearly any place on earth. We spent five days at the lovely Great Heron Lodge on Big Fish Lake—swimming, boating, fishing, canoeing and watching the sun rise and set over our little piece of heaven. We were truly blessed.

While I'm certain none of you are the least bit interested in the details of our honeymoon adventures (oh, I hope you'll excuse my bawdy humor!), I must share this favorite moment with you:

One afternoon, we decided to head over to neighboring Little Fish Lake, so I packed a simple lunch in our picnic basket (a lovely shower gift from Aunt Helen—thank you!) while Ed loaded the canoe onto the car and tightened the straps (an eight-foot canoe on a Volkswagen Beetle—can you imagine?!). It was a picture-perfect day, and as we floated, listening to the waves lap against the side of the boat, my dear Ed turned to me and said, "Violet, I may not have been able to buy you the most expensive or exotic honeymoon, but I'll make it up to you. Someday we may even find ourselves paddling together in Hawaii."

Can you believe it? To say that I was flabbergasted doesn't even begin to capture the moment. Not only did I marry a smart, upstanding man who makes me as happy as can be, I married a man who thinks I deserve more than what I already have. And so I keep that moment in my heart, a reminder of my blessings as I work to fulfill the expectations of a happily married life, of being a good wife to my husband, of making a house into a home. (Goodness, I'm getting philosophical! I beg your patience!)

So now, life has begun. We've settled into a sunny, one-bedroom apartment a few blocks from Lake Nokomis in Minneapolis, a lovely corner flat in an eight-unit brownstone. Ed takes the car to his laboratory every day, but our location allows me to walk to work. For those of you wondering, yes—I plan to keep my job until Ed finishes his degree. My salary doesn't pay much, but I'm proud of my work and even more proud to donate to the family funds. (Although, who am I kidding? I can't wait to leave it all behind for motherhood!)

I do struggle some days to keep the stresses of work and life from getting the best of me. Every once in a while, it's all I can do to push my worries aside before dear Ed walks through the door, lest I spread my mood to him like a case of the pox.

So it is only fitting that I close this very first of many Christmas letters with the verse Pastor Berendtsen read at our wedding, that wonderful passage from Ruth, chapter one, verse sixteen:

"Where you go I will go, and where you stay I will stay. Your people will be my people and your God my God."

May we each be so blessed as to be surrounded by those we love.

Christmas blessings to each and every one of you,
Ed and Violet Baumgartner

14

Richard

DAMN, IT FELT good to be out. Like he could breathe again. No, more than that. Like his blood was no longer sludge, a pooling residue behind his eyes, draining the color from the world.

How could he have forgotten the feel of life after dark? Life in the dark had its own vibe—did they even say *vibe* anymore? Who the hell could keep track?—all drawn shadows and isolated echoes in the silent air: a single car door, a smoker's cough, a woman's drunken laugh and her companion's "Aw, c'mon."

He'd known the night, the younger Richard. Lived it. Breathed it in. Not so long ago, but well before he'd grown wise to its fleeting tease.

Aw, hell.

He'd said goodbye to his cohorts close to an hour ago. Packed the equipment into the back of Ted's minivan, ignored the cramps in their overripe muscles and pretended they weren't glad the night was over. Cash work wasn't as easy as it had once been. Age put its stamp on everything. But they'd done it. Finished the gig and got their money.

The rest of the crew all made straight for their car keys as soon as the evening was done, grabbed them from their pockets like paid tokens to the respectable life, passes to home and family and stability.

Not Richard. He was blocks from his car and leaving it farther behind with every step.

It was cold, *goddamn January*, but so what? His lungs woke with every breath. He imagined the hop-to underway deep inside him: millions of microscopic air sacs filling with oxygen, begrudgingly sending faint signals of life to cells that had been lying listless and bored for years, lifeboats without a passenger, aimlessly afloat amid the river of his veins.

He was waking up. Every night, every step, every breath. He was coming back.

And he hadn't even known he was gone.

Eldris, though. That Eldris. Always with the worrying and the fussing and complaining about nothing in particular. Like the tile in the entryway. That was his particularly favorite *nothing* lately. As if he didn't have anything bigger to worry about. As if anyone gave a damn.

He turned the corner onto Washington Avenue. He guessed he was headed for the Stone Arch Bridge, the one in all the photographs, the one that connected downtown to the north side. There hadn't been much of anything on the north side during his previous tour of duty as night owl, but now it was every young hipster's treasure to discover, microbreweries sharing the same square of land as a Greek Orthodox Church and the Polish butcher.

His stomach growled. *How good would a Kramarczuk's with mustard and slaw be right about now?*

"What'you doing out so late, old man?" It was a kid, no more than twenty, the patch of whiskers on his face no more purposeful than a worn toothbrush. He stepped from the shadow of a storefront awning and held his palm out to Richard. The seam on his glove was torn straight down through to the skin. "You got a cigarette?"

"You got a loaded gun?" answered Richard. He kept walking, though he knew the exchange wasn't over yet.

"What if I did?" The kid was following him now, a lonely dog on his heels hoping for scraps. "What if I stuck it right in your back and made you empty out your rich-man pockets? You're trying to look like you ain't got nothing, but I know better. I bet you own one of these buildings here. Hell, I bet you own more than one."

The kid was as dumb as he looked. Richard kept walking.

He climbed, the hound close behind, onto the wide pedestrian lanes of the former railroad bridge. Down below, the Mississippi crashed lock over dam, filling the hollow night with sound—a single, monotonous roar.

Richard stood silent, awash in sensation. His pores, raw with cold, opened themselves to the great river's power while his mind, finally quiet, closed down in contemplation of—what? *Aw, hell.* You couldn't stand here and not be taken over by something.

Minneapolis had been founded *right here.* Good old Father Hennepin—lucky son of a bitch had found the only falls on the whole damn Mississippi. *The whole goddamn river.* Named them St. Anthony's falls—or some crazy French equivalent—St. Anthony, the lone guy responsible for finding missing things and lost people.

All these ancient guys and their fascination with the saints.

Richard's teachers had always bent themselves over backward to point out that Hennepin was a priest, a missionary and an explorer—in that order. Always in that order. Standing here, though, Richard knew that couldn't be right. All those teachers for all those years had gotten the order wrong. Hennepin had used God, worn him as a foil on his way to adventure. Being a priest had just been his ticket to ride.

"Getting farther an' farther away from home, old man." *For chrissake,* the kid was still with him, waiting for more. "Something tells me you've got a secret."

Well, *hell.* Richard turned.

"Here's what I'm gonna tell you, kid, so listen up. Wherever I am—wherever it is you think you found me tonight—I sure as hell wasn't the one who drew the X on this part of my map. But here I am. Maybe it was karma. Maybe it was luck. I don't goddamn know. Did I do something wrong? Or, did I do something right? Nobody knows. And that's God's honest truth."

He reached into his pocket and pulled a bill from the top of the night's pile. It was too dark to see and he didn't know if he was handing the kid a five or a twenty. What did it matter? This pup needed more than he could ever give him. "Here," he said. "Have a Coke and smile."

The kid took it without looking.

They stayed there for a few minutes more. The kid seemed content just for the company. Richard was content just to keep him quiet. There was too much talking in the world now. Too much *I know better than you*. But it all just came down to words. These days, words weren't worth shit.

Eldris, though. She'd be wanting a few words with him in the morning. Hadn't told her where he was going. Just *out*. Just *back later*. He should've done better. He knew. She'd probably lain in bed fuming herself to sleep.

Yeah, he knew.

She wouldn't be awake when he got home, but the fact that she was there would help. Allow him to settle. Fall into his slot in the puzzle. The way it had been for Kyle as a kid. Nights he'd spent between the two of them during a thunderstorm or after a bad dream.

"Hey, kid," he said, turning to go. "It's the middle of the night. Where you gonna be in the morning?" He pulled his coat high up on his neck against the wind and made his way back the same direction he'd come. "Take it from this old man—strangers only get you so far."

Whether you
Fly like Charles Lindberg
Walk like the Jolly Green Giant or
Dance like Charles Schulz's Peanuts,
Make your way to the Land of Sky Blue Waters!
Saturday, September 1st

For the wedding of two true-blue Minnesotans

Mary Richards
(aka Rhonda Nelson)

&

Jesse "The Body" Ventura
(aka Kyle Endres)

Save the date.

F. Scott says,
"It's sure to be a Gatsby of a time!"

15

Violet

"I GAVE HIM a piece of my mind, all right." Eldris was on her hands and knees, scrubbing Violet's kitchen floor and sputtering herself into a good lather. "I said, 'Richard Endres, if you ever disappear on me again you'll be sleeping at Kyle's house until he kicks you out, too.'"

Violet had never been so confounded. Should she be thankful or appalled? Eldris was at least five years her senior—though a good bit trimmer, as she'd never seen her put more than a single bite of anything into that narrow little mouth of hers—and yet here she was, risking a week of back pain just so Edward and Violet weren't forced to walk atop the colonies of bacteria reproducing underneath their feet.

Even more, she wouldn't soon be able to forgive Eldris if she took her marital distress out on the delicate grain of their hardwood flooring.

"Well, I can hardly blame you," Violet said, hoping a supportive comment would calm Eldris's growing churn. "Ed used to disappear for days on end, but at least I had the comfort of knowing he was just working out a problem in the lab."

It was true. She never worried he'd become a philanderer—or worse—but even so. Violet didn't think she'd ever forget the morning Ed came down for breakfast sporting a fresh head of salt-and-pepper hair. It seemed he'd left the house a young man and returned, days later, flecked with age.

Cerise had asked, "What's in your hair, Daddy?"

Violet had answered, "Wisdom and responsibility, dear. That's how people can tell Daddy takes such good care of us."

Ed had only winked and tucked into his plate of food.

So, yes, many days his presence felt like nothing more than an empty seat at the family table. But that had been their bargain since the first day they'd met—Ed a young teaching assistant at her university's chemistry department, Violet his undergraduate laboratory tech. She received a weekly stipend for washing test tubes and proctoring his exams; he found a partner capable of clearing his path toward professional success. After all, she hadn't gone to college for the academics. She'd gone because she believed it would ignite something within her, a purpose, a picture of who she really was. Which it did, the moment she met Ed, and so their partnership began—she managed, he strove, they all won. The Baumgartner trio they created felt unstoppable.

And then there were the Endreses. Kyle was *fine*, of course, and Eldris never gave up, but what Richard was doing running around town all hours of the night at this age, she could only imagine. Her poor friend was obviously sick with worry.

"Of course," said Eldris, "it helps to know he's not out womanizing or having an affair." She moved like a water bug, skittish and determined at once. "He's far too practical for that. He'd never spend the money!"

She thrust her energies into cleaning a waxy buildup from one of the legs on the kitchen table. Violet heard her knees crack.

"Eldris, there are people I can call to do that."

She shook her head and went on scrubbing. "But you fired them, Violet. And Ed told me every time he leaves you alone for more than five minutes he comes back to find you cleaning or fussing with something or otherwise engaged in a way specifically prohibited by your doctor." She tossed the sponge into the bucket at her side and wiped a cocked wrist across her forehead. "You, Miss Violet, have been very naughty."

Honestly.

"For goodness' sake, Eldris. You make it sound as if I've been training for the Olympic figure skating team. I was just doing a few dishes."

Eldris disappeared under the kitchen table. "That's not what I heard," she called.

It had been more than a month since the accident and still, Violet's nasal-toned doctor had refused to clear her for normal activity. Concerns about a neuro-some-nonsense in her exams and fidgetiness in her balance. And Ed tattling on her sleepless nights. As if anyone could sleep with all that rest.

The doctor had at least allowed her to leave the house for Christmas Eve services at church, but had forced her to spend the rest of the holiday being scolded back to the couch by her husband and daughter. She would not forgive the indignity.

"You're doing too much," the doctor said, every visit sounding the same alarm. "Slow down. Don't rush the recovery. This is not an overnight process."

Of all the advice she'd been given over the years, his was the most maddening. Of course recovery wasn't going to happen overnight. She knew better than anyone the level of injury she'd sustained in her fall. After all, wasn't she the one experiencing its painful effects?

"Dr. Hartz," she'd said during her last visit. She put on her *let sanity reign* voice, the tone she typically reserved for DMV workers, Cerise's teachers and political boosters who made the mistake of soliciting her support during the dinner hour. "While it is true that I sustained quite the knock to my head, I am anything but feebleminded. Nor am I too shy to say that I'm simply not interested in your course of treatment. Extended immobility, as I'm sure you'll agree, comes with its own significant consequences."

She'd yet to succeed in convincing him of his shortsightedness.

Eldris emerged from under the table and went to work scrubbing Violet's baseboards. "To tell you the truth, I'd much rather be here scrubbing these floors than nearly anywhere else. Richard's moods and Kyle's wedding. It's been so stressful around our house lately I'm about to lose my mind."

Violet clutched at the locket at her throat and inched her way to the edge of the couch, hoping to get a better look at Eldris's work from where she sat in the living room. From the sound of her scrubbing, she worried she might be close to stripping the paint from the wood.

"I mean, I'm absolutely thrilled for Kyle, but you saw their 'Save the Date' card—according to Rhonda, those cards were *worth every cent of the six thousand dollars they cost.* Six thousand dollars! Can you imagine? Who spends six thousand dollars on postcards?"

Violet had to agree, though the issue for her wasn't so much the cost as the postcards themselves. Whose grand idea was it to put the Jolly Green Giant into the heads of their wedding guests? They'd be lucky if they didn't end up with cupboards full of 1970's kitsch.

"And how are Richard and I supposed to help pay for all of these extras? Did I tell you that they've planned a Lake Minnetonka cruise for all of their out-of-town guests the day after the ceremony? Kyle and Rhonda won't even be there—they'll be off on their honeymoon."

Violet craned her neck farther over the couch. "Eldris, dear. Gentle with my woodwork—"

"Rhonda calls the guest cruise a *Toast to their Caribbean Adventure*—did I tell you they've chartered a private sailboat for a ten-day honeymoon? I mean, they haven't asked for money yet but I just know it's coming." She threw her sponge into the bucket and it landed with a splash, tossing a spray of dirty water into her face and hair.

"Eldris, you're working yourself up into a royal mess."

She sighed and leaned her back against the kitchen wall.

"You're probably right. It's just that none of this is happening the way I'd imagined it would. Kyle's hardly involved us in any of the planning. And Richard, well—I'm mad at him for so many reasons right now, I could just spit."

"Well," said Violet, "don't do it on my floor after all your hard work."

Eldris smiled. "You don't know how good you have it."

Good Lord. She ought to have seen this coming. Eldris could go from hysterical to melancholy in no more than a heartbeat. "And what, pray tell, is it about my very unfortunate situation that I should feel so lucky about?" She made a sweeping gesture about the room, reminding her dramatic friend of just how confined her world had become of late. Not just confined, but constrained. No connection to what was really happening beyond her walls. No ears. No eyes. No insight. No influence.

Ed was hopeless. He continued to answer the phone but refused to update his speaking points with the questions Violet really wanted answers to, like what else the Dorcas Circle had begun scheming behind her back.

And of course she'd asked Eldris, but she'd invested all of five breaths promising nothing untoward was afoot. Eldris said people had returned to talking about themselves—their holiday visitors, their too-dry turkeys purchased from butchers they'll never trust again, their New Year's diets in advance of the medical procedures they'd tried but failed to apply to last year's deductible.

And, as was always the case with Eldris these days, their children.

"But think of it, Violet. You don't have to deal with any of this wedding nonsense. You're going straight to grandparenting. You really don't know how blessed you are."

Violet suddenly wished for shoes so she could throw them at Eldris. The now-familiar burn of her postinjury life needled its way up the back of her neck and her peripheral vision blurred, the curtains and walls of her living room bending like blacktop under the heat of a hundred-degree day.

She closed her eyes. *One…two…three…four…five…six…*

"I mean, you don't have to worry about any of it—like which of your cousins you'll invite and which you'll be forced to snub because you've been reminded again and again that you are only allowed a portion of the guest list. 'Space is limited. We can't invite everyone we love. We'd prefer if you only included people who mean something to Kyle's life.'"

…seventeen…eighteen…nineteen…twenty. She ought to sue her doctor for malpractice. How long was she going to have to live like a cave dweller to prove that nothing he prescribed was working? If she could stand up without toppling over right now she'd find her notebook and write *File lawsuit* in the first available slot.

"'Oh, and it's soooo sweet of you to offer your mother's china, but Kyle and I have our own pattern on the wedding registry. It's very special to us. I've been looking at it in the Tiffany's catalog since I was a child.'"

And Ed, bound by this medical quackery to be always underfoot, always appearing with offers of tea and reminders that he is perfectly capable of doing laundry. If that were true, she'd clearly have spent the last thirty years of her life very differently. When had everyone around her grown so confoundedly thick? She'd had a fall. Period. She wasn't suddenly simpleminded.

"Can you imagine my son getting excited by anything at Tiffany's? He's not that type. He's a good boy. He keeps people's eyes healthy. He loads the dishwasher without asking. He works weekends at the Community Health Corp. He cares for poor, blind children in *Africa*, for heaven's sake! What could he possibly need from the Tiffany's catalog to help him with *that*?"

Meredith Turner had taken her by the elbow at church on Christmas Eve. *By the elbow*—a woman at least a decade older than her acting as if she wasn't, as if she was the picture of health. Heavens, Meredith didn't even drive herself to church. Violet knew she got a ride from Howard and Alice Tobler. And that Alice, eyeing her like a woman with a delicious, dark secret. "How is Cerise?" she'd had the nerve to ask. "How is she doing with the *baby*?"

"I know I ought to be accepting. I know I ought to love anyone who loves my son. But I just can't. I cannot understand how my son ended up with a woman who bought a bottle of fourteen-dollar ketchup as a hostess gift. Who spends fourteen dollars on ketchup?"

Violet had told Cerise this would happen. If she'd told her once she'd told her a hundred times. People cannot be trusted to draw proper conclusions with inadequate information. And it was happening, just as she warned—Meredith Turner and Alice Tobler were but the tip of the iceberg. The knowledge that they were out there, people speculating, gossiping, tearing her poor daughter's reputation to shreds. And all while Violet was stuck inside her redbrick fortress, unseen and voiceless. The heat surged red-hot across her skull.

"And yet, I know I have no choice. I'd better just get over it. Be the adult. Love her for who she is."

Love. Where had it disappeared to in this world? When had it been swallowed up by judgment, by holier-than-thou know-it-alls who act as if they had the right—the *right*—to determine what *ought* to be? If she'd had that right, she would have ripped that atrocious plastic mistletoe broach off Alice Tobler's sweater and thrown it directly in the trash.

"Maybe I ought to just write her a nice note. Ask her how I can be more involved. Ask her how I can help."

Yes. A note could certainly help.

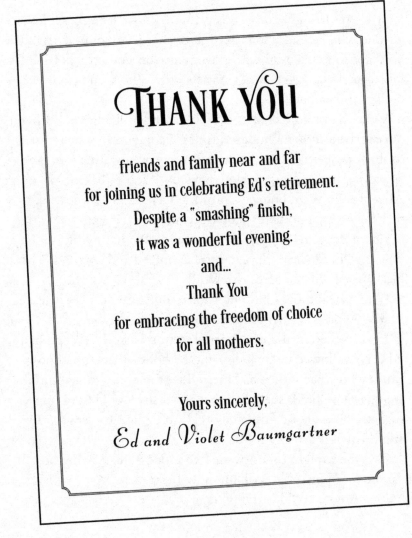

THANK YOU

friends and family near and far
for joining us in celebrating Ed's retirement.
Despite a "smashing" finish,
it was a wonderful evening.
and...
Thank You
for embracing the freedom of choice
for all mothers.

Yours sincerely,

Ed and Violet Baumgartner

16

Cerise

"SOMETHING YOU'RE NOT telling me?"

Barb flicked a piece of the mail she'd been sorting across the kitchen counter at Cerise. She knew at a glance who it was from—same card stock, same engraving as the retirement invitations. Add to that the look on Barb's face, and her stomach went into free fall.

"What the f—" She read the lines again, hoping they'd change before her eyes.

"Yep. Kinda sounds like you went and got yourself an abortion."

Cerise reached for a chair and fell into it. "Can you make dinner tonight?" she said. "I need to concentrate on not killing my mother."

A WARM BATH and a mug of hot tea later, Cerise felt ready to re-enter civilization. The pause hadn't granted her the clarity she'd sought, but it had dampened the red she'd been seeing. Now thoughts of her mother's latest announcement only shaded the world in tones of hot pink and orange.

The retreat had also convinced her there had to be a way to short-circuit her mother's behavior. Almost certainly. The key was to find out why she was stuck. Eventually, Cerise would be able to flip the right switch. She'd done it before.

Like in high school, when they had fought over Cerise wanting to go to Pink's concert. Her mother had predictably balked at the risks—she'd ruin her hearing, she'd be fooled into taking drugs, she'd be abducted—then she got one look at the singer's glitter-caked bras and spiked heels in the newspaper and dropped the hammer. *No daughter of* hers *was doing* that. Even more, it was as if Cerise's mere interest in the event had sounded the gong on future misadventures, causing her mother to begin a well-coordinated antisubversion campaign.

Cerise came home from school one day to discover that all of her jeans had been replaced by chinos, all of her above-the-knee skirts replaced by below-the-knee ones. Dinner, which had always been accompanied softly by the Minnesota Public Radio classical music station, evolved into a guided tour of the composers—a week of Stravinsky, a night of Vaughan Williams, a century of Bach. Her mother never explicitly addressed the change, but it was so obvious that Cerise began to refer openly to their mealtimes as "dining with the old, white dead guys."

None of which dampened her desire or determination to get to the concert. In fact, she had a ticket. She'd had her friends buy her one and had secretly paid for it with cash earned babysitting. Worst-case scenario, she figured if she couldn't convince her mother to let her go she'd turn around and resell it; the concert had sold out in less than two hours and fans were clamoring. Regardless of the outcome, go or sell, the risk on her end was minimal but the payoff was huge.

Then Jenny Fielding decided to cure cancer. She was only a year older than Cerise but had already lost all four of her grandparents to the disease. So when senior projects rolled around, Jenny grabbed ahold of her fund-raising crusade the way a televangelist grabs his Bible. Cerise's mother didn't know Jenny, but she did cluck consolingly every time the local cable commercial Jenny produced flashed pictures of her dead grandparents across their television. "That dear child," she'd say.

Cerise spotted opportunity.

When Jenny distributed flyers for a "Take the Heat Out of Cancer" bake sale, Cerise made sure hers landed on the Baumgartner kitchen counter. When Jenny promoted the "Kick Cancer to the Curb" community garage sale, Cerise asked her mom if their family *happened* to have anything to donate. When Jenny's "Scrub the World of Cancer" car wash needed an empty parking lot, Cerise made sure to muse aloud that the Faithful Redeemer parking lot looked practically deserted on Saturday mornings.

Before long, Cerise's mother was dropping less-deserving commitments from her too-crowded calendar to make room for cake baking, closet clearing and car wash supervising.

Then came the comparisons—"Cerise, just look at how Jenny takes full advantage of everything life has to offer. She's not too scared to dream big. Learn from her. Never back down from a challenge. Make every moment count."

When the lectures reached their crescendo, Cerise told her. "I have the chance to go to Pink's concert."

What could her mother say?

Cerise had flipped the right switch on her mother's psychology back then and she could do it again. In fact, she thought, wrapping herself in her bathrobe, she might already know how.

She padded on bare feet into the kitchen and watched as Barb stuck her head into the oven and pulled the grocery store rotisserie chicken from the rack.

Cerise held up a hand. "Wait, why does that chicken look like it's wearing rain boots?" Ribbons of black plastic, shiny with chicken grease, wound their way around each of the bird's legs.

Barb shrugged sheepishly. "I forgot to put a cookie sheet under the plastic tray when I put it in."

"What?" Cerise made for the oven and flipped down the

door. "Don't tell me it's melted all over the inside, too." She scanned the shelves and the grease pan, but didn't see anything other than the burned remains of previous dinners.

This was one of the few things about Barb that confounded her. How could a woman with a pristine professional reputation be so careless as to put plastic in a hot oven?

"I remembered that you could reheat the chicken in its store packaging," Barb said, reading her mind. "Only, I forgot those were microwave instructions." She picked at the bird's encased leg with a fork. "We can just eat the breast."

Cerise scowled. "Shrimpy doesn't feel like carcinogens for dinner tonight." She laid a hand on the underside of her belly and briefly considered their restaurant options. But she was too tired to think about putting her clothes back on, let alone everything else that came along with a dinner out. "You pull out the bread," she said. "I'll get the peanut butter."

Barb shook her head and gently ushered her over to the table to sit. "I'll make the sandwiches."

Cerise watched as Barb smoothed the peanut butter to the edge of the bread with even measure, its lines parallel to the bread's crust. She then did the same with the jelly. Such a paradox, her partner—so cavalier and yet so precise. She couldn't make sense of it, except to be glad that in the home they'd made for themselves, life didn't have to be perfect.

Barb placed the sandwich and a glass of milk in front of Cerise, who said, "Speaking of my mother."

Barb cocked an eyebrow. "Not funny."

"As much as I want to strangle her, I was thinking… She's stuck on this paternity thing because she's bored. I mean, she's never had to live without a project. I can't remember a single day when she wasn't organizing a bake sale at church *and* heading up the PTA *and* hosting a charity luncheon for missionaries in Sierra Leone." She chewed a bite of her sandwich and washed it down with the last of her milk—she'd come to learn that baby loved all things dairy. "The key is to distract her."

Barb nodded. "True. And then strangle her?"

"Funny." She rolled her eyes. "Keep this up and I may just find myself a job in Ohio. Make *you* live in your family's shadow for a change."

Barb put up her hands in mock surrender.

Cerise continued, "I think our best bet may be to get my mother involved in other baby stuff. Keep her engaged, productively."

"Like what other baby stuff?"

"I dunno. Baby showers. Baby gear. Baby's room."

Barb paused and put her sandwich down. "You're not even going to call her out for making it sound like you got rid of a baby you didn't want? Tell me you're not going to let her get away with that."

"I'm not letting her get away *with* something, I'm trying to get her away *from* something. I mean, we've been denying her answers for weeks now and look where that's gotten us. I'd rather distract her with a new topic than become the next pro-choice poster child of Hennepin County."

Barb smiled. "Sorry, babe. You're too late for that one."

Cerise groaned. "Trust me, the fight's just not worth it. What could I even say?"

"That she just made you the pro-choice poster child of Hennepin County."

"Yeah, right. Play that out. I say, 'Hey, Mom. Don't love the fact that you just made several hundred people think I had an abortion.' Then she says, 'I did no such thing.' Then I say, 'Oh, yeah? Well, it sure seems to me like you did.' To which she says, 'If you mean to imply that I don't have the right to say whatever I wish to my own friends in my own words on correspondence for which I paid, then you are not the grateful and rational human being I raised you to be.'" Cerise dropped the last of her crust to her plate with demonstrative flourish.

Barb shook her head. "Your mother's a piece of work."

"That is a known truth."

Barb leaned back in her chair and drummed her fingers lightly against the side of her glass. "So, say we do involve her in more of the baby stuff. Aren't we just causing a new headache for ourselves?" She stood and walked to the pantry, returning with a bag of barbecue-flavored potato chips. "It's one of the reasons I've never been eager to get married." She popped a chip in her mouth and crunched it gone. "God, can you imagine planning a wedding? Your mother would invite five hundred people and impose a dress code on each and every one of them."

"That's not true—" Cerise began to protest out of duty, though Barb was right. Her mother had asked each of the hundred guests invited to her high school graduation party to bring a gift representing their favorite element on the periodic table. The request had resulted in Cerise heading off to college with four bottles of zinc tablets, a cast-iron skillet, several rolls of antacids "with added calcium" and, thanks to one of her father's colleagues, a prep kit for a barium enema.

Barb shrugged and offered her the bag of chips without apology.

Cerise sighed. "If I had a better idea, I'd offer it."

"What about your dad? Can't you enlist his help in getting her to rein in the crazy?"

Cerise paused. The thought hadn't crossed her mind. Her dad was rarely even in the equation when dealing with her mother. "Well..." She fiddled with a piece of potato chip that had fallen to the table with one of Barb's more energetic bites. "To be honest, I don't know how much help he'd be. I think his strategy all these years was to just say yes. Easier than fighting her."

"Worth a try, though. No?"

Cerise guessed it was.

Feds Greeted with Second "Watchers" Statue

by Harvey Arpell,
staff reporter, *Minneapolis/St. Paul Standard*

January 31, 2018

Minneapolis, MN—A second statue appeared overnight on the lawn facing the Federal Reserve Building in Minneapolis, this time depicting a woman, raising her fist to the sky and cradling a child in her lap. Last month, a statue depicting a child beggar was discovered in the same location. City personnel removed both pieces within hours of their discovery.

"The Watchers," a previously unknown activist group, again claimed responsibility for the installation, posting several pictures of the chicken wire statue on Instagram. Within hours, the hashtag #whatthewatcherssee began trending on Twitter, driven mainly by its use in online social activism.

Minneapolis Police declined to comment on the group or their recent activity.

17

Violet

"READ THAT AGAIN, ED." Violet pulled the washcloth from her eyes and tossed it aside. The cloth had been warm and calming when Ed sat down to read the paper to her—a lovely new tradition of theirs—but now it was giving her the chills.

"Which part, dear? About The Watchers' statue downtown?"

She groped at the cashmere throw around her shoulders. "No, the weather." She wasn't interested in frivolous political shenanigans, nor could she even begin to imagine the chicken wire monstrosity. "Read the weather again. I want to know when this cold snap is going to end. I'm worried about my hydrangea bushes."

"Ah." Ed flipped the pages. "Warming up tomorrow, from the looks of it. Back into the teens by Thursday."

"Good. I don't want to spend the spring replanting." They would be welcoming a baby in a few months and she intended to be ready. She'd already missed so very much. "What time is Cerise coming?"

"Just after lunch." He folded the newspaper into a tidy square. "Which reminds me—would you prefer turkey or ham on your sandwich? It's nearly noon."

"Both," answered Violet. "I'm feeling frisky today."

"That's a good sign, then." He stood, but showed no indication of moving toward the kitchen.

Violet eyed him. "Yes?"

"Well…" He began to flick the newspaper against his leg with a nervous twitch.

"For goodness' sake, Edward. Spit it out. I'm not a delicate flower."

"Of course not, Violet. It's just that, well, I suppose I ought to prepare you that there seems to have been some kerfuffle over the thank-you notes." He slapped the newspaper with such aggravation it lost its rigidity and slumped flaccidly at his side.

"A kerfuffle?"

"Of sorts, yes. That's what I gather, anyway."

"From whom?"

"Whom?"

"Gathered from whom, dear? From whom do you gather there was a kerfuffle?" She groped for the washcloth she'd thrown aside a moment before.

"From Cerise. When she called. Said she and Barb hadn't ap-preciated being mentioned."

"But I didn't mention them."

"Well, Violet. I don't think it's a stretch to say you were re-ferring to Cerise's pregnancy."

"Of course I was."

"Then we agree."

"We most certainly do not." Her fingers located the wash-cloth and she laid it across her forehead. The moisture cooled her rapidly rising temper. "I was simply making a clear statement of support for our daughter and our future grandchild. In case any of our guests assumed otherwise." She pressed the cloth to her temples. "You, on the other hand, make it sound as if I'd published the contents of her medical records."

"Now, I didn't say anything like that and you know it."

"And what would you have had me do, Edward? If I asked you once, I asked you a hundred times to be more forthcom-ing in your phone conversations. But never once did I hear you advocate for the still-outstanding reputation of your family."

"That is quite possibly the most ridiculously unfair thing you've ever said to me."

He was raising his voice now. Her brain was about to overheat and Edward was screaming. What had become of their life together?

"Meg Thompson asked Eldris if they'd used a donor."

Ed shook his head. "Who on earth is Meg Thompson?"

"A *donor*, Ed. People are speculating about how our dear, sweet daughter got pregnant! Doesn't that bother you?"

"Not as much as the fact that Meg Thompson needs a lesson in human biology. How else would two women have acquired the necessary spermatozoa?"

For heaven's sake.

"Forgive me if I've grown old and out of touch, Edward, but I thought the method you and I used still worked just as well as it used to." She waited to let the point sink in. "From the sounds of it, our daughter's sex life is the topic du jour at the Faithful Redeemer Sunday Coffee Hour."

Ed sighed and walked to the couch, sitting down in such a way as to not jostle her. "People will talk, Violet. It's just the nature of things." He put a hand on hers, but she pulled away. She was still overheating and his body temperature ran furnace-hot at all times.

"After all I've done. All the committees I've chaired, the funds I've raised. It's the cruelest turn of fate I've ever experienced."

The moment struck her.

"Tell me I'm not becoming my father." Her voice was barely a whisper.

"Violet."

"I mean it. Every cell of my being is screaming. Telling me to fight. Reminding me that *even as I sit here*, rumors are becoming truths." She threw the blanket off her lap, feeling suddenly hot enough to ignite. "When they did it to my father, my mother let it happen." She looked at Ed. "I won't."

Ed drummed his fingers on his kneecaps, formulating his words carefully. "I can certainly understand why it may feel that way." His fingers appeared to mark the pace of his thoughts. "You are vulnerable—"

Violet opened her mouth to protest.

He stopped her. "No, now hear me out. You are upset—*understandably*. You are worried. You haven't slept well in weeks." *Well, obviously.*

"Anyone in your position would feel as you do."

She nodded. *Yes, they would.*

"What I'm asking you to consider," he continued, "is that the problem feels bigger than it actually is."

Violet shot him a look. This was not a turn she appreciated.

"I know you don't like hearing me say that. But this isn't the same as what we experienced with your parents. Your father was accused of plagiary. Maybe he wasn't guilty of all of it, but he was guilty of some."

Some, yes. Segments of two—*perhaps three*—of some of his best-known publications seemingly lifted from other historians' work. But not all. Certainly *not all.*

"Cerise and Barb, however—" Ed's fingers stopped their drumming and he quietly folded his hands in his lap. "They're not guilty of anything. They're having a child. We're about to be grandparents." He turned and smiled at her. "If we show the community how much we love this child, how can others not do the same?"

Love was exactly what she was trying to show, of course. A fierce, protective love, yes, but when had protecting the ones you loved become wrong? Ed would agree in theory, she knew, but he wasn't prepared for such an indirect assault. His was a life of science—measurable, provable, repeatable. Violet, however, had other skills. She could see the unseen.

"Dearest Ed," she said, giving his face an affectionate pat. "How I do cherish you."

He watched her carefully for a moment. "Does this mean you're feeling better about the situation? Calmer? Cerise is due to arrive shortly and I want to be sure you're not going into her visit upset."

Violet demurred. "Thank you, love. This has helped a great deal."

BY THE TIME Cerise arrived, Violet had positioned herself at the dining room table with her calendar, a fresh notebook, three colors of Post-its and a new Sharpie. She'd allowed Ed to gather the supplies for her and had even acquiesced when he wouldn't let her clear the lunch dishes from the table.

She was ready.

A new member of her family, their first grandchild, was coming into the world in a matter of months. Preparing to become a grandmother was serious business, and fulfilling her responsibilities as the mother of a mother-to-be, even more so.

After all, if there was one thing Violet knew for certain, it was that Cerise had no idea what she was in for. But then, how could she? No woman in the history of time ever had. It was one of humanity's greatest conspiracies. Our whole lives spent listening to women spin tales about the wonders of motherhood, of its miracle and majesty, but none of them ever quantifying its darker truths—that every ounce of a mother's hopefulness and joy is matched, drop for drop, by the darkly crippling weight of her ultimate helplessness, by the profound isolation that comes with one becoming two. That every moment is haunted by motherhood's twin ghosts, Guilt and Failure.

And yet, she would never withhold motherhood from Cerise. To not be a mother seemed as inconceivable to Violet today as it had all those decades ago when she longed so deeply for a child of her own. Ironic though it may seem, the joy she'd felt when Cerise came along was unspeakable, the reward worth the years of heartbreak.

The front door squealed open and shut, releasing Violet from her thoughts and capturing with it a pocket of winter's cold glare.

"Hi, Mom." Cerise kissed her quickly on the cheek and she could feel the chill on her lips, just as she had all those hundreds of afternoons after school.

Cerise dropped a pile of books onto the table and Violet wondered whether she should be carrying all that weight at this stage in her pregnancy. She held her tongue. There were too many other items to discuss.

"Hello, dear. Have you eaten, or can Daddy make you a sandwich?"

"No, thanks." She gave her belly an affectionate pat. "We just finished lunch."

Violet's breath caught unexpectedly in her throat. She'd patted her belly the same way when she was expecting Cerise— a gentle *Hello, I'm here* from Mom to baby. Her daughter was about to become a mother. Oh, the joy of it.

"Cerise, I—" There were so many things to say, so many fundamental things. Cerise looked at her, expectant, and she knew they were having a moment, unspoken but clear, the lifelong resonance of all that had begun with a gentle pat on her belly.

And then, she couldn't. The words would not come. She felt the threat of tears, a great knot of them, naughty toddlers knocking about behind her eyes, ready to tumble.

"—I think you ought to let Daddy make you a sandwich, anyway. Just in case you do get hungry."

"All right. Baby does love turkey and Swiss."

Violet took a deep breath and restraightened her collection of supplies. Then she began their work with a calendar discussion.

Cerise was due on May first—the perfect date.

"Wonderful. You'll have all summer to take long walks together, go to the park. You'll have your baby weight off in no time." It had taken her far too long to shed the weight she'd gained with Cerise, though things were different in those days. She was lucky to have had her daughter during a slice in time in which elastic waistbands were easy to come by. These days, if you weren't being forced to wear a belt so tight it took your breath away, you were struggling to keep your waistband where God had meant it to be—which, as she'd told more than a few saleswomen, was certainly *not* just above the buttocks.

"I think we should begin by making a list of items you'll need. Eventually, you'll have to create a baby registry and this will serve as its core."

Cerise nodded agreeably.

"Now, your father and I have already discussed it and we would very much like to buy the crib for you."

"Wow, Mom. That's very generous. Thank you."

"You're welcome." She smiled and reached for the locket at her throat, taking its chain gently between her fingers. "We love you very much, Cerise."

"I know. I love you, too." She reached across the table for Violet's hand, stroking her thumb along the veiny ridges that ran from her knuckles to her wrist, just as she'd done as a girl. Violet paused and closed her eyes, silently scolding the toddlers again for threatening to misbehave. She regained control and looked up.

"Of course, that only takes care of one crib. You and Barb will need to make plans for buying the second."

"A second crib?"

Violet nodded.

"Why would we need another?"

She had figured this could be a sticking point. "For when baby sleeps elsewhere."

"You mean, like a portable one?"

No, that was not what she meant, but she was willing to play this out. "If that's how you'd like to treat the child, then, yes, a portable crib could suffice."

Cerise's nose wrinkled with confusion. "I don't think I understand. If you're not talking about a portable one, then—"

And then it was there, the light of recognition in her eyes.

"Are you trying to imply that we'll need a second crib for the father's house?"

Violet sat motionless. This was not her burden to sort.

"Mother, we've told you a hundred times—" She picked up a pen and began pounding its clicker on the table. *Open, shut. Open, shut. Open, shut.*

"Cerise, please do not abuse my Stickley."

"Uuugghh!" She threw the pen across the table and collapsed violently against the back of her chair. Violet heard a tiny crack as she hit and the sound of it made her grimace. The dining room set had been her tenth anniversary present.

"I should have known." Cerise had lost the pen but continued to abuse the table with her index finger. She glared at Violet, the chill on her face as obstinate as the mid-winter weather outside their dining room window.

This was bait, Violet knew. Cerise wanted nothing more than to draw her into an argument, to distract her from the real, more pertinent subject at hand. Of course, as a young mother she would have fallen for such nonsense, but decades of experience had taught her that this was simply the rhythm of things between mother and daughter. Today, she remained still, ready to wait out the storm.

"Heck, I did know. I did! Even Barb warned me this would happen."

"For heaven's sake, Cerise." She did not allow her voice to pitch or rise, but let serenity guide the moment. "We're simply making a list of things you'll need for the baby. There is no need for a tantrum."

"Then why are you obsessing on where this baby comes

from?" Cerise was now working herself into a near fit. "It comes from me—I'd think that would be perfectly obvious." She motioned at her growing belly as if Violet were some sort of simpleton.

"You know, Mom. I think I finally get it." Now with the finger wagging. Violet wanted to grab it with her fist like she did when Cerise was a child. "Silly me. I always considered myself fairly transparent about my relationship with Barb. We never specifically talked about it, of course, but you knew. You and Dad both knew. And you never made it an issue. But now, you just can't seem to see it as real. That two women can make a *real* family."

Violet stiffened. "Do you mean to imply that I have a problem with your being gay?"

"I don't know, Mother. You tell me. Because considering your reaction at Dad's party, you either can't stand the fact that I'm gay or you hate the fact my partner and I are about to have a baby together."

"Of all the things," Violet sputtered and wound her locket tight around her finger, feeling the rush of pain as she pulled. "Honestly, Cerise. I can't even begin to tell you." She opened her hands to the heavens and looked up. God help her.

"Tell me what?"

"What?" Despite her best efforts to restrain herself, she let out an exasperated huff. "Where do I begin? Let's start with the fact that *Rhonda Nelson*—who, if I'm not mistaken, is not even a close friend of yours—knew about the baby before your father and me. And then she had the nerve to share the news with two hundred of our closest friends."

Violet made a face. Did Cerise need her to go on?

She went on. "And your poor father. At his own retirement party. During a toast, of all things."

"So, it's not that I'm gay or that I'm having a baby. You just couldn't stand being embarrassed in front of all your friends!" Cerise huffed and color swept her cheeks like wildfire.

"Oh, but you think it's just fine to tell the world that you trust the weather girl more than your own mother!"

Cerise threw her hands in the air as if in surrender, though Violet knew she was far from it. "Oh, that's rich, Mother. You can't forgive me for embarrassing you at Dad's party, but it's perfectly fine for you to send a note to your two hundred closest friends implying that I'd had an abortion!"

So, Ed had been right. Their daughter had gone tattling to Daddy. Talk about rich. As if he'd been home for any of the big issues when Cerise was a girl. And hadn't there been plenty? Toddler tantrums turned to adolescent sulks turned to outright teenage assaults on Violet's authority as a parent. And now he was supposed to step in and play the hero? No, this would not stand.

"I refuse to tolerate such a vindictive accusation in my own home." Her head was buzzing with stimuli—ringing in her ears and stars in her vision—but she wasn't even close to finished. She'd never allowed insolence from her daughter when she was a child and she certainly wasn't about to start tolerating it now.

"It's such an interesting predicament you find yourself in, Cerise. In fact, I was just discussing it with your father before you arrived." She began ticking evidence off on her fingers. "You're not married. You've never talked about wanting children. For all anyone knows, the baby could have been the result of a—" she leaned in and hissed "—one-night stand."

"You know I'm gay!"

At long last, Ed appeared in the doorway wearing yellow dishwashing gloves and an apron that read, "Minnesota Lutheran Jell-O Society."

"Ladies, what on earth is going on in here?"

Violet waved away his concern and buttoned her lips tight. She'd always been responsible for guiding their daughter's behavior and she saw no reason to change roles now.

Cerise, on the other hand, chose not to control herself. "We were talking about my being gay. Or were we, Mother?"

Violet could feel Cerise's eyes on her from across the table but refused to meet them.

Ed snapped the rubber gloves from his hands and pulled out a chair. He sat down beside Cerise and tugged thoughtfully at the resilient yellow fingers. "Why? Has something changed? Did you and Barb split?" His eyes went misty and he looked as if he might tear up.

For goodness' sake, he had never been poised for the difficult moments. Every snapshot the photographer had taken at the retirement party had Ed looking as sorrow-jawed as a man who'd just shot his most loyal retriever while out on a hunt. This from a husband who'd never even picked up a shotgun.

"No, Dad. Nothing's changed."

"Well, then, I'm afraid I don't understand the issue."

Of course he didn't. Just one more thing she'd have to explain to him about their daughter. Like when Cerise went off to college and came home a lesbian. And why Barb moved in with Cerise and never moved out. And now, why this wasn't just *any* pregnancy, but one that required aggressive sheltering.

"It's just," said Cerise, looking up at her dad, "we've never talked about me being gay. I assumed you knew. I assumed we didn't need to talk. But now everything feels so, well, backward. Barb and I are about to become parents—committed, loving parents who want this child so much—and yet, I feel as if I'm being punished for something wonderful and good."

Of all things. "Babies are wonderful and good," said Violet, exasperated but willing to look her obstinate daughter squarely in the eyes to settle a point. "They're nothing but bundles of innocence. But like I've told you for years—ever since the boys started calling in middle school—babies *don't* just appear out of nowhere. I do not want this father showing up out of the blue one day, upsetting our lives all over again."

"Now, Violet—" started Ed, but she held up a hand, hushing him. She intended for this moment to sink in, for her daughter to understand that she wanted no more surprises. She'd had absolutely enough.

"Secrets will destroy this family, Cerise. Take it from me. I'll have no more of it."

No one spoke for several moments until Ed finally broke the silence. "We do love you, Cerise. We love you and Barb and this baby." He put his hand on hers and squeezed. "I guess our generation just lives by different rules than yours. We believe some stuff ought to be talked about and some stuff is better left unsaid."

"I know, Dad. That's why it's such a mystery to me—" she shot her mother a direct look "—why Mom is determined to get me to talk about all the stuff I intend to keep private. I'd have thought this was exactly the sort of thing you didn't want to hear about."

"Well, now, that's a good point." He nodded slowly and caught Violet's eye with a pleading look.

Oh, for Pete's sake.

"Cerise, now listen. We love Barb, we love you." Violet reached out and patted her on the arm. "And if you really want to sit and talk with us about your being gay with Barb, that's fine. Just so long as you sit and listen to your father tell you about all the women he dated while he was in the army."

That ought to settle things.

Cerise reached for the first book on the pile and opened it. "No, thanks. Those are details I'll never be able to un-hear. Which is exactly why I expect this to be the last time you ask me about where this baby came from. There was sperm. There was an egg. Someday very soon, there will be a baby. And that's all you need to know."

February 10, 2018

Dear friends and supporters of EyeShine—

2017 was a wonderful year for our organization. Thanks to you, Eye-
Shine collected more than 400 pairs of new and used prescription
eyeglasses and received more than $10,000 in monetary donations.

Your extraordinary support has allowed us to plan our next mission
trip, scheduled for May. This year, founder and president, Kyle Endres will be joined by three optometrists, each of whom have volun-
teered their time and skills to this mission, and who, together, will
provide eye exams and prescription eyeglasses to the members of
three poor and remote villages in the African nation of Ghana.

In the spirit of full transparency, the EyeShine Board of Directors
also wishes to announce that it has hired accounting firm, Rivera,
Rivera, & Craft to perform a five-year audit of the organization. The
work is expected to be complete by the end of Q2 and the findings
will be discussed at the Q3 Board of Directors meeting.

With heartfelt thanks,

The EyeShine Team

18

Richard

"YOU COULD AT least tell me where you've been." Eldris was at it again. Always with the questions. He'd told her before he left that he had an appointment, said it about a dozen times.

She'd walked in the door to find him in the kitchen eating leftover macaroni casserole. She hadn't wasted any time in swatting his fork away from the pan, then dished him out a plate and stuck it into the microwave, all the while going on about having spent the afternoon helping Kyle—some business with his charity fund EyeShine.

"He could use your help, you know, Richard. Kyle's doing practically everything for EyeShine by himself. Let alone running his practice during the day. Told me he hasn't gotten more than a few hours of sleep at a time for weeks."

"He has my number," he said, carrying his plate of casserole to the table. "If he wants help, he'll pick up the phone."

"Oh, because you're so dreadfully busy. Do you know what I just spent my day doing? Matching donor's checks against a paper printout of every single donation EyeShine has ever received. Five dollars. Twenty dollars. Two hundred dollars. Doesn't matter! It all has to add up." She rubbed at a splotch of ink on her finger. "But not you. You couldn't possibly make time to help our son."

"How was I supposed to know, Eldris? Like I said, the kid hasn't exactly been ringing my phone off the hook. And anyway, a man has a right not to be hounded about his own business." He stuck a forkful of macaroni into his mouth. Eldris had been right. It did taste better hot.

"And in case you haven't noticed—which you obviously have since you won't quit with the questions—I'm not exactly home much lately."

"Oh, far be it from me—*your wife*—to want to know where you're off to at all hours."

They'd been down this street so many times lately he ought to name it. "For cripes' sake, I said just give me time. I'll tell you when there's something to tell."

"Do you have a job interview? Is that what you're not telling me?"

Like a dog with a bone, this one.

"I'll bet that's it. You think you're being clever, but don't forget I know you, Richard. I can see right through you. You were gone for two days straight—not to mention that one of them was Valentine's Day."

Damn it. All right, so the holiday had slipped his mind.

"We'll go out to dinner tonight. You and me. Where do you want to go? Feel like steak?" Maybe he'd even take her to Murray's for a jumbo shrimp cocktail and a plateful of pierogi, like they used to do, back before Kyle and the four-door sedans and having to show up at church every goddamn Sunday morning to push the offering plate down rows of men who'd only agreed to come because their wives promised they'd be home in time for kickoff.

"Steak! Where on earth did you come up with that kind of money?"

"We have an income, for God's sake, Eldris. As much as you like to think otherwise, I'm not completely useless."

Again with Eldris pouting and him apologizing and all of it ending, like it always did, with him feeling like an altogether rotten son of a gun. *Aw, hell.*

"Let me worry about the money. Really. We're fine." Richard stood and pulled her to his chest. "I'm sorry I hollered. You just gotta trust that I'm taking care of things."

And he was. Plans for March and April were shaping up, though he knew better than to share them with Eldris just yet. Advance planning gave her too much time to stew.

He was beginning to wonder if there wasn't a book in all this—*Baby Boomer Goes Boom,* or something like that. He'd have to think about the title. But the story line wasn't so far-fetched: middle-aged executive puts the brakes on his career and makes a name for himself on a completely new adventure.

Hell, plenty of well-known people must have hit the reset button.

While Eldris went upstairs to change her clothes for dinner, he escaped into the office. He opened his laptop and went straight for Google: *famous midlife career changes.*

Ronald Reagan. Yeah, everybody knew that one. But politicians, they didn't really count. Colonel Sanders, though—that one caught his eye. Turned out, the Colonel didn't open his first chicken place until he was in his forties. And even then he didn't get rich until after he went out of business and was forced to franchise his recipe. There was George Foreman, too. Hell, his body was probably so beat up by the time he retired, he could hardly walk.

Those were the comeback stories he could relate to.

He closed the laptop and grinned for what felt like the millionth time in as many breaths.

Not that he should have been smiling. There'd been another rejection last week. Two punks barely out of diapers needed a "seasoned" executive—their words, not his—to steer their upstart digital advertising firm. They'd launched no more than two years ago but were already throwing rolls of cash at their staff with no more concern than a guy buying a round of Cokes from the vending machine.

"We need someone who's been there, done that." This from the guy with the slicked-up hair and the ridiculously pointy shoes. Richard's toes ached just looking at them, which he had plenty of opportunity for because the kid wasn't sitting at the table, but several feet back from it, like a territorial dog making a point. The iPad he'd carried into the room sat dark on the conference table, but his right thumb hadn't stopped strumming the screen of his phone since he'd sat down. "Word around town is that you've been around and done plenty."

That's how they got rich, exploiting clichés for cash? And hadn't anyone taught this kid the importance of eye contact? Richard hadn't wasted his breath on a response. Instead, he'd worked up half a smile and aligned his gold pen more perfectly with the edge of his legal pad.

"How would you react to being the oldest person in the office every day by, say, thirty years?"

This was the second kid, the one with the paunch and the greasy ring around the collar of his faded T-shirt. He was device-free, but he'd already drained a sweating can of Diet Mountain Dew and Richard could hear a tinny clang every time he forgetfully raised the empty can to his lips, only to bring it back down to the ring it bled into the table.

Eldris would have sputtered herself blue over that water stain.

Everything in this office, he'd suddenly noticed, was old: the table was constructed from some sort of reclaimed wood, and the offices were really a repurposed warehouse. Even the conference room looked out onto a gutted boxcar whose rusting railroad tracks served as the boundaries of a community garden. Everything, Richard included, came from another time and place.

Everything except the two upstarts staring at him, waiting for an answer.

"You ever go work in that garden out there?" Richard had thrust his chin toward the oversize windows lining the wall behind them.

Ring-Around-the-Collar appeared briefly confused, but turned and looked. "I'd like to, someday." He scratched at the back of his neck. "But I really haven't had time."

Pointy Toes kept his face buried in his phone and added, "A bunch of the team goes out there every summer and posts pictures of the produce to our Insta feed. Some great exposure."

Richard wasn't a gardener himself, though Eldris managed a few salads each year from the tomatoes and basil she grew in pots on the deck. They were called "caprese" salads. Until this very moment, just knowing the term had kept him feeling young and smug.

Their rejection hadn't taken long to arrive, a tidy letter—on letterhead and mailed USPS, he was amazed to see—thanking him for his time and wishing him well in his search.

Aw, hell. He never would've been the legendary Richard Endres there, anyway. Never would have been the guy who laid out new accounts in front of him like dominoes. But there had been a time, *goddamn it.* Those two punks had said as much when they'd hauled him in to check his oil and gauge the tread life on his tires.

Sitting in that warehouse—that wannabe office straight out of his father's cigarette-smoking, fedora-wearing, punch-the-clock-at-five existence—he'd felt like a Pontiac waiting for parts. He'd once been everyone's favorite ride to the drive-through. Now, they didn't even make his kind anymore.

But here's what they'd missed, those kids: Richard Endres still had plenty of miles left in him.

"Eldris!" he hollered up the stairs. "What's taking so long? Steaks are all gonna be burned up by the time we get outta here."

He picked up his overnight bag, pulled out two hundred dollars in cash and pushed the bills deep into his pocket. Then he grabbed a stack of Post-it Notes, wrote a few words to himself and stuck it on his computer screen. "Kyle—inventory pickup?"

19

Violet

THERE JUST WASN'T any sense to this planning business. How could Violet possibly prepare her daughter for a baby when she refused to tell her if the child was a girl or a boy?

"You didn't know when you were expecting me, Mom," Cerise had said. "You did fine."

"I'd hardly call your infancy 'fine,'" Violet huffed. "You spent the first six months of your life dressed like a turtle." And she had. "To see that beautiful little head of yours poking out of nothing but green-and-yellow jumpers every day nearly made me crazy."

That was, of course, before ultrasounds were handed out like Halloween candy. Now the technology was so advanced, Violet could practically match an outfit to the baby's skin tone. Not that Cerise seemed to care. "Why does it matter?"

"Why?" Violet hadn't even known where to begin. "It matters because—" She found herself sputtering, her thoughts as slippery as a wrestling alligator. "It matters because it matters, Cerise." *Of all the questions.*

And if it were just simply a matter of wardrobe... But, no, there was also a room to design, equipment to purchase, parties to plan, invitations and announcements and thank-you cards, every single decision coming down to one basic question: Blue or pink?

People were already asking. At least that was the one thing

they could wonder to her face. Or, in her current situation, to her *ear*.

Violet swept her fingertips across her eyebrows, pressing gently at the pressure points her hippy-dippy concussion clinic nurse had recommended—with unsettling enthusiasm—and resolved, yet again, to remain stress-free. She breathed in and blew out, as she'd been instructed.

DING.

Her twenty-minute timer chimed, another of the nurse's suggestions. When she announced that she'd be helping with the baby planning, Ed had dragged her into the clinic for yet another evaluation before allowing her to so much as open a Pottery Barn Kids catalog. The timer and stress-reduction techniques had been the broadest compromise to which her doctor would agree. She could look at books, browse the internet, write in her planner, but for no more than twenty minutes at a time. On and on he'd gone with the eyestrain lecture. As if she were a child. As if she weren't smart enough to have already purchased a magnifying glass to help her make sense of the blurs that sometimes appeared on her page. No, she didn't need to pay a neurologist to lecture her about a problem she could fix at the dollar store.

And yet, she'd agreed to his terms. She'd let Ed buy her a fancy new timer and listened as he'd reviewed the rules because her reality was this: she had but one daughter to prepare for motherhood, and if she was ever going to be freed up to do that one job the way it ought to be done, she was going to have to pass that doctor's ridiculous tests.

This twenty-minute break was good timing, anyway. She'd just seen Eldris pull into the driveway.

"Ed hasn't summoned you to clean again, has he?" Violet held the door open for her friend, widening the gap when she caught sight of the bulging shopping tote Eldris carried with her. "What on earth?"

Eldris bobbled and sighed. "Oh, I know. I'm in an absolute stew, Violet."

Violet hadn't needed to be told. "Oh, dear. Come in." She waited as Eldris stomped the snow from her boots and set them in the tray by the door. "I was just going to take a short rest—all of this baby planning, you know. You can keep me company, as long as you won't be offended if I close my eyes."

Eldris made a show of helping her to the couch, but Violet swatted her away. She wasn't decrepit.

She settled into Ed's favorite chair, the wingback with the nearly invisible collapsible footrest. She'd been mortified when he'd brought it into the house—a La-Z-Boy, of all things—but she'd soon admitted that not only was it attractive in a masculine sort of way, it was deceptively comfortable.

Eldris took half of the love seat for herself and gave the other half to her overflowing tote bag.

Violet pointed. "Well, dear, like I said—what did you bring?"

Eldris's face clouded. She clutched her fist around the bag as if its contents might leap out with no warning. "Is Ed home?"

"No. Did you need him for something?"

"Actually, I'd hoped to get his opinion."

Violet went to raise a skeptical eyebrow, but her muscles responded by shooting torrents of pain across the crown of her head and down the back of her neck. She immediately tightened both hands into fists, then relaxed them, once, twice, three times. She took a deep breath and released it to the count of ten. The pain eased.

Eldris eyed her warily. "Anyway…" Apparently satisfied that Violet wasn't going to pass out or worse, she released the tote from her grip and opened it, pulling out a red satin blouse dotted with insufferable blue paisleys.

"You came to ask Ed for fashion advice?"

She shook her head. "No, it's Richard's. I found this in his closet—and I want to know why."

Violet stared. She'd never seen Richard Endres wear anything other than a Sunday suit or Saturday golf attire. "What do you mean, it's Richard's?"

"I mean, he's been gone so much lately—days at a time. You know he missed Valentine's Day?"

Violet nodded. That had taken up nearly an hour on the phone last week.

"And when he finally did take me out to celebrate, he was pulling wads of cash out of his pockets like some mobster on TV. He ordered two vodka martinis before the appetizers even arrived. *Appetizers*, Violet. He won't give me the money for new carpet, but he'll order crostini and tapenade."

Her volume was rising like the tide and Violet held a hand up to stop her. "Eldris, my head."

"Sorry." She straightened her bangs with the back of her wrist and took a deep breath. "Anyway, I got curious. I deserve to know what my own husband is getting up to."

"Of course you do." No wife should have to fear for her husband's health or fidelity.

Eldris threw the shirt aside and dived again into the seemingly bottomless sack. This time she pulled out a ragged bunch of who knew what.

"Is that a—"

"A *hairpiece*." Eldris positioned the dark-furred oddity on her own head. Front pieces spiked sadly to one side while longer strands fell in clumps down the back.

"That is possibly the most ridiculous-looking toupee I have ever seen." Not possibly, definitely. But she was trying to restrain herself.

"And hidden at the back of my husband's closet." Eldris's bottom lip began to tremble.

"Oh, Eldris, I'm sure it's, well..." *Dear Lord.* Grant her the energy for one of Eldris's crises today. She forced her eyes shut, imagining her body as a thermometer, the mercury falling with each breath. When she felt the calm flush from fingers to toes, she opened her eyes and looked at Eldris. "What do you think is going on?"

Eldris sniffed, then tossed the hairpiece back into its sack. One of the strands hung limply over the side like an octopus tentacle. "That's just it. I'm fresh out of ideas."

"Well, I still think it's safe to say he's not cheating. He wouldn't wear any of that to impress a woman."

Eldris shook her head. "No. We can definitely rule out an affair."

"And you're certain you haven't seen any of this before? It's not some sort of costume?"

"He's always refused to dress up for Halloween. Even when Kyle was young." She cocked her head, paused in thought. Then her face brightened like she'd caught a fleeting thought by its tail. "Oh, that can't be it."

Violet waited, knowing it would take her friend a moment or two to shake her words into place.

"But I bet it is. I bet I'm right."

Almost there.

"I can't believe I didn't think of this sooner. The odd hours. The late nights. The promising to tell me something when there was something to tell…"

And, here it came.

"I'll bet he's in a play. Or at least auditioning for one. That would explain why he keeps telling me to wait—wait till he knows if he's gotten the part. Of course, he hasn't been in a production since college, but he loved it. Said the stage was the only place I'd ever catch him wearing tights."

Eldris grew ever more animated as she spoke. Violet wasn't convinced by her theory, but it wasn't a ridiculous possibility, either. "So, this is some sort of theater costume, then."

"Well, don't you think? I mean the wig practically screams it."

It was screaming something, all right.

"I wonder if Kyle knows. I haven't said a thing about this to him, of course, but I wouldn't put it past him. Then again, he's been so busy lately that any news like this would probably go in one ear and right out the other."

She took the wig from the sack again and smoothed it, replacing it with far greater care than she'd shown it just a moment ago.

"I just hope he can make time to come see a performance or two. I know it would mean the world to Richard to have us both there."

Violet drummed a finger lightly on her thigh. Yes, yes, yes, the theater speculation was all good in theory, but the picture was still incomplete. She raised her finger to the air. "The only part of the mystery this doesn't explain, I suppose—" she paused, ensuring she had thought the idea through before articulating it "—is why he's gone for days at a time."

Eldris collapsed, positively deflated, into the back of the couch. Violet hated to see her this way, but what good would it have done to let her continue on down fantasy lane?

"I didn't think of that," said Eldris.

"Of course not. You're understandably upset."

"That's why I was hoping Ed was home. I thought maybe he'd have more, well, insight." Eldris paused and straightened herself on the couch. "Being a man and all."

"Well, quite frankly, I doubt very much—" Violet stopped. Eldris might have just inadvertently touched on something brilliant. "You know, of course, Edward has played nursemaid ever since my accident. Hardly leaving the house for more than a few minutes at a time."

Eldris nodded, then turned her head to scan the room. "Where did you say he was now?"

"I sent him to a matinee. Told him I'd be busy with baby planning. But really, I couldn't even stand to hear the man breathe anymore." And it was true. They'd gone from years of stolen moments together directly to an endless morass of inseparability.

Eldris dropped her head, though it took Violet a moment to understand why. When it clicked, she could have kicked herself. "Oh, listen to me going on about having my husband underfoot when you can't even keep yours at home."

"Violet!"

"Well, now you know I didn't mean that." She put a palm in the air, calling for a change of subject. "I'm simply saying, I have a husband who spends too much time at home, and you have a husband with a secret. Why not join forces?"

"You're suggesting I spy on Richard?" Eldris looked as forlorn as when she'd first arrived.

"Not exactly. I'm suggesting Edward spy on him."

Eldris sat, silently considering. "That could be interesting. But would he agree to it? I mean, would Ed know he was spying? Or not?"

Well, that was the question, wasn't it? Violet paused. "Not, I think. He'd only try to talk me out of it. Accuse me of interfering. But with a little coordination on our part, I see no reason why he'd have to know."

Now it was Eldris's turn to pause. "I don't know, Violet. As much as I want answers, all this sneaking around could just lead to more trouble in the long run."

"That's one way to look at it, certainly. But if there's anything my current situation has taught me to remember, Eldris, it's how quickly people jump to conclusions. It would be awful to let your suspicions ruin your marriage." She reached for the cashmere throw folded beside her chair and pulled it across her lap. "Secrets are never healthy."

Eldris dropped her head to the back of the love seat and sighed. "I suppose you're right."

CEDAR-ISLES NORTH STAR SAILOR

April 16, 1992

Cerise Baumgartner, age 4, and her father, Edward Baumgartner, of Cedar-Isles, attended the Faithful Redeemer Lutheran Church Father-Daughter Banquet on Saturday where they performed the duet "I Don't Need Anything but You" from the musical *Annie*. When asked if her father reminded her of Daddy Warbucks, the younger Baumgartner replied, "No, my dad's still got a little bit of hair left."

CEDAR-ISLES NORTH STAR SAILOR

April 7, 1994

Cerise Baumgartner, age 6, and her father, Edward Baumgartner, of Cedar-Isles, attended the Faithful Redeemer Lutheran Church Father-Daughter Banquet on Saturday where together they performed the song "Edelweiss" from the movie *The Sound of Music*. Said Cerise, "I was afraid at first because I thought edelweiss was actually a poisonous flower, sort of like mistletoe. But then my dad explained that it's not, and he knows because he's a scientist. So then I liked it again."

CEDAR-ISLES NORTH STAR SAILOR

April 11, 1996

Cerise Baumgartner, age 8, and her father, Edward Baumgartner, of Cedar-Isles, attended the Faithful Redeemer Lutheran Church Father-Daughter Banquet on Saturday where they performed a vaudevillian routine of knock-knock jokes. "My favorite," said the younger member of the team, "is the joke that goes, 'Knock, Knock. Who's there? Broken pencil. Broken pencil, who? Aw, who cares? It's a pointless joke.'"

CEDAR-ISLES NORTH STAR SAILOR

April 20, 2000

Cerise Baumgartner, age 12, and her father, Edward Baumgartner, of Cedar-Isles, attended the Faithful Redeemer Lutheran Church Father-Daughter Banquet on Saturday where they performed "This Little Girl of Mine" by the Everly Brothers. Edward sang vocals and Cerise played piano. Said Cerise, "It was my mom's idea."

20

Cerise

"A Liberty Bell on one wall and Betsy Ross sewing the American flag on the other?" Barb dropped the magazine she was reading, a glossy photo of a dog wearing a ballerina's tutu on the cover. "That's her idea for the baby's room?"

Cerise nodded. "Something about 'freedom being our greatest blessing at birth.'" Frankly, she was surprised her mother hadn't also announced that she, herself, would pose as the model for Betsy Ross. Her closet held so much red, white and blue that Cerise had once threatened to salute it.

"I warned you about involving her," Barb chided. "Your mother has a *Minimum Safe Distance* greater than a transcontinental convoy."

Cerise rolled her eyes. "You would think I'd know that by now. But somehow a lifetime of honing my Violet management skills keeps me fooled into believing otherwise."

"So, then—" Barb stretched her arms behind her head and yawned. The move knocked loose the bun into which she'd twisted her curls and she groped for the rogue strands in an effort to rewind them. "What's next?"

"Same as before. Keep her involved just enough that I know what she's up to."

"In other words, keep your friends close and your enemies closer?"

Cerise flung a pillow at her but missed by nearly a foot. "Be nice." She straightened the remaining pillows behind the small of her back and sat up. "Actually, I think there's a hitch to the whole suggestion."

"Why am I not surprised?" Barb stood and walked to the kitchen. The house still smelled of the grilled cheese sandwiches they'd eaten for dinner, all buttered and toasty. "Are you going to be offended if I pour myself a beer? Something tells me I'm going to need it."

Cerise waved her approval. Alcohol was the perfect response to what she was about to unveil. "I think she knew we'd hate the idea, so she pitched it first, hoping to make her alternative suggestion sound more reasonable."

"Which was?"

"To cover the walls with an illustrated family tree."

Barb returned and sat down on the couch next to Cerise. A spot of beer foam danced on her upper lip. "So?"

"So...all the branches filling in all the names of baby's entire heritage..." She dabbed the foam from Barb's lip and waited for her to catch on.

Her eyes lit. "No."

"Yep, baby's *entire* heritage." Cerise cocked an eyebrow, punctuating her point.

Barb stared back—just a beat or two of blank face while she played the various scenarios through in her mind—*what could come of this news?* Cerise loved to watch her when she did this, cinema verité à la Barbara.

"Oh, well, let her. I'm *that* part of the tree. Shrimpy has two parents: you and me. Your family gets one side of the tree, my family gets the other." She kicked her feet up under her butt and leaned in. "That's how it works."

"I know. I'm just preparing for the inevitable." Cerise fluffed the knitted throw that had been keeping her warm so that it fell across the two of them. She smoothed the blanket's corner across Barb's bare feet and tucked them in tight the way she knew she liked it. In bed, Cerise was a blanket kicker, but Barb burrowed—a dweller of their bedding's greatest depths.

Barb took a long drag on her beer, then looked apologetic. "Sorry. I really wish you could have some. I think it's helping."

Cerise smiled and teased at Barb's knees with her toes. "No worries. I made it through my childhood without drinking. I can manage for a few more months."

Barb took another drag. "You know, my mom will probably love this idea. And it won't be hard to get our information. The Hesse family documents its heritage like we're expecting a call from the Smithsonian. Half the shelves in my parents' library were occupied by leather-bound genealogy books."

"Half?" Cerise'd made a habit of checking Barb's hyperbole ever since she'd heard her compare her childhood home to Arlington National Cemetery in its "population of swallowed souls."

Barb shrugged. "At least half. The rest of the shelves were filled with my mom's self-published anthropological studies of semi-nomadic Incan tribes and my dad's Kama Sutra art collection."

Cerise wasn't sure which direction to turn first. "Your mom's an anthropologist?"

"Not officially. Not any more than my dad's an art historian." She raised a conspiratorial eyebrow. "Never be fooled by the prestige money can buy."

Cerise let the subject drop. Nor did she and Barb discuss Violet's latest angling any further. They didn't need to. Well before they'd even chosen a donor, Cerise and Barb agreed never to disclose the identity of the father. Of course, if Shrimpy asked someday—and was mature enough to process the information—then, yes, they'd tell. But other than that, it wasn't anyone's business.

THE NEXT DAY at work, Cerise downloaded a file with the results from her team's latest round of testing. She scanned the data and sighed: more bad news. They'd been testing a new biodegradable compound for months, and with the trend she saw now, they were headed back to the starting line.

When her cell phone buzzed, she was in a foul mood and knew better than to pick up, but there was something about a ringing phone that she'd never been able to resist, an etiquette drilled into her as a child.

Anyway, if she didn't answer, the phone would ring every few minutes until she did.

"Hi, Mom."

"What does Barb think about the options for the baby's room? I'll need to get moving if I'm going to hire someone to paint."

Cerise dropped her head onto her hand and ran a thumb along her forehead, smoothing her worry creases. "Well, I think the patriotic theme is definitely out. But, we were both sort of fond of the family tree—our family on one side, Barb's on the other." It was an obvious point but she felt it necessary to specify, given the question she suspected was coming.

Her mom *hmm*'d on the line. "I thought you might like that option. You've always been family-centric." Cerise could hear the shuffle of books on the other end and she imagined the oversize wallpaper binders that constituted many a childhood afternoon at Benjamin Moore.

"Of course, an accurate family history comes with complications, you know," her mom said.

And there it was. Not so much an interrogation as an insinuation, one that she'd let rise and curve like a question mark.

Cerise, however, refused to play her game. Instead, she waited quietly.

And so did her mother.

The grandfather clock in her parents' entryway ticked away seconds of their lives.

"Cerise?"

"Yes?"

"Neither one of us is ignorant to how nature works."

"Obviously not."

"So you know what I'm asking."

"Yes, I do."

"And you're obviously choosing not to tell me."

"Yes, I am."

"So, perhaps it would help you to know why I'm asking."

Why, indeed.

Cerise waited, knowing her mother was going to continue regardless.

"DNA can be extremely consequential."

"You don't think I know that?" She let out a tiny, derisive snort. She couldn't help it. Her mother called her at work—in a world-class scientific laboratory, no less—then tried to claim superior knowledge about the significance of DNA.

"I do not appreciate your attitude, Cerise."

"Would you appreciate it more if I told you I was too busy for this conversation and hung up?"

"Don't be cute." She paused, but just for a moment. "What if there's something awful in baby's DNA? Or, even more, what's if there's something wonderful? A predisposition to extreme intelligence or being the descendant of a famous historical figure?"

She paused again.

"Did I ever tell you about my great-aunt Tabitha?"

"About a million times. I know all about her grandfather spying on George Washington as he crossed the Delaware."

"It wasn't her grandfather, it was her great-great-great-grandfather. And he wasn't spying on General Washington, he'd single-handedly infiltrated the Hessian troops waiting to ambush them on the other side."

Cerise heard her mother speaking but she wasn't taking in the words. Instead, she pulled out her notebook and reviewed her notes from the morning's team meeting, determined to multitask her way through this latest lecture. It did not improve her mood. Their project timeline looked close to hosed.

Damn.

"Cerise, are you even listening to a word I'm saying?"

"Of course, Mother, but I have absolutely no idea what the Hessians or our relatives who spied on them have anything to do with you acting so—" She stopped, forcing herself to get control before she said something her mother would refuse to forget. "We've asked you to drop this. Why do you insist on making it an issue?"

"My great-aunt Tabitha was offensive and a bully. No matter who was speaking to her."

"And?"

"And she got away with it because everyone knew her history, that she came from the same stock as a man brave enough—and, quite frankly, just foolish enough—to infiltrate the Hessians and in so doing help win one of the most decisive victories of the Revolutionary War."

Cerise felt her heart drop and her hands begin to shake, a sure sign she was near the end of her patience. "What is your point?" Her pitched voice rang back at her through the phone.

"Family is the face we bear to the world, Cerise. Don't let your child's—" She paused. "Don't let your child's origin story be the most interesting thing people hear. Wouldn't you rather baby be known as sharing the same DNA as a world-class historian instead of that of some faceless *donor*? Give baby a story."

She went on, but Cerise couldn't hear beyond the roaring in her ears. How dare she? The audacity to assume she knew *anything* about this decision. This was Cerise's child. Hers and Barb's. Why wasn't that enough?

"Frankly, Mom, I know you have your own good reasons for being so hung up about family, but I've got to be honest—it's become just short of pathological. Your past is your past, but this baby is happening now. And you can't seem to get on board.

You say you're supportive of our choice, but you refuse to respect our privacy. You say you're not interested in discussing my sexuality, but you seem pretty fascinated by just how I managed to get the sperm and egg together at the same baby party."

She'd become aware of a silence on the other end of the line, followed by several seconds of what sounded like an elephant blowing through a straw.

"Are you all right?"

"Of course I am," said her mother, though her voice was tight and Cerise knew she'd better get to the point.

"So this is how it's going to be from now on. You keep asking. You keep pushing. You stay all hung up on this family issue of yours. But Barb and I aren't going to play along. We're going to smile and turn the other cheek and bring this baby into the world happy and healthy."

She waited for a response but the line was silent.

"Got that? Have I made myself perfectly clear?"

"Crystal." She could tell the word had to be pushed from between taut lips.

"Delightful. And before I hang up, Barb wanted me to tell you that the Hesse family keeps an extensive history of its genealogy. Has done for generations. I'm sure Mrs. Hesse would love to share it. Would you like me to put you in touch?"

"If that's what you and Barb would like to do."

Ugh. Her mother's passive-aggression was enough to melt the phone line.

"Terrific. I'll send you her contact information just as soon as I get home. Oh, and, Mother? It wasn't just *some* donor."

She hung up, only to realize what she had just done.

"Watchers" Group Expands to Kansas City

by Harvey Arpell,
staff reporter, *Minneapolis/St. Paul Standard*

March 1, 2018

Kansas City, MO—"The Watchers," the activist group that claimed responsibility for the construction of two statues outside the Federal Reserve Bank in Minneapolis late last year, now claim to have erected a statue outside the Federal Reserve Bank in Kansas City. The installation was found early this morning.

Photos posted to the group's Instagram show a statue of a man lifting his face to the sky and cupping his hands behind his ears, as if listening. The Kansas City installment differs slightly from the Minneapolis statues, both of which depicted women and children in poverty. All three figures have been constructed primarily of chicken wire and eyeglasses.

Kansas City Police declined to comment, though they did confirm that the statue has been removed.

21

Violet

VIOLET SAT AT Eldris's kitchen table and picked at her chicken salad. Not that she wasn't hungry—she hadn't eaten breakfast—but her head was full of the previous day's call to Cerise, leaving little room for appetite.

A mother could never fix the world enough to put her heart at rest for her child.

Despite the mood, Eldris buzzed about the kitchen, opening cupboards and offering crackers or a dash of salt and pepper, which Violet waved away one after the other.

"Sit down, Eldris. You're making me dizzy, all this back and forth."

"You know I'm not a very good sitter. Have you checked your phone? Has Ed called?"

"He's hardly been gone twenty minutes."

Violet put down her fork and closed her eyes against the commotion. There were so many balls whirling about in her head, so many worries to catch. The consequences of dropping one felt nearly too much to bear.

It didn't surprise her that Cerise had grown obstinate about the baby's paternity. She hadn't ever been a pushover, not even as a child. During Cerise's third grade year, Violet had received no fewer than three phone calls from the mother of Robert Brewster, a boy on her bus. "Cerise hit Robert in the face with her backpack and gave him a bloody nose." Then it was, "Cerise ripped Robert's coat from his hands and nearly tore off his entire fingernail."

When she got the last call, "Cerise left Robert with bruises all up and down his arm," she sat her daughter down and wouldn't let her leave until satisfied she'd learned the truth. It took several hours and a threat to withhold her lasagna dinner before a confession finally came.

"He teases Jake Engquist," Cerise had said, refusing to meet her mother's eye.

"The boy with Down syndrome?"

"Yes. He stutters and mixes up his words and Robert makes fun of him. The whole bus laughs. Nobody sticks up for Jake. And sometimes I don't even think he understands he's being teased."

"Are you telling me you beat up on Robert Brewster because he teases Jake Engquist?"

"I guess." Cerise had shrugged and nodded. Violet still couldn't see her face but saw early tears begin to gather on her chin.

"Cerise, you know we've taught you there are better choices than violence. Why didn't you come talk to me?"

"Because I knew you'd make me stop." She'd finally raised her head and Violet could see, yes, she was crying. "It felt good to see Robert scared for once, instead of Jake."

Violet had nodded and hugged her for several long minutes. Then she sent her daughter to bed without dinner and told her there would be far greater consequences if she ever caught wind of more fighting. After Cerise was asleep, she dialed Mrs. Engquist and advised her of the teasing. Said Cerise had stepped in once or twice, but didn't explain how. That much of the story, at least, she could fix.

So of course she knew Cerise wouldn't back down on the paternity issue. And yet, this was a worry Violet couldn't seem to let go. Where was the line between worry and wisdom in mothering?

She opened her eyes in time to see Eldris scooping more chicken salad onto her already-full plate.

Violet took the bowl and spoon from her hands and set them aside. Then she patted the place at the table beside her. "If you don't come sit down, I'm going to have to go lie down."

Eldris surrendered and took a seat.

"He'll call when he's on his way home, Eldris. But remember that won't be for a good couple of hours."

Today was the first opportunity they'd had to set Ed onto Richard's trail. Eldris had come downstairs this morning to find her husband in jeans and a sweater, stuffing his laptop into his briefcase. When she pushed him for answers, he said he was just heading up to St. Cloud to "meet a guy."

"St. Cloud is at least an hour and a half drive," Violet reminded her. "Maybe closer to two, given how much snow we got last night."

"I just hope Ed finds him. You're sure you told him River City Brews? I'm almost positive that's the name Richard gave me. I mean it could have been River City News. That would make more sense, I guess. But not if they were going to lunch, which he said they were."

"I told him River City Brews and even made him look up the address on the internet. He has a printed map and a phone number in case he gets lost." She nodded, pleased and a bit surprised at her ability to concoct a compelling story on such short notice. This had all unfolded in less than an hour. "I told him I'd overheard Barb talking about their beer and that I very much hoped to give her some for her birthday. It's coming up."

"Oh, I didn't realize. Is that true?"

Violet couldn't remember exactly. She changed the subject. She needed to think about something lighter. "What did you ever decide about your mother-of-the-groom dress? Are you going with the sea foam or the navy?"

Eldris had been back and forth to Violet's house at least a dozen times in the past week with armloads of options. Violet had rated most of them a solid C+, though it was nearly impossible to judge since Eldris insisted on wearing a T-shirt throughout the entire process.

"If I leave deodorant stains I can't take them back," she'd said.

"And just how am I supposed to determine what's flattering or not when your shirt is hollering at me to *Call Dean to Keep Your Plumbing Clean?*"

The parade continued until they'd narrowed it to two choices, each at least a solid B+.

"I'm going with the sea foam. Though… Oh, I don't know. Are you sure it doesn't wash me out? I've been told green isn't my color."

"Who on earth told you that?"

"My mother. Every year I wanted a green dress for Easter but she always said, 'That color makes you look as if you're about to turn your stomach.' Of course, my sister can wear anything."

Dead and gone for nearly twenty years and her mother's ghost still haunted Eldris's head, as cranky and judgmental as ever. Even at the funeral, there was poor Eldris in tears because the Ladies Auxiliary had used thick-sliced ham in the sandwich buns rather than thinner deli slices.

"She hated gristle!" she'd wailed, as Violet shoved a tissue into her fist and ushered her out of the rapidly filling Fellowship Hall.

"Well, I say this wedding is your chance to finally have the green dress you've always wanted. If it had washed you out, I would have told you so."

As if on cue, the door leading to the basement opened and Kyle emerged holding a manila folder and looking like he had spent the better portion of the morning on hands and knees. His jeans were caked with dust and he had what looked suspiciously like a spiderweb hanging from his brow line.

He brushed at the web-ish strand with the back of his hand.

"Hi, Mrs. Baumgartner. I didn't realize you were here."

"Nor I you, Kyle. We were just discussing your wedding, in fact."

"Oh? Good things, I hope."

"We were just deciding on my mother-of-the-groom dress," said Eldris. "I think I'm going to wear green."

"Great," he said, though Violet suspected from the blank look on his face that if she asked him in ten minutes what his mother planned to wear to his wedding, he'd have no recollection this conversation ever took place. Kyle always struck her as somewhat synthetic, the male version of those cheese slices she'd watched Eldris put on his sandwiches as a child—real-looking, but wrapped in a flimsy plastic shell. In fact, perhaps the abundance of those cheese slices was one of the reasons he'd developed as he had.

He placed his folder on the counter and flipped it open to the top page, losing himself in whatever he found there.

"Taking inventory again?" Eldris had made her way to the refrigerator and seemed to, as if by reflex, be pulling the ingredients for a sandwich from its shelves.

"Yeah." He traced the rows of data with his forefinger. "There's just something I still can't make sense of."

"Don't you worry." She slathered mayonnaise across one slice of bread then reached for the mustard. "You'll get to the bottom of it."

"And such a great year for donations." He said the words aloud but Violet sensed he was in his own head.

Eldris placed a plate with two sandwich triangles in front of him and made for the fridge again, this time pulling out the milk.

Catching sight of the carton, he put his hand out to stop her. "No, thanks," he said. "Rhonda has me off dairy."

Violet watched as Eldris's face fell, a sentinel stripped of her charge. At least Barb had the decency to allow Violet a voice in her daughter's life.

"Kyle," she interceded, "I've been wondering if you could shed some light on a subject about which I am a complete novice."

He looked up from his inventory studies and, after a brief, blank-faced pause, blinked at her, coming to.

"Sure," he said. "Shoot."

"Sperm donation," said Violet. "How does it work, exactly?"

Kyle dropped his sandwich and stared at her as if she'd just stripped naked and asked him to tea.

"Excuse me?" he said.

"Well, as you know, Cerise and her partner, Barb, are expecting their first baby. And we all know that they needed assistance. Simple human biology. So naturally, I'm curious about the process. The sperm. Its origins."

Kyle stuttered and shook his head. Just like his mother. Violet hadn't ever seen that trait in him before. Genetics were amazing.

"I'm certain he doesn't know anything about that, Violet," said Eldris, who, for the first time all morning, finally stopped moving.

"Oh, I'm not implying as much," said Violet. "But certainly—as a man—he's more informed about the process in general than either of us?"

Kyle finally shook himself loose of his shock and answered her question, sputtering his way through a flurry of speculative and less-than-descriptive descriptions of the process.

"Well, from what I've heard..." He must have equivocated a hundred times. For heaven's sake, she hadn't asked for a first-person narrative. She simply wanted a man's knowledge of where one would donate *quality* sperm—the Bergdorf's of DNA, so to speak.

"Well, there was a clinic near the medical school when I was at the university. Rumor had it that's where the male med students went when they needed rent money."

But again, he didn't know from experience.

Of course he didn't. His profession didn't require an MD.

But he did give her what she needed: a name. A name attached to an address, which, it turned out, was more serendipitous than she could have dreamed.

22

Richard

So, NEWS OF their group had spread all the way to the Philippines. How goddamn crazy was that?

Richard would've been tempted to think the email was one of "Phil the Filipino's" jokes, an I'll-try-anything guy he used to work with who once dropped a half-dozen raw eggs into a pint of beer and drank them down in exchange for one month of Richard's executive parking space. Only these days, Phil had taken a job with the Peace Corps and traveled the backwaters of the globe meeting with warlords and dignitaries and all sorts of greedy sons of bitches. So it definitely wasn't Phil.

He wrote back and took the meeting. "I'll bring one of the guys, too."

They pulled into the parking lot of River City Brews and found a spot next to the door. Good thing, since whoever the restaurant hired to plow their snow hadn't done more than a half-assed job.

The guy on the other end of the email was just inside, waving at them through the window from a table near the door.

The guy was Gus Severson, about two heads taller than Richard and pale enough to burn under a high-voltage lamp bulb. He had the gray hair gone white typical of Minnesota Scandinavian transplants and it was thinning just enough Richard could see his pink scalp beneath.

"Knew you two as soon as I saw you. You guys are getting

a reputation," he said, pulling a beefy hand from thick gloves and extending it.

Richard shook it, and then introduced his colleague.

"This is Ted." They shook hands. "Our third guy, Julian, has a real life, which means, unlike us, he can't drop everything for an 11 a.m. lunch on a Thursday."

Gus nodded. "Understand. Anyway, I'm really just here because I've been asked to find out if you're interested in hitting the road."

He and Ted had spent the last two hours talking about nothing else. Because, really, it wasn't just the road, it was the other side of the world.

"How long is the flight to the Philippines?" he'd said. "Twelve, fourteen hours?"

Ted didn't know. He'd only been as far west as Hawaii, when he took his wife along to a medical sales conference and called it their twentieth anniversary trip. That flight had been six hours out of LA and they still spoke English in Hawaii. This trip had to be a hell of a lot farther.

"Gotta be honest, Gus," said Richard. "At our age, it feels like a long shot."

Julian was just now able to sit for ten minutes at a time, a result of some quack surgeon clipping the wrong nerve endings while grabbing for his swollen prostate. And Ted, his knees were so shot he couldn't carry any of his own equipment. They'd have to hire a crew for his things, alone.

"Sorry, Richard," he'd said about a half-dozen times on the trip up. "The last thing I want is to slow down the momentum we've got going."

"Nah," Richard assured him. "None of us expected this to be a long-term gig."

For his part, Richard would probably handle the travel just fine. His back flared like an angry pisser every once in a while, but he could manage that with a few decent muscle relaxants and two fingers of Jameson. Ultimately, though, the decision about whether or not to hit the road came down to one question for him: Was this what he wanted?

He'd only agreed to the first outing for the cash. Their band of aging misfits had needed one more person and he'd needed a reason to escape Eldris's suffocating brooding. Not to mention, it was only supposed to be a few nights, a few places. Then people started to notice and they got more calls, more emails, more requests. And more money. Cash in hand at the end of the night. *Goddamn intoxicating.*

So, not bad, right? A hell of a long way from the life he'd expected, but not so bad. Anyway, how were men like him supposed to spend their final decades? Old age used to be so black-and-white. His father worked until his joints gave out. Then he took his pension and parked on the couch for ball games, in the pew on Sundays. He took his wife on a one-week vacation every summer and played nice when the grandkids came over at Thanksgiving and Christmas.

This, though. Richard didn't have enough cash to retire, but his months spent pounding the pavement only proved with high-def precision that he lacked the hipster cool of today's ad exec. Still, he wasn't ready to put his life into Park like his father had. But neither was he eager to let go of the luxuries he'd earned—a man his age deserved a beer fridge and a monster hot water heater, environmentalists be damned.

Was he up for red-eye flights and crap-hole hotels? There was a time when the idea of the international jet set would have sung to him to him like a circle of flight attendants humming the Pan Am tune. Now he wasn't so sure.

And what would Eldris say? If she were upset with him now, she'd shake her brain loose with worry once he started leaving for weeks at a time. Nah, it wouldn't be fair to either one of them.

He had done one thing right recently, though. Last week

he'd taken Eldris's pleading to heart and called Kyle about all the trouble with EyeShine.

"Your mom's pretty worked up. Says she's worried you're not sleeping."

"I'm not. Whatever time I'm not at the office I'm spending answering Rhonda's wedding emails, and whatever time I'm not online I'm spending trying to work through this EyeShine donations mess."

"You know, we're around if you need us."

"Yeah, I know."

"All you gotta do is ask."

"I know, Dad."

Neither of them said anything more.

"Well, kiddo, I'll see you soon, then."

"See you soon, Dad."

So he'd said his piece. The kid knew he was in his corner. Knew he had people looking out for him. He and his mom both. And his fiancée, Rhonda, too, of course. Hell of a catch, that one. At least, he hoped she was. Sometimes Richard wondered, got a zing in his gut like he'd eaten too fast and needed a Zantac—maybe it was something Rhonda said, maybe it was the look in her eye. He didn't know, and he sure as hell wasn't going to bring it up. If his dad had warned him about all the hours he'd lose trying to talk Eldris off a ledge, it wouldn't have made one goddamn difference. He would have married her anyway—call it love, call it spite—either way, he would have walked that aisle and not looked back.

"So, what about families? Enough cash for them to come along? You could say I'm newly retired, and my wife's been waiting twenty years to travel."

Gus said he'd look into it.

Ted said, "I don't know. Doesn't seem like this would translate internationally. And anyway, I'd wanna know who's paying us first. I'm not about to take it on the chin for some mysterious dude across the Pacific."

Richard nodded. The cash would have to be pretty darn fantastic for the kind of deal Gus was talking.

"We'll get back to you after we discuss it, the three of us," Richard said. "Anyway, regardless of how it shakes out, thanks for getting in touch."

He stood to go and Ted followed his lead, though slower, giving his battered knees time to adjust.

"It's the cold," he explained. "Maybe a trip to the tropics would do me good."

Ted and Gus said their final goodbyes. As for Richard, he was distracted. He could have sworn he'd just seen Ed Baumgartner get into his car and pull away.

Maybe the world was smaller than it seemed.

23

Violet

"WE'RE RIGHT HERE, ED. Why on earth wouldn't we go in?"

Violet and Ed stood outside a dark wood-paneled door, the words *NextGen Cryolabs* the only identifiers on its small, discreet nameplate.

"Your checkup is in twenty minutes. We'll be late if we stop."

When Kyle had given Violet the name and location of the sperm bank yesterday, she'd immediately recognized it to be in the same building as her nasal-toned neurologist. She didn't believe in signs, but if she did—well, no. She didn't believe in signs.

"For heaven's sake, Ed. When was the last time it took an elevator twenty minutes to go up two floors?" She reached for the doorknob, but he stopped her, his hand on hers.

"What's going on, Violet?"

He didn't know, of course, because she hadn't told him. She was making the plan up as she went along. Her first excuse had come as soon as they stepped on the elevator.

"You pushed the button for seven," he'd said. "Dr. Hartz is located on the ninth floor."

She thought fast. "Oh, didn't I tell you? Kyle Endres told me to check out a practice on seven. Said it was highly recommended by the medical students when he was in school." She shot out of the elevator as soon as its doors opened, knowing Ed would have no choice but to follow.

"Yes, but what is it, Violet?"

She could hear him struggling to catch his breath behind her and she made a mental note: *Explore couples' yoga.*

"Just what I told you." She glanced over her shoulder. He was several paces behind. "Kyle said it was very popular. The least we can do is stop by."

Ed finally caught up as she slowed to read the office numbers. Suite 710. She'd found it.

Ed read the nameplate aloud. "NextGen Cryolabs. NextGen— why on earth would Kyle be sending you to—" Ed turned to look at her, and she watched as the gears of his mind turned and caught.

"Explain," he said.

Oh, for heaven's sake. "Cerise may have said she would no longer answer my questions about baby's father, but she specifically did not prohibit me from finding the answers on my own."

She reached again for the doorknob, but Ed inserted himself in front of the door.

"Violet, this is madness."

"Oh, madness, is it? And do you suppose it's mad of me to wish to proactively protect my grandchild from a host of genetically derived health risks?"

She felt the bees begin to stir in her head but she pushed them away, forced them quiet.

"My father was dead and gone by the time we discovered his secrets. But they come out. And when they do, they take innocent lives with them."

She'd said these words before, but they burned just as much today as they had the first time they'd exploded from her lips.

Ed sighed and dropped his head. He used to be her champion, her stalwart against this awful pain. But somewhere over the years, he'd grown tired. Looking at him now, he was nearly exhausted.

Violet had learned this awful truth—that her father hadn't been nearly the man they'd believed him to be—years after becoming a mother herself. Cerise was in third grade, meaning Violet was well on her way to raising a happy, successful child of her own. His failure shouldn't have rattled her so badly. But it did. Nothing could ever remain unquestioned.

"Edward," she said, squaring her hips so she could meet him eye to eye, "this is a mystery I cannot abide."

He didn't move an inch. "They're not going to be able to tell you a thing. All that will come of this is further upset."

"Oh, really?" She saw a man turn the corner at the end of the hallway and head in their direction. She smelled opportunity.

"Are you sure, dear?" Violet raised the volume on their conversation several notches, ensuring the man approaching could hear them clearly. "I'm certain this is exactly where we need to be."

Ed shot her a furious look and growled under his breath, "Violet..."

The young man was upon them now and he paused, edgy like a fawn, eyeing the door.

Without so much as a breath, Violet turned to the man and asked, "Are you going in?"

"Well, um." He seemed barely able to lift his eyes from the carpet. "Yes."

"Wonderful." She nodded and stepped aside, pulling Ed along with her by the elbow. "We'll follow you."

Ed held back but she answered his retreat with a look that said, *Follow me or not, I'm going in.*

He followed.

In the waiting area—a lovely modern Danish design, all right angles and blond wood—they queued, waiting their turn for the receptionist. From Violet's estimation, the young man must have been a regular, as it took no more than a nod and a friendly *Hello* before he was invited to take a seat. Expediency was such a lovely thing.

"Good morning. I'm Violet Baumgartner and this is my husband, Edward."

The woman's smile was warm and welcoming. She wore a
trim suit jacket over a neatly pressed shirt and Violet spotted the
pale pink blush on her fingernails. Oh, yes. *This was the place.*

"You know, I bet you're looking for Suite 720. This is Suite
710. You want the office just around the corner."

"Excuse me?"

"Midwest Urology Specialists. Suite 720—around the corner. Happens all the time."

Oh, dear.

"No. You see, we are, in fact, in the right place. This is Next-
Gen Cryolabs, is it not?"

The woman flustered and began knocking her fingers about
on her computer's keyboard.

"Do you have an appointment? I'm sorry—tell me your name
again?"

Violet did not have time or patience to waste; their twenty
minutes were dwindling.

"Our daughter used your—" she paused, realizing that she'd
never actually said the words aloud in public before "—your
sperm bank. She's now expecting her first child and we would
like to know more."

The woman began just where Violet expected she would.

"Oh, I'm sorry but all of our donor information is kept strictly
confidential. I can't possibly share—"

Again with the wasting time.

"I'm aware. I simply need to know more."

Ed, she saw out of the corner of her eye, had wandered and
was now behaving conspicuously innocent, scanning the rack of
magazines on the wall. As if there was time for reading material.

"More *what*, exactly?"

"We've been advised that this is a premier bank. Your donors are of the highest caliber in education and profession, are they not?"

The woman nodded silently, her mouth slightly agape. Violet fought the urge to reach across the desk and nudge it closed.

"A phalanx of doctors and scientists among your ranks?" said Violet.

Again with the nodding.

"Then what I'm here for is a sampling of your most prominent donors."

"A *sampling*?" said the woman.

"That's what I said, yes. A sampling. A selection. A small taste."

"A small *taste*?"

Ed was back. "Please. You must be right. We have the wrong office. So sorry to have bothered you."

He reached for Violet's elbow but she was too quick for him, pasting it to her side.

"Well, of course," Violet said, "we could make an appointment, if that would help."

"You have an appointment?" Then again with the punching at her keyboard and the flustered questioning about names and were they sure they weren't looking for Suite 720?

"Oh, for heaven's sake," said Violet. "We're not here to *donate*. Like I told you, we simply would like to get a look at the men our daughter may have chosen with which to impregnate herself."

What language was she going to have to use to make herself clear? She made a mental note of the girl's name so as to include it in the letter of complaint she was going to be forced to write to NextGen Cryolabs management.

Violet continued her attempts to clarify. "Don't you have a library? Flip books? A computer database? Anything?"

As she spoke, a door just beyond the reception desk opened and a man emerged, fiddling with the tuck of his shirt.

"Peter?" Ed stopped tugging at her elbow and stepped toward the stranger.

"Ed?"

Violet noticed her husband was chuckling, the same nervous twitter that always surfaced when beset with nerves. The same way he'd behaved when performing with Cerise at the Father-Daughter Banquets or when giving his toast at the retirement party. At least this time he hadn't chosen to lead with his awful clown joke.

"Well," Ed said, "I certainly hope BiolTech hasn't cut paychecks so drastically you're forced to supplement your income."

For gracious' sake.

Violet didn't know this man. At least, she couldn't recall meeting him at the retirement party or at any of Ed's corporate picnics. But she did know enough about human behavior to see that he would rather die than stand there for one more second with what she could only assume was his sperm in a bag.

"No, well," the man started. "Angie and I are trying to jumpstart a family. So to speak."

Ed was now at his side and, Violet was horrified to see, shaking his hand.

"Say no more. Say no more. Went through a bit of the troubles ourselves back in the day. I found it helpful to push a diet high in folic acid—kale, spinach, beet greens. Your swimmers will be back in the game in no time." He gave the man a nudge, shoulder to shoulder. "Your colon won't complain, either, come to think of it."

Violet looked at her watch. Twelve minutes. It would take Ed at least five to wrap up his conversation, even in the face of that poor man's desperate glances toward the door. There just simply wasn't enough time.

"Well," she said to Cynthia, the rough-and-tumble receptionist about whom she would soon be writing her complaint. "What a pleasure to have benefited from your brilliant insight."

Violet allowed herself to admit defeat.

At least for today.

Christmas 1996

Dearest loved ones, far and near—

Evergreen Tidings from the Baumgartners!

I hope this letter finds you surrounded by family and friends, steeped in the joy so abundantly offered us each holiday season.

We all send reports of good health and interesting work this year. Our dear Ed, of course, remains tucked away in his laboratory. His research into common bowel disorders is now showing great promise and he believes the team is within sprinting distance of a breakthrough. I hope to have bountiful news to share in next year's letter.

Lovely little Cerise is hardly little anymore (though she'll always be a petite speck of a thing, tiny feet and all (oh, how I envy her!)). Her 9th birthday just passed us by, leaving this awestruck mother to wonder, where did the time go?

Unfortunately for us, third grade has been an exercise in perseverance. The biggest obstacle is not the work, but keeping Cerise challenged—I can't tell you the number of phone calls I am forced to exchange with her teacher each week (a well-intended but past-her-prime warhorse). I can say with certainty that no other mother faces such unnecessary schoolmarm commentary with unnerving regularity.

"Cerise is letting other children copy her work."

"Cerise corrected my spelling in front of the whole class."

"*Cerise brought a copy of* Lady Chatterley's Lover *in for silent reading time.*"

Obviously, anyone with eyes can see that the child is not disruptive, but bored! (Though where she found a copy of that book, I've yet to discover.) She's already tested out of her grade level in math and reading. So until this school of ours learns to create an environment in which her industrious brain is fully engaged, our little Cerise will find ways to do it herself.

On the bright side, I continue to keep myself busy while Ed and Cerise are out of the house. This fall I had the good fortune to sit on the Parent Advisory Committee for the Minneapolis Public School Board of Education—an enlightening experience, to say the least. You can't imagine the complaints parents raise! Therefore, as an Advisory Parent, let me remind those of you reading this humble letter that it is not the school's job to make sure your son enjoys his homework (it is called "work," after all) or that your daughter be allowed to skip first period due to her late-evening dance class. I, for one, refuse to grant permission for lazy parenting, and said as much to my committee colleagues, freely and often. (Oh, how I could go on about this! But I will refrain, for fear it would kill your Christmas spirit.)

All of this cheerful banter, however, is but a screen to mask the devastating sadness we feel at the passing of my father, Thomas Odenbach, two weeks ago. One minute he was asking my mother for tuna salad on toast, the next minute he was gone. The Lord's hand was swift and decisive and the doctors told us there was nothing they could have done.

Needless to say, not a day goes by that I don't mourn his loss. He was a pillar in the community, in the church and in my life. He held his standards as high as his head and expected no less of me or my brothers. I can still hear his voice reminding me, "Violet, the truth may not be pretty, but it must always be told." And so you have my father, Thomas Odenbach, to thank for the knowledge that you can always trust me to be truthful.

Christmas blessings to each and every one of you,
Ed and Violet Baumgartner

24

Violet

VIOLET THRUMMED HER fingers on the locket at her throat, lost deep in her worry. She could feel her pulse, beating like rain through the locket's gold heart, quickened with questions to which there were no simple answers. *What.* Thudump. *Was.* Thudump. *She.* Thudump. *Going. To. Do.* Thudump. Thudump. Thudump.

Yesterday had not gone at all as planned. It had begun with the fiasco at the lab and ended with her having been shocked and not a little bit horrified by her disaster of a neurologist.

"Two more weeks, I oughta think. Then you can ease back into normal life. See how it goes."

Two more weeks. Just what did he think he was playing at? In fact, she'd asked him that very question.

"Well," he'd said, "I'd like to think I'm *playing at* getting you back to full neurological function."

He and his laissez-faire care. As if there wasn't a baby coming or a nursery to decorate or a daughter keeping secrets or a husband who couldn't get the sheets on the bed without entangling himself to the point of near choking. Not to mention a best friend whose married life was beginning to show as much wear and tear as her living room carpet.

Ed had, sure enough, found River City Brews and brought home the requested six-pack. But he hadn't said a word about bumping into Richard. "Didn't see anything unusual," he'd said, picking Violet up from Eldris's house. "Nice day for a drive, though. A good excuse to get out of the house. And come to think of it, isn't Barb's birthday in July?"

Plus, ever since yesterday's foray into Fertility 101, Violet hadn't been able to shake the picture of her daughter knees-up on some cold slab of an exam table, vials and tubes and bright lights and doctors speaking in hushed tones all around her. The thought that her grandchild had begun its life in such a stern, sterile way haunted her every thought.

Though, too, she knew that if Cerise had conceived the baby in the *natural* way she wouldn't have wished to picture that event, either.

Perhaps a baby's conception just wasn't anyone's business.

Then as resolutely as her thoughts had come, she pushed them aside and pulled a blank sheet of paper from the binder in front of her. She picked up a freshly sharpened pencil and began to sketch the Baumgartner family tree.

Sometimes, there was no answer but to move on.

She began with Ed's side, which was fairly easy. He was one of only two siblings and his sister had not married. Violet's family, on the other hand, was larger. She was the eldest of four children, though the only girl among them. Growing up she'd thought of her brothers like a litter of puppies, careless and messy and wrestling about on the floor. Thankfully they'd grown into decent family men.

She sketched a few more generations as best she could recall—she'd need to check her genealogy before it went permanently onto the nursery wall—and noticed something she hadn't before. Her side of the family was broken only by death. There were no divorces. Delightfully unusual, she thought, when in this day and age people seemed willing to toss aside their responsibilities for a wink and a nod.

She skimmed the diagram and noticed that Ed's family hadn't suffered many divorces, either—only one, and that was his great-uncle Oscar who fathered three children in swift succession, then joined the World War II Navy and never came home. He didn't die; that would have been too easy. He was simply convinced that life at sea was preferable to home, wife and family. So after four years of waiting, his wife, Martha, marched down to the courthouse and got her walking papers.

No wonder neither of Martha's sisters married.

That made three unmarried women on Ed's side: his sister and two great-aunts. Violet looked at her own side of the tree and counted four unmarried women—three great-aunts and her favorite, Auntie Tate. She'd been asked to marry several suitors but she said she never considered any of them suitable enough. Instead, she taught school in Southern Minnesota for forty years and shared a spacious two-bedroom apartment for twenty of them with a fellow teacher and spinster named Rube. Violet loved Tate and Rube. Visits with them meant summer picnics on the lawn and walks downtown to the taffy shop and the chance to run her fingers gently along Rube's collection of delicate china dogs.

Wasn't it funny the things you'd never considered before.

Could it be that Tate and Rube were something more than just Auntie Tate and her loyal friend Rube? Could it be that maybe, just maybe, Cerise hadn't been the first in their family to find love in another woman?

In a moment of inspiration, she pulled a new sheet of blank paper from her portfolio and began:

Dear Mrs. Hesse,
My name is Violet Baumgartner and I have the pleasure of knowing your daughter, Barbara Hesse.

Cincinnati Independent Times

March 17, 2018

Historic Mount Auburn Home at
Center of Preservation Debate

Hesse House, one of the many Gilded Age mansions built high atop the hills of Mount Auburn, is at the center of a debate about how to preserve the city's history and, moreover, just who should pay for the building's upkeep.

The home's current owners, Elliott and Amanda Hesse, were in the final stages of selling the property to the Frontenac Group, a boutique hotel developer known for its small but upscale properties, when the sale was abruptly halted last month by a joint lawsuit from the Ohio Preservation Alliance and the Preserve Cincinnati Foundation. The suit argues that the property cannot be sold for development, as the neighborhood in which it sits is listed on the National Register of Historic Places and is thereby federally protected.

"Hesse House is a near-perfect example of Romanesque Revival architecture and represents Cincinnati at the height of its stature in America," said Preserve Cincinnati's Director, Ellsbeth Mariner. "To lose it to developers is unthinkable and we are determined to prevent that from happening."

Historians and architects throughout the nation would seem to agree on the home's prominence, as the Hesse House boasts numerous citations in architectural textbooks and on websites for house-obsessed Americans, which name it as one of the country's best and only remaining Romanesque Revival homes. The style is recognizable by its exteriors of large, square stone, dramatic rounded towers and Roman arches over windows and doors. "Traditionally," says Mariner, "Romanesque Revival is found in public buildings such as courthouses and universities. Only the wealthiest few could afford the heavy, grand materials required for that sort of design."

Albert Ingersoll Hesse was one of the men who could. A wealthy German immigrant who claimed to have been sent to America by parents frustrated with his insatiable lust for horses and women, he made his immense fortune—once estimated at more than two billion dollars by today's standards—by dominating Cincinnati's waterways, shipping crops up the Mississippi from the south and, more importantly, iron ore and steel to mines and factories along the Missouri.

The Hesse family sold off its shipping assets in the 1970s and '80s, and that financial shortfall is felt most prominently, according to Albert Hesse's great-great-grandson, in the maintenance of his family's hand-me-downs.

"I am burdened with Hesse House simply because of my last name," says Elliott Hesse, the home's current owner. "The stone is crumbling, the electrical is a mess. When we inherited the house, it was still steam heated. If these organizations want the home preserved, they are either going to have to step in with the money or let us sell to a party who is willing to pay."

This isn't the first time local preservation agencies have intervened to stop the loss of buildings they consider of historical and architectural value. A number of homes throughout the Cincinnati area are now under the care of nonprofit organizations or maintained through public-private partnerships. Hesse House, however, is the first case in which the family seems willing to walk away from the property in order to prove a point.

"I'm here to remind them that no one has ever been able to tell a Hesse what to do," says Elliott Hesse.

A decision on the pending lawsuit is expected in June.

25

Violet

VIOLET REREAD THE letter a third time.

Dear Mrs. Baumgartner,
I was surprised and honored to receive your letter and would be happy to comply with your request. Please see the attached list of questions, which, in so answering, will allow me to narrow the information we provide, as our family maintains more than 300 years of genealogical detail in its archives.

Such language. Such sophistication. It made her spine tingle. The Hesse family didn't simply track its history; it *maintained genealogical detail*, a family *archive*. People of this stature would never have settled for the spiral-bound, mimeographed mish-mash the Baumgartners passed from one generation to the next.

How wonderful that you've made acquaintance with our daughter, Barbara. We have always called her Gigi and, as it was only after her departure to Rensselaer that she became Barb, I assume you do not know her full name to be Barbara Ambrose Ingersoll Greer Hesse, names richly woven throughout the tapestry of our history.

Barb had grown up a Gigi? She couldn't picture it. Though that lovely red hair of hers did have a regal nature about it, reminiscent of days long gone, of feudal principalities and castles and velvet-clad princesses who cut locks of hair for brave knights as a talisman against death in battle.

For heaven's sake. She didn't have time for daydreaming.

Now, did Mrs. Hesse mention their family tapestry in the literal or figurative sense? She penciled a note: *Hesse crest?*

Oh, how Violet loved names. Always had. She'd been told she was named after her mother's favorite flower. Though, who knew how much of her family lore to trust.

But long before she'd been taught to doubt, she'd met a handsome young man by the name of Baumgartner, which literally meant "gardener." She couldn't help but swoon. What could be more romantic than to become Violet Baumgartner, the gardener of her mother's favorite flower? Over the years, several German speakers had pointed out that Baumgartner was more accurately translated as "tree gardener," but she found that lessened the charm.

And, oh, how she'd loved choosing a name for her daughter. Cerise, of course, was French for "cherry," and while they didn't have any French heritage in the family, the name came to her the instant she saw her daughter's face. There couldn't have been a more fitting name for her beautiful rosy-cheeked baby, nor a more wonderful complement to the Baumgartner name. This time, cherries even had the added benefit of growing on trees.

Violet simply loved names. The history. The imagery. The discovery.

She pulled a fresh piece of stationery from her supplies and began.

Dear Amanda,

Please forgive my forward nature and allow me to call you by your first name, as your letter led me to believe we can be good friends. In exchange, I hope that you will call me Violet.

Please find enclosed a list of specific details requested for the nursery project.

Additionally, I wonder if you may be willing to help me solve a mystery most pertinent to both of our families…

26

Cerise

It was the smallest item of clothing Cerise had ever seen. She'd called it a shirt but Vicky—the only female research lead in their entire building with kids—had been quick to correct her as she pulled the tiny white gift from the box.

"It's a *onesie*. See," she said, pointing to the three sturdy snaps along the bottom. "It snaps just under baby's butt. Keeps them snug and warm—like a one-piece. Get it?"

Cerise ran a gentle finger along the yellow-and-green thread embroidering the words *Say Mama* on the front. She felt as if she'd just been handed someone else's dry cleaning.

"Uh-huh."

"I couldn't find your registry in any of the stores, so I just got you something small for now."

"Yeah." The cotton seemed no more than a swatch, no bigger than a handkerchief. "We started to register, but got sort of overwhelmed and never finished."

Vicky laughed and took a sip of her iced tea. "A lot to take in, I know."

They were sitting in the same retro-chic diner where they'd gone for lunch dozens of times, eating the same wild rice chicken salads they always ordered. Their favorite waitress, a woman whose name tag read "Marge," but her real name was Maggie, sat them against the far wall under the ancient tin sign that read, *Restroom for paying customers only. Outhouse out back for everyone else.*

Everything was just as it had always been. And yet...

"I haven't been able to shake it lately, that overwhelmed feeling. Like I don't even know my own body."

"Just wait till baby is born. When Audrey came, I cried for a month. I remember sitting at dinner one night saying, 'No one warned me about how much these things poop!'"

Cerise paused, midbite. "What?"

"Oh, yeah. Newborns, especially. You just get a clean diaper on its butt and baby's gone and filled it again. Serious poop machines."

Cerise lowered her fork to her plate.

"You'll be fine." Vicky waved a dismissive hand and reached for the last piece of bread in the basket. "Look at it this way—at least there's one thing you'll know going into motherhood that I didn't."

Cerise felt her salad stick in her throat and knew that no sip of water was going to clear it. The feeling had been there for weeks. Not a physical problem like a rogue kernel of popcorn or a cold virus setting up in her sinuses, but a sensation. She wanted to call it dread but that felt too drastic. What kind of mother would dread the birth of her own child?

"Do you ever wish you hadn't become a mother?"

Vicky nodded vigorously as she chewed, making her blond waves ping-pong across her shoulders. "Of course!" She paused to wash down her food with her iced tea. "I talk about selling Adam to the circus about once a week. Yesterday I came upstairs to find that he'd cut holes in all of his sheets."

Cerise suddenly couldn't remember how old Vicky's son was. Could he possibly be old enough to play with scissors? How does one know a thing like that?

"I thought I was about to blow a gasket. Every single sheet ruined. When I asked him why he did it, you know what he said?"

Cerise couldn't begin to guess.

"He said, 'But I need peepholes for when I get scared and have to cover my head.' Genius, right? I couldn't get mad at him for that."

"But you just said he ruined them."

"Well, yeah—to me. But to him those holes were entirely necessary."

Cerise could feel the lump in her throat settle in and make itself at home. Her colleague-turned-friend—a woman she'd long trusted and who, the first day they'd met, told Cerise about the box of emergency tampons she'd stashed in the women's bathroom—seemed to be speaking a foreign language. She was an experienced working mom, a woman achieving the successes Cerise hoped for herself.

Yet her brain couldn't process a word she was saying.

"But didn't you punish him? What if he does it again or cuts up something else like your curtains or his clothes?"

"What if? I mean, sure, I told him that fabric was not for cutting and blah, blah, blah—but even grounding him for a year is no guarantee he won't ruin something else next week. Heck, the only guarantee is that he probably *will* ruin something next week."

Vicky breezed on, certain about her son's destructive genius.

"But—" Cerise stuttered. "There must have been consequences." She flashed to the afternoon as a child that she sat at the kitchen table coloring all of the polka dots on her place mat with a brand-new Bic pen. The ink glided in seamless circles around and around each fat dot. It had felt so natural, so satisfying. Then her mother discovered what she'd done and sent her to her room.

"Like what? Make him patch the holes?" Vicky paused and studied her from across the table. "You can't let children run wild, but it's unrealistic to make a big deal out of every little thing."

But, that was just the problem, wasn't it? What was little and what was very, very big?

"WHAT IF WE have a boy and he turns into a juvenile delinquent because neither one of us understands what he needs?"

Barb shrugged off the question. She'd picked up pulled pork for dinner from the BBQ joint down the road and was busy scooping it onto buns.

"Do you want your slaw on your sandwich or on the side?"

"I'm serious. What do we know about boys? I mean, really— I don't think you could ask for two people who have exhibited less interest in the opposite sex."

Barb looked over and waved the coleslaw container. "Which one?"

"On the sandwich, please."

"Memphis-style it is, then." She slopped slaw onto the steaming piles of pork and carried the plates to the table.

"I mean, a girl we'd understand. But boys are different. I can't tell you the first thing about what makes a boy tick."

Barb took a bite and chewed slowly, looking as if she were in deep contemplation.

Cerise couldn't stem her flood of questions. "Should we be lining up male mentors? Reading books on raising boys? It's like people are all fixated on what bedding pattern we've registered for while completely overlooking the larger issues."

"Which are?"

"Which are—*huge*." She dropped her sandwich to her plate with a messy splatter.

Barb smirked and handed over an extra napkin. "I mean, what are they specifically? These myriad of issues."

"Raising a child, for starters. And doing it well. Giving the child the emotional support and confidence it deserves. Heck, even understanding *what that is* in the first place."

"So you're worried we'll screw it up."

"Of course. Aren't you?"

Barb bobbed her head noncommittally. "I guess I assume that's a risk for every parent. But I certainly don't think you and I are at any greater risk than anyone else."

Cerise let go a haughty gasp. "Yeah, right. Two lesbians, one of whom hasn't even seen her parents in as long as she can remember."

Barb looked up from her dinner with such shock that Cerise wondered if she'd just broken a tooth.

"What has that got to do with anything?"

Oh, god. Now she'd done it.

"Nothing. I take it back." If only she could.

Barb flicked a rogue bit of pork from her fingertip and Cerise watched as it flew across the table and stuck to the pepper mill her mother had given her as a housewarming gift.

Barb scraped at her BBQ-stained fingernails with a napkin. "At least I don't need my mommy's opinion every time I want to buy a new pair of shoes."

What?

"I don't need her approval."

"Yeah, right. And you haven't spent every night on the phone discussing paint colors, either."

"That's keeping her involved, not gaining her approval."

Barb rolled her eyes and shook her head. "Whatever."

Never in all their years together had their tide of emotions turned so swiftly. She couldn't believe the anger filling the room, both of them suddenly puffed up and venomous like two snakes facing off on a *Wild Kingdom* special.

"Well, since you're such an expert on parental relations, Barb, tell me—how should I be dealing with my mother?"

The question in its very supposition was preposterous. For as long as they'd lived together, Barb's relationship with her parents had been limited to Christmas cards, a birthday check and a list of financial instructions for the various Hesse family holdings that arrived via registered mail each fall. Cerise had met them once, at graduation, and they'd left after a single congratulatory cocktail at the President's Club.

And yet, Barb deigned to advise.

"Try being honest with her, for starters."

"So you'd prefer I *say it like it is*. Like you do. Tell the truth no matter how much it hurts."

"If it prevents living a lie—yes!" She threw her napkin down and pushed her plate away. "You and your dad dance around your mother with such ceremony you'd think you were at a Victorian ball."

She lifted her arms into a formal dance pose and mimicked a stiff bow. "Yes, m'lady. If it so pleases you, madam."

"Oh, for chrissake." Cerise wanted to scream, wanted to throw her mess of a sandwich against the wall and leave it for the family know-it-all to clean up.

"My parents have been nothing but good to you. But do you ever give them any credit? No—it's always, 'My god, your family is so dysfunctional, Cerise.'"

What had she been thinking, trying to do this? Getting pregnant and acting as if the blue line on the test strip was miracle enough. The real miracle would be raising a child who didn't want to either kill or institutionalize them both.

And what gave her the right to be a mother? What gave them both the right? Two messy, career-driven frauds who pretended to have it all together but who, underneath, were nothing but a swamp of contradiction and confusion, simmering to a boil.

This was never going to work.

"You think I'm so weak?" she said. "Try facing your own parental issues for once. I dare you."

How was that for honesty?

"The Watchers," Elusive and Everywhere

by Harvey Arpell,
staff reporter, *Minneapolis/St. Paul Standard*

April 2, 2018

"The Watchers," the elusive protest art group with a talent for completing its work under the cover of night, has set its sights on cities as far-reaching as Minneapolis, Kansas City and, most recently, New York City. Investigators, though, seem to have little information about the group or its intentions.

"Their message seems to be poverty-related," says Kansas City Police Chief Ben Renken. "Though at this point, even that conclusion appears speculative. We really don't know much about them."

The group has been erecting statues outside of Federal Reserve Banks since December of last year. All of the installations have been constructed of chicken wire and eyeglasses, and all of them have depicted scenes of individuals and families in need.

"So far, the group is still considered a nonviolent threat, as we've had no indication that they aim to strike out with anything more powerful than words and images," said Renken. "Though, I might add that their interest in Federal Reserve sites is of some consideration."

There is plenty of historical precedent for what officials are, at this point, calling protest art. English artist Banksy, for example, gained international recognition in the early 2000s with his darkly humorous graffiti. Today, Civic Park in Hong Kong is becoming a creative hotbed of antigovernment through the construction of several statues featuring umbrellas and sticky notes.

Of less precedence, however, is the group's insistence on remaining anonymous and its ability to keep its work out of the public eye until its ultimate unveiling. It's this secrecy that seems to have officials most concerned.

Domestic terrorism expert Sam Kleven, however, warns that the greatest danger may not lie with the group, but the people attracted to the movement. "Even if their intentions are purely peaceful, they are still gaining the attention of groups and individuals throughout the country—and if there's anything history has taught us, it's the dangers of an unpredictable crowd. Attract the wrong fans to your work and anything could happen."

27

Cerise

"Ever feel like you're walking face-first into a disaster of your own making?"

Cerise handed Kyle a cup of steaming coffee and followed him to a table in the far corner of the shop. It was late Sunday morning, so the room was a mishmash of yoga pants, cable-knit sweaters and proper-person church attire—an ecosystem of her Minneapolis neighborhood.

"When you grow up with a mother like mine you learn to expect it." Kyle pulled a chair out for Cerise and waited for her to settle before sitting down. "In the *Book of Eldris*, disaster lurks around every corner. There is no avoiding it."

Cerise couldn't help but laugh. "I've never had a conversation with your mother that didn't start with who died and end with who has cancer."

"Lois Jacobsen has cancer," said Kyle.

"Who's Lois Jacobsen?"

"I have no idea. But my mother told me yesterday she has cancer." Poor Lois Jacobsen. No one was without trouble.

Tensions had run high between Cerise and Barb for several days following their argument—silent dinners and single-word answers to questions that couldn't be avoided. But with the passing days, life had moved on. They were talking again, though the unspoken still echoed in the emerging cracks of their life together.

"I don't know if I can do this."

Kyle looked at her from across the table but thankfully didn't move to grab her hand or make more of the moment than she could handle. Tears were too easy these days and she'd grown tired of their company.

"Do what?"

"Any of it. All of it. Barb and I suddenly feel worlds apart. Like I never knew her to begin with. But now here we are, acting like the sort of people who are capable of giving a child everything it needs."

Damn it. Tears again. Hot streaks fell down her checks and she wiped them away on a coffee-stained napkin.

Kyle pulled a clean one from the dispenser and handed it to her. "Well, you know my thoughts on the matter."

She did. He was her ever-unwavering friend.

"How'd you get to be such a cheerleader when your mother acts as if she expects life to end at any moment?"

"Let's just say I've earned a certain sympathy for the down-trodden."

He winked.

Good old Kyle.

She wiped the last of her tears away and arranged the growing mess of napkins into a pile at the edge of the table. She really wanted to grab Kyle's coffee and chug it—caffeine be damned. It had been so long.

Instead, she picked up the wad of napkins and pushed them deep into her near-full cup of herbal tea.

"Sometimes I wonder if I haven't spent my entire life stifling a scream. Like those dreams, you know? Someone's broken into your house and grabbed you and you try to yell but nothing comes out."

Kyle shook his head. "I have the opposite problem. My dreams are too real. The last time I was in New York I pushed Rhonda out of bed because I thought it was swarming with spiders."

"You did not."

"I did. I woke up to her knocking me over the head with a shoe and yelling, 'Get off!' I had her pinned to the floor."

"Shut up."

"No, serious. She called her shrink the next day. I thought she was trying to get me medicated or something, but the appointment turned out to be for her."

God, she should have known. Rhonda was one of those women to whom things always happened. It didn't just rain; it rained on her new Ferragamos. The flight she was on didn't just get delayed; it prevented her from receiving a text with a potentially career-changing scoop. The ozone wasn't just disappearing; it had caused a change in her skin tone dramatic enough for her to have to reorder her wedding gown in a different shade of white.

Still, she was the woman her best friend had chosen.

"Aren't we a pair, you and I?" said Cerise, laughing through the last of her tears. "Did you ever figure it out? With the dreams, I mean."

Kyle nodded. "I've had them since I was a kid. They're stress induced. High school exams. College finals. And now, with everything happening..."

"The wedding planning?"

"That doesn't help, but no." Kyle shook his head and rubbed his fist back and forth across his forehead. "Remember that book-keeping issue with EyeShine I mentioned a few months back?"

Cerise nodded. She'd forgotten at first but was reminded when reading Kyle's end-of-year note to donors.

"We've been killing ourselves to figure it out. And I think I may have stumbled across a possible answer."

"Well, that's good, isn't it?"

Kyle sighed. "Not exactly. Because if it's what I think is—" He stopped and sat back.

"What?"

He frowned, the look on his face not so much angry as drawn

in disbelief. Still, he didn't speak, but stared across the room, lost in his own thoughts.

"Seriously, what?" Cerise suddenly felt a bit panicky. Kyle never withheld on her.

Kyle rubbed his forehead again and leaned back in. "It may be nothing." He was whispering and Cerise had to come in closer to hear him. "But the firm I hired and I have gone over every single donation we've ever received. We've accounted for every check, every cash donation, every pair of glasses we've gotten."

"And?"

"And, there's a big chunk of our physical donations missing. A half-dozen or so boxes of glasses."

"So, good. Now you know that much. Can you trace them? Figure out where they went?"

"That's the problem," said Kyle, dropping his head nearly to the table. "We have traced them. All the way back to my parents' basement. But now they're gone."

"What do you mean, your parents' basement?"

"I stored the first few years of donations there. I didn't have room in my condo and I didn't want to spend a bunch of money on storage."

"And now they're gone?" Cerise could see that he was upset but didn't understand why this would be causing so much stress. Just a few boxes of used glasses.

"Some of them are there, but some aren't. And my mom swears up and down she didn't do anything with them."

"And your dad?"

"I mean, he said, 'What the hell? What does anyone want with used eyeglasses?'" She noticed Kyle avoided the question.

Cerise watched him for a minute, rubbing his palms against his jeans and distressing his forehead with his fist. She didn't know what to say.

They sat quietly until Kyle finally broke the silence. "Anyway, thanks for letting me vent."

Cerise didn't realize that's what she'd been doing but, sure.

Plus, she wasn't sure how to gauge her worry meter. He seemed stressed, but Kyle always landed on his feet. He wasn't exactly an underachiever, after all. He'd work it out. There would be a logical explanation to what now seemed like a mess.

She opted to stay light. "Hey, I was the one in tears when we got here. I owed you a good venting."

Kyle laughed. "Yeah, well, one more thing," he said, cocking an eyebrow. "Your mother sort of interrogated me about sperm."

"Yeah, I'll bet." She loved Kyle's knack for easing a moment.

"No, I'm not kidding. Sperm banks, in particular. Wanted to know how the process worked."

Cerise stopped. What in the world was her mother up to now? Same old busybody she always was? Cerise shouldn't have expected anything different. Her mother was stuck, and Cerise finally understood where. It was this: it takes a man and a woman to make a baby. That's the math. And she was never going to settle until she had the full equation.

"What did you tell her?"

"That there's a popular sperm bank near the university campus where all the med students go."

Cerise smiled. "Nice." She paused for a second. "Is that actually true?"

"Of course." Kyle was smiling now, too. "But I'm not going to tell you how I know."

"Please don't."

Her instincts told her to pull out her phone, to get ready for an uncomfortable conversation. Though, with who? If she told Barb, they'd argue again. But confronting her mother would be an exercise in frustration.

And anyway, what was her mother going to find?

"Meh," said Cerise, waving off the issue. "Let her poke around. It'll keep her busy. My dad will probably thank me for it."

28

Violet

THE ENDRESES' AGING Buick pulled into the driveway and Violet hurried to climb in.

Not that she was terribly excited to put her life in Eldris's hands. Her attention as a driver was questionable at best, constantly drawn from the road to everything alongside it—the *Semiannual Sale!* sign in the front window of Gilbertsen's Good Home Goods or Marty Hendrickson's frost-stricken gladiolas. *Look at that. They're an absolute heartbreak!*

But, Violet reminded herself, Eldris was a wonderful friend. She was loyal. Never boastful. And wasn't that a priceless blessing?

Plus, they'd shooed Ed off again today, hoping to set him on a collision course with Richard. Eldris called with news that she was sending Richard to Wuollet's bakery to pick up the cake she'd special ordered for Solveig Thompson's funeral luncheon. She'd told him it had to be picked up precisely at noon.

Violet, in turn, had sent Ed to Wuollet's to pick up a coffee cake for their neighbor Jeanne whose husband had broken his collarbone falling from a ladder while trying to loosen the ice dam above their entryway.

"I thought you hated store-bought cakes," he'd said.

"Are you saying you'd like me to dig out all of my pans and begin the three-hour process of baking one, then?"

He left the house shortly before noon.

That left Eldris as the only person available to drive Violet to her appointment at the painter's studio. If she didn't get there today, the nursery wouldn't be ready in time for baby.

Violet closed the door with a thunk and smiled at her friend. "My goodness, Eldris, don't you look pretty today." A peach turtleneck poked up from beneath her faded wool coat and she wore a pair of slim gold hoops in her ears.

"Oh, I just pulled out the first thing I could find. You know me. I don't like to fuss."

Violet *hmm*'d vaguely and busied herself digging through her handbag.

"Anyway, I was in such a state this morning that I just pulled out the first thing I laid eyes on."

She paused and Violet knew she was waiting for her to chime in with a complicit note, a *Do tell*. Only, Violet couldn't focus on anything besides the stop sign Eldris was about to blow through at thirty miles an hour.

"Stop!"

Eldris slammed on the brakes and the Buick screeched to a halt midway through the intersection.

"Uff. I always forget about that one."

Violet closed her eyes. She took a breath and said a prayer of thanks that they hadn't seen another car for several blocks.

"Anyway," said Eldris, stepping on the gas, "Kyle was over at the house checking his inventory again and he discovered a large chunk of his donations have gone missing. I told him I didn't know a thing about it. He was terribly upset."

Violet lowered her purse to her feet for fear that it would fly from her lap with the next episode. She smoothed the pleat in her slacks and took hold of the passenger grab handle with both hands.

"Someone stole money from EyeShine?"

"No, bifocals. Whole boxes of them."

Violet waved a dismissive hand. "I'm sure he just misplaced

them. Or maybe he gave them away on his last trip. I can't imagine anyone is out to steal used eyeglasses."

She couldn't help but wonder whether the bifocals she'd donated were among the missing.

Eldris shook her head and the accelerator responded in-kind. Violet's stomach lurched.

"That's just it. Kyle keeps meticulous records. You know—you've seen him, yourself."

Technically, yes. Violet recalled the afternoon she'd seen Kyle poring over rows of what looked like inventory data. But was it accurate? He'd also given her the name for a sperm bank that led them on nothing but a ridiculous goose chase.

Eldris went on, "Stolen from under our very noses. I'm absolutely convinced of it."

Violet closed her eyes, thinking it better to focus on the list of to-dos in her head than the rows of houses careening past her.

She needed to ask the artist about the paint she used. Baby was not to sleep in a room tainted with carcinogenic air. But what had the Sherwin-Williams man called the safest alternative? Low VOD paint? Low COD? She'd need to refer to her notes when they arrived.

Eldris continued, "I know it seems like a trivial matter, but it's not. EyeShine has to document the value of its donations with the IRS every year. That's why Kyle is so careful. If he misrepresents the organization's charitable income by even a trivial amount he can be investigated for fraud. *Fraud.* I'm just sick about it."

Violet opened her eyes in time to see Eldris speeding through a yellow stoplight. She squeezed them shut immediately and held on, waiting for the impact of a crash.

Then, nothing. Praise God. She opened a cautious eye and confirmed the all clear. She blew out a slow and steady breath—*one...two...three...four...five.*

Better.

Now, then.

She'd actually spoken to Amanda Hesse on the phone last night, the first time they'd connected in person. So far, their correspondence had been limited to lengthy and detailed exchanges through the US mail, but there was one very important detail she wanted to ensure was captured exactly right before her meeting at the artist's studio.

"Yes," Amanda had confirmed. "Francis Ingersoll, my great-great-grandmother's cousin thrice-removed, was a member of the Mayflower Colony."

The Mayflower. Violet swooned. Now that was a wonderful story for baby.

"Lore has it, of course," continued Amanda, "he had a hard time keeping his prick to himself and was nearly thrown to sea with his pants around his ankles halfway across the Atlantic."

Violet choked. Had she just heard what she thought she'd heard? Couldn't be.

"Now," Amanda had said. "Remember that he was not on the first voyage. He arrived on a later ship, but we do have documentation of his name on a passenger list from 1621 and documentation of his Plymouth land purchase."

Violet felt tears welling. Her grandbaby was of founding stock.

As soon as Eldris stopped talking, she'd be able to share the news.

"Kyle is supposed to leave for Africa soon. Just what is he supposed to do with a quarter of his donations missing?"

"Oh, dear."

"Exactly. That's what I'm saying. It's an absolute nightmare."

Violet had to concur, but not because of Kyle's dilemma. Her cell phone was ringing and she didn't dare loosen her hands from their death grip on the handle to reach for it.

"And Richard—well, you'd think this sort of thing happened every day at our house. The most he has to say about it is that maybe Kyle ought to delay his trip. Can you imagine?"

"Oh, no."

"So you agree? Thank you. I mean, it's an absolutely absurd suggestion."

Violet's phone was ringing again. Was this a second time? Who could concentrate with all this commotion?

"He called the airline, of course, but the change fee on his flight to New York, alone, is four hundred dollars. I mean, for heaven's sake, what business are these airlines in? Highway robbery?"

Her phone seemed to be playing her *Für Elise* ringtone in an endless loop.

"Eldris, I think this may be an emergency."

"Well, that's what I told Kyle to tell the airline. But did they care? Absolutely not! Apparently they aren't in the business of caring for poor African children or anyone else. They're just out for a buck. It's an outrage."

Violet's head was beginning to spin and the trees lining the road seemed to be flying past her at insane speed, blurring into an unbroken streak of green.

"No, I'm telling you, Eldris. I think there may be an emergency. Pull over. I need to get to my phone."

Now there was a second screeching—an obnoxious electronic version of Beethoven's Fifth coming from the depths of Eldris's purse on the bench between them.

"I mean it—pull over, Eldris. Someone needs to get ahold of me."

"Oh, for gracious' sake."

Eldris thrust a hand into her purse and began scrambling for her phone.

"That's not a phone call, Violet. It's a text. Which means it's probably Kyle. He's the only one who texts me."

She continued scrambling about blindly in her purse, the steering wheel matching every sweep of her hand, and soon the Buick was weaving back and forth across the centerline.

"Eldris—pull over!"

Violet let go of her death grip on the door handle and began grabbing at Eldris's purse.

"Let me find it!"

She gave the purse a hearty tug, but Eldris was tangled in the handles and Violet ended up pulling her—and the steering with it—wildly to the right. The car zigzagged. Eldris yelped. Violet whooped. Then there was a swerve and a bump, and the Buick came to a stop halfway onto the lawn of Everette Bob's Real Tasty Bar-B-Que.

"Sakes alive, Eldris! You nearly killed us."

"You were hitting me, Violet!"

Both women dived for the phones in their respective handbags. Both gasped in unison.

"Cerise is in the hospital. She's gone into preterm labor."

"It's from Richard. Kyle's been taken in for questioning by the police."

29

Richard

RICHARD PULLED A tattered business card from his desk drawer and dialed its number. The line picked up immediately.

"Browning, here." The voice resonated with the tenor of a man deaf to doctors' warnings about fat cigars and fattier steaks.

Thank god some people still answer their own phones. "Al, it's Richard Endres."

Al roared with all the *sonnuva guns* and *how the hell are yas* Richard had expected. He waited until Browning exhausted himself, then got to the point.

"I need the best lawyer you know."

The agents had shown up at the door at one o'clock sharp, two of them, in crisp dark suits and well-shined shoes. Richard hadn't seen gloss on a pair of loafers like that since the '80s. Had they been anywhere but his front door, the sight would've made him goddamn nostalgic.

They were looking for Kyle who, fortunately or not, was down in the basement resorting his donations inventory in search of the missing bifocals.

"It's the government, goddamn it." Browning was always good for a righteous fuming. "Did they search your property? Did you see a warrant?"

That was just it. They hadn't wanted to search. They only wanted Kyle. And he'd gone willingly before Richard could talk him out of it.

"Bottom line, Al—I need the best name you've got. And then I need you to help me figure out how to pay for it all."

Browning, as it happened, was Richard's on-again, off-again accountant. Not this year. Richard didn't want anyone to see the financial cost of his *involuntary retirement*, as he'd taken to calling it. But the years when he was feeling flush—got a bonus or a raise or scored in the stock market—Browning made sure his funds were tied with a neat bow and tucked away where Eldris wouldn't be tempted to spend them.

They'd also been racquetball partners since long before the days their orthopedists began tethering their failing joints with pig tendon and wire. Richard knew the influence wielded by the high-rolling ass-kisser crowd Browning kept on speed dial. Hell, thanks to Browning, he'd wrapped his naked ass in a steam room towel alongside Vikings coaches, mayors and Fortune 100 CEOs all in the same week.

"Only one guy you want," said Browning. "O'Neill. Government connections that'd make James Comey blush. He's your best defense when the feds fill your dance card."

"I figured he'd be your recommendation." Richard reached for the bottle of Tums he'd opened last night while balancing the checking account. It'd been new; it was now half-empty. "Now tell me how I'm going to pay for this."

Browning roared with laughter. "Hell, Endres. That's the easiest question I've had all day. Like I've told you before, you don't need an accountant—you need a good shrink."

He was still laughing when Richard hung up.

He took a minute to consider his next move. Then he opened his phone and found the number he needed. This time, though, he wouldn't call. He knew if he found himself on the other end of the line from a live voice, he wouldn't be able to control what came next.

Richard here.

Thought you might find it interesting that the feds just showed up at my door.

Lots of questions about EyeShine donations suddenly popping up on federal property.

And it got me thinking.

About a certain few boxes you picked up.

And I can't help but wonder about the coincidence.

¿Qué? ¿Quien es este?

30

Violet

Eldris had hardly rolled to a stop before Violet was out of the car and up the hospital sidewalk. The automated doors whooshed open to the lobby, a glass cathedral radiating with natural light, its every detail engineered, she knew, to induce a calm in its passersby.

She would have none of it. Her daughter was in danger.

She made a direct path to the center of the room, to the woman who'd smartly chosen to wear a crisp, dark suit for her day's duties at the Information desk. Violet stated her business and the woman tapped her keyboard with the rapid-fire intensity of a telegraph operator. Violet took the first easy breath she could remember since leaving the house.

"Room 422. That's in our birthing center. Take the elevators on your left to the fourth floor."

"And where do I *gown up*—isn't that what you call it?"

"Ma'am?"

"Gowns and gloves and those dreadful shoe covers? My daughter may be having the baby as I stand here."

The woman's face betrayed nothing. "Check in at the nurses' station when you arrive on-floor."

That was one option.

Instead, she went directly to Cerise's room.

She opened the door to a cacophony of crises. Monitors screeched. Women in candy-colored scrubs rushed about as the lone man in the room stood at the end of the bed shouting directions. She spotted her daughter's manicured toes peeking out from the paper draped across her body.

Violet's brain seized and her vision narrowed to a tunnel. She looked desperately for a chair.

Then, above the din, she heard Cerise, her voice no more than a tiny whimper.

"Cerise! I'm here."

Violet could do nothing. But she was there.

When Cerise was three years old, the two of them spent a lovely spring afternoon making mud pies from the freshly turned flower beds in their front yard. The sun leaped across the sky like a happy dog chasing sticks and their hands grew pink and raw digging in the chilly dirt. Violet was rarely prone to encourage such messy play, but that day all judgment fell aside like ribbons from the gift of life.

Every moment felt ripe for the picking.

She watched as Cerise scooped handfuls of dirt into a pink Tupperware bowl and dribbled it with water. She ran her palm across the top, smoothing its surface, and then poked dainty points all along its edge with her fingers. Her nails were caked with mess, her hands streaked with black. It would take a week of baths to soak it all out. And yet, was there anything more beautiful than a child's perfect skin? Dirt held no power over its radiance.

"Mama?" Cerise handed her the small, pink pie. "Would you like to take a bite?"

"Oh, yes please." She brought the bowl to her lips and pretended to chew, moaning as if she'd never tasted anything like it in her whole life. "Where did you learn to make such delicious pie, sweet girl?"

Cerise giggled and returned to her flower bed kitchen. "Just wait until you try the next one. It's my es-specialty."

And so the play continued, Cerise offering treats to Violet, who acted as if each were more amazing than the last.

"Wait, Mama." Cerise stood and scanned the yard. "I need a special ingred'ant for this one."

Violet watched as she wandered toward the lilac bush at the corner of the yard. Ed had planted it only a few years before and already its lower branches spread like a canopy, a perfect place to hide.

"Come and find me," Cerise teased, dropping onto hands and knees.

Violet laughed and pitched herself up from where she'd been sitting. Her backside was chilled from the spring soil and beginning to ache.

"I'm gonna get you."

She crouched and held out her arms as she trotted toward her giggling daughter. Cerise played along, scooting back farther and farther into the lilac's canopy.

Their commotion startled a bird from its perch and it fell to the ground, panicked and flapping.

"Look!" Cerise called, scrambling toward the frightened creature. "It won't fly."

"Don't touch it!" Violet's voice went from merry to harsh in no more than breath. "It might be sick."

Cerise, however, advanced. And the bird—a robin with its bright red breast—took one more lunge toward survival. It heaved itself into the air, low to the ground but in flight.

"Birdie!"

Cerise chased it. Blind to the curb, the street and the car headed straight for her.

There are some moments as consequential as lifetimes. Seconds that begin and end all at once. Awareness in which there is neither breath nor thought—only the observation of what is to be.

The afternoon of the mud pies was Violet's first.

This moment in the hospital—with the doctors and the noise and the electric rush filling the very air—was the second.

"Cerise!"

She was screaming. Screaming and not moving.

She knew she could not get there in time. Knew her feet were not fast enough, her arms not strong enough, her reactions not nearly quick enough to do what needed to be done.

At age three, Cerise's life was saved by an alert driver who swerved just in time. Today, Violet waited for the miracle again.

"Violet?" She felt a hand on her arm. "Everything will be all right. Calm down."

It was Barb, still in her street clothes but looking every bit as official as the rest of the professionals swarming about in their scrubs.

"What's happening? She's not due for another month."

Barb took her by both elbows and moved her to a corner, out of the path of commotion. She didn't let go, even as she began to explain.

"Cerise has preeclampsia. The doctors are trying to determine just how much trouble she's in. Thankfully they spotted it early."

Violet craned her head over Barb's shoulder, trying anew to gauge the level of crisis in the medical team's activity. Mercifully, the doctor had moved out from between Cerise's legs and now scanned the long paper tail streaming from the monitor beside her bed.

"Him—the doctor. Who is he? Where is Dr. Chung?"

She knew Cerise's obstetrician because she'd recommended her personally. Not only had Dr. Chung been featured three years running as one of Minnesota's top doctors, she was also the daughter of Ed's lead researcher.

That man with the banana yogurt face was not Dr. Chung.

"She's not on call today. Dr. Edmonds is her partner. He's very good."

"How?"

"How what?"

"How do you know he's good? Have you researched him? Have you assessed his reputation among his peers?"

The shrill pitch of a monitor filled the room and they both turned. Violet watched as a nurse silenced it with no greater concern or effort than the push of a button.

"For heaven's sake. Not a single professional in this room appears to be aware of the seriousness of the situation."

"No, I assure you…" Barb let go of her elbow as if to explain. Violet, instead, made a break for it.

"I need to gown up," she announced to the room.

She didn't know who she needed to talk to, so she resolved to keep talking until someone took action.

"I am the mother. I need to gown up. Is anyone listening?"

A pretty thing in pale pink scrubs glanced up from her work preparing a tray of instruments. She glanced at Violet. Then at Barb.

Violet knew that look, and she wasn't about to be quieted or controlled.

"That is my daughter you have on that bed. I am her *mother*."

She felt a stab in her chest and realized it was coming from her own finger; she'd been jabbing herself with it.

"I am her mother and I have the right to be here."

Again, she saw the nurse's eyes flicker and she felt Barb's arms pulling her away from the action.

This time, Barb made no effort to soothe her.

"Violet," she barked. "Cerise is the only mother we're concerned with right now."

The words hit with a magnitude of force.

Cerise was a mother. Not going to be. Not soon to be. She already was. She was on that journey, responsible for the life and health and safety of the child they would all soon meet.

Cerise was a mother.

"All right," she said, fixing her eyes on Barb's steady face. "Please help me find somewhere I can sit quietly and wait."

❋

BY THE TIME Ed arrived, Barb had been out to the waiting room twice to faithfully update her on the situation. Violet relayed the details to Ed.

"It's a condition called preeclampsia. I had to practically haunt the nursing staff to tell me anything about it, but it has to do with the blood vessels and high blood pressure..."

What had the nurses told her? The details skidded across her mind like tires on ice; she couldn't seem to grab on.

"Yes." Ed nodded. "They called it toxemia back in our day."

Aha! Of course. That was the clue she'd needed. She reached for Ed's hand.

"The doctor says baby appears strong. Thank heavens. But they're having to monitor Cerise closely." She felt her throat grip the words, not wanting to release them.

Ed repositioned her hand, taking it more fully in his own.

Violet squeezed—harder, then harder still, until his wedding ring pressed painfully against her knuckles. A reminder she was not alone.

"Violet—" he squeaked.

She loosened her grip, but only slightly. "This can't happen, Ed. We can't welcome our only grandchild the same day we lose our daughter." Thoughts raced at her, white-hot and screaming.

"We won't lose her," he said, patting their joined fists with his free hand. "The doctors know what they're doing."

Violet shook her head. "I can't. I can't go from celebrating a new life to planning a funeral." That was not the way of things. It was too cruel. Too awful to bear. "I'm not strong enough. I won't make it."

Ed brought his arm up to her shoulders and pulled her close. "It's not time to panic. We have to believe."

"But what if? What if she's just gone? Our beautiful daughter, just—gone. With a child who will never know her, who will never know the wonderful, beautiful person she was. Never be held by her or comforted by her or even kissed. A child cannot grow up without her mother." The words weren't even out before newer, bigger fears piled in behind them.

"Is," said Ed.

"What?" She looked at him, calm, as if none of this were happening, as if he were on an entirely different planet.

"The wonderful, beautiful person she *is*. Not was." He squeezed her hand. "We don't panic until we have reason to. And it's not time yet."

No, it wasn't. It wasn't time yet. Cerise wasn't due for nearly a month. This baby needed more time. Baby wasn't ready, wasn't fully developed. They shouldn't be here. It wasn't time.

"It's not time—" She stopped, looking up.

Without notice, Barb stood in front of them, her red hair still piled into a sterile scrub cap, holding a bundle all wrapped in blue. "Cerise is doing just fine. Everyone is just fine. Would you like to meet your grandson?"

ANNOUNCING

Edward Thomas Benson
Hesse Baumgartner

Born this day
April the eleventh, in the year two thousand eighteen

Measuring
Five pounds, ten ounces and twenty-one inches

To delighted parents
Cerise Applewhite Baumgartner
&
Barbara Ambrose Ingersoll Greer Hesse

And to humbled grandparents
Edward and Violet Baumgartner
&
Elliott and Amanda Hesse

*"For all those who exalt themselves will be humbled,
and those who humble themselves will be exalted."*
Luke 14:11

31

Cerise

CERISE ROLLED OVER and felt the warm bundle at her side.

"Careful," whispered Barb. "You'll squish Chuck."

She let out a fatigued moan and gingerly propped herself up against her pillows, her belly quick to remind her that her muscles had only recently been sliced open and stitched back. She was awake now. Nothing sounded more delicious than sleep, but her maternal senses had been piqued at the sight of the baby. There was no quieting them.

"I wish you'd stop calling him Chuck."

"I will," said Barb, her face covered by hair and pillows. "Just as soon as we name him."

Because they hadn't been able to yet. They'd become one of those *can't agree on the fundamentals* couples. Cerise didn't want to blame their son, but she worried that everything had changed as soon as he'd made his presence known. As if the moment she got pregnant, she and Barb went from best friends and lovers to the creators of to-do lists and doctors' appointments.

They never talked about anything. They talked, sure—about baby's weight and feeding patterns and Cerise's daily intake of folic acid and whether or not she needed Barb to pick up more of the heinously oversize postdelivery maxi pads. Why hadn't anyone warned her about that humiliating delight?

She knew, though, that those were the easy topics, the ones that kept them from having to discuss the bigger stuff. Like why

Cerise wanted her parents—even as invasive and obnoxious as they could be—involved in baby's life, when Barb was content to leave her parents in Ohio, silent as statues in the park.

Cerise could handle the fact that the nursery was yet unpainted. She could handle the dark-of-night feeding calls. But their son would need a name. Even more, their son would need parents who could manage their emotions long enough to give him one.

"I thought you were stuck on Jax," she said.

"You called it *one of those made-up names.*"

Cerise bristled. "No, I just said I like the classics—Joseph, Edward, Thomas, Benjamin, Albert, Andrew. Pick one."

"Okay, then. Cerise," Barb said.

"What?"

"No, I mean I pick the name, Cerise, since around here we do things the Baumgartner way."

Had Barb really just done that? Attacked her with such ease? She felt the rise of emotions so sharply, as if she'd been punched in the throat. She swallowed, fighting it all back.

FOR HIS PART, baby was performing like a champ. He took to nursing immediately and ate until Cerise's breasts were drained of their last drop. He pooped with astounding regularity, as Vicky said he would, and when swaddled in a blanket like a burrito, he slept more than he was awake. Seven days into life, he'd upheld his end of the bargain.

Cerise, on the other hand, was the one crying into her soup at night. She couldn't shake the private sensation that the most beautiful thing she'd ever created had ruined her life. She couldn't make a decision, she couldn't sleep, she wandered the house as if looking for something she'd lost.

Where had her confidence gone? Her whole life she'd been a

land dweller, her feet on solid ground. Now she was standing at the edge of the water, the waves licking at her bare toes. Never had she ever felt the stakes so high and the future so unclear.

If she could just get a handle on what worried her she could act to fix it. Was it motherhood? Was it her relationship with Barb? Was it the fact that she would never again be responsible for just herself alone? Yes, all of those things. And none of them. No one instrument of doom stood out from the symphony of worries playing in her head.

She sat at the kitchen table sorting through the accumulating pile of cards and baby gifts, but realized she hadn't really seen any of them. She was simply going through the motions.

Barb brought over a mug of tea and sat beside her.

"Did you see the gift from Abby and Stephan? It's a T-shirt with a crown on it that says, *Sir Poopsalot*. Pretty cute."

Cerise *hmm*'d. "Did you add it to the thank-you card list?"

"Think so." Barb flicked through a few of the cards atop the pile. "So many congratulations and we haven't even sent out his birth announcement. Amazing."

That reminded her. "My mom's coming by this morning. Just to warn you." She caught the glimmer of a frown crimp the edges of Barb's eyes, but she must have caught herself in time to change course.

"Okay. Did she tell you what time she'd be here?"

Cerise glanced at the clock on the kitchen wall. Nearly ten. "Soon," she said.

The doorbell rang at ten fifteen.

"Helloooooo!"

Cerise came around the corner to see her mother's face peeking through the half-open door.

"We're letting ourselves in because you shouldn't be up on your feet. You need your rest." Violet opened the door wide and stepped into the foyer. Cerise could see her father hesitating on the front step.

"C'mon in, Dad," she said. "Hi, Mom."

She waited for her mother to slip off her shoes and stand upright before giving her a kiss on the cheek.

"I see you're leaning over these days," Cerise said. "Are the headaches gone?"

Violet handed the bundle of bags and papers in her arms to her dad and none-too-ceremoniously ushered Cerise toward the couch in the family room.

"No more fretting about me. You need your rest so you can care for your son."

Before she had the chance to resist, her mother was propping up her feet and tucking a blanket across her lap.

"Have you been drinking plenty of water? You need it for recovery and for the breast-feeding, both."

Cerise saw her father stiffen and blush at the mention of her breasts. She smiled.

"Barb's been chasing after me with tea and Gatorade all week."

Violet nodded her approval. "What did the doctor say yesterday? Is your incision healing properly?"

"All according to plan," she answered. Cerise couldn't take her eyes off of her father shuffling uncomfortably at the edge of the room. All this talk about his daughter's girl parts. He'd never had a problem peppering her with intimate questions about her colon, but the female-only regions were anathema.

"Dad," she said. "Come in and keep me company while Mom does her thing. I'm sure she's got plans to reorganize my kitchen or teach the baby French while she's here."

Her dad gave her a wink and sat down in the armchair opposite the couch. Then he called after her mother, "Don't overdo it, Violet."

"I'll just put water on for tea," she called back from the kitchen.

Cerise and her father sat without speaking. He picked at the crease in his khakis, and she wondered why. They looked freshly dry-cleaned.

Cerise shifted on the sofa, crossed and then uncrossed her legs.

Her father cleared his throat. Looked at the ceiling above the fireplace. "Well," he said. It was a statement, more than a start. A word to fill the silence.

"Well," Cerise answered, filling it some more.

The kitchen rattled with pans and cupboard doors.

Barb walked across the bedroom floor above their heads.

Cerise crossed her legs.

Her father took a deep breath. He smoothed his pant leg with his palm.

Cerise looked him over in his freshly dry-cleaned polo and khakis, just the sort of outfit she'd have expected on a retiree of his age.

"You think you'll ever trade in those loafers for a pair of sneakers, Dad?"

He gave her a half smile and lifted the leg of his trousers, revealing an ankle as naked as if he'd just stepped from the shower.

"No socks." He chuckled. "Just wait till your mother discovers what a rebel I've become. It may send her back to the hospital."

"Your mom has to go back to the hospital?" Cerise turned to see that Barb had entered the room and stood behind her. "Did something happen?"

"No, no," said Ed, waving a dismissive hand.

"Dad's just gone a bit rogue in his retirement, is all," said Cerise, offering no more detail than her father had. She gave him a private half smile.

"The two of you and your secrets." Barb came around the side of the couch and sat down. The bounce of the cushion sent a zing through Cerise's recovering belly and made her wince.

"Sorry, babe."

Violet reappeared carrying a selection of teas arranged in a neat circle on a plate.

"I'll let you each choose your own flavor," she said, arriving in front of Cerise first. "Hello, Barb. I didn't even realize you were home." She waited for Cerise to pull a tea bag from the plate, and then offered the remaining selection to Barb.

"I was upstairs checking on baby," said Barb, taking Earl Grey.

"You two girls have such a system going. It's just wonderful. Admirable, really."

Cerise closed her eyes, knowing she was going to hear about the "girls" reference later.

"We certainly are a team." Barb's tone was jovial but Cerise recognized the lightly veiled dig for what it was.

"Well, now, that's going to become increasingly important as baby grows up. The moment your support for each other breaks down, the entire family is in trouble. I've seen it happen a hundred times."

She offered the tea selection to Cerise's dad, but he waved his hand to decline.

"We've had too much coffee today," Violet said, explaining for him.

She placed the plate on a side table and assessed the room. Everyone seemed to have what they needed. "Very good."

Still, she made no move to sit.

"Anyway."

Cerise recognized that halted stutter—it meant her mother had a story to tell. It also meant she wanted them to ask for it, saving her from looking like a gossip.

Cerise took the bait. "Someone you know breaking up?"

Violet frowned and pursed her lips like a disapproving librarian.

"No. Not breaking up. Not that extreme." She looked to Cerise's dad as if for permission, but he didn't seem to recognize the signal. Or if he did, he wasn't going to offer it.

Her mother waited a full breath before going on. "It's the Endreses. You know, Kyle's parents."

Cerise couldn't help but roll her eyes at her mother's constant need to place people in social context.

"Yeah? What about them?"

"*Uff.* Such a mess. But it's not my place to speak."

Barb egged her on. "Though you're worried about them?"

"Of course I'm worried. Eldris pinches every penny since Richard lost his job—and he's gone every night to Lord-knows-where—and with Kyle being arrested, who knows—"

Cerise and Barb both interrupted.

"Kyle's been arrested?"

Ed interjected. "*No.* Now, Violet, you have to be careful about what you're saying." He palmed the air as if clearing it of misinformation. "His nonprofit appears to be under investigation. Apparently, some of his donations have been showing up in all that 'The Watchers' business. But—as of yet—they haven't charged him with anything, and Richard's hired a very good lawyer, just in case."

Cerise felt an ache in her belly that, for the first time in a week, wasn't related to her incision. She hated that they'd been so consumed with the baby they hadn't even known.

"We need to call him," she said. Barb gave her a sidelong glance and nodded.

"All in good time," said Violet. "I shouldn't have even said anything. Your worrying isn't of any help to Kyle or his parents."

She reached for one of the bags she'd brought with her.

"Now, then. A few items of consequence that we can do something about." She pulled an elaborately colored piece of card stock from the bag and handed it to Cerise.

"You printed birth announcements?"

"Not printed. Drafted. Just to get you started with some ideas."

"He doesn't even have a name yet," said Barb.

"Which is the next item on the agenda," said Violet, pointing at Barb as if she'd just made the most salient point of the morning. "I'd like to get a date on the church's calendar for the baptism, but I can't do that until they at least have a name to put in the datebook."

Cerise felt the heat in the room begin to rise and knew immediately that its source sat beside her.

Barb put a hand on Cerise's knee as if preemptively restraining her. "Violet, stop."

"You don't like that one? I have more samples." She reached for her bag, every bit the innocent. Cerise suddenly recognized how skilled her mother was at playing every turn, every moment to her advantage. How many times in her life had she witnessed the same phenomenon without recognizing the source and depth of its power?

"I'm not talking about the announcements," said Barb.

"No?" Violet blinked once but otherwise did not move.

She was going to make her say it aloud.

"No," Barb said.

Lord, this was becoming the showdown at the O.K. Corral. Cerise wanted to intervene. At least, she knew she ought to want to.

Instead, her eyes glued themselves to the carpet. The corner of the rug was beginning to fray. Maybe she ought to do something about that.

How long had baby been napping? He was due to wake up soon—she could feel the pressure in her boobs.

"We appreciate all you're doing to help." Barb patted Cerise's knee, establishing their we-ness. "But we haven't decided these things yet—especially his name."

"Of course you haven't had time to decide," said her mother. "You've been doing exactly what you should be doing—giving all of your love and attention to your infant son."

Cerise wanted to nod. Yes, that's what they had been doing. Yes, that's exactly what they needed to do. Could they move on now?

Was that crack in the ceiling new?

"That's precisely why," her mother continued, "I do these things. To help. To allow you to keep focusing on all the truly important work."

Cerise felt Barb shift beside her.

God, the room was stifling hot.

"To be perfectly honest, Violet," said Barb, "we don't even know if we're going to have him baptized."

Cerise looked at her. She couldn't disguise her shock. It was true, yes. They'd considered forgoing the ceremony. Did it even mean anything to her? She didn't know. But.

Crap.

"Cerise, is this true?"

"Well, I— It's just— You know. We have to discuss it."

Damn it, Barb!

"Well," her mother said, physically closing herself off to the rest of the room, all folded arms and crossed legs. "I can see you think I'm intruding."

Cerise opened her mouth to argue, but Barb squeezed her knee. She squeaked.

"Thank you, Violet," said Barb. Cerise eyed her, never having noticed before her partner's ability to mimic sincerity with her mother's nearly identical victorious undertones.

"Of course." Her mother was clipped, the smile on her face kept in reserve for moments like these. "You just let me know when you do want me to help."

"Absolutely," said Barb.

"Wonderful," said her mother.

"Yes," said Barb.

"Family is so very important," said her mother.

"It is," said Barb.

"And you are family," said her mother.

"I'm blessed," said Barb.

"Yes," said her mother.

"Yes," said Barb.

God, someone stop them.

"Did you know," said her dad, finally, blessedly stepping in, "that it remains commonplace in many cultures for the mother to eat the placenta after giving birth?"

32

Violet

"YOU'RE GOING TO have to dig, Ed. They're all the way in the back." Violet had dragged her unwitting husband into Cerise's childhood bedroom in search of clues.

"How many are there?"

How many are there? For all his smarts the man could be dumb as a stick.

"Four. Four years of high school, four yearbooks."

He climbed down from the chair he'd been using to reach the back of the closet and handed her a stack of cleanly creased, leather-bound books. He returned the chair to the corner of the bedroom and pulled one of the books from Violet's hands.

"Looks like she hardly ever opened them," Ed said. "That was a perfectly good waste of a hundred dollars."

"Nonsense. Memories are never a waste of money."

They headed out the door toward the kitchen.

"What are you looking for, anyway?"

Violet registered the question but didn't answer.

The idea that the answer she sought may lie within these books had come to her last night in bed, when she suddenly remembered something Cerise had said—that the baby's father wasn't just *some donor*. Cerise knew him. *Of course!* Why had she overlooked the possibility? It was so obvious upon reflection.

Granted, Violet wasn't back to her old self yet. Sleep eluded her since the accident, though she tried her best to keep that fact to herself. If she lay still until Ed's breathing fell into its raspy, lazy rhythm, he remained none the wiser to her insomnia and, therefore, unable to tattle on her to the doctor. So she'd begun a daily ritual of compiling a list of all the subjects she'd contemplated during her late-night solitude—and last night's list was dedicated to the health and security of her family.

Of all the wonderful things Cerise and Barb had already done for their son—and they were becoming such loving, responsible parents—it turned out they'd neglected to legally protect him should his biological father someday choose to make a claim on him. And if there was anything that getting to know Amanda Hesse had taught Violet, it was the importance of maintaining a family line. Working with a woman so historically rooted made her ever more resolute about one fact: no two-bit absentee sperm-only father was going to waltz into their lives and claim what was only his by a force no more natural than a *sneeze*. It was up to her to root him out and size him up. She would be ready, come what may.

She put her stack of yearbooks on the kitchen counter and went to the coffeepot to refresh the cup she'd poured nearly an hour ago.

"Can I warm yours up?" she asked, motioning toward Ed's cup with the pot.

"No. Thank you." He thumbed loosely through one of the books, stopping on a black-and-white photo of girls in polyester athletic uniforms and perfect ponytails.

"I forgot Cerise played volleyball."

"Three years." Violet returned the coffeepot to the warmer. "You were never able to make it to her games."

"Ah..." Ed nodded, continuing to flip pages. "I remember the science fair, though. She borrowed one of my lab coats."

"That was middle school, Ed. Not high school."

"Right."

"Hand me the one from her senior year. I want to start there."

Ed shuffled through the pile, calculating.

"Two thousand and five. Your daughter graduated in the year 2005."

"Yes," he said, handing her the correct book. "Right again."

Violet flipped immediately to the senior class photos.

"You never told me what you're looking for."

More questions. Had he always been like this, with the, *what are you doing now?* And all the rifling through the cupboards for a snack. The calories were beginning to show at his belt line.

"Violet?"

She looked up, knowing that he'd keep at her until she relented.

"You never told me what you're looking for."

"Names," she sputtered. "Just—names. The baby shower. I need to know who to invite." She hated to lie to him but he'd left her no choice.

"Can't you just ask Cerise?"

"As if she and Barb have time to make lists."

She hated snapping at him and yet, here she'd gone and done it, anyway. The shock flashed across his face.

"I know I missed a lot while Cerise was growing up. That's not news, Violet. But it also doesn't mean I'm incapable of being an integral part of her life now. And our grandson's."

Violet retreated immediately and smiled at him.

"I know it's been very difficult for you since the accident," he said. "But don't forget that I've been here, too. And that's new for me. I don't know what my next chapter holds. Except, of course—"

She could hear the words swell in his throat.

"Except that I wish it to include more time with family."

Dear Ed. Always such good intentions. "Of course, dear. Forgive me."

He cleared his throat and nodded, a sign he'd said all he intended to for the time being.

She switched tack.

"You know, I just remembered." She reached for his hand. "I promised Eldris I'd swing by and pick up the volunteers list for the Mother's Day brunch at church. Kyle has her worried sick. She's in no shape to make phone calls." She took a sorrowful breath and shook her head slowly. "Just imagine what she might end up saying."

"I need to swing by Home Depot later. We can go then—after lunch."

Violet raised her voice by half an octave.

"Do you think you could possibly go now?"

That worked. He shrugged and fished his keys from his pocket. She waited until she heard the front door click.

She flipped the yearbook open to where she'd left off.

Daniel Anderson wrote, "Have a great summer and a great life." *How truly inspired.* Given that level of eloquence she assumed his career had peaked as manager of the car wash.

Brent Barnes. Calvin Bundtworth. Derek Carter. None of them did much more than sign their names.

George Clark scribbled his initials over his face.

Finally, Erik Clarkson. Violet remembered him—Enid Olson's grandson. He'd been confirmed with Cerise at Faithful Redeemer but had hardly graced the sanctuary since.

"Knock 'em dead at college," he wrote. "Remember, E=MC2, except after C."

Well, he was obviously bound for a state school.

When would this agony end? And how on earth had she gotten here, a grandmother forced to wade through pages of barely postpubescent men who, none of them, hadn't shown even the remotest potential to become a father. To make babies, yes—she was certain they'd been up to plenty of that nonsense. But to become a man of character enough so as to eventually father her grandchild—not a single one.

She wouldn't even be in this predicament if they'd done the same as the Hesses and sent Cerise to private school. She'd argued for it for years. But her words fell mute upon Ed—his belief in public schools as the core of a strong democracy. A respectable argument, certainly, except when it's your child whose IQ is suffering.

Nor could she deny that her current predicament was also partly the Hesses' fault. After all, they'd sent Barb to an all-girls boarding school. So when Violet wrote to inquire about any potential donors stemming from their daughter's earlier friendships, Amanda Hesse replied with the obvious biological impossibility.

And then, curiously, she'd added, "You should know that I make it a policy to stay clear of my daughter's vagina business."

The vulgarity shocked her.

But the letter had come, too, with documented proof of their family's Mayflower Colony ancestry. Violet had chosen to dwell on that good news.

She returned to her research.

Donald Davies wrote, "It was a blast at prom with you."

Violet stopped. Cerise hadn't gone to prom with any boy named Donald Davies. She'd gone with a group of single girls, and only after Violet had bought her a dress and threatened to wear it herself if Cerise didn't at least make plans.

She looked again. Could she have misread? No, his penmanship was as clear as her own. "It was a blast at prom with you."

She picked up a pencil and wrote, "Donald Davies—prom?" on the yellow legal pad at her side.

Ed would be back in no more than ten minutes. She had to pick up the pace.

Seth Davison. Christopher Doyle. Allen Dwight. Eric Eastman. Kyle Endres. Evan Erickson.

Wait. She backtracked. Was that Kyle? She could hardly believe Eldris had let him wear a Looney Tunes tie for his senior portrait. Would that child ever grow up?

G... H... M... O... S... She'd flipped nearly to the end and still, not a single standout. Her list gave only three vague clues:

the faux prom date, a boy named Jeremy Michelson, who looked to be about twelve years old but who took the time to include a decent and wise quote from Benjamin Franklin next to his signature, and a classmate named Barry Thomas, who, himself, was headed to Princeton and considered Cerise a member of his "Eastern Time Zone posse."

Nowhere on these pages did it look as if she'd discovered the father of her grandchild.

She reviewed her notes. Nearly an hour's research and she'd discovered only two flimsy possibilities. *Uff.* There was Kyle, too, of course—the bile rose in her throat every time she considered him—but he was engaged long before baby happened. There was no ethical path to him fathering a child outside of his relationship with Rhonda.

She heard the front door just as she flipped the book closed. "Violet?"

"Right here, Ed. Just where you left me."

He appeared at the kitchen door.

"Ah, here you are."

"Yes, dear. Here I am."

She noticed immediately that his recently dry-cleaned shirt now sported a yellow blotch down the middle.

"How did you have time to stop for a hot dog, Ed? You weren't even gone long enough to get out of the car." She stood, soaked a clean cloth with water and immediately went to work on the stain. "Dare I ask whether you picked up the list from Eldris?"

"Funny you should say that."

Was it? That was to be the entire purpose of his trip.

"I stopped by the house but no one was home. Knocked. Rang the bell. No cars in the garage. So I headed over to Home Depot to look for that piece I need for the sink."

Ed had been trying to fix the sink in the guest bathroom for going on two weeks now. Preretirement, Violet would have called the handyman and had it taken care of within a day. Now, though...

Good gracious. Her landscape was shifting on too many fronts.

"I was going to resist, I really was. But it was the good hot dog vendor today. The one with the cheddar dogs."

Well, that explained it. She was fighting cheese grease, not mustard. She added a dab of dish soap to her rag and got back to work.

"Anyhoo…long story short, I decided today was as good a day as any for a cheddar dog."

She waited for a punch line.

"And?"

"And what?"

"And…you said it was a funny story."

"Who did?"

"You did."

"No, I didn't."

"For heaven's sake, Ed. I asked if you'd picked up the list from Eldris and you said—and I quote—'funny you should say that.' So what's so funny?"

"Well, now I'd argue that my saying that was more of a turn of phrase. Not so much a statement of fact."

Violet felt the urge to grab a fistful of shirt and twist until his face turned blue.

"Ed, what happened at the Home Depot between the time you ordered your cheese dog and your destruction of this shirt?"

"Ah, yes! Now I remember."

She waited.

"Edward!"

"Oh, sorry. Just had an idea for the sink. But, yes, I was just finishing my lunch when I saw Richard walk out."

"And?" She couldn't believe they'd actually crossed paths by chance. After all their attempts.

"A man was handing him cash in the parking lot. I think he must be picking up odd jobs in his spare time. With all those legal fees, who can blame him?"

33

Cerise

THIS TIME SHE'D really done it. She'd sat silently on the couch and watched the women she loved face each other down. Now the price she was paying for her mute cowardice was further silence; she and Barb had hardly said a word to each other in days.

Her parents hadn't stayed much longer after the face-off. Baby woke up and Cerise needed to nurse him, which provided a convenient excuse to leave. She knew her mother would have considered it ill-bred to argue with a baby present, and her father still couldn't stomach being confronted with the utility of his daughter's nipples.

It all felt so strange to her now, as if she'd grown up while none of them—she or her parents—had even noticed. In many ways she still felt like a twelve-year-old girl, one who wanted a Christmas stocking and to go trick-or-treating on Halloween. And yet, she'd grown a baby in her belly, used her uterus for its expressed natural purpose and chosen to feed the child with the very same body that had created it. How was that even possible? Her boobs themselves had only been around a few years and now they had the power to drive her father out of the room.

Her physical and emotional selves couldn't seem to make any sense of each other.

She'd owned a house and had a job and lived happily with her partner for years. She'd mastered the stuff of adult life, but she realized now she hadn't felt like a grown-up in the midst of any of it.

Because this new life—motherhood—was nothing but sheer, overwhelming, helpless terror.

And yet...

She was now part of a select group, those with the honor of being able to tell a child, "I was there the very moment you came into the world."

The magnificence of it made her shiver.

She opened the door to the nursery and peeked in. Barb sat in the rocker with the baby. He was fast asleep but she looked wide-awake, mesmerized by his face.

Here was the only other person who would ever be able to say the same to their son—"I was there the moment you came into the world." She and Barb had chosen this road together and she knew they could not falter, couldn't allow themselves to screw this up.

That was just the trouble, though. When everything was changing so quickly, who could tell right from wrong? Was it her responsibility to mitigate every disagreement between Barb and her mother? They were both grown women. They could speak up for themselves. They were capable of managing their own relationship.

That was rational terrain, the terrain Cerise had revisited several times over since the argument. It was a safe place, where she didn't have to worry about anyone except herself.

Now, however, she'd decided to leave that place behind.

"I'm sorry," she said.

Barb turned to look at her and even in the dim afternoon light Cerise could see the lack of sleep piling up around her eyes.

"For what?"

God, that was a good question.

"I wish I knew."

The two of them remained quiet for a moment.

Cerise said, "It's really hard. All of it. And I think I've been acting as if I'm in this alone. As if I'm the only one dealing with it."

Barb gave her the pleasant, glazed smile she typically reserved for elderly people and toddlers. "But you're the mother. It is harder for you."

The words went directly to Cerise's gut, where she felt their immediate churn.

"Please," she said. "Don't be cruel."

Barb did not respond.

"You and I have never been this distant," said Cerise. "Never." She saw Barb's face soften, if just slightly. "I didn't plan to do this without you and I don't want to."

Barb smoothed the blanket around baby's shoulders and tucked the corner in on itself. Baby puckered his lips, still asleep and dreaming of food.

"I don't think you get it," she said. "It's like I've been left out of some game. Like you and your family have your own rules, your own language and I'm just expected to figure it out on my own."

This wasn't the first time they'd had this conversation. Barb once described Baumgartner family holidays as being like a days-long charades tournament, everyone wordless and guessing at clues.

For her part, though, Cerise wanted to understand Barb's frustration and confusion—and she'd tried. Trouble was, she didn't feel as if she knew the game any better, herself. "I don't mean to leave you out. And I don't feel like I do. Not intentionally." Which was true. "I'm trying to figure this out just the same as you are."

"Then why does your mom get to dictate everything?" Barb's tone rose just enough above a hush that baby frowned and kicked his legs.

"You love to say that, but she doesn't." Yet another conversation they'd had countless times before.

"She tried to name our son."

"She did not. Those were just samples. And be honest—if it were up to us, we'd never even get the announcements out."

"But that's just it." Barb was rocking ever more quickly and Cerise worried that soon the sheer velocity of the chair would wake baby. "Did we even talk about doing announcements, the two of us? It just so happens that, yes, I'd like to announce the birth of our son. But that's not something we decided together. Your mom went full speed ahead on her own."

"So?"

"So, I don't always want to be in reaction mode. I don't always want my parenting decisions to be in response to something your mother thinks."

Cerise put her palm up to stop all the talk. She needed a second, the span of a breath, at least, to process.

It wasn't as if she'd never agonized over her mother before. She'd been doing it since she could remember. She learned to walk, learned to go potty, learned to look to her mother for approval—it was that fundamental. She could remember being thrilled as a child by the Dr. Seuss "I can read it myself" books at the library. It wasn't until years later, as a teenage babysitter, that she realized the actual purpose of those labels—to guide beginning readers toward books they were capable of reading. She'd always shown them to her mother as proof that she'd used her library time wisely.

Plus, her mother was useful. It was as if she just knew the way of things in life—what to do and how to do it—and that lifted a burden from Cerise. School and work were enough to think about. "You just focus on your studies," her mother always said, "and let me worry about the rest." Who wouldn't want to accept that deal? Her father certainly had.

But motherhood changed all of that. She'd suddenly been forced to switch roles. She was the one worrying now.

"I don't know that I'll ever be able to leave my mother out of all this. Honestly, I don't think I'd even know how."

Barb nodded as if that's what she'd expected her to say.

"You know that I'll never understand your relationship with your mother."

Cerise shrugged.

"And I'm not asking you to leave her out of it. I am asking for you to put me first."

"But I do put you first."

Barb shook her head. "No. Not when you treat every decision we make as preliminary. As if it's pending Baumgartner approval."

The churn in her gut wasn't going away and, in fact, gave no sign that this argument was getting them anywhere. Still, here they were.

"What does it feel like?"

"What?" said Barb.

"To not need your mother's approval?"

Barb smiled and thought for a moment.

"Lonely," she said finally.

That was not the answer Cerise had expected. She crossed the room and sat on the floor next to Barb and baby, her back supported by the wall. She realized that her recovering belly wouldn't have allowed this a few days ago, and she was glad now that it did. She reached up for Barb's hand but they were both tucked under baby, holding him. Cerise took his foot, instead.

He was their bridge.

After several long minutes of silence, Barb said, "How do you like the name Adam?"

"Adam," repeated Cerise, considering.

"I've been thinking about all the firsts for this kid—first child, first grandson, first boy on both sides of the family."

"First boy in our lives, for sure," said Cerise.

"Adam," said Barb. "I like it. It's strong."

"I agree," said Cerise. "And he's gonna need it."

Christmas 2000

Dearest loved ones, far and near—

Evergreen Tidings from the Baumgartners!

As I write, the December snow is blowing in great gusts, winter's own drama playing out just beyond our windows. But here we sit, Ed and Cerise and I, safe and warm and happy. I hope this letter arrives to find you equally blessed.

    2000 was filled with milestones for our family—of the emotional, familial and professional varieties, all.

    First and foremost, this was a monumental year for our dear Ed. As most of you are probably aware (thanks to recent coverage in the Minneapolis-St. Paul Standard, *but who am I to brag??) Edward has received the first series of patents for his F8 Tri-scope Method, which he and his team worked on tirelessly. Needless to say, Cerise and I missed him terribly during those late nights and weekends away, yet our family's sacrifice is but a tiny thorn when compared to all the millions of people who have, for years, suffered the pain and humiliation of chronic gastrointestinal disorder. It simply gives me chills to think about the lives that will change because of one man—and we are just lucky enough to call him our own. Dearest Ed, we are so proud of you!!!*

    I must admit that the outpouring of congratulations has been truly humbling. It began when BiolTech held a lovely reception at their recently renovated corporate headquarters (Oh, the glass! Oh, the chrome!) to celebrate—and even found it fitting to invite Minnesota's very own governor! (Sadly, he was unable to attend (as I have been told by a discreet little birdie) for reasons related to a last-minute summons to a house of a particular color in our nation's capital. But I shall say no more!)

As if that weren't excitement enough for one year, we have news on the familial front, as well: Our little Cerise has finally become a woman. One Sunday in May, while all dressed in white, our lovely daughter celebrated the Rite of Confirmation at Faithful Redeemer Lutheran, our church home of many years. It was a joyous day and we watched with pride as she and her fellow confirmands stood for the first time as full members of the congregation, publicly professing their faith and thereby reaffirming their baptisms. Cerise, this marks the end of a serious, thought-filled journey for you and we could not be more proud.

Which brings me to the milestone I met this year: I am now the mother of a teenage girl. Oh, why didn't you warn me, dear friends??!! The emotional turmoil of parenting a teen girl is relentless. How many days must I feel like the lone keeper of the lighthouse, fighting in vain to guide her embattled ship safely to shore amidst a hurricane that rages and storms without warning?

Those of you who know me, of course, know that chaos is not a state in which I prefer to operate. It is, in fact, a state I actively work to avoid. I am proud to have earned my reputation as a woman who can be trusted, who comes through in a pinch, who knows how to get things done. Is it any coincidence that I carry a calendar in my wallet and a spare pair of stockings in my purse? If life is a course to be run, may I forever choose to be its mapmaker.

That is, after all, the mind-set required of excellent parenting. If you think it was easy for Cerise to earn a Five-Star Student award for nine quarters running, you are sorely mistaken. Yes, she is bright and works hard, but the foundation for those awards began in her earliest years: musical immersion programs as soon as she could walk, preschool interviews as soon as she could talk, children's book clubs as soon as she could read. Some may call me overbearing, but I am a mother who is prepared, come what may.

And yet…I was blindsided by the day she chose friends over family. (Ed tells me that growing apart is a way of growing up, but I can't settle for a trite euphemism, especially not when I've worked so hard for so long to help our daughter achieve so much.)

The trouble arose when I made plans for a wonderful mother-daughter outing a few months ago. Cerise and I were to go see the theater rerelease of Disney's Fantasia, a movie we'd watched together countless times on the VCR, followed by reservations at the Russian Tea House in St. Paul. We were both excited and had been looking forward to our mother-daughter adventure for days.

And then the phone rang. (I was prepared for boys to begin calling someday, but who would have known that passing into the teen years meant a fivefold increase in the time our daughter spent chatting with girlfriends??!!) The call, of course, was from Cerise's newest best friend (who shall remain nameless (even though I'm certain she would have remained clueless about her mention in this year's Baumgartner Tidings, as her family is not included on our Christmas card list, nor is she the brightest bulb in the pack)). To my consternation and extreme surprise, Cerise hung up the phone and canceled our day! Even more, she announced her intention to see the movie Never Been Kissed (for the fourth time, I might add!!) with ~~Brittany~~ her little friend! Can you imagine my reaction??

Well, any mother will relate to my shock, not to mention the betrayal I felt at the hands of my very own daughter. We weren't simply dashing out to the store together. We'd made plans. I'd confirmed and reconfirmed our reservations for tea. I'd special ordered low-cholesterol piroshki to go for our dear Ed. We'd made <u>commitments</u>—and now our daughter's friend was encouraging her to toss them aside without a second thought.

You'll be glad to know, fellow parents, that I put a stop to what I imagine could have become a highly unfortunate collapse of integrity <u>that very day</u>. I made clear in <u>no uncertain terms</u> (and, yes, a few tears—I am human, after all) that FAMILY COMES FIRST.

I'm pleased to share that we've had no further recurrences of what I can only describe as a misguided, teenage brush with disloyalty. And if my story lends any guidance or faith to any of you reading this, please know that I am one friend who will always support your choices as a parent, as difficult as they may be. Stand firm. Stick to your principles. Learn from our pain.

May 2001 bring you every blessing and every abundance that this wonderful world of ours has to offer.

Christmas blessings to each and every one of you,
Ed and Violet Baumgartner

34

Richard

WELL, HELL, IF that wasn't Ed Baumgartner in the car behind him. How many times had he seen him lately?

There was the Home Depot—*twice*. Man, that guy loved a messy hot dog. Both days he'd seen him, his chin was dripping with mustard. Like a kid caught sneaking chocolate syrup out of the refrigerator and pretending he wasn't up to anything, only his mom knows it's a bald-faced lie on account of the evidence dribbling down his face and shirt. Ed was that kid. Only, Richard suspected—no, he *knew*—that Ed was trying to avoid his wife.

That Violet. She was always around these days, too. She'd spent more time at Richard's house in the past few months than all the twenty years they'd known the Baumgartners, combined.

Ever since they'd been married, he'd never known what Eldris got herself up to on, say, a Tuesday afternoon. He was always gone. At work. Earning the money she spent while he was away.

Richard, though, was finding it easier and easier to adapt to the idea of early retirement. Who wouldn't want to spend a Wednesday morning at the movies? Theaters handed out incredible discounts while the rest of the world was at work.

He hadn't had the time before. But now he did. Now he and Eldris could actually spend some time together, actually escape life's drudgeries for a bit. Except, she claimed he wasn't retiring. She refused to even discuss it. All she wanted to talk about was the wedding and why couldn't they landscape the front lawn before then and how was she going to manage all of her church responsibilities and the wedding, both?

The stoplight turned green and Richard put his foot to the gas. He couldn't remember if it was easiest to turn right on the next block or the one following that. The theater he was heading to today had always been tricky to find. Of course, Eldris had pitched a holy fit when he announced his plans—*how could he just go running off willy-nilly*—yeah, she had said exactly that—*when there was so much to do?* But he was heading to the movies, anyway. Clint Eastwood had a new film out and who knew how much longer that old son of a bitch was gonna be around to make them? He had to be ninety at least.

Clint Eastwood sure as hell hadn't settled for any early retirement.

Richard shook the thought from his head. *Don't ruin this.*

Damn it. He should've waited until the next street before turning right. Now he was going to have to do that crazy backtracking nonsense through the bank that never should've been allowed to screw up the thruway so goddamn much in the first place.

He swung wide around the drive-through tellers and back onto the street.

Was that Ed behind him? *Sunnuva gun.*

Ed Baumgartner was following him.

He took the next right and checked his rearview mirror. Yep. Still there. Shoulda known.

Of all the miracles Ed Baumgartner could pull off—and judging from how many times he'd been in the newspaper, there was a goddamn lot—a successful tail wasn't one of them. All right, so maybe he wasn't tailing him. Maybe it was a total coincidence that Ed just happened to be at Home Depot the day Richard met his buddy Scooter there. And maybe he just happened to be there again when Scooter's friend paid him for their last engagement. And maybe—just maybe—Ed happened to be heading to the movies this morning, too. But he sure as hell wasn't likely to have forgotten which goddamn right turn to take off Nicollet Avenue.

Eldris must've put him up to this nonsense. Her and all her questions about where Richard was getting the money to pay for movies and dinners out when he'd been unemployed for twelve goddamn months. And there was the bag he carried back and forth. He'd noticed it moving across the floor of his closet. Just a few inches at a time, but it was moving, all right. He knew Eldris was in and out of that bag, checking up on him, as if it had anything to tell her about what he was up to.

Best he could figure, Eldris had opened her big mouth to Violet, who just couldn't resist getting her fat little fingers into the whole mess. It would've been Violet who recruited Ed to tail him. After all, anyone with a brain knew Violet was no selfless do-gooder. Nah, she never did anything that wasn't good for Violet. She probably figured she'd save the day—solve the whole mystery of what poor Eldris's husband was getting himself up to—and then swoop in to claim all the glory, all the while rubbing it in his face.

Yeah, well. It could be that. Or it could be that this whole FBI business had him feeling tight as a tick on a fat man's ass. He'd gotten the call yesterday he'd been waiting for and the news hadn't been good.

"They definitely got something," his lawyer told him. "Looks to me like they feel pretty solid about it. And it looks to me like they got it on Kyle."

Just thinking of it made the eggs Eldris scrambled him for breakfast turn in his stomach. He swung wide into a parking space at the back of the theater lot and threw open the car door.

The fresh air cleared his head just in time. At least cleaning his upholstery wasn't one more goddamn thing he had to worry about today.

Because there was enough, for chrissake. Kyle wasn't involved in all this Watchers business the feds were questioning him about. And he knew for damn sure.

Yeah, they'd traced some of the EyeShine glasses to The Watchers. That wasn't any news to Richard. But it wasn't Kyle. He had the proof. He could tell the feds everything they needed to know.

Problem was, that tidy piece of intel was certain to make it worse for all of them—Kyle, Eldris and his goddamn self, included.

He pulled a napkin from the wad of drive-through leftovers Eldris kept in the glove box and wiped the sweat from his face and lip. He was going to burp those eggs through the whole friggin' movie if he couldn't find himself some Tums but quick. Maybe he ought to just skip the whole thing. Turn around and go home and call the lawyer for any updates.

He went to pull his car door closed but a hand grabbed the window, stopping him.

"I never can remember if this theater is the first right off of Nicollet or the second."

Well, hell. Wouldn't you know. Ed goddamn Baumgartner had pulled up and parked right beside him.

35

Cerise

BARB CAME HOME from work with a story. "You'll never guess who called me today." She dropped her bag to the floor and made a beeline for the restroom. "I'll take Adam in a sec, but I've had to pee since I left the shoot." She hustled down the hall and continued talking from behind the half-open bathroom door.

"So, I'm waiting for the guy to adjust the lighting on a sectional couch when I see my mother's number on my phone."

Cerise remembered. Today was a furniture sale commercial for a new client and the money was good, a positive influx of cash just as the paid portion of her maternity leave was ending.

"And like, no matter where the lighting guy moved his setup, the leather kept picking up a glare. So since I'm just standing around, I think, 'Why not add to the crazy?' and I picked up."

There was a pause and Cerise could hear the toilet flush followed by the water running in the sink. A few seconds later, Barb reappeared in the kitchen and held out her arms for the baby. He'd refused to nap all day and Cerise was aching for a break. She'd tried all of her best tricks—taken him for a walk in the stroller, given him a warm bath and driven him around in the car for more than an hour. Finally, exhausted and out of ideas, she'd lain down with him on her chest in the bedroom, where they'd both fallen asleep.

Now she was starving. She handed over the baby without a

second thought and began pulling a mishmash of leftovers out of the refrigerator as Barb continued her story.

"First thing out of her mouth, she says, 'I do hope I haven't caught you indisposed, Gigi.'"

Cerise laughed. "Ironic, given that you were in the restroom while telling me this story." She loved Barb's old-timey family nickname. Plus, Barb always mimicked her mother with a husky, golden-age-of-Hollywood drawl à la Katharine Hepburn, and Cerise couldn't help but picture Mrs. Hesse in wide-bottomed pants and a hat, punctuating her opinions with the cigarette dangling from her fingers.

"Isn't it?" said Barb. "Anyway, she says—" Barb became Katharine Hepburn again "—'We'll be arriving for the christening on the eighth and of course Hesse family tradition would hold that Adam wear the family gown. But we won't be bringing it.'"

"Oh." Cerise hadn't realized there was a Hesse family baptismal gown. "Are you disappointed?"

"Not really. It hadn't even occurred to me to ask for it. But now I was curious. So I said, 'Any reason you wish to share?'" Hepburn again. "'It appears to have yellowed.' To which I said, 'Too old, I guess.' To which she replied, 'Actually, bourbon.'"

Cerise rolled her eyes and continued scooping the leftovers from their plastic containers. "And they say being on set with kids and animals is bad."

Relations between her and Barb had warmed considerably since the blowup over the birth announcements, as if just the airing of their conflicts had lessened their stink, like musty carpets hung out to breathe. Together, they'd chosen a birth announcement and agreed to have Adam baptized in two weeks on June 10—he would be nearly two months old. She couldn't believe it.

Her mother, of course, hadn't changed a bit. She was still head over heels with baptism plans.

But it had been Cerise's idea to invite Barb's parents to the ceremony. She knew her mother would be at least suggesting—if not attempting—the idea soon and Cerise wanted to get ahead of the action.

Barb resisted at first. Then reconsidered almost instantly. "I want them to meet Adam. And maybe they'll be easier to tolerate in a group. Dilute the crazy."

Cerise asked her mother to mail an invitation the next day. And, as of this afternoon's phone call, the Hesses had accepted.

"Kids and animals are a nightmare, it's true," said Barb. "But I promise you, even eighteen hours of baby barf and puppy turds is easier than just five minutes with my parents. You really don't know what we're in for."

"They're hardly that bad."

"Really?" Barb shifted Adam from her right shoulder to her left, but he didn't stir. "That's your first mistake in dealing with my parents. Never, ever assume you know what they're thinking. They deal in inference. That's their conversational currency."

"Okay…" Cerise wondered suddenly if she had the brainpower to take this in tonight.

"Then she tells me they've made reservations at the Westin and did I think they'd be happy there?"

Again, Cerise faltered. "I just assumed they'd stay here. Or with my parents. Won't they want plenty of time with Adam?"

Barb crooked a finger at her. "Aha! Mistake number two. When dealing with my parents, never—and I mean *never*—fall for the guilt."

God, now Cerise was certain she didn't have the brainpower for this. "I just assumed—"

"Nope!" Barb threw her hand up and Adam responded by squawking his displeasure. She sat down at the table and laid him across her knees, gently bouncing him back to sleep. She lowered her voice to a near whisper. "See, you got caught assuming again. Rule number one. Never assume you know what they're thinking."

Cerise waved off the theatrics and popped their dishes into

the microwave. She hadn't realized how hungry she was. Had she even eaten lunch?

"I consider that a good rule in any relationship," Cerise said. "The not assuming..."

"Yes," said Barb, again with the finger crooking, "but it's different with the Hesses. Their game is to keep you guessing. And they love it. They thrive on it. I think it's better than sex for them."

Gross. Cerise had never liked picturing parental sex, no matter whose parents were doing the deed.

"Barb, seriously. I'm about to spend three days with them. The last thing I want when I see their faces is to picture them naked."

"Why? I'm sure my mom's pictured us hundreds of times. I think she finds my lesbianism *fascinating.*"

This was getting creepy. And she said so.

Barb continued, anyway. "I told you that my parents were trust-funders-turned-hippy-types, right?"

Cerise nodded, unsure if she really wanted to know where this conversation was headed. She plucked their dishes from the microwave and put one down in front of Barb. She sat down and started in on her own.

"But did I ever tell you that from about the ages of two to four, I thought my mother was actually a woman named Joyspark?"

"What?" Cerise felt a spaghetti noodle slide dangerously close to the back of her throat and she had to gag it back up.

"Yeah, well," said Barb. "Imagine how I felt." She twirled a bit of pasta onto her fork while a smile—was it shock? Mirth? Bitterness? Cerise couldn't tell—crept slowly across her face. "I never told you about her because I never wanted you to know. But it's true. Every glorious bit. And since you're about to experience Elliott and Amanda Hesse in person, you may as well know everything."

Cerise felt her head begin to spin but she made a motion

with her hand like, *keep going.* There was no choice now but to hear this out.

"Apparently, after I was born, Amanda decided she wasn't *hacking* it as a mother. Too much work. So she booked a steamer ticket to Europe—you know, like old-money style—and told my father that he was 'free'—" she made air quotes with her fingers while keeping an eye on Adam so he didn't tumble from her lap "—to find a surrogate 'mother and lover'—" again with the air quotes "—until she came back."

Cerise didn't know what to say. So she just kept quiet and let Barb set her own pace. It was Barb's story to tell, and Cerise could hear from the tightness in her voice that she hadn't done it often. If ever at all.

"And that's when he found Joyspark." She raised her eyebrows, as if the woman with the ridiculous name had been a foregone conclusion.

"Where?" asked Cerise.

"Where what?"

"Where on earth do you find a woman named Joyspark?"

Barb popped a forkful of pasta into her mouth. "How do I know?" She put a hand up to her mouth to keep from spitting. "I was three. I probably thought she was the babysitter for like the first year."

Cerise nodded. She couldn't even remember being that young. What does a child know at that age?

Barb took a few more bites, thinking and chewing. Finally she said, "You want to know the biggest irony in all this?"

Cerise knew she wasn't looking for an answer, so she just waited for it to come.

"She was a pretty good mother."

Cerise held up a hand. "Wait. Amanda? Or Joyspark?"

Barb snorted. "God, no, not Amanda. *Joyspark.* She was really fun. And gentle. Granted, I was little so I don't remember much." She spun her pasta around and around on her fork without eating it. "Mostly, we just hung out. Cooking. Walking to the park. She loved to fly kites, I do remember that."

"And your dad?"

"Came and went. I didn't really know any different." She began to bounce Adam gently on her knees again, as if waiting for the motion to travel up her body and knock free tiny bits of memory from her brain. "And he liked to grab her butt. I remember that, too. She always wore these flowy, colorful dresses and the fabric would all gather up in his fist."

They sat quietly for several minutes, Barb gazing down at Adam, and Cerise watching Barb. She didn't want to push, for fear that her questions would unravel the threads slowly encircling them.

"And then, one day," she said, "Amanda just walked through the front door and announced, 'Mother's home!'" She laughed with a pinched, bitter gasp. "I was like, 'huh?'"

"You must have been so confused." Cerise felt her heart tighten at a memory that wasn't even hers.

"I'm sure I was, but it was like, the whole situation was already so crazy, you know? And I was so little. I didn't know what to think. My parents acted like nothing happened." She took a deep breath. "It's only now as an adult that I look back on it that I'm like, *what the fuck?*"

She paused for another bite and a sip of water. "I mean, I know we're new to this parenting stuff, but can you even imagine doing that to Adam? Sometimes on my drive home, I suddenly think, *oh, my god, what if I get in a car accident between here and the house?* I get panicky just being away for the day. I can't—"

She stopped and waved the rest of her thought away. "Anyway, the Hesse family is a piece of work. You should know what you're in for."

Cerise had the sudden sensation that she was simply listening to a story, something out of a novel. She couldn't connect the depth of its emotional well to the real life of the woman she'd known, loved, slept beside—and was now parenting with. Wouldn't bits of this story have slipped out before? Even a tiny hint dropped when they'd had too much wine. But she hadn't heard any of it.

God. Had she even been paying attention?

She felt her heart tighten another notch at the prospect of having failed her partner so fundamentally.

"I don't want to live with secrets like this between us anymore," she said, looking Barb in the eye. "Your parents betrayed you."

Barb nodded slowly. "You understand now why I've kept them at arm's length for so long." She moved Adam back up to her shoulder and rubbed small circles into his back. He pulled his legs up into his chest and settled in, content and happy.

Cerise felt tears rush her eyes at the sight of it. Whatever scars Barb's mother had left on her soul, the woman had not even touched her daughter's deep, driving need to care for those she loved.

Feds Watching "The Watchers"

by Harvey Arpell,
staff reporter, *Minneapolis/St. Paul Standard*

June 9, 2018

Minneapolis, MN—"The Watchers," the activist group that has claimed responsibility for a series of art installations erected outside Federal Reserve buildings across the United States, are reportedly under investigation by the FBI, ever since the first statue appeared in Minneapolis December 26 of last year. According to unnamed Bureau sources, the agency is now zeroing in on the group's Minnesota roots.

Investigators have traced the eyeglasses used in the Minneapolis, New York and Kansas City installations to Minneapolis-based EyeShine, a nonprofit providing used eyewear to villages throughout Africa. It is not known whether the eyeglasses were obtained illegally, though there is no report of theft or burglary on record for the organization. Executive Director, Kyle Endres, could not be reached for comment.

The last statue for which "The Watchers" claimed responsibility was erected in Denver on May 9, though suspected copycat installations have appeared in San Francisco, Atlanta, Denver, Des Moines, Boston and Ann Arbor. In Portland, Oregon, an activist group claiming solidarity with "The Watchers" attempted to erect what they called the "Leaning Tower of Democracy's Power" atop an Interstate 405 overpass. The structure toppled, forcing the Oregon State Patrol to close all but one lane of the freeway for nearly four hours until the discarded yard and farm machinery from which the tower had been constructed could be cleared from the roadway.

36

Richard

"Why in the world do we have to go tonight?" Richard stood at the bathroom mirror as Eldris fussed at his waistline, tugging and tucking at his shirt, *tsk-tsk*ing at the way it fell. He let her. If she didn't finish now, she'd go at him again at the party in front of a room full of strangers.

"Why on earth would we not go? Kyle is the child's godfather," she said. "The Baumgartners are our dearest friends. Of course we're invited to the prebaptism dinner."

Of course. Every answer to every question he ever asked about Violet Baumgartner got answered with the same two words. *Of course* they did.

"Not to mention that Violet is an absolute mess. Trying to make sure everything is perfect for the Hesses. They come from very old money, you know. Shipping money, I believe. Did you know they came across on the Mayflower? Violet just can't believe it. She's absolutely convinced herself everything has to be perfect. I mean, if this doesn't put her back in the hospital, I don't know what will."

"Well, they could've come across on the Love Boat, for all I care." He adjusted the knot in his tie. A Full Windsor. Symmetrical and strong. "It still doesn't justify my having to spend the evening jammed into a suit when I just have to turn around and put it on again in the morning for church. Once oughta be enough. One kid, one baptism, one to-do."

"You're wearing your sport coat tonight. You don't even need a tie."

For cripes' sakes. She could have at least told him before he went to all that work.

"I'm only going, you know, so I can talk to Kyle." He pulled the loosened tie from around his neck. "Lawyer won't answer my calls and I don't know what the hell is going on."

It had been weeks of the same. No charges. Nothing. Just a single directive on repeat from the attorney: "Wait until we know more."

"Richard, please don't say anything at dinner. I'm certain the investigation is the last thing Kyle wants to talk about tonight." She took the tie from his hands and walked into the closet to return it to its hook. She reemerged with a gray twill sport coat.

He turned and extended an arm, letting her slip it on.

"For cripes' sakes, Eldris, I know better than to air our family business in front of Gilligan and his three-hour crew." Like he would ever expose his kid's vulnerabilities in exchange for a glass of Scotch and a decent dinner.

"And don't get all wrapped up in Violet's business tonight," he said, sliding a loafer onto his foot. "Kyle so much as whispers he's leaving and we're outta there, too."

Eldris grabbed her purse. "I can't imagine we'll be home later than nine o'clock. You may even be back in time to catch the end of the baseball game."

37

Violet

"I'D USE THE blue toile, but I don't want to look like we're trying to impress." Violet stood in front of her china hutch, a plate in each hand. "Ed, do you think the Wedgwood will be too plain?"

"Whatever you think is best." He was hollering from the other room again. Plus, she could hear him working the knob on the toaster.

"You're not eating, are you, dear? I'm serving appetizers in less than an hour." She'd already let out the waist on his black suit last week; there wasn't time for another intervention before morning.

There wasn't time for much of anything, in fact. Eldris, and presumably Richard with her, would be arriving in thirty minutes to help with preparations. Between now and then, Violet had to choose her dinnerware, set the table, pull the flower arrangements out of the refrigerator and put on her face.

"I hope you won't forget to open the wine, Ed. Remember you need to do it at ten minutes before the hour. The man at the shop said it's best—"

"If we give it just an hour to breathe. Yes, Violet, I know." He was in the dining room with her now, taking each stack of dishes from her hands as she pulled them from the hutch.

"You have crumbs down your front," she told him. "You'll have to go change."

"I assure you I wasn't planning to wear a Hawaiian shirt when meeting our Adam's second-favorite grandparents." He winked.

Violet harrumphed. "Now, Ed. These are sophisticated people we're hosting tonight. The won't be accustomed to your—" She paused, implying he ought to know what she was referring to without being forced to say it.

"Yes, I know, Violet. Mind my mouth!"

ELDRIS AND RICHARD were not the first to arrive. In fact, they were inexcusably late and Violet had barely managed to zip her skirt—they were both losing their waistlines, though at least her filling figure was the result of medically mandated rest—when the doorbell rang.

She heard Ed's newly resoled loafers tap the length of the foyer. Then a man's voice—though for the life of her she couldn't understand what he was saying.

Did no one teach their children proper diction anymore?

"Violet!"

Ed with the hollering. She was at the mirror, already exasperated by her hair, which insisted on bulging out above her right ear. In her mother's day she would have had the option of a wig, but those sensibilities had long flown the way of the dodo. She didn't need his hollering on top of everything else.

"Violet, dear. Our guests are beginning to arrive."

She ran her comb under the faucet one more time and tried in vain to de-poof the right side of her head. In desperation, she reached for a bottle of hair spray, unscrewed the cap and dipped the comb in. She would glue her hair down if she must.

Yes, there. That was working. She dipped the comb again.

"Violet!"

Ed again. This time not calling from downstairs but from the doorway of their bedroom. It startled her so that she jumped, the comb tipping the bottle of hair spray all down her front.

"Edward Baumgartner! You've soiled my skirt!"

It didn't strike her until the words left her mouth that whomever just arrived could also hear her screeching.

"I'm sorry, Violet. But a man named Donny has just arrived."

She didn't know anyone named Donny. "He's probably selling something. For heaven's sake, don't leave him to prowl the house unsupervised."

She grabbed a washcloth, soaked it with water and blotted furiously at the puddle.

"He says he's a friend of Cerise."

"Not any friend that I'm aware—" she stopped. "Donny or Donald?"

"He said Donny, dear."

She brushed past him and stuck her head out the bedroom door.

"Donald? I'm just settling a wee issue. I'll be down to greet you in a moment."

"Yes, Mrs. Baumgartner," came the man's reply.

She turned and swatted at Ed's arm.

"Don't just leave him down there, Ed. Go and sit. Make him a cocktail."

"I don't know any cocktails, Violet. I picked up beer yesterday."

Violet was twisting herself in knots—turning this way and that—trying to get a look at the stain infecting her lap like a contagion.

For goodness' sake.

"Not beer, Ed. We'll look like the traveling circus." She spun her back to him and flapped her hand at the zipper of her skirt. "Unzip me, dear. Unzip me."

She sucked in deeply, easing the tug of the zipper, then stripped down to her slip.

"Now, shoo!" She pushed Ed into the hallway, then cracked the bedroom door just enough to speak through the crack.

"Make him an Old Fashioned. The one with the orange slice. All the young men are drinking them."

He opened his mouth to protest but she shut the door and began a second assault on her closet.

By the time she descended the stairs in a fresh skirt, Eldris had arrived and was flitting about the kitchen, reading aloud from the to-do list Violet had left out for her.

"Not that chip and dip, Eldris," said Violet. "The Mariposa." What grown woman considered it appropriate to serve artisanal artichoke-Gruyère dip on a plate shaped like a cactus? Ed had won it in an Optimist's Club raffle years ago and loved it, but that was no excuse.

"Don't you look nice, Violet. You've always looked good in black."

Violet demurred and excused herself to the living room to greet her guests.

Four men plus Ed sat in awkward silence, each staring at the various corners of the room—and each with a beer in hand.

For heaven's sake.

She reached for the reassurance of the locket at her throat, then scanned the side tables for coasters.

"Richard," she said, "wonderful of you to join us this evening. Kyle, you're looking well." He was wearing a navy sport coat and slacks. Perfectly acceptable for an evening such as this, but she hoped he owned a suit. He'd need it for the baptism tomorrow. And possibly for court.

Both men nodded and helloed back.

Cerise, it turned out, had chosen Kyle as sweet Adam's godfather, an unusual B+ decision that continued to puzzle Violet. But so far, Cerise was providing no justification. So here he sat, unspectacular as ever and beer in hand, awaiting the arrival of one of America's oldest families.

"No Rhonda?" Violet asked. She hadn't seen the woman who'd effectively tried to kill her since the retirement party and she lighted briefly—even she hated to admit—at the prospect of not facing her tonight. *Of all nights.*

"Her flight doesn't arrive for another hour or so," said Kyle. "She got a last-minute scoop on a story she's been developing that she couldn't pass up. But she's promised to catch the first cab out of the airport after touching down." He smiled proudly, as if having managed a miracle. Violet, on the other hand, knew that if Ed had inflicted the humiliation of an airport taxi on her as a young fiancée, she would have dropped his engagement ring directly into the mailbox and not looked back.

"Well, we're just so pleased she can join us at some point." The sentiment, she supposed, was not entirely untrue. She'd recently watched Rhonda's exclusive report on the rapidly disappearing blue poison dart frog from the Amazon rain forest and had nearly been convinced to mail a check off to the Nature Conservancy that very evening. The woman looked like she could convince a dying man to sing.

She turned her attention to the other two men in the room. They were a sad reality, now that she was able to lay eyes on them. As different from the creatures she'd imagined as could be.

One was tall and lanky with thinning hair, looking like the sweat pooling on his pale skin might cause him to slip right out of his discount suit. The other one, much stockier, wore jeans and a luau shirt on which the words *Cheeseburger in Paradise: Maui* blazed across his left breast.

The disappointment filled her lungs like water.

"Mrs. Baumgartner." The cheeseburger advert stood and extended a hand. "Donny Davies." He pumped her arm as if he intended to rip it from its socket. "Thanks again for inviting me. Exciting time for Cerise."

"Yes, Donald." She withdrew and gently flexed her fingers,

encouraging the blood flow back to her joints. "Thank you for joining us."

Smile.

"I was surprised to hear from you. Cerise and I lost touch after high school. But I just moved back to town a few months ago. Good to reconnect."

Violet mentally made a large X across his forehead. So—not Donald Davies.

She moved on.

"Erik? Nice to see you again. How is your grandmother?"

Goodness, had this boy's sweat glands always raged with such ghastly determination? The droplets of perspiration on his upper lip were quickly coalescing and a single, fat drip quivered on the small patch of whiskers he'd missed while shaving.

"Well, I think she's doing better now. My mom says she doesn't have to go to the bathroom so much ever since they switched her antibiotics."

"Yes."

Smile, Violet. If she weren't able to cross this boy off her list by the end of the evening she might just throw herself off the I-494 overpass.

"Urine or fecal?"

Violet turned violently in Ed's direction, but was too late.

"Sir?"

"Urine or fecal? Lots of senior citizens are affected by the medications they're given. Most often it's fecal. Throws off the intestinal biome. Quite dangerous, actually. Diarrhea and de-hydration and the like."

"Um." Violet saw the droplet of sweat break free and cascade down the boy's lip. "I'm not actually sure."

"Been the downfall of entire armies, diarrhea. Quite serious."

"Yes, sir."

Violet practically leaped at Ed.

"Isn't that someone at the door, dear?"

"I didn't hear anything."

The doorbell rang. *Thank heavens for small miracles.*

Cerise and Barb stood on the front stoop with sweet Adam asleep in his infant carrier at their feet. Beside them stood two people she could only assume were Barb's parents.

"Welcome!"

Amanda Hesse was exactly the woman Violet pictured her to be. Crisp, ivory linen suit, tasteful red manicure, beige ballet flats. Cole Haan from the looks of the delicate leather. Or Prada. Violet reached instinctively for her hair. Bulging again.

"Violet." Amanda Hesse didn't simply speak. She cooed. "Your home is just lovely. Lovely."

But she hasn't even seen it yet.

Violet smiled and offered her hand, pushing away her willingness to second-guess herself. "We've been so looking forward to your visit."

Amanda cooed her thanks.

Elliott Hesse, on the other hand, was not entirely the man Violet had pictured—though not as far from expectation as those two disappointments in her living room. He left every bit of the instant impression as his wife, but in his own way—more swagger, more intimidation, the sort of man who'd say *ka-pow!* in casual conversation.

Not to mention, he was wearing jeans.

"Violet." As if he'd spent his life as a carnival barker. "Amanda here nearly refused to come if I insisted on wearing jeans but I told her, I said, 'If I know Minnesotans, I know Ed and Violet. And I know they'll welcome yours truly no matter what I'm wearing.' Come as you are, am I right?"

He winked. Then without warning, he reached out and pinched Violet on the waist.

Of all things.

She stifled a squeal and looked at Ed to see if he was going to do anything about the man taking liberties with her body.

Then, as if he'd read her mind, Elliott said, "Don't mind me." He held his hands in front of his chest in surrender. "No harm, no foul. I'm just a bit of a hugger."

Violet realized then that Ed hadn't seen any of it. His head was in the infant seat, pulling Adam free.

Amanda, however, had seen it all and whispered conspiratorially in Violet's ear, "My husband tends to be *hands-y*," she said. "Beware."

Lord, give her strength.

38

Cerise

APPARENTLY, BARB HADN'T been exaggerating.

In the twenty minutes her parents had spent at the Baumgartner house—they'd never met their grandson nor seen where their daughter had lived for the past decade—Elliott had pinched Barb in the hip-almost-butt-region at least once, and had wandered from the kitchen, where they all stood, midconversation, to the living room, where he proceeded to let loose a wildly expressive fart. Without apology.

"It's our agreement," explained Amanda. "He goes into the other room to do it, or I get to increase the limit on my credit card." She grabbed Cerise's wrist and pulled her in close. "I highly recommend it, sweetie. I'm up to nearly twenty thousand."

Cerise couldn't remember a time she was so relieved to see her parents.

If only they'd been the sanctuary she'd hoped for.

"Mother." They were in Violet's kitchen pulling cellophane from tiny appetizer dishes. "What on earth are Donny Davies and Erik Clarkson doing here?" She picked up a dish of something she didn't recognize and sniffed it.

"Caviar," explained Violet. "They say it was Fitzgerald's favorite."

Cerise scowled and set it aside. "Don't avoid the question."

Violet huffed. "You were so distracted with Adam that I decided to take the burden of a guest list off your shoulders." Her voice had a lilt to it that made everything—even the most ridiculous statements—sound logical. It had always amazed Cerise. Tonight it infuriated her.

She opened her mouth to argue, but her mother was gone, off to the living room holding a platter overloaded with crackers and dip.

Damn it.

She spotted Barb at the far end of the room, in a corner talking to Erik and Donny. She was smiling and nodding but Cerise knew that look. It was the look of a woman who'd prefer to stick each of her ten fingers into a pencil sharpener, one after the other, rather than to stand there for even one more second.

Double damn.

"Erik. Donny. Great to see you both." It hadn't taken her more than five seconds to cross the room but Barb had watched her the entire way, pleading with her eyes for Cerise to *hurry, hurry, hurry.*

"Long time, no see, girlie-girl." Donny gave her the one-armed side hug she remembered from her past life. "Last I knew you were off to solve the world's scientific mysteries. Next thing I know, you're a momma and—" He stopped, turning to look at Barb, then back at Cerise. "And *everything.*"

"Yep." Cerise nodded. "And everything."

She was now solidly convinced this evening was never going to end.

"Good to see you, Cerise." Erik pulled at the collar on his shirt and Cerise could see that he'd sweated enough to leave a ring. "I—uh." He shuffled and scanned the room with his eyes. "I was sort of shocked when your mom invited me," he said, lowering his voice. "But my mom was worried she'd be offended if I didn't come."

"Yep, she's just as scary as ever these days," said Cerise. She played it light for Erik's benefit—the poor guy looked ready to faint—but her mother *was* just as scary as she'd ever been.

"Anyone else due to show up?" Now Donny scanned the room. "Looking forward to seeing some of the old faces again."

"Well, I don't know, to be honest." Cerise caught Barb's eye. "But I have the feeling that if she did invite anyone, they'll be fully male."

Barb snorted. At least she was laughing.

There was a hand on Cerise's elbow and she turned to see Kyle. "Oh, thank god," she said, practically falling into his arms.

"Yeah." He laughed and she could hear in his voice that he understood every bit of her pain. "Crowded room tonight."

"You have no idea," said Barb.

The clinking of a knife on crystal filled the air.

"If I may interrupt..." Violet stood at the doorway dividing the living room from the dining room, holding her glass aloft. "Dinner is now served."

As the guests made their way to the table, Barb took Cerise gently by the arm and whispered in her ear, "Methinks the only strategy we have for surviving tonight is to *float above the crazy*."

Cerise laughed, relieved more than anything else that Barb's instinct was to turn toward their relationship rather than to retreat. She leaned in and kissed her. Then added, "Methinks you're right. And when that fails, there's wine."

There were name cards at every place. Cerise was in a corner at her mother's end of the table and sweaty Erik Clarkson was on her right. Until Barb walked up and switched her place card with his.

"This way we can pass the baby back and forth," Barb said with a wink.

Violet spotted the change immediately and scowled, but said nothing.

Barb's father was seated directly across from them. Eldris was on his left and next to her was Amanda. Then there was Kyle,

Donny and Erik, who were all lined up in a row at her dad's end of the table.

Lucky them.

It was cramped quarters, and as Cerise sat, she found that she had no choice but to straddle the leg of the table. Her parents' dining room was really only meant to seat ten, but her mother had squeezed in two extra place settings. It was some relief that Rhonda still hadn't arrived, but the guests were elbow to elbow, nevertheless.

Adam, in fact, had the best seat in the house. He was fast asleep in his infant carrier in the corner.

"I hope everyone is pleased with white wine for the salad course," her mother announced. "We'll switch to red with the lamb."

Cerise hated lamb.

"I'm a complete novice when it comes to wine," said Eldris, loudly enough for the table to hear. "I'm afraid you could serve me communion wine tonight and I wouldn't know the difference."

Cerise watched as Kyle's dad rolled his eyes, then flinched. Best she could figure, Kyle must have given him a swift kick to the shin under the table.

"No worries," barked Elliott. "Just drink whatever my wife drinks. She's an expert."

"Oh," said Eldris, turning to Amanda. "How did you develop your expertise? Do you study, like a chef would?"

"Hardly," said Elliott, answering for his wife. "You just drink until you can't think straight anymore. Then you're an expert on everything." He laughed as if he'd just made the funniest joke of the entire evening and didn't seem to care in the least about the silence encircling him.

"Dad," growled Barb.

Elliott held his hands up in defeat.

"Edward?" said Violet, her voice almost shrill with intent. "Please do say grace."

Everyone bowed their heads.

"Heavenly Father," said her dad. "We thank you tonight for bringing us together in honor of this dear child, Adam."

Ever since she was a little girl, Cerise'd had a thing about keeping her eyes closed during prayer. People just looked so funny when they were trying to commune with the Lord. Like Kyle's mom right now, trying to mumble silently along with the words—as if this were a scripted prayer—but looking like a crazy person talking to herself on the bus.

"May you bless his life, just as you have blessed us."

Plus, it felt like cheating, watching people. She sneaked a quick peek at her mother and caught her with her own lids half-open, scanning the table for secret nonconformists.

"Guide us, as we strive to live as you have taught us."

Her mother had caught her cheating prayer a few times as a kid, and Cerise had just claimed to have something in her eye, blinking like a mad fool until the scolding stopped.

"Full of grace and peace."

Cerise closed her eyes briefly, then couldn't help but peek across the table again. Kyle's mom had surrendered and gone still. But not Barb's mom. Cerise saw Amanda use the moment to slip a tiny white pill into her wine.

"In Jesus's name we pray."

Good grief. Why couldn't she just pop it into her mouth like a normal lush? Cerise looked quickly at Barb, but she'd actually bowed her head and closed her eyes and missed the whole thing.

"Amen," her dad said.

"Amen," the table replied.

Amanda lifted her glass and took a long swig.

"I never have been able to cook lamb very well," said Eldris, restarting the conversation. "Always too dry, no matter what I do."

"It's the fat," said Amanda. "The fattier, the better when it comes to lamb."

Cerise noted the tiniest slur grabbing hold of Amanda's *S*s. She wondered if Barb heard it, too, but saw no reaction.

"Do you cook a lot, Mrs. Hesse?" Cerise asked, more curious about where her sobriety was headed than her culinary pursuits.

Amanda gave her a dreamy smile. "Only when my husband is gone," she said.

Elliott snorted. "Yeah, I'm afraid it's liquids-only dinner when I'm around."

The silence that followed threatened to swallow the table whole.

Then Donny. Until that moment Cerise had forgotten what she'd always loved about him—his willingness to take on a room, no matter what the stakes. He'd done it as a teenager, forever derailing classroom bullies with a joke at his own expense. One time, she suddenly recalled, he'd even intervened on Mrs. Spurloch, the school nurse who came into classrooms every spring to warn students about STDs, using the same scared-straight stack of full-color slides she displayed via overhead projector year after year.

"Mrs. Spurloch," he'd said. "I know everyone has seen your pictures before. But I'd be happy to stand in as a real-life model of what genital warts can look like if gone untreated for too long." He stood and made for his zipper and the whole room fell apart. He was sent immediately to the principal's office, but his sacrificial act had effectively taken the wind out of the nurse's sails and spared their class a painful afternoon.

"So, Elliott," Donny said. "I noticed the insignia on your ring. Is that Harvard? Yale? I was just barely lucky enough to make it through junior college, myself, so you'll have to school me."

"St. Sainsbury," said Elliott. "The men in my family have attended for six generations now." He cleared his throat. "Amanda and I, of course, had daughters. So they attended Lady Augustine's."

As he was speaking, Cerise thought she saw Eldris reach for her glass of wine, only she could have sworn that she grabbed Amanda's by mistake.

Oh, crap. Everything was so tight at the table, who could tell what from what?

"Ah, the sweet days of Lady Augustine's," said Barb. "Or, as we called it, 'Lady Blow-out-my-jeans.'" She hooted at her own joke. "Because there were basically two types of girls there— you were either too fat from the cafeteria food to wear anything except the skirt that came with the uniform or you popped so many laxatives trying to keep from getting fat that you couldn't risk wearing anything else." She looked around the room. "You know, 'cuz jeans, well—" she stopped.

"Don't be coarse, dear," said Amanda.

Cerise thought Barb's mom was definitely beginning to slur now. She looked at Amanda's wineglass. It was nearly empty. Had it been so low before?

"I always thought boarding school would be so glamorous," said Eldris. "Remember when we looked into private school for Kyle?" she said, looking down the table at Richard.

"Nope," he said, refusing to meet her glance.

"Well, I do. It would have been a wonderful opportunity for him."

She reached for her wine again and this time, Cerise was sure of it—she was definitely drinking Amanda's tainted brew.

Eldris returned the empty glass to the table. "Oh, my heavens," she said. "Did I drink a full glass already?"

Cerise watched Amanda's face as she put the pieces of the ill-fated mix-up together in her addled head. She flushed a deep crimson, but said nothing.

"It's a funny thing how laxatives actually work," said Ed, circling back to Barb's boarding school days. "The commercials would have you believing it's all about the fiber, but it's really a matter of water being drawn into the large bowel."

Cerise saw her mother stiffen. "Edward," she said, cautioning.

But it was too late. He was in his head and sauntering down whatever path he saw in front of him. "Although, stimulant laxatives work quite differently in that their job is to stimulate the intestinal muscles. Productive spasms, really, all the way down the bowel."

"Really?" Barb was egging him on. Cerise went to nudge her under the table but only ended up smacking her knee against the hard, wooden leg.

Damn it.

"Oh, yes. They're quite effective. But of course, overuse comes with a high risk of overstimulating—you could say *deadening*—the intestinal lining. Then a person is left with a total loss of bowel control, a state of constant constipation. *Lazy Bowel Syndrome*, it's called."

"Aha!" said Donny. "I knew there was an official name for it. That's what my dad used to call me growing up. Except he used the term, *Lazy Little Shit.*"

Richard, then, who hadn't said more than a single word all evening, howled as if he'd never heard anything so funny in his whole life.

"*Richard!*" Eldris scolded.

He harrumphed but didn't apologize.

Donny, though, did. "Gosh, I'm so sorry, Mrs. Baumgartner. That was crude of me."

Violet stood. "Who is ready for lamb?"

She gathered the guests' salad plates and Ed stood to pour the red wine. "The man at Surdyk's assures me that this is the perfect Pinot for chops." He had to squeeze between the guests and the wall and Cerise saw him struggling to suck in his belly as he went. "I followed his instruction to open it one hour before drinking." He glanced at his watch. "Should be perfect."

He reached their end of the table and poured. Amanda's white wine was, of course gone, and he refilled her glass with the red. Cerise glanced at Eldris's glass. It was empty, too.

Now she was thoroughly confused. Had Eldris actually been drinking Amanda's wine? Or worse, had she drained two glasses of white on nothing but a bellyful of lettuce?

Oh, god.

She tried to catch Kyle's eye, but he was on the same side of the table as her, all the way down at the other end. She leaned over to Barb, instead.

"Your mom slipped a pill into her wine and I think Kyle's mom drank it."

Barb looked at her like she was crazy. "What?"

"I saw your mom slip a pill into her wine. And then I think Kyle's mom drank it by mistake."

Barb looked at the two women across the table. Eldris was busy trying to engage Amanda in a conversation about her dream of making a trip to New England for the fall colors.

"It mus' jus' be gorgeous." Cerise could hear the same slur grabbing ahold of Eldris's words that had first grabbed on to Amanda's. Only, Eldris seemed to be fast-tracking.

"All the orn'jez an' redz an' yellz an' golz. Perplz? Izz'ere perpl, too?"

Amanda replied, stone-faced, "I wouldn't know. We live in Ohio."

Barb was now apparently convinced of trouble. "Mom," she hissed. "What did you do?"

Amanda turned to Barb and smiled. "Are you enjoying yourself, dear? Such a lovely family."

From Cerise's angle, it appeared like Amanda had a faraway glassy look to her eyes, but now she wasn't entirely convinced it hadn't been there all night.

"She's clearly been into your wine," said Barb, flicking her head in Eldris's direction.

Eldris, in the meantime, was visibly sliding down the seat of her chair.

"Up you go!" Elliott now, with his carnival barker voice.

Cerise saw him reach over and pinch Eldris at the waist.

She squealed and bolted upright. "You're naughty!"

The attention of the entire table was now squarely tuned to Amanda, Eldris and Elliott.

"Everything all right down there?" asked Ed, having returned to his seat.

"Oh, I thin' I may've had too mush onnan empty tummy," said Eldris.

"She'll be fine once the lamb comes," barked Elliott. "Always seems to perk Amanda right up, at least."

Amanda turned to Richard. "I think your wife may have dipped into my wine. You'll want to give her an aspirin before bed, I'm afraid."

Richard leaned down the table to look at his wife, who was now sliding back down her chair toward the floor.

"Eldris!" Now he was barking.

"I got her," Elliott barked back. And, once again, pinched her squarely at the waist.

"OH!" Eldris squealed, this time not just sitting up, but standing. Just at the moment Violet arrived with the platter of lamb— and just as the front door opened with a clatter.

"I'm finally HERE!" called Rhonda.

Cerise watched in horror as Eldris's shoulder clipped the plate as she stood and twelve chops flew into the air, each one catching a beautiful glint of the light from the dinner candles in their mint glaze as they fell.

SPLAT! SPLAT! SPLAT! The cascade of meat splash-landed onto the table piece by piece, a few of them even hitting Violet's prized Stickley with such angular precision that they bounced into the air again and swan-dived onto the freshly shampooed Berber carpet below.

No one moved. Not a single guest appeared to breathe or lift their eyes from their chests. No one, at least, until Cerise suddenly had no choice but to duck as a chop flew from her mother's hand and headed directly for Rhonda's face. The guests all shrieked as it hit, a chop-shaped bull's-eye at the center of Rhonda's gleaming white shirt.

Violet, her lips quivering with ghoulish green globs of mint jelly pointed a gnarled, angry finger at Rhonda and screamed in a pitch Cerise had neither heard nor elicited from her mother in all of her thirty years on this earth.

"You. Ruin. Ev-e-ryTHING!"

39

Richard

Damn, if all hell wasn't breaking loose.

"This is a three-hundred-dollar shirt!" Rhonda screeched, dripping green grease in the Baumgartners' entryway. "And SILK!"

No one had yet to move. But Violet, still holding half of the broken chop platter in her hand, stirred, raising her head at the sound of Rhonda's voice. Then, hand-to-God, if she didn't create one of the craziest goddamn spectacles Richard had seen in his whole life—Violet opened her mouth and began to roar, pure, resonant rage filling the air, a literal lioness defending her territory.

All right, so maybe *hell* wasn't the word for it. The night had turned full-on primal.

Then Kyle, as if called by an animal duty, leaped to his fiancée's defense. Like he could even do anything to help her. Like any of this mess was his fault in the first place. Didn't matter. The kid decided to rush to Rhonda's side, only to send his chair, as he stood, careening into Violet's glass-fronted china cabinet.

SMASH! Richard heard the unmistakable sound of another thousand bucks down the shitter.

He and everyone else at the table ducked, instincts kicking in enough to shield their eyes from the flying glass. When he looked up, he saw that whatever parts of the table weren't splattered with lamb chop guts now glistened with shards of Violet Baumgartner's china hutch.

Ed, standing and doing his diplomatic best to calm the mayhem, said, "Now, then. Not the end of the world. I'm sure we can have this cleaned up in just a few minutes." But there was no salvaging the night. The baby was wailing, Rhonda was screeching, Violet thundered into the kitchen and Eldris—goddamn drunk or high or both—had somehow managed to slide into Elliott Hesse's lap.

"This one's yours, Dick," he barked, snapping his fingers in Richard's face. "Too sticky for my taste, I'm afraid."

If he'd had a better angle on the son of a bitch, he would have punched him right in the face. Instead, he stood, picked Eldris up by the waist, threw her over his shoulder and walked directly out the front door.

He could hear the din of the ongoing mayhem spill from the open doorway, all the way down to the corner where he'd parked.

Now Richard sat in his favorite chair, a tumbler of Scotch in his hand, waiting out Eldris's hysterics. She'd holed up in the bedroom as soon as they got home and refused to come out. He'd tried knocking but she started in with the name-calling and that never led anywhere good. So he'd retreated, and here he sat.

The front door opened and Kyle's voice echoed from the hall. "Hello?"

"In here," he called back.

Kyle peeked his head around the corner of the living room. "Hey."

"Hey yourself."

He made his way to the couch and collapsed as if his legs could no longer hold him. He sighed and rubbed the heel of his palm across his eyes. Poor kid looked like hell.

"No Rhonda?"

"She's in the car. Threatened to fly back to New York tonight but she couldn't get a flight. Now she's madly searching the internet for a hotel room."

"That mad, huh?" Not that it surprised him, considering the greeting she'd received back at the Baumgartners', but still. Wasn't Kyle's fault Violet had gone full-blown Looney Tunes.

"How's Mom? That's why I stopped by. To check."

"She'll be fine."

Kyle nodded. He knew. The kid had been here before, too. Still, Richard couldn't let the moment pass without trying to save his son from an evening as dour as his own.

"Don't let Rhonda go to a hotel tonight. You do that and you'll magnify this whole mess. Apologize. Suck it up. Settle this before you go to bed."

Kyle shrugged.

Richard looked at his deflated son. "None of this is your fault, you know. That group of crazies was loaded for bear before we even walked in the door."

The kid chuckled like he couldn't help himself. A good sign. "God, I should have known as soon as I saw Donny Davies there. Do you remember him? He was the one who streaked the homecoming football game my senior year. Ran up and down the field naked and doing the chicken dance. The cops hauled him away but he was back at school on Monday saying his brother paid him a hundred bucks to do it."

Now Richard was laughing. "Christ, if I'd known that, I'd have paid him double—no, triple—to repeat his performance tonight." The picture of naked Donny Davies squawking and strutting across the Baumgartner dining room took hold of his brain and wouldn't let go. Before he knew it, he was clutching his stomach and laughing so hard tears streamed down his cheeks.

Didn't take more than a few seconds for Kyle to catch the fever. "And we think Mrs. Baumgartner was mad at Rhonda. Can you imagine what she would have done with those chops if she'd come after a naked Donny?"

"Lamb chop laxative."

"Mint jelly jailbreak."

"Full moon fillet."

Richard put up a hand, begging for surrender and a chance to catch his breath.

Kyle laughed himself out on the couch, then stood and reached for his dad's drink. He took a deep pull and handed the glass back. "You're gonna be at the baptism in the morning, right?"

Richard nodded. "I'll get a few aspirins in your mom before we go to bed." He looked at his watch. "Barely past ten o'clock. Plenty of time between now and then."

He stood up, wanting to accomplish at least one thing tonight. He reached out and pulled his son in for a hug. "You're a good man, Kyle. I'm proud of you. Remember that. No matter what."

He gave him a strong one-two on the back. He knew Kyle knew he was talking about more than just tonight's tragedies. But there were no words to add, nothing helpful he could say about anything other than this moment, the one right in front of them. He gave Kyle one more squeeze and released him.

"Thanks, Dad." Kyle turned for the door, but stopped. "There is one thing I'm responsible for, though. I think it's pretty obvious after tonight."

Richard nodded and waved the implication away. "It's just a china cabinet. Don't worry about it."

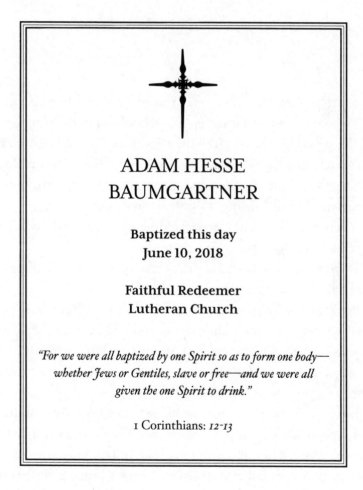

ADAM HESSE BAUMGARTNER

Baptized this day
June 10, 2018

Faithful Redeemer
Lutheran Church

"For we were all baptized by one Spirit so as to form one body—
whether Jews or Gentiles, slave or free—and we were all
given the one Spirit to drink."

1 Corinthians: *12-13*

40

Richard

AMAZINGLY ENOUGH, THE next morning, there they all were, the whole lot of them lined up like schoolkids in the front pew. Violet posed on the end like the Queen of England. A ridiculous circle of a hat no bigger than a Ritz cracker atop that lopsided pouf of hair. A sullen and ibuprofen-quelled Eldris beside her, with Richard sitting on Eldris's other side.

Then came Ed, and Cerise holding the baby, and Barb and Kyle and Rhonda and Barb's alien parents.

Boy, those two. Poor Ed; forty years married to Violet and now this.

No sign of the two saps from Kyle's high school. Richard wasn't surprised they didn't show—couldn't blame them, really. Still, the wicked schoolboy in him couldn't help but hope Donny Davies would decide to pop in for a naked chicken dance before the morning was over.

But as for now, there they were, and not a single one of them had looked at each other all morning. They'd gone nearly the whole service without passing hymnals or bulletins or even the baby, who squirmed and fussed in Cerise's arms. The tension wasn't just palpable—it had assumed physical form, a gray judgmental haze clinging to every surface.

All they had to do was play nice for five more minutes.

Pastor Norblad stood and called the baptismal party to the font. "Will the parents and sponsors please join me?"

He'd said, *parents and sponsors*, which to Richard's count meant four people plus the baby: Cerise, Barb, Kyle and Rhonda. Heck, maybe even just three, since he wasn't sure Rhonda had been asked to serve as the baby's godmother. Was godmother-in-law even a thing? He didn't know.

Instead, an entire pew's worth of people herded their way to the front of the church, every one of them stepping over and squeezing past Richard and Eldris as they went. Violet and her tiny hat went first, followed by Ed, who looked ready to burst from his shrunken suit. Then Cerise and Barb and Kyle and Rhonda and Barb's dad, Elliott. Last came Barb's mom, Amanda, who, grabbing the back of the pew with every step, looked more post–Saturday night than Sunday-morning fresh.

By the time the hoard of them congregated at the baptismal font, Pastor Norblad looked like he'd just been invaded. He cleared his throat and raised his hymnal.

"In baptism," he read in his booming pastor voice, *"our heavenly Father frees us from sin and death by joining us to the death and resurrection of our Lord Jesus Christ."* Quarters were tight, and Pastor Norblad had to elbow his way in past Elliott, who'd positioned himself at the helm—if one could call it that—of the proceedings.

Elliott grunted. "Watch the jewels, Father."

Pastor shot him a look, but ultimately ignored the warning and picked up a large earthenware pitcher and began to pour its contents into the font's basin. *"By water and the Holy Spirit we are born again as children of God and made members of the church, the body of Christ."*

The baby startled audibly at the boom of the pastor's voice and the congregation responded with an enamored giggle. They were used to Pastor Norblad waking sleeping babies. Even the babies who slept through his thundering soliloquy inevitably woke screaming to his cold-water dousing. But as Cerise bounced and shushed and rocked, Adam calmed.

Across the font, Amanda Hesse began to sway and hum.

Eldris leaned in to Richard's ear. "Is she trying to calm the baby? Or is that an evangelical thing?"

"Neither." He, too, had been watching her. "Looks solidly pharmaceutical to me." The dopey smile, the weaving in and out of sight. No one was ever that moved by emotion during a baptism. "She's high as a kite."

"Nooo, couldn't be. We're in church, for heaven's sake."

"Eldris, don't be daft. You saw her. Practically had to drag herself out of the pew. She's out of her head."

She swatted him quiet and began furiously scooting her behind to the end of the pew closest to the goings-on.

"Pssst." She raised her hands to her face and wiggled her fingers. *"Kyyyy-le."*

Richard, too, edged his way down the end of the pew and grabbed her hand, shoving it into her lap.

"What do you expect him to do about it?"

Eldris grunted her disapproval but relented.

"Parents and sponsors, together today we offer this child in the ceremony of Holy Baptism."

Richard watched as Amanda's head wove figure eights atop her shoulders.

"If they're not careful up there she's gonna end up playing motorboat in the baptismal waters."

Richard made to stand but Eldris nicked the corner of his suit coat and pulled him back down.

"You're being ridiculous. Don't make a scene."

"Oh, so I'm the one making a scene even though you're the one *yoo-hooing* our son from twenty feet."

He made to stand again, just as Amanda lost her balance, catching herself mere inches from landing face-first in the pastor's hymnal.

"Pardon me, Padre," she said, as the acoustics of the sanctuary carried her words to each of its four corners.

The congregation, now alerted to the fact that all was not well, began to twitter and chirp like waking birds at dawn.

"Back pills," she said dreamily. "I think I may have taken one too many."

"Maybe it was the vodka you washed them down with." Elliott reached for his wife's elbow and pulled her sharply to him. Her head snapped from side to side, a rag doll to his touch. "Suck it up for two more goddamn minutes, would you please?"

The congregation sounded suddenly and fully awake.

Pastor Norblad cleared his throat. "Would you like a minute?"

"No, Padre," she cooed. "He's always been like this. *Hands-y.* It makes him feel like a man." She gave her husband a droopy smile, visibly, drunkenly thrilled at her bravado. Then she wiggled her pinkie finger in his face—a tiny, pink wriggling worm, full of accusation and innuendo. "Doesn't it, darling? Makes you feel manly in at least *one* important way."

All sound in the sanctuary ceased, swallowed whole by the congregation's collective hush.

Everyone except twelve-year-old Pete Olson, who piped up to clarify for his younger brother. "She's talking about his dick."

Richard laughed out loud. Couldn't help it. *Hell yeah!* He'd known within five minutes of meeting that son of a bitch Elliott last night. He deserved everything his wife dished out—and more.

Eldris swatted and shhh'd him. Like he was the only one laughing. The entire sanctuary had begun to hum with it. Without even turning around Richard could identify stifled laughs coming from Bob Olson, Ned Jacobs and Andrew Johns.

There was another sound, too.

"Oooooooh!"

"Is that Violet?" Eldris was making to stand now, but Richard pulled her back down.

"*Of course* that's Violet." On top of the howling, she'd begun swatting indiscriminately at the air around her as if under attack by a swarm. "What the devil is she up to? She sounds like a cow about to calf."

"Oooooooh!"

Eldris picked up again with the twiddling fingers and the *Kyyyyy-le's.*

"Oooooooh!" continued Violet. "Bees, Edward. The bees!"

Ed Baumgartner now, helping to wave away the imaginary swarm attacking his wife, made pleading eyes at the pastor. "Perhaps—" he started.

But Amanda was only gathering steam. She began twisting her hips and shoulders in opposite directions, as if trying to hula-hoop herself free of her husband's grasp.

"Quit trying to hold me back," she hissed. Then, clearly singing, though incapable in her altered state of any particular pitch or tune, bellowed, "I am a lady, hear me roar!"

Elliott grabbed her by the waist so swiftly it made her yelp. "Amanda, so help me God."

"Oooooooh!"

"Pastor?"

"Parents." Pastor Norblad again, his voice a battering ram against the disintegrating scene.

The group, the congregation and even the baby suddenly quieted, obedient.

Aw, hell. Richard couldn't help but be disappointed that the best circus he'd seen in years was suddenly over. And it was just getting good. Leave it to a pastor to kill a joke.

"Do you desire to have this child baptized into Christ? If so, please answer, we do."

All Barb and Cerise had to do was to say "I do" and they could all get out of there. Go home. Get out of the monkey suits. Finally enjoy some peace and quiet and get on with their own lives. Two simple words from the child's two very female parents. Only there wasn't a single person in that whole blessed mess of a sanctuary who didn't recognize the voices of the three people who answered: Cerise and Barb and Kyle.

Goddamn, thought Richard. He knew he'd seen that baby's nose somewhere before.

Nah, couldn't be.

After all those chances the kid hadn't taken in high school.

Cerise was gay, anyhow. Hell, practically married.

And he was cool with that.

So what the hell did Kyle have to—

Oh.

Right.

Of course.

Mr. Nonprofit had made a donation of his own.

It didn't take Richard more than a nanosecond to put it all together, but by the time he did, Kyle was desperately trying to walk the moment back.

"I, uh," he said.

The kid was never any damn good at lying, all freckles and splotches and sweat at the mere hint of indiscretion. "Go ahead, Pastor Norblad. I…uh…just lost my place."

Richard himself didn't even know where to look anymore— one look at his poor kid, stuck in a corner of his own making, made him want to cry, but to look at poor Pastor Norblad, who never in a million years could have foreseen the rise of the vaudevillian farce now taking control of this most blessed of ceremonial rites, made him think he might actually piss himself laughing.

Well, wasn't this just one helluva day?

And then…

"Was it intercourse?"

Richard snapped to. So did everyone else. There was no mistaking that voice. And there was no mishearing what she'd just asked.

"Violet!"

"Mother!"

"Mrs. Baumgartner!"

Ha! So Richard hadn't been the only one putting the pieces together. Queen Violet had just ID'd Kyle's baby makers, too.

"I would like to know the truth." She was practically shouting now.

Then again with the outrage. "Violet!"

"Mother!"

"Mrs. Baumgartner!"

"Oh, don't get your panties in a bunch." Amanda sounded as gleeful as a witch headed for Oz. "It's obviously obvious. Kyle gave the juice for this child." She ran a finger down the baby's cheek and clucked like a mother hen. "We're merely curious if it happened naturally or by way of Federal Express."

Elliott. "So help me God, Amanda! We're going home by way of Betty Ford."

Then Ed. "Actually, Hazelden is closer."

And finally, like the canary in the coal mine, Rhonda the weather girl dropped the curtain on the whole charade.

SLAP!

The sound reverberated throughout the sanctuary.

"How DARE you?" Rhonda screamed. She lunged at Amanda, apparently ready to keep hitting her until she'd slapped the words back into her face, but Kyle grabbed Rhonda by the elbow, stopping her short.

Amanda, however, simply grinned and dabbed gingerly at her swelling cheek. "Dearie," she cooed. "The sooner you accept reality, the better." She swayed and steadied herself on the font. "There isn't a goddamn man in the world who can keep his pecker in his pants." She laughed. "Adam may not even be Kyle's first."

What happened next, Richard wasn't exactly sure, though he laid it out as best he could during his later statement to the police. He knew Barb hadn't reacted well and had quickly stormed out the side door. Cerise followed, practically smothering the baby as she shielded him from the unfolding chaos.

He knew, too, that Ed must have grown some balls in the midst of it all because Richard heard him laugh. Not a *ha-ha*, but a literal guttural explosion, the kind of release he seemed to have been waiting a lifetime for.

And he knew Kyle hadn't thrown the first punch.

No, if he'd had to put money on who threw that first punch, his money would be on Elliott Hesse. Sure, Rhonda had started with the slapping, but Elliott had escalated.

"What other son of a bitch would throw a punch in church?" He must have said as much to three different cops. Only, since he hadn't seen Hesse do it, they didn't much care to believe him.

"I'm telling you, if Kyle threw a punch, I didn't see it. And if Ed Baumgartner got a punch off in all this mess, well he god-damn deserved to."

Problem was, the only person headed to the hospital was Pastor Norblad—and his nose hadn't been his greatest blessing even before someone broke it.

Part
Three

CEDAR-ISLES NORTH STAR SAILOR

February 18, 1988

Edward and Violet Baumgartner of Cedar-Isles baptized their daughter, Cerise Applewhite, on Sunday, February 14, at Faithful Redeemer Lutheran Church in Minneapolis. The infant became the fourth generation to wear the heirloom baptismal gown, whose lace was hand-crocheted by Edward Baumgartner's great-grandmother in 1879.

CEDAR-ISLES NORTH STAR SAILOR

October 31, 1996

Cerise Baumgartner, daughter of Edward and Violet Baumgartner of Cedar-Isles, celebrated her First Communion at Faithful Redeemer Lutheran Church in Minneapolis on Sunday, October 27.

Says her mother, "Cerise chose to wear the same white gloves that I also wore at my First Communion in 1959. I was quite humbled to be so honored."

CEDAR-ISLES NORTH STAR SAILOR

May 11, 2000

Cerise Baumgartner, daughter of Edward and Violet Baumgartner of Cedar-Isles, was confirmed on Sunday, May 7, at Faithful Redeemer Lutheran Church in Minneapolis. With her she carried the handkerchief with which she'd been baptized at the same church in 1988. "Tradition is very important to our family," said her mother, Violet.

41

Cerise

THE DOORBELL RANG just after three o'clock and Cerise wasn't the least bit surprised to see it was Kyle on her front step.

She and Barb had driven Elliott and Amanda directly to the airport from the police station. They weren't due to fly out for a few more days, but not a single person in the car suggested they stay.

"Mother, I hope you'll consider getting help," Barb said as she pulled the car up to the airline's curbside check-in.

"Help for what, dear?" said Amanda. Then she opened the door and stepped out, surrendering her hand to the smiling sky-cap who stood ready to assist her.

Elliott grunted. "Always on the lookout for a tip, those guys." Then he leaned forward and shoved a fistful of cash into Barb's hand. "For the baby," he said.

Barb stared at him.

"You're gonna need it. Kids are expensive." He pushed the door open and stepped out, but stuck his face back into the car before closing it. "Almost forgot. I got Adam's name onto the list at St. Sainsbury's. Lemme know if they give you any grief."

Barb scoffed as her father slammed the door behind him, and Cerise knew one thing for certain: there wouldn't be any more contact with the Hesses until the annual call from the family accountant in the fall.

As for her parents, they were too mortified after the day's fiasco to even leave their house. Baumgartners weren't shy, except when it came to scandal, and Cerise suspected that the final three weeks of her maternity leave were not going to unfold as she'd hoped. Instead of finally getting Adam onto a manageable feeding schedule, she would be fielding calls from her mother followed by calls from her father followed by calls from her mother again in which she would try to convince Cerise to discount everything her father just said about her state of mind.

That drama could wait until tomorrow, though. Today, the person ringing their doorbell was in irrefutable need of some TLC.

"You okay?" She opened the door and Kyle stepped in, still wearing the same suit he'd worn to church that morning.

"Been better," he said.

She led him into the living room and told him to take a seat. Then she went to the fridge to grab beer. She was still breastfeeding, but she'd give the baby a bottle of the milk she stored in the freezer. This was an occasion that called for alcohol.

Barb came in holding Adam, freshly changed and wide-awake from his nap.

"I hope at least one of those is for me," she said, nodding at Cerise's armload of bottles.

"Kyle's here," she whispered, guiding Barb with her eyes to the man now moping in their living room. They had expected him. They just hadn't known when.

After everyone was settled with their respective bottles—Adam included—Kyle got straight to the point. "Rhonda called off the wedding. Gave me back the ring and took the first flight out."

He plucked the brilliant platinum and diamond band from his pocket and flipped it back and forth in his fingers. The stone caught the afternoon light and tossed a prism of color across the room.

Barb and Cerise were so, so sorry.

"She blamed it all on me, of course. Said she couldn't—" He stopped. "Actually, she said she *wouldn't* marry a man who kept secrets." He flipped the ring onto his palm and dropped it back into his pocket. "And you want to know the funny thing? I always sort of knew this was going to end. Whether I told her about the baby or not. Only, if I had told her, then her excuse would have been that she *wouldn't* marry a man who had children with other women."

"You still should have told her," said Cerise, gently.

"I know," Kyle said.

They were all quiet for a beat. Then Barb said, "Not to throw salt on this, Kyle, but you don't actually have a child with us. We'd always agreed that you would remain essentially anonymous." She hooked a thumb in the air between her and Cerise. "Adam has his two parents."

"I know that, too," he said again.

"So," Barb continued, "what gives?"

Kyle sighed and fell back in his chair. He looked like a defeated man in every sense.

"I wish I knew," he said finally. "I've made a mess of everything." His eyes went from glassy to red and Cerise could feel the weight of his confusion overpowering the room, filling every space.

"Look," she said, wanting to quell the tension. "Barb and I can deal with people knowing. Our mothers are going to have a field day with this, but we'll manage. We always said we'd tell Adam when it was time, anyway." She looked at Barb for confirmation that what she'd just said remained true. Barb nodded. "But I guess now we need to know that you're going to be okay with the boundaries we set out from the beginning. That there isn't something bigger going on."

Kyle shook his head with a quick, firm assurance. "No. Nothing. I never meant to mess with you guys or the baby at all."

Cerise believed him. He was telling the truth. It was one of the reasons they'd chosen Kyle all those years ago—his honesty—though Rhonda, she realized, had reason to disagree. Because it *had* been years, ever since the day Cerise had an abnormal pap and a cancer scare and the sudden realization that she may never be able to bear children. She and Barb made their plans quickly—who to ask as donor, what to do if the cancer got bad. Yet, only one of those two things came true. The cancer had been a false alarm, but Kyle had readily agreed and the donation was already on ice.

"Well, for what it's worth, I think you were just looking for a way out with Rhonda," said Barb. "And frankly, we're fine with it." She hooked her thumb in the air again and looked at Cerise.

Cerise nodded. She was very fine with it. Kyle had gone from dating to engaged in a matter of months, having invested little more effort in finding Rhonda than an eye exam. Cerise had already undergone her procedure at the ob-gyn by the time they even met her. In fact, for a time, Cerise had even wondered if she and Rhonda weren't both pregnant. It would have explained their rush. Not to mention the absurdity of the match.

Kyle laughed. "If I were looking for an excuse—and that could well be true," he said, "then that was the most bullshit, cowardly way I can think of to break off an engagement."

"Go big or go home," said Barb.

"I did that, all right," agreed Kyle.

"You think Rhonda will be okay?"

Kyle hooted as if that were the funniest thing he'd heard all day, as if the last twenty-four hours hadn't already been an around-the-clock circus of the absurd. "She was onto the next thing before I even dropped her at the airport. Like the end of our engagement was no more traumatic than canceling a doctor's appointment. She screamed at me, gave back the ring, told me I ought to learn to be a 'better man,' then picked up her phone and ordered her assistant to get working on tomorrow's calendar. That was it."

He tossed his head against the back of his chair and blew out a long breath. "Oh, my god. What has become of my life?" Then again with the laughter, followed by another deep breath. He couldn't seem to stop—breathe, laugh, breathe, laugh. He was nearly hysterical. But was it grief? Or relief? Cerise suspected maybe a bit of both.

"You've been under an enormous amount of pressure lately," she said, doing her best to inject a touch of sanity. "Give yourself a bit of a break. Not everyone plans a wedding under the watchful eye of the FBI."

Kyle rolled his eyes. "God, that. I'd almost forgotten for a moment."

"Sorry," said Cerise.

"Heard anything more?" asked Barb.

"Another *interview*." He emphasized the word as if it were a farce. "Later this week." He ran a hand through his hair but it didn't help. He still looked like a henpecked rooster. "Something tells me it's not gonna be pretty."

42

Violet

VIOLET'S HEAD WAS splitting again. Not from the crack she'd taken to her skull months ago, but from the cleaving of what she'd always believed to be a safe and perfect world.

How on earth had that happened?

The weight of it all was still far too much to process and she thanked her brain for allowing her to do so gradually—in bite-size pieces—each one difficult to swallow, but not big enough to choke on and die.

First, she'd come to terms with the fact that Barb's parents were awful human beings. Drunken, addled, groping, self-entitled heathens. It dumfounded her to think that she had been so fooled. But if that's what money did to a family, she would have none of it. She was ready to donate Ed's entire 401K to charity. Only, the Baumgartners weren't nearly as well-off as the Hesses. And there was so much goodness that lay ahead for her and her dear Ed. No, she wouldn't let Elliott and Amanda strip them of their golden years. She would stand firm. For baby Adam's sake. Against selfishness and ego and the graying of the lines between right and wrong. She would teach him that good was good and evil was evil. She would show him that family was love, no matter what he saw in Ohio. The baptism, she knew now, had granted her a mandate. And she would not fail to fulfill it.

She'd come to terms, too, with the knowledge that life at

Faithful Redeemer would never feel the same for her or dear Ed. Yes, people had been calling to offer their condolences, to offer their support. But she knew. She knew that those calls were just the prelude to the subsequent calls those friends would make to each other to gossip and *tsk* and whisper, *Isn't it just such a shame?* As if this could never happen to them. As if their families were somehow immune to the shame the Baumgartners had been forced to bare before them. As if the Baumgartners were now a caste apart from the rest.

But so be it. She and Ed had raised a smart, beautiful, brave woman, who'd committed herself to a woman no less her equal. Together, Cerise and Barb had humbled themselves before God, had brought their son to His very altar and asked for His blessing in Holy Baptism. Even in the midst of her mortification— *and, oh, it was crushing!*—even when she could hear nothing but her own jeering thoughts, taunting her and pushing her back into the darkest corners of her mind, Violet felt the presence of grace, of wonder and of pride.

Yes, this weekend had shown her that she had two daughters now—two daughters and a grandson. And her daughters were lesbians to be admired among lesbians.

She made a mental note: *Establish a lesbian fund in Cerise's name?*

Despite all the progress she'd made, she had not, however, come to terms with the facts of Adam's biology. To think that Kyle Endres, the vanilla ice cream of men, the boy she'd always worried in high school would *in fact* impregnate her daughter, had done just that. It didn't matter to Violet the pregnancy hadn't happened in the exact physical manner she'd always feared, it had happened nevertheless. She and her family were forever inextricably bound to Kyle Endres.

Of all things.

Thankfully, Adam hadn't inherited Eldris's knobby knees. And he certainly seemed calmer than both Eldris and Richard.

He was a prince of a baby, after all—sleeping and eating and playing exactly the way he ought to. He was a Baumgartner.

With 50 percent of Kyle Endres's DNA.

She squeezed her eyes closed against the blood suddenly rushing from her head. *One...two...three...four...five...*

The phone startled her alert once more. She waited for Ed to answer it. He knew she wasn't ready to screen sympathy from cynicism, and he'd been an absolute guardian angel all day. The stack of phone messages he'd taken for her sat neatly on her desk, ready for her just as soon as she was ready for them.

The phone, however, was still ringing. *For heaven's sake.* Where was Ed?

She closed her eyes and let her breathing block out the noise. *Six...seven...eight...nine...*

Where on earth was Ed?

She couldn't stand the sound of even one more ring.

"Hello. Baumgartner residence. Violet Baumgartner speaking."

"Violet? Oh, I'm just tickled pink you picked up."

The voice stumped her and shot a prickle up her spine. She knew this woman. Was she a friendly caller or a fellow congregant calling to gloat?

"And to whom do I have the pleasure of speaking?"

"It's Meg, silly. From Dorcas Circle."

Of course. That explained it. The end of the mutiny was at hand. The final coup. The last stab. Her *Et tu, Brute?* moment.

"Hello, Meg." She would not make this easy. Meg would have to do her own dirty work.

"Violet, I just hope you know that I've been thinking of you."

Of course she had. Waiting for Violet to fall. To be at her weakest. "Well. Thank you. How very nice."

"No, I mean it, Violet. I've always looked up to you. You work so hard. You believe so deeply. It broke my heart to see what happened this morning."

"Yes, well. It certainly didn't go as planned." If understatements were money.

"No," Meg said gently.

They were both silent for a moment.

Violet waited for the sword to fall.

"Anyway," said Meg. "I thought an encouraging word might be just what you need."

What on earth?

Violet felt herself release the tiniest bit of the air she'd been holding hostage in her lungs. She wanted it back. Now was not the time to let her guard down.

"Well," she said, using a tone she knew would bring an end to this call before it was too late. "Thank you again, Meg."

"Just—before you go, Violet. I hope you know, no one is laughing at you. I mean it was shocking for all of us, yes. And in retrospect it seems absolutely ridiculous—"

Good gracious.

As if this woman had experienced anything but glee in the face of Violet's pain. As if this woman hadn't in fact called as some sort of territorial move, a reminder that Violet was weak, but she was strong. As if Violet should have to be on the receiving end of this woman's emotional self-cleansing.

This would not stand.

"Yes. Like I said, thank you for calling."

"Violet, wait." The woman suddenly sounded urgent. "I'm sure you know that not everyone sees it the way I do. But I want you to know that if Sylvia grows up to be even half the woman that Cerise is, I'd be immensely proud."

For heaven's sake.

What in the world was she to make of this? Violet felt the air in her lungs swell and threaten to topple her.

She closed her eyes and breathed in slowly. *One…two…three… four…five…*

And out.

Huh.

There.

She felt it again.

Like a hum on the breeze. A whisper. The same sensation that had been breaking through since the baptism. Wisps of grace.

She held her breath, willing the moment to stay.

But now a question crashed its way through. She couldn't ignore it. So loud and insistent.

How? Her mind raced. *How had she not seen her daughter for what she was?*

Because Cerise had always been this person, even as a child. Strong. Absolute. And true.

Able to stand without apology. To say, *This is me. This is my family. This is love.*

Today Violet had watched her daughter become whole. Barb and Adam had made her whole.

Violet suddenly realized she'd never cried over the disaster at the baptism. The tears were there, yes, but they had yet to break through the emotional battlements holding them back.

Until now.

She took a wavering breath and felt the first tear tumble down her cheek. "Thank you, Meg." Her voice was no more than a whisper. "Thank you so very much for calling."

June 11, 2018

Dear friends and supporters of EyeShine—

Due to recent news coverage, you are likely aware that eyewear known to have been donated to EyeShine in support of our mission to provide prescription eyewear to the poor in Africa has been discovered at the sites of unlawful protest outside US Federal Reserve Banks. The group claiming responsibility for these events calls themselves, "The Watchers."

As the EyeShine Board of Directors, we wish to assure you we are cooperating fully with the federal authorities investigating this matter. Included in this cooperation is our surrender of a recently completed five-year audit by our accounting firm, Rivera, Rivera, & Craft.

We also wish to inform you that we have no current or prior knowledge of anyone within the EyeShine family engaged with or supporting The Watchers' efforts.

We believe EyeShine will ultimately be exonerated of any wrongdoing, and we ask for your continued support as we fulfill our commitments for 2018 and beyond.

With heartfelt thanks,
The EyeShine Board of Directors

43

Richard

R<small>ICHARD</small> <small>WANTED</small> <small>ANOTHER</small> cup of coffee but didn't know if he could make it across the kitchen. He'd had to sleep in the den on that sinkhole of a pullout couch Eldris insisted they buy when her mother slipped on her obsessively mopped floors and broke her collarbone. Now his back was screaming like a witch and he could barely walk.

Not that Sunday's mayhem was even his fault. But Eldris still wouldn't listen to reason. Wouldn't open the bedroom door. Wouldn't eat the food he left for her. Wouldn't even tell him where she kept the extra coffee filters—which meant he could now say with firsthand certainty that coffee brewed in toilet paper tasted like shit.

Maybe he didn't even want another cup.

He'd talked to Kyle, though. Kid had called late last night and given him the what's up. Rhonda was gone. The ring was back. Another appointment with the feds.

Richard couldn't believe it. Yeah, Rhonda left. That was no big surprise, all things considered. But the investigation—the pace was intolerable. Like the fed's best strategy was to wear them all down, kill them with worry, hold a magnifying glass to their heads and let the sun's concentrated rays burn the fight out of them. All right, so Kyle was the one in the spotlight, but this hit him, too. They'd waited weeks for news and when it came, it was just more of the same: more questions, more time, more worry.

Richard would've done whatever he could to help his kid out of this mess, but he was no better than a beetle stuck on his back. Six legs and nothing to kick but air.

He hobbled over to the fridge and pulled open the freezer. He was either going to have to swallow half a bottle of Jack Daniel's or put his muscles into a cryogenic freeze if he ever wanted to walk upright again. Maybe both. Either way, he needed ice.

Not to mention, he couldn't go anywhere until he was certain his wife wouldn't change the locks while he was gone.

The home phone rang and he reached for it—*easy, easy, easy, goddamn it*. He looked at the number.

Friggin' Violet.

"Endres," he barked into the receiver.

"Richard. Ed Baumgartner here."

So—apparently Violet wasn't talking to her husband, either. Yeah, he knew. He didn't need a map. He and Ed were both men of a certain age, which meant they didn't talk on the phone unless someone was dead or in jail.

"You're in the doghouse, too, eh?"

"Well," said Ed. "I'm back on phone answering duty, if that counts for much."

Frigging Baumgartners. Why couldn't they just spit it out, say, *Yeah, life's a pile of dog shit and I just stepped in it.*

"To what do I owe the pleasure, Ed?"

"Yes, well, I believe it would be in everyone's best interest to come together and discuss what happened yesterday." Ed cleared his throat. "It appears we are—*family* now."

Well, how about that? "Yep. Sure looks that way."

"Shall we say Friday night, then? At our house. I will ensure Cerise and Barb can join us. If you can do the same with Kyle?"

Richard said he would.

"And, one more thing before I go?" said Ed.

Now Richard was especially intrigued. "Shoot," he said.

"I was wondering if I could hire you to help me with some plumbing issues we've been having here at the house. There's a sink I just can't seem to fix."

"Hire me?"

"Hire you. Yes." Again with the throat clearing. "I thought I saw you at Home Depot recently—in an exchange with a man for whom it appeared you may have done some work. And I just assumed—"

Well, hell. Maybe poor old Ed hadn't been tailing him, after all. And yet, only a fool gets fooled, meaning, Richard had a few questions of his own. "I noticed you at the Home Depot, yeah. Easy coincidence. When you showed up at the movie theater, though…and were you at a brewpub in St. Cloud recently? I gotta say, Ed. I think you might be tailing me."

"Why on earth would I do that?"

"You tell me. Just seems awful coincidental to keep bumping into you."

Baumgartner was quiet on the line for a beat. "Well, at the risk of making us both sound like stereotypes, Richard, we were hardly the only retired men in that movie theater last week."

The theater had been dark, of course, but as far as he could recall, Ed was right. It was a full of old gray fools just looking to escape the house for a few hours.

Ed continued, "I don't even like Clint Eastwood movies, as a rule. But I think you can relate when I tell you—in confidence, of course—that sometimes the walls threaten to close in on a fellow."

"Or your wife threatens you with another item on the Honey-Do list."

"Yes, well. Anyway…" Ed got back to his original question. "When I saw you at the store I figured you were picking up extra work as a handyman. I know—at least Eldris tells us it's been…" He paused. "Difficult. Financially."

Richard didn't respond. He was tempted to let Ed flail on the line while he sat back and enjoyed the sound of the struggle. But he knew better. Baumgartner wasn't one for financial one-upmanship. This wasn't a game he was playing.

"Not that," added Ed. "Not that we mean to imply that you need our money, of course. I simply—"

"You didn't see what you thought you saw, Ed. But I'll be happy to help you with your sink. Shouldn't be a problem."

They said their goodbyes and hung up.

So they'd both been wrong. How about that?

His back was now in full-blown mutiny—a posse of angry villagers throwing their torches at the ogre that had become his hunched and screaming spine—but he grabbed the back of one of the kitchen chairs and pushed it, inch by inch, across the floor like an old man with a walker. The ten-foot journey took him longer than a hippie hitchhiking to Vegas, but he finally made it to the couch.

Down, down. Easy. Damn it.

He hit the sagging cushion with a plop and moaned as the villagers raged.

He knew that what his back really needed was a few hours on the hard floor, but he didn't trust that once down, he'd be able to get back up. And Eldris sure as hell couldn't be relied on to rescue him. Even if she did show him even the tiniest kernel of human decency by trying to lift him, she'd snap her bones in two and end up falling there next to him, injured and moaning and begging to be put out of her misery.

God, wouldn't it just be Kyle's luck to walk in on that.

What a year. He'd gone from unemployed sap to involuntary retiree. Eldris was as ornery as ever. And Kyle, well... They couldn't let their guard down yet. Their kid was wrapped in a package he didn't buy but that had his name stamped all over it.

Literally. That's why the feds started asking questions. Several of the glasses used in The Watchers crap had tags on them.

This gift of sight brought to you by EyeShine! He couldn't believe it. Whatever brilliant criminal overlooked that small detail deserved to get caught. It's how Richard knew this wasn't Kyle's fault. The kid wasn't dumb. A little naive, yeah. But not flat-out stupid.

Meanwhile, all Richard could do was sit his ass on the couch. The sagging, faded couch that Eldris had picked out the day she learned she was pregnant with Kyle. She'd come home from the doctor that day in tears, hollering at him about how could he even think about bringing a child into the world when he wouldn't even provide decent seating for the child's soon-to-be grandparents.

Goddamn it. He just realized that made two couches Eldris had forced him to buy on account of her mother.

But that's why he'd married her, wasn't it? All right, so she could be strong-willed and he admitted to letting her push him around on the home front. So what? It was her territory. That was the unspoken agreement. She'd created a space where Kyle felt safe and Richard knew his place. No one bossed Eldris around in her own house. Not even him. And that mattered. It meant she loved her family as much as he did.

When it came to Richard's territory, yeah, he'd made a different map for himself. And he'd followed it. He'd trudged all the way to the top of the advertising mountaintop, all the way to Senior VP, hauling ass the whole way like a good soldier should. Then he turned left, took a single goddamn turn off course and walked his ass right off the face of that mountain. Not because he wanted to. Because they'd shoved him. Coaxed him all the way to the highest, most dangerous peak and pushed him right off.

Which wasn't to say he hadn't saved himself. Because he had. He'd grabbed hold of the strongest limb he could reach and clawed his way to safety. He wasn't falling anymore. He was stable. His feet were both on solid ground.

He paused the rushing of his thoughts for a minute and

twisted slightly to the right, trying to work a muscle or two loose in his back. They answered by hissing fire. But he didn't retreat. He twisted to the left.

Easy. Easy. Damn you.

If Richard survived this last year, he had to trust Kyle would make it through this feds business. It looked bad, yes. But they'd see. This wasn't Kyle's doing—the kid was all heart. Too much, probably. Too much wanting to help the helpless and foster world peace and all that. All heart was right. He'd dated Rhonda, what, six weeks before popping the question? Look where that got him. A broken engagement and a ring he couldn't return.

Well, now.

That was a turn of events he hadn't considered.

He sat for a moment, mulling.

Richard edged his hand slowly into his pocket, cursing the villagers and their fires as he went, and pulled out his cell phone.

Richard again. A little birdie tells me there's been a change in your status. And it just struck me: I don't have any reason to keep your borrowing habits a secret anymore.

Que¿

Yeah, that's right. Keep up the charade. But you and I both know. I've got your number.

Richard waited for a response. He let a minute tick by. Then a few more. Nothing. Good. He had her attention.

Turns out I also have the email. You remember that, don't you? The one where you say you need to swing by to pick up a few of Kyle's boxes.

322

And?

I think you and I both know those are the donations showing up on the feds' doorstep.

And I've had a lot of time to think lately. I'm a pretty smart guy. So I did some math.

Never did like math much, but I'm actually kind of a whiz at it. Fancy this equation: Ambitious young broadcaster + an eye for opportunity x social media phenomenon = biggest "scoop" of her career.

You have one hour to fess up to the feds, Rhonda. After that, I'm doing it for you.

Christmas 1985

Dearest loved ones, far and near—

Evergreen Tidings from the Baumgartners!

Sadly, I'm afraid you will find me to be the bearer of bad news this year. Not a single snowflake has yet to fall and the world outside our window hearkens none of the Christmas cheer manufactured in department store displays or newspaper circulars. Here, ground meets sky as a stretch of dreary, deadened gray.

Oh, but I must depress you with such doleful news! And to do so when the annual Baumgartner Tidings are meant to bring good cheer and reports of a year well lived. But I'm afraid I must admit that 1985 has not felt glorious nor joyful for dear Ed and me, but has been one of heartbreak and tears.

For my dearest and I, two babies have already come and gone. Neither child was with us for long—the first miscarried during my fourth month, the second even sooner, during my third. But both were ours. They were our children, whom we loved from the very moment we knew of their presence, whose lives we treasured and anticipated with every breath, whose faces we pictured, even though they were not ultimately ours to see.

They were our babies. Do you understand?

On my stronger days, I am reminded of what God said to Abraham:

"And He took him outside and said, 'Now look toward the heavens,

and count the stars, if you are able to count them.' And He said to him, 'So shall your descendants be.'"

—Genesis 15:5

Who am I, I ask myself then, to question God's plan? Who am I to despair when He asked so much more from Abraham and Isaac and Israel?

And yet, my brain argues with my heart and makes me question: What if it's all just words?

Fear not! I say to myself then. Shake your head loose of its gray clouds, Violet, and remember what the angel said to Mary:

"For nothing will be impossible with God."

—Luke 1:37

Oh! But if only I were strong not just of faith but also of nature. If only my body could keep our children safe until it was time, until the day their father and I were due to welcome them into this glorious world.

If only I did not wonder if our babies, themselves, made the choice to leave us.

"He gives strength to the weary, And to him who lacks might He increases power."

—Isaiah 40:29

Dearest friends, I ask you to please keep Edward and I in your prayers, as we are so terribly weary. My beloved has been my rock, my center, and yet I fear my burdens may become too much even for him. We ask your grace to carry us.

May 1986 be a year of God's richest blessings for us all.
Ed and Violet Baumgartner

44

Violet

"I'VE BROUGHT YOU some soup."

Violet looked up to see Ed setting a tray of food on the side table next to the couch in the family room where she sat. Her afternoon tea was still in her hands, now long cold. She wasn't hungry but she didn't have the heart to tell him.

"Thank you, dear." She sat up straight and brought the tray to her lap. Before retirement, her family had never eaten a single meal outside of the kitchen or dining room. Cerise had begged, certainly, when a favorite show or some other *can't miss* television event was due to air, but Violet had strictly forbidden it. "The only distraction allowed at the Baumgartner table is a sparkling conversation," she'd said.

Her stomach now roiled at the irony.

Even so, in recent months she and Ed had become quite adept at "lap lunching," as she called it. Violet coined the term herself, convinced that activities were considerably less boorish when given a title.

"Will you join me?" She looked up at Ed and smiled.

He nodded. "Back in a jiffy."

Soon, they were both tucking into warm bowls of wild rice soup.

"Ham in the soup tonight," said Ed. "I know it's an odd choice for June, but this seemed a good way to use up some of the leftovers."

Violet *hmm*'d. She'd ordered five-dozen ham buns, six pounds of pasta salad and two relish trays for the postbaptism reception at the church, which, of course, never happened. Ed took much of the unused food to the Glorious Savior shelter downtown, but with the warm weather setting in, nearly half of their beds were empty and they couldn't use but a portion. Now Ed would have to put ham in everything from omelets to salad.

"Probably two or three ham meals left, I figure. How would you feel about egg and cheese bake for breakfast tomorrow?"

Violet chewed quietly, considering.

"Dear?"

She snapped to and realized she'd been staring at a small piece of carrot on her spoon. She lowered it to the bowl and turned. "Yes?"

Ed's face clouded with concern. "Don't go dark, Violet."

She wanted to play the naïf, pretend she didn't have the slightest idea what he was talking about. Only, she did know. It was the term they'd used since the beginning of their marriage when one of them sensed the other turning away, isolating. Like she was doing now. "I realize," she said, "it may look that way." She picked up her napkin and wiped it across her lips. "But I'm not trying to."

Ed wiped his own napkin across his mouth, and then slid his tray off his lap onto the couch beside him. He turned and gave his attention to Violet, waiting for her to say more.

"I suppose I'm simply feeling—directionless." She sighed and followed Ed's example, moving her tray to the side table. Then she pulled the gray merino wool blanket Cerise had given them for Christmas years ago across her legs. Summer was here, but she always ran chilly. "I'm afraid this year has left me with more questions than answers."

It was Ed's turn to *hmm* and nod and she appreciated his quiet patience while she sorted her thoughts.

"We were supposed to be off enjoying our retirement. Traveling. I'd hoped to go to Scandinavia this summer. Remember?"

"Yes."

"Instead, I feel like I've spent the year—quite literally—out of my head."

Ed chuckled and took her hand. "At the risk of offending you, I have to agree."

"For heaven's sake, you hadn't been retired five minutes before you had to play nursemaid. Twenty-four hours a day. For months. And let me just say, at the risk of offending *you*, there were times I never wanted to see or hear you again."

She harrumphed, thinking of all the occasions Ed had checked on her in the bath or forced her to lie down for a rest or sent Eldris over to babysit. *Gracious.* "It felt like motherhood all over again, only this time, you were me and I was Cerise."

Ed laughed. "At least you didn't require toilet training."

"Edward!"

He reached for her hand and stroked a thumb along her knuckles. "It wasn't easy for either of us, Violet." He waited for her to meet his eyes. "Once you get a bee in your bonnet, there's no shaking it loose. You have exacting expectations and you don't suffer fools." He paused, not breaking eye contact. "Imagine what it was like being locked in the house with you all winter long."

Violet crooked an eyebrow, and for once, she felt no zing, no pain. "I presume you're about to make a point?"

Ed nodded. "I never resented caring for you and I would—will—do it again, should it become necessary. I don't take my wedding vows lightly." He brought his face in to hers, intensifying his point. *"However..."*

Violet waited, too exhausted to even get her defensive dander up.

"I would like you to repeat after me: *The earth rotates at nearly 1,000 miles per hour.*"

Violet pushed him back. "What in the world?"

Ed rebounded, leaning in again. "Say it, Violet. *The earth rotates at nearly 1,000 miles per hour.*"

"I will not."

"Why?"

"Because it doesn't have anything to do with what we're discussing."

Ed waited.

As did Violet.

The grandfather clock ticked.

Ed, finally, was the first to break. "All right. But I know who broke Pastor Norblad's nose and I'm not going to tell you until you say it."

"Fine!" That nugget had provided more incentive than she expected. "*The earth rotates at nearly 1,000 miles per hour.* What is your point?"

He was grinning now, practically licking his lips at his delicious victory. "It's what I tell myself when I need a reminder that I can't control everything. I say, *Ed, no matter what you do, no matter how badly you want this, the earth is going to go on spinning—1,000 miles an hour, twenty-four hours a day, seven days a week.*"

Violet eyed him. "You're saying I have control issues?"

He eyed her back. "You're saying you don't?"

Of all things.

"I hardly think petty accusation is helpful, Edward. Frankly, I resent it." She could hear her voice rising.

Ed didn't rile, not even a twitch. "Hmm. So your compulsion to discover Adam's donor father didn't lead to any disappointment or upset."

Violet scoffed. "And you're thrilled about the child sharing Kyle Endres's DNA?"

Ed shrugged. "At least we know he's a decent human being. At least we know what we know. We wouldn't have any information if they'd used an anonymous donor."

Exasperating, this man! Violet threw her hands in the air. "That's what I've been saying for *months*."

"But…" Ed squeezed her hand—too hard, though she wasn't about to let on. "Don't you see? That's our opinion, not our right. Cerise and Barb are his parents. These are their choices. We have to trust they'll do what's best. And they will."

Of course he was right. It was one of the only positive revelations from the horrors of the past weekend. Cerise and Barb didn't turn on each other. They stayed cool. Even as the earth turned to salt around them, they kept their focus exactly where it needed to be: on their family.

And then the call from Meg.

Even so.

"It's unnatural for a mother to give up on her child." The words stuck in her throat. "I push Cerise because I love her. And if I don't push—" She stopped, her throat closing its gates against a rising emotional tide.

This loop. She knew it so well. Push because you love, know you're loved because you were pushed. It felt as familiar as an old housecoat. Practical and necessary.

"Letting go isn't the same as giving up," said Ed. "I don't think that's news to you, but I do know it's difficult to accept."

Violet nodded, but put her hand up to stop him. He was getting too far ahead, while she lagged behind, still wading through her last set of thoughts.

"It's like," she said, "I started pushing the day my mother stopped. While I was growing up, she was our family's biggest cheerleader. Always the first to sing my father's praises. Always prepared to ensure our accomplishments were properly recognized. And as soon as Daddy was gone, as soon as we needed her the most—poof! She just walked away. Just let him die and his reputation along with it."

Ed closed his eyes. He recognized the trope and Violet knew

what he was thinking—*Here they were again, back spinning the same yarns.*

He opened his mouth to speak, but Violet stopped him.

"I know. I know. I'm not going there again. It's just that I realize—I don't want my mother's old housecoat."

Ed screwed his face, confused.

"Never mind." She waved the metaphor away. "The point is—" She took a deep breath. "Oh, Ed. The point is—I just farking *hate* getting *old!*"

Ed, who until that moment had been so present, so intimately concerned with her thoughts, suddenly opened his mouth, peeled his eyes back and howled with laughter.

His voice rang around the lip of her water glass and up the tinny brass candlesticks of her coffee table display.

The couch cushions shook as he shook, the two of them bouncing up and down, and their stomachs with them.

Violet, desperate to get her words out, howled back, undeterred. "I do! I farking hate it! I hate having to write every blasted thing down because I can't remember any of it. I hate having to go to bed by nine o'clock, knowing that I'll have to get out of bed at least twice to go to the bathroom. I hate that Alice Tobler—that old biddy who wears the same plastic mistletoe pin every blasted Christmas—looks at me like I'm decrepit."

She had to stop to breathe, trying to find a gasp of air between heaving sobs of laughter. "And," she added, pointing directly at Ed, "I HATE that you saw me wearing a diaper in the hospital!"

Ed howled again, clutching his stomach and collapsing against the back of the couch.

"I hate that it took me thirty years to discover that you're a wonderful cook. I hate that I can't even hire a cleaning service because no one can do it the way I do, even though I *hate* scrubbing the floor and if I never cleaned another toilet in my life I'd be perfectly happy. I hate that I'm now the age my mother was when she checked out so spectacularly, and I hate that my daughter—at just thirty years old—is already a better mother than I ever was!"

The room suddenly died.

Ed looked at her, wiping tears from his eyes with the back of his hand. "Why do you say that? You're a wonderful mother."

She hadn't planned to—the words just came. "I don't know." She reached for the box of tissues on the coffee table. She offered one to Ed, and then took one for herself, wiping her cheeks. "It's just that as each year passes, I'm acutely more aware of all the mistakes I may have made in life and how little time I have left to fix them."

"Violet," Ed said softly.

"Yes, yes, I know. We are not our pasts." She blew out a long breath and steeled her spine against the cloud of self-doubt clinging to her. "And I know that being a grandmother is different. Things change for me now." She smiled. "I don't understand those changes yet, but I will do my best to accept them." She patted her knee as she spoke, accentuating her final point.

Ed smiled. "I know you will."

Violet cocked her head, feeling oddly proud. "Yes, I will."

"Things are going to change around here for both of us, you know." Ed stood, gathering his tray. "You don't want me underfoot and frankly, I have no desire to be." He patted his growing middle. "Besides this lovely addition, I worry all this time at home has also made me a bit thick in the head."

"Nonsense." Violet stood and gathered her own tray, then followed him into the kitchen.

"No, I'm afraid it's true. Life has to involve more than mowing the lawn and trips to the Home Depot." He turned on the sink and squeezed a dash of dish soap into the basin. He set the soup pot under the running water, letting it fill with suds.

Violet loaded their bowls and spoons into the dishwasher. "You may be underfoot but I certainly can't complain about all the help around the house." She pulled a clean dish towel from the drawer and waited while Ed scrubbed the pan and rinsed it clean. She looked at the towel she'd chosen. "Do you remember this?"

She held up the towel for him to see. It was crisp white linen, embroidered with the words of *Matthew* 25:35.

For I was hungry and you gave me food,
I was thirsty and you gave me something to drink,
I was a stranger and you welcomed me

"If I remember correctly, that was a gift from Barb," he said.

"Yes," Violet said, smiling as she recalled the day. "The very first Christmas she spent with us."

That reminded her.

"Now, what do you know about Pastor Norblad's nose?"

45

Cerise

BARB WENT BACK to work on Monday afternoon. Her new furniture client liked the work she'd done for their Luscious Leather Days Sale and hired her back to shoot the spots for their July 4 Exploding Savings event. She warned Cerise it was likely to be a late night.

"Just do a good job," Cerise said. "We could use a new mattress and I want their *cr-aaay-zy-est* discount." She winked and shooed her out the door.

Anyway, Adam had just woken up and Cerise was in the process of packing him into his car seat to head over to her parents' house. She'd spoken to her dad that morning and he said the mood at their house was still a bit grim. Maybe some baby love would help.

She and Barb were feeling shaken by the weekend's events, themselves. At times, it felt to Cerise like she had a news ticker running at the base of her brain, constantly reviewing the headlines: *Fistfight at the font, Suburban housewife drugged at dinner party, High school reunion hopes to answer the question, "Who's the daddy?"*

And yet, she and Barb also both admitted to feeling a bit numb. The weight was still settling. "Like, I'm thinking," Barb said as they lay in bed Sunday night, *That happened to someone else, right? That could not have been real.*

Cerise nodded and thought about the moment Kyle said, "I do" at the baptismal font. She couldn't shake the look on Rhonda's face, like she hadn't been the least bit surprised. But also like she was ready to murder him. How could it be both?

She pressed Pause on the memory and erased Rhonda's face from her mind. Kyle had the ring back; Cerise could forget her now.

"I'm sorry I pressured you to invite your parents," she said after a moment. "I had no idea."

Barb put a hand on hers and squeezed. "Neither did I. They've always been complicated, but never this much of a mess." She shook her head as if replaying her own nightmarish collage of memory. "And for what it's worth, you didn't pressure me. I ought to be able to invite my parents to come visit without expecting them to bring the apocalypse."

"Has your mom always—" Cerise wasn't exactly sure how to finish without accusation.

"Always liked her vodka, yes," said Barb. "The pills are new." She stopped. "Or maybe they're not. It's like I told you—they like to keep you guessing."

"For what it's worth, I think their visit reminded me of why I fell in love with you." She moved in close and nestled into the warm nook at Barb's side. "Why I love you still."

"Because surely I've had plenty of practice mixing a strong vodka martini?"

"No." Cerise laughed. "Because it reminded me of how steady you are. Watching the chaos your parents created reminded me that I've never doubted you. You've never given me reason to." She pulled herself up out of her Barb cocoon and kissed her. "You're exactly who you say you are."

"So—boring, in other words." Barb winked, both accepting and deflecting the compliment.

"Strong," said Cerise, kissing her again before nestling back down. "And smooth. What you just said, like a good martini."

Barb nestled in, too, turning her face to Cerise and smiling. "Make it a *gin* martini."

Cerise smiled back. "A *gin* martini."

"Hello!" Cerise knocked on her parents' front door but didn't wait before walking in. She peeked through the entryway into the kitchen and spotted her dad pulling yellow rubber wash gloves from his hands.

"Just finishing the washing up, dear," he called. "Come in, come in. Your mother is in the living room. Say hello, Violet!"

Her mother stood to give her a hug but didn't say a word. Then she reached for Adam and brought him directly to her nose.

"Is there anything sweeter than the smell of you?" she said, kind and soft and looking directly into his eyes.

Yes, baby love seemed to be just the thing she needed.

"How is Barb?"

Cerise was momentarily taken aback. Barb was never foremost on her mother's mind, not to mention that she almost always began a conversation with an agenda.

"Well, her head is still spinning, I think," said Cerise. "But she's open to talking about what happened, at least."

"Good," said Violet, adjusting the collar on Adam's jumper. "Keep talking and don't let her quit until it's all out there. I had no idea what she'd faced as a child."

"Nor did I," answered Cerise.

In another time and place, she might have been tempted to force her mother to look at the role she, herself, had played in the whole fiasco—pushing the paternity question to its breaking point and, worse, imagining a universe in which Adam shared DNA with Erik Clarkson or Donny Davies. There was no denying that her mother had created a carnival of her son's whole start to life.

So, yes, she would have to address it someday. Only, not today. Adam was safely tucked away in his grandmother's arms and life, *for just a moment*, felt quiet.

She sat back on the couch and closed her eyes.

"Cerise?"

"Yes, Mom?" She resisted the temptation to open them, hoping her mother would take the hint.

"I've done some very serious thinking and I'm afraid I have two very important apologies to make. I'd like to start with you."

Cerise opened her eyes and sat up. This was interesting. "What for?"

Violet smoothed the tufts of hair just beginning to grow above Adam's ears. "It's hard being a mother," she said.

Cerise nodded. "Yes, but also rewarding."

"Rewarding, of course. But what I'm trying to say is that I understand. I watched you and Barb this weekend, caring for Adam and dealing with her parents' nonsense, and I just..." She looked at Cerise, then reached for the locket at her throat, enclosing it in her fingers. "Sometimes it's hard to accept I'm not needed anymore."

"I'll always need you, Mom."

Her mother held up a hand and waved the words away. "Yes, I know. But not in the same way. And that's what I'm saying. That's how it's supposed to be. Adam needs you now—and Barb—the way you once needed me. I want you to know that I see that. I understand. And I'm sorry if it's taken me some time to adjust."

She nodded her chin with the word *adjust*, as if reassuring herself that, yes, it was the correct choice of word. She'd just needed some time to adjust.

"I appreciate that, Mom."

"I want you to see something," she said, raising a hand and pointing toward the den. "Go in there and open the closet."

Cerise gave her a skeptical look.

"Go on," said Violet, shooing her off with a wave of her hand.

Her parents' den had always felt like a room where time stood still. The walls were lined with the same bookshelves her father had installed the very first year they moved in and the shelves, themselves, were lined with encyclopedias, atlases and every hardcover collection, treasury and do-it-yourself book published by *Reader's Digest* since 1980. The computer, which her mother had resisted until Cerise's teachers started sending notes that "homework must be submitted via email," still sat on a desk in the corner under a yellowing plastic dust jacket. Her father had owned and worked on a laptop for years, but never in the den; perhaps he sensed the anachronism.

She pulled open the closet door, realizing that she'd never had a reason to go in it before. She didn't know why. Perhaps she assumed it was full of—what? She really had no idea.

The shelves inside were neatly stacked with plain, white stationery boxes, not unlike the paper aisle at Office Depot, and the side of each box bore a number—*was it a year?*—written in black marker. She took a closer look at the box at the very top. It read, "1978." Below it were "1979," then "1980," "1981" and so on. Dozens of them, all the way up to 2017.

She pulled out the box labeled, "1978" and opened the lid. She hadn't been wrong—the box was full of paper and she flipped through the stack. Every page was the same.

She pulled the first sheet from the pile and began to read.

Christmas 1978

Dearest loved ones, far and near—

Evergreen Tidings from the Baumgartners!

SHE WASN'T EXACTLY sure how long she sat on the floor reading, but it had to be hours. She heard her mother feed Adam a bottle, sing him to sleep and lay him down for a nap. Cerise heard him wake just as she reached the letter in which she'd graduated from high school.

The boxes were just what they appeared to be—a lifetime of Christmas letters, each written by her mother and each photocopied and boxed. The printer, Lake City Press, taped its invoice to the inside of each lid and every year it was the same: two hundred copies.

It looked as if her mother had never mailed a single one.

Cerise stood, stretched the cramps out of her back and neck and walked into the living room, where her parents both sat, drinking tea and playing with their grandson. The sunlight had shifted from bright afternoon to early dusk.

"You wrote a Christmas letter every year?" She sat down next to her mother and looked at her face. She felt as if she'd just spent hours swimming inside her mother's head, listening to her narrate the ups and downs of their lives.

"Well, that's a silly question," said Violet. "You just saw for yourself."

"But you didn't mail any of them?"

Her mother stiffened and shook her head. "No."

There were a million questions urging themselves from Cerise's lips, but she stayed quiet and let her mother speak.

"I was going to. At first. I was a newlywed, going by script. But it felt too—" she searched for the right word "—assuming."

"What do you mean?"

"I mean, who am I to assume people even want to hear about our lives? What if I sound as if I'm bragging? What if people don't even care?"

For the first time in as long as Cerise could remember, her mother didn't look as if she were formulating the next argument in her head, as if this conversation were nothing but a battle she was prepared to win. Instead, she looked resigned. Not beaten, exactly, but simply—*maybe*—peaceful.

"But if you never mailed them, why did you keep writing? For heaven's sake, why did you keep paying to have them printed?"

"Like I said, the first few years, I thought I was supposed to write a Christmas letter. It was a wife's duty. Then, after a time, I realized that I was simply doing it for myself. It felt good to put my thoughts down on paper. And many years, I actually enjoyed doing it. I liked reliving our life." She paused. "Other years, it was just—necessary."

"And the copies?"

"I know. Ridiculous. But somehow, they made the letters feel less self-indulgent. Something I was supposed to do." She looked at Cerise. "I'm very task-oriented. Ask your father."

Ed, who had been listening quietly, nodded.

"Did you know, Dad?"

"Oh, eventually," he said. "I didn't see much harm. If she enjoyed it." He looked at Violet and smiled. "After forty years of marriage, a closet full of boxes seems pretty insignificant."

Violet smiled back at him and Cerise watched as they enjoyed a private moment. She'd always been reasonably sure she grew up with decent parents. Overbearing, certainly out-of-date with the times and probably a little bit nutty, yes. But the unfolding of the last few days made her certain of this: she loved them fiercely.

"Thank you," she said, first to her mother, then to her parents, both. "Thank you for—everything."

Adam squawked, hungry and ready for bed. There were no Hallmark card moments when a baby ran the schedule, no time to belabor her thanks. So she took her squirming son from her mother's arms and began to pack up.

Then she remembered.

"Hey, Mom, you said there were two things you had to apologize for." She snapped Adam into his carrier. "What's the second?"

Violet huffed as if she wished she'd never mentioned it. She looked at Ed, who nodded his *Go ahead.*

"Your father and I have compared notes. And we believe I may have been the one to break Pastor Norblad's nose."

"You?" This was more than delicious. "You punched Pastor Norblad?"

"Of course not." She sounded disgusted at that mere suggestion. "Something brushed my hip and I thought it was Elliott. Getting *hands-y.*" She wiggled her fingers. "So I swatted him with my hymnal."

"Only—" Cerise laughed, putting the pieces together "—you missed and hit the pastor."

Violet scowled. "Well, I say I did him a favor," she said. "In fact, his wife ought to thank me for finally giving him an excuse to fix it."

Cincinnati Independent Times

June 13, 2018

Court Says History Has Rights, Too

A federal district judge ruled in favor of local preservation groups yesterday, declaring that Hesse House, the historic Mount Auburn Romanesque Revival landmark, cannot be sold for development.

"The ruling could not be more clear," said Preserve Cincinnati's Director, Ellsbeth Mariner. "The land on which Hesse House sits is federally protected through the National Register of Historic Places. Developers, or other people just looking to make a buck, can no longer pretend that their destruction of these treasures doesn't have a lasting impact on our city."

The home's current owners, Elliott and Amanda Hesse, had been on track to sell the house to boutique hotel developer the Frontenac Group, but yesterday's ruling permanently derailed the agreement, according to a company spokesperson.

The court's decision ultimately leaves the Hesse family fuming and scrambling for options on how to deal with the historic liability.

"These so-called preservation groups owe me money," said Elliott Hesse from his second home in Naples, Florida. "And they better get their act together soon because I'm not putting one more cent into that place. I'd certainly hate for something to happen to it in the meantime."

46

Violet

So, here they were again—Violet and Ed, and Cerise and Barb with the baby, and Eldris and Richard and Kyle—all seated around the dining room table and all wondering what on earth was going to happen next.

Violet had never been so horrified as the last time they'd gathered guests around this table. She'd even considered selling the entire set—or burning it, but she couldn't do that to a Stickley—for fear that it would forever remind her of that night. Elliott's groping hands, and his wife, slurring her words like a snake in the grass. These were deeply troubled people, no doubt, and had they been anyone other than her grandson's relations, she would have tossed them out the door and turned the lock.

But that was not an option. No, it was now indisputably clear that Elliott's and Amanda's failed moral characters made her and Ed infinitely more important as grandparents. The Baumgartners would have to pick up the slack. And they would do it—for Adam, obviously, but also for Barb. She was a mother now, yes, but with what guidance? Certainly she wouldn't be looking to Amanda as a role model. *Lord, help us!* No, it would be Violet's job to guide these young mothers—Cerise and Barb, both. She owed it to her family.

Even Ed hadn't been the same since the baptism. He'd always been efficient, but for the last few days he'd displayed the energy of an old Hollywood business tycoon, the sort of character you'd see on Turner Classic Movies, making phone calls and saying ridiculous things like, "Make it happen!" She was happy to see him busy again, but for heaven's sake, did he have to be so boisterous about it?

He hadn't even told her he'd invited guests this evening until mere hours before the doorbell rang.

"And what on earth am I supposed to feed these people, Edward?" As if she could produce dinner from five loaves and two fishes.

"I've taken care of it. Two salads and a lasagna from Vescio's, which I'll pick up at five o'clock."

For goodness' sake. "Never in my life have I served take-out food to guests." Vescio's was solid, yes, but honestly.

"You don't, but I do," answered Ed. "I didn't tell you because I didn't want you to fuss."

He assured her there was nothing to do. He would set the table. Eldris was bringing dessert. Kyle was bringing the wine. Violet had no choice but to acquiesce. Only, not before making him agree to transfer the contents of each and every take-out container to her Wedgwood serving dishes.

The guests arrived promptly at six. Even the Endreses.

"I've invited you all for a meal," Ed began, holding his wine-glass aloft, "because I believe there's nothing better for smoothing ruffled feathers than to break bread together." He raised his glass. "A toast. To friendship. And family."

The table echoed its reply.

Ed continued, "The Baumgartners and the Endreses have been friends for many years. Decades, really. And, thanks to little Adam here…" He paused and looked at Cerise as if waiting for a signal that he was approaching dangerous water. Her face betrayed nothing, but he appeared to change course, nevertheless. "Well, let's just say it looks like we have reason to stay friends."

He raised his glass again and the guests each took a sip of their own drinks in return.

Eldris shuffled in her seat and Violet knew she was just burning to ask.

"What role will Kyle be taking in Adam's life?" Violet hadn't waited for Eldris to work up her courage.

Cerise, Barb and Kyle exchanged knowing glances, and then said in near unison, "Godfather."

"Yes, of course," said Violet, scooping at the air with her hand as if digging for more. "But what does that mean?"

"It means," said Cerise, "that he's his godfather. As simple as that." She turned to Barb and smiled. "Right, Momma?"

Barb grinned. "Right." Then she leaned over and kissed Cerise on the lips. Right there at the table.

Of all things.

Oh, well. Violet wouldn't complain. That Barbara was made of nothing less than steel. It was very impressive.

"I don't suppose I can call him—" started Eldris.

"No." Violet stopped her short. "You heard the kids. Kyle is the godfather. Nothing more." Adam was Violet's grandson. He was not a piece of coffee cake they could divide and share at the church fellowship hour.

Then she remembered, softening. Kyle wouldn't be giving Eldris and Richard any actual grandchildren anytime soon.

"I am sorry, Kyle," Violet said, turning to him. "I heard about the wedding."

Kyle shrugged in his typical Kyle-like manner. "Yeah. Well. Turns out I'm more relieved than I expected." Then he filled his mouth with lasagna as if giving himself an excuse to say no more.

There was a pause in the conversation and Violet strained to keep herself from blowing up with exasperation. Why couldn't the Endreses ever just say what they meant?

Finally, Richard picked up where his son had left off. "It was Rhonda."

The guests murmured their assent. Violet looked around the

table, quickly realizing that she was the only person who didn't understand. "Rhonda, what?"

"Rhonda rousing all the suspicion with the feds. Stupid girl. Had her cronies faking all those 'Watchers' hijinks only to find out they were trespassing on federal property." He shoved a piece of bread into his mouth and chewed it only halfway gone before speaking again. "Did you know they were actually investigating Kyle for domestic terrorism?"

"What on earth?"

Now Richard's mouth was full of lasagna, so Cerise picked up the story. "Apparently, Rhonda planned The Watchers group as a way to advance her career. Hired some guys, tried to ignite a social media frenzy. Her plan was to be the reporter who scooped the whole thing. Big exposé. Make a name for herself and ditch the weather-girl life for a network news career."

"Except she nearly landed our son in prison!" Eldris sputtered and bobbled, her face red with anger. "I just knew that anyone with the nerve to put a twelve-hundred-dollar ice-cream maker on her bridal registry wasn't any good for my son. Selfish. That's what I'd call her."

Violet knew exactly which ice-cream maker Eldris was referring to. The Dream from Sur la Table—and she had to agree. She'd found the price tag outrageous. Although it was supposed to make exceptionally delicious sorbet.

"But how did they find her?" Violet looked from guest to guest, not knowing who to turn to. The entire table seemed to be enjoying their food immensely.

"You think the feds figured this out?" Richard again. "Ha! No way. I'm the one who nailed her. I'd suspected for months, only— Well, I didn't want to mess things up for Kyle."

Eldris gasped, as shocked as Violet had ever heard her. She looked about ready to bobble her head right off her shoulders. "You *knew*? Why on earth didn't you say something? Our poor son was nearly incarcerated." Eldris suddenly went so pale that

Violet wondered if the poor woman was going to slide off her chair—again.

"Well, obviously I never thought they were going to nail Kyle for this, Eldris!"

He tossed the piece of bread he'd been fingering to his plate. "Okay, so maybe I didn't know for sure how Rhonda made it all go down. But I damn well suspected. On account of one day, she emailed to ask if anyone would be home because she needed to pick up a few boxes for Kyle. I never thought to ask the poor kid about it until one day he's missing almost exactly a trunkful of donations and the feds are knocking on our door."

"What?" Eldris again. This was most definitely not good for the poor woman's blood pressure. She dropped her head into her hand, looking ready to either scream or sob.

Violet waited briefly, then gently nudged Eldris's wineglass out of the way for fear she'd strike out and break one of her Waterford stems.

Kyle rubbed a hand across his mother's back. "Mom, it's okay. Dad was stuck. You see? If he ratted out Rhonda, he knew it would end our relationship. Plus, the lawyer never thought the investigation would go as far as it did. As soon as Dad knew we'd broken up, he went straight to the FBI."

Violet rolled her eyes and sighed. She was relieved about Kyle, of course. Not only could Eldris quit sputtering to her about how to pay for a wedding on Richard's unemployment check, but sweet Adam was no longer at risk of having to visit his godfather in prison.

Still, she couldn't believe that yet another dinner party was unraveling before her eyes. At least this time she didn't have anything at stake. Except for her crystal. She scanned the table to ensure no other pieces were in danger.

Richard again. "Well, to be clear, I didn't exactly head straight to the feds."

"What?" Now Kyle and his mother both looked like they wanted to attack him.

"I still thought there was a chance it might blow over. Then I talked to Ed." He glanced over. "And it just became clear how things can so easily get blown out of proportion."

Violet looked at Ed. How on earth had he become involved in this mess? And he must have read her mind because he didn't hesitate before offering an explanation.

"I thought Richard was picking up odd jobs as a handyman, remember?"

She nodded slowly, waiting for more.

"Well, it turns out I was wrong. He did help me fix the sink, though. I was buying the wrong size washer. All that mess and it came down to just a tiny bit of rubber—"

"Edward! Get to the point." Violet knew she wasn't going to like what was coming any more than she liked the feel of the ice pick digging its way into her skull.

"I've agreed to become the manager for Hair Supply." He straightened, as if daring her to argue.

"What on earth—" Violet wondered if she could even spit the words from her mouth "—is *Hair Supply?*"

"It's my band," said Richard, answering for him. "With some buddies. We're an Air Supply cover band and we're doing great. Getting very popular. May even head over to the Philippines in a few months if the money's right."

Eldris began making tiny squeaking sounds, but kept her face buried in her hands.

"Mom's not so sure about it all yet," explained Kyle. "But the good news is that Dad's also agreed to start taking on a leadership role with EyeShine. Frees me up to keep building my practice while we build the organization at the same time. I'm psyched."

He shot a grin at his dad, who shot one right back.

Well, weren't they just peas in a pod?

"Does this mean you're leaving advertising?" Violet couldn't help but feel a tiny twist in her gut, knowing that neither seedy roadside bars nor charity work would even come close to covering the salary Eldris had grown accustomed to. Not that it was a terribly impressive salary. Eldris hadn't changed her kitchen wallpaper in years.

"In a way," said Richard. "Except that I'll be bringing all my advertising expertise along with me to EyeShine. It'll be a great asset for building the brand."

"And the money..." Violet was doing her best to be discreet.

"Yeah, well, you could say I've been a bit of a tightwad over the years. We're fine to retire, if we're careful. Plus, we'll have a bit of income to cover the gap."

"He's been more than a tightwad," said Ed, interjecting. "I brought him over to Harry Saels's office and Harry said he'd never seen accounts so neat and tidy at Richard's. He called it an 'open-and-shut case of financial constipation,' but I think the metaphor was just for my benefit."

Eldris punctuated Ed's joke for him, stifling an agonized moan. "I'm still getting new vinyl in the entryway, Richard," she squeaked. "Maybe even tile. You just wait!"

Violet couldn't believe it. All these years her dear friend had pinched and scraped, only to find out that life could have eased up years ago. She felt a renewed rush of thanks for her dear Ed. Not that he, of all people, was going to get away with this band manager nonsense without a thorough talking-to, of course. Nor would she at any point or under any circumstance allow her Ed to wear one of Richard's ridiculous wigs. Or a vest. Equally ridiculous.

There was, she had to admit, though, a certain intrigue to the idea of international travel. She'd never been particularly drawn to the Philippines, but she could be persuaded of Japan. Possibly. And definitely Norway. Yes, and Germany. They could make a global tour of it. Maybe even take Adam. Expose him to the cultures of the world. Immerse him in Mandarin and French and Swahili. Where was it that they spoke Tamil?

She made a mental note: *f/u foreign languages.*

That reminded her. She made a second mental note: *Adam on waiting list for Academy of the International Baccalaureate?*

Oh, and a third: *Infant vaccination protocol.*

For heaven's sake. She was already behind.

Epilogue

Violet

SHE WOULD HAVE preferred they'd stayed overnight.

"They only live ten minutes away, Violet." Ed sat next to her on the couch, each of them nursing a warm cup of coffee. "It won't be long."

"I know." She sighed. There was a melancholy in her voice this morning. Even she could hear it. "It's just that this is the most magical part of the morning."

And it was. The white lights of the tree danced in the early-morning dark, as the pink sky outside their windows announced: *Christmas has come again.*

"Well, I like to think they're doing just what we are right now." Ed leaned in and nudged her with his shoulder. "Enjoying the glorious quiet of Christmas morning together."

Violet smiled at him. Dearest Ed. Head to toe in his red plaid holiday pajamas.

He nudged her again. Always a nudger, her husband. Never overly conspicuous with his affections but hardly withholding of them, either. "I love you, Violet."

She leaned in, feeling his warmth. "I love you, too."

He nudged her yet again.

Oh, for heaven's sake! "Edward Baumgartner, you just spilled coffee all over my lap!"

FINALLY, THE ENTIRE FAMILY—all five of them—gathered at the tree. It was late afternoon, several hours past the time they typically sat down to open presents, but Adam had napped longer than usual. In the time he'd slept in the crib Violet kept in the guest bedroom, they'd finished off last night's Swedish meatballs, a full pot of coffee and half a tray of Christmas cookies, all while opening and reading aloud the pile of holiday letters received at the Baumgartner house over the past several weeks.

As usual, people had very little to report other than more gray hair and a growing list of grandchildren.

The Endreses, however, had forgone the typical family photo this year in lieu of a picture of Kyle and Richard standing beside a bland concrete structure, surrounded by strangers. The caption read, *EyeShine brings the gift of sight to Togolese refugees in Monrovia, Liberia. August 2018.*

Well. That was different.

Violet had feared Eldris would call and ask to include a picture of Adam in this year's family photograph. But in fact she hadn't. Hadn't even asked to put a present under the tree or donate something to his stocking.

Eldris, it appeared, was playing by the rules. And Violet wasn't exactly sure how she felt about that.

Anyway, now Adam was awake and hungry, drinking a bottle in Ed's arms, and dressed in a green-and-red jumper that read, *Grandpa's little elf.*

"I'm just so glad he slept," said Cerise. Violet could now see she'd done her best to cover the dark circles under her eyes with makeup. "I don't know if he's teething, or what, but he's been up two or three times a night all week."

"He's awfully flatulent," said Ed, patting baby's bum. He lifted Adam diaper-side-up to his nose and sniffed. "All this rich holiday food passing through your milk, making him gassy. Try a hot water bottle on his belly. Should loosen him up."

"Merry Christmas to us," said Barb, handing Cerise her mug of warm mulled wine for a sip. "Any chance there's a full night's sleep wrapped up in any of these boxes?"

Violet smirked. "Perhaps." Oh, she couldn't stand herself, she was so smart. There was, in fact, a gift certificate under the tree for one night at a lovely boutique hotel downtown. She'd seen it featured in the newspaper for its amazing brunch menu and called that very afternoon. Now their getaway-for-two was wrapped in ribbon and bows with a tag that read, "Sweet dreams, Cerise and Barb."

"Mom," said Cerise, "open yours first." She handed her a gift wrapped in lovely silver paper with a white satin ribbon running long tails below its bow.

"How lovely. Thank you." She took the box from Cerise, and nearly dropped it. It was the size of a shirt box, so naturally she'd expected it to weigh as much. Only, it felt as if it were full of bricks. "What on earth?"

Cerise and Barb exchanged pleased, knowing glances.

Those two. "I see you enjoyed yourselves." She smiled and pulled at the ribbon, which slid loose with the luscious feel of silk. She wrapped the yard or so of ribbon carefully around her palm and set it next to her on the side table. Most definitely reusable.

Now, where to begin? She turned the package over and examined its wrap for the best point of entry. The silver paper was thick and the tape barely translucent against its sheen. Perhaps it was best to begin at one of the ends.

"Just rip it, Mom!" Cerise was practically hollering, though laughing as she went.

"Hang on," said Barb, leaping to her feet. "I'll get a knife."

"No need," said Violet, running a fingernail along the back

center seam. "I think I've got it." She had torn the paper slightly, but she assured herself it did not matter. As it was, she'd had to toss out several rolls of wrapping paper this year in order to make room for the new rolls of child-appropriate paper she'd purchased to wrap Adam's gifts. Life, she reminded herself, was bountiful.

The silver paper, once freed, fell to the floor at her feet. Inside it, as she suspected, was a plain white shirt box. She pulled off the lid and stopped at the tissue paper layer. "Edward," she said, looking for him. He was just over her shoulder, still bouncing the baby. "Are you watching? This is from Cerise and Barb."

"Yes. Go ahead. Adam and I are both watching."

She pulled back the tissue and found a book. Coffee-colored leather binding. On its cover the words *Adam Hesse Baumgartner.*

"Oh." She heard herself cooing. "A baby book. How wonderful." She looked at Cerise and Barb, being sure to make eye contact with each of them.

"Um, sort of," said Barb. "Open it."

Violet didn't have to be told twice. The leather crackled as she pulled at the cover, working itself a new crease. Ivory paper pages, at least 32-pound stock. The first several were blank, but then came a surprise—a triple-fold insert.

"Pull it out, Mom," said Cerise. She was practically bouncing with excitement. If Violet didn't know better, she'd ask if she needed to use the restroom.

Nevertheless, Violet pulled open the insert and discovered that across her lap lay a family tree with two major branches, Hesse and Baumgartner. At its top, the name, Adam.

"With all the excitement of Adam being early. And the baptism—" Cerise shot Barb a sideways smirk. "Anyway, you never got to do the family tree for Adam's room. So we did it for you."

Violet found herself without words. All she could do was run her fingers along each branch. They were all there—she and

Ed, their parents, her aunts and uncles. Even crazy Aunt Tabitha and wonderful Auntie Tate.

"How?" she asked. One word was enough.

"Dad knew most of it," said Cerise, smiling at her father, who still stood, looking over Violet's shoulder.

"And my parents had the rest," said Barb.

Gracious. That meant— "You spoke with your parents?" Violet did her best to keep her voice light, free of judgmental inquisition.

"Well, yes, I have spoken to them. But not about this. We received an entire library's worth of genealogy books on our doorstep when they moved out of the house in Ohio."

"No notice," said Cerise, nodding. "Just twelve boxes of books and a sweaty delivery guy wanting a tip."

The two of them laughed, and Violet watched them briefly share a private moment.

"Anyway," said Barb, "it gave us the idea."

"Do you like it?" asked Cerise.

She did. She loved it. The intricacy of the hand-drawn tree. The dates and details and names. How many generations? She'd have to take the time to count.

"The tree is only part of it," said Cerise. "The rest is any written documentation we could find. Newspaper articles, government records, letters, whatever."

"But how—with Adam and work and—"

"Like I said, my parents had most of our information already," said Barb.

"And Dad helped with the rest," added Cerise, again nodding in her father's direction.

Violet felt a warm hand on her shoulder. She reached up, covering it with her own. She couldn't turn to look at him. That would lead to tears, and tears would stain the precious gift open across her lap. "Thank you, love," she said, leaning into him as best she could. "And all that time you spent squirreled away on your computer I thought you were busy with Hair Supply nonsense."

Ed patted her. "Oh, there was plenty of that," he said. "But mostly this. I was happy to do it." She felt a kiss land on the top of her head. "Merry Christmas, Violet."

★ ★ ★ ★ ★

Acknowledgments

THIS BOOK MAY never have come to life if my father hadn't once written a Christmas letter about my mother's new can opener. He was my first teacher, and I'm forever thankful he encouraged me to find the humor in (nearly) everything. Thanks to my mom, who allowed her family of characters to be just the people we are.

Thanks to my cheerleaders—a whole lifetime of them. Most recently, my incredible agent, Holly Root, who's one badass woman and human being. To my editor, Natalie Hallak, whose love for these characters is contagious and her editorial insight spot-on. Thanks to my fellow writers: Karen Cimms, Laura Broullire, David Williams, Josh Moehling, Laska Nygaard, Katherine Dickinson, Tim Hennum and Bree Powers. And to my bestest readers: Bethany, Vicki and Renee. Brian and Tracy, every story is better with you in it.

Finally, to Chad and our boys with love. Yep, it's real now.

EVERGREEN TIDINGS FROM THE BAUMGARTNERS

GRETCHEN ANTHONY

Reader's Guide

PARK
ROW
BOOKS

1. Violet is a matriarch with high expectations and very specific tastes, who greatly values her social standing and family history. Why do you think these things are so important to Violet? Why do you think she constantly needs to feel in control? How did your feelings about Violet and her actions change as the novel progressed?

2. Discuss the evolution of Cerise's relationship with her mother. How does it change over the course of the book? Are there aspects that remain the same? How do their perspectives on family evolve?

3. The unexpected news of Cerise's pregnancy brings Violet's world crashing down—literally. Do you think Violet's reaction to the news would have been different if Cerise was straight? In what ways does her being gay affect her relationship with her parents? Do you believe them when they say they already knew she was gay?

4. Violet is forced into an uncomfortable isolation after her accident. How does this is affect her? Does it affect her social standing, or does she only believe that it does? Would she have

behaved differently during Cerise's pregnancy if the accident had not occurred?

5. At various points in the book, Barb encourages Cerise to be more honest and direct with her parents. Yet the behavior of her own family comes as a surprise to everyone. Do you think she would be able to follow her own advice? How does her family and history affect her vision of herself as a mother?

6. Discuss the ways in which parenthood alters Cerise and Barb's relationship. What issues does it force them to address? What strengths and weaknesses does it reveal?

7. It seems like everyone was keeping a secret at some point in the book, such as Cerise and her pregnancy, Richard and his band, Rhonda and her Watchers scheme. Are there any secrets that you felt were justified? Do you think keeping secrets always has consequences? Do most families keep secrets from each other?

8. At first, Edward and Richard seem like opposites. What characteristics do they share? What do they respect about each other? How does their friendship serve them?

9. Discuss the reveal that Kyle is the one who helped Barb and Cerise become parents. Were you surprised? Do you think Rhonda was justified in ending the relationship? In your opinion, would their relationship have worked even if Rhonda hadn't found out?

10. Do any of the characters resemble real people in your life? Which character did you relate to the most? Who would you be most likely to have as a friend?

11. Why are Violet's Christmas letters critical to the book? What do you think the discovery about them at the end says about Violet? What does it say about Edward? About their marriage? Do you write or receive holiday letters?

12. What will you most remember about *Evergreen Tidings from the Baumgartners*?

Evergreen Tidings from the Baumgartners tells the story of a formidable matriarch who goes to wild efforts to wrest back control of her family, and the antics that ensue. What was your inspiration for the characters and story?

We've always loved Christmas letters in our family. My dad and I used to sit in the living room together and read them aloud, saving the ones we knew would provide the most entertainment for last. To this day, my brother and I have an ongoing competition for who can write the funniest letter. He says I always win; I say he does.

Even so, the very nature of the holiday letter is disingenuous. A year in the life of your entire family on a single page—that's not even possible! No one can capture ups and downs of all that living with absolute honesty. And even if they could, who would want to read it?

We've all read those letters, too. The Violet kind. The ones that leave you thinking, Yeah, right. She was the seed of my inspiration. I wondered, what if someone actually believed the high-gloss story she presented to the world? And I wondered, how would she react if she was forced to acknowledge the growing cracks in her facade?

The novel has a great Minnesota flavor, filled with details that bring the setting to life. Can you talk a bit more about why you chose this setting and what it means to you?

Well, geez, you bet! That's so nice of you to ask. Are you sure you've got the time?

Translation for non-Minnesota readers: Sure. I'll tell you. But remember, you asked. Don't blame me if you get bored.

I'll be the first to admit: this place has got a hold on me. I was raised in Minnesota, then moved away for nearly twenty years and swore I'd never come back. The winters really are crazy cold. But like my husband says, there's a siren call to those of us who move away. We can't imagine raising kids who don't know the summers here—great blue stretches of lake and sky, broken only by trees. We love our schools. We love our theaters and our music. We love our woods and our water and—oh, heck! Listen to me going on and on.

Everything non-Minnesotans say about us is true: we manage to be both passive-aggressive and genuine, outwardly nice and subtly cutting, unwilling to admit to the cold while equally preoccupied by the weather. We Minnesotans are a complex bunch. It's what makes us so interesting. I imagine that, for anyone raised elsewhere, trying to understand us must feel like cracking the Enigma code. And yet, as a Minnesotan, I'm obligated to give you as many clues as possible. We just can't help ourselves.

What was your toughest challenge writing *Evergreen Tidings from the Baumgartners*? Your greatest pleasure?

Writing this book was a years-long exercise in maintaining my momentum and confidence. This isn't the first novel I've written but it's the first book I felt I might have a shot at publishing, and with that realization came long periods of fear and doubt. Thankfully, I have terrific writing group partners and they kept me inspired and moving forward. If it weren't for my colleagues, this book would still be scattered chapters on my laptop.

The most fun I had was writing Richard. I can't remember a character who flowed more easily onto the page. I think he may even be my alter ego. Originally, I called him Dick but my fabulous and smart editor, Natalie Hallak, suspected the name was too "on the nose." I'll let the reader decide.

Can you describe your writing process? Do you write scenes consecutively or jump around? Do you have a schedule or routine? A lucky charm?

For me, writing fiction is the process of answering the question, "What if...?" What if a perfectionistic mother began to see her facade crumble? What would she do? How would the people around her react? What consequences would their reactions ignite? It sounds as if I focus on plot first, but I find that my characters drive plot. To put them in realistic situations, I need to understand them first. I develop the emotional plot well before the action plot.

It takes me about two years to complete a book, and only about half of that is writing. The first year, I spend my time thinking about the characters—imagining them in various situations, trying to hear their voice, reading other books or watching movies that may help to inspire them. My kids find it hard to believe that when they find me watching a movie, I call it "work."

When I am writing, I try to write about a chapter a day. I'm deadline driven, so daily goals help keep me on target. I don't have a lucky charm, unless you count all the great friends, family and fellow writers who keep me going. I'm certainly lucky to have them.

Do you read other fiction while writing or do you find it distracting? Is there a book or author that inspires you the most?

One of the best moments of my life was when my agent, Holly Root, told me, in essence, It's your job to read. Until then, I'd always looked at reading as an indulgence, something I did to avoid the stuff I was really supposed to be doing. But my job? That changed everything!

I'm always reading something. When my writing feels stuck, I look for books or characters to inspire me, to help me look at an issue differently. When the writing is going well, I read to relax—it quiets me and allows my mind to rest.

Since my books tend to have big, quirky characters, I have a few books I return to when I need a master course in how to ensure they're also redeemable: A Prayer for Owen Meany and The World According to Garp by John Irving. Where'd You Go, Bernadette?

by Maria Semple. Last year I was enthralled by Gail Honeyman's *Eleanor* character in *Eleanor Oliphant Is Completely Fine; I think that may go into master class rotation, too.*

How did you know you wanted to be a writer? Can you describe the journey to publishing your first book?

I've always been a writer, but I think that's different than being a novelist. I had a career in corporate communication for nearly twenty years and I loved it because the job is both strategic and creative.

I only had the courage (or maybe the drive) to try to establish myself as a novelist about ten years ago. (Those of you doing the math at home know that I'm much older than your average debut novelist.)

Sometimes, when I read an article about a breakout young writer I think, Should I have taken that path? Was I exercising some sort of fear by not pursuing my fiction career earlier? But, no. I realize now that I wasn't always interested in writing fiction. I never dreamed of writing the great American novel or becoming the next Fitzgerald. I did, however, always enjoy writing first-person essays. The funnier, the better. And those, I did write. Some years it wasn't anything more than a Christmas letter or a well-buried blog, but I wrote. I wrote because I enjoyed the stories I could tell.

Eventually, my interest in writing humor led me to the novel. Long-form fiction gave me the freedom to build my characters and the space to spin out their stories. I can still tell stories that make people laugh, but they don't have to be things that happened to me. And even if some of those ridiculous things did happen to me, I get to blame the people in my book.

What do you hope readers will most take away from *Evergreen Tidings from the Baumgartners*?

My parents were big believers in the power of laughter. Several years before he died, my father suffered a traumatic brain injury during a ski accident that nearly killed him. After several days of watching machines keep him alive, my mom, brother and I sat together and began to laugh—at the crazy things he did during the rare moments he spent awake, at what he would say if he could see himself. It was such a release! To finally feel something other than fear and pain and confusion.

Even so, a friend of my father's who'd come to visit scolded us. "Laughter is hardly appropriate at a time like this!"

I've always been proud of my mom for how she reacted. She looked at him and said, "Without laughter, there's only tears."

That's what I want readers to take away from this book—resilience. Really bad things will happen. And when they do, we get to grab on to whatever lifeline gets us through, to prove that even our worst moments can hold more than awfulness and pain.